The Critics Praise
KITEWORLD

"*Kiteworld* is the first novel in years that has compelled me to re-read the first chapter upon finishing the last. That says a lot . . . the climax is violent and breathtaking."
—*Denver Post*

"A gripping book." —*Hartford Courant*

"This is one of those novels where the society is so real that the reader feels the author must have somehow managed to visit it. Roberts has always been one of the more interesting authors working in the genre. *Kiteworld* is one of those novels from which scenes will pop up in our memory months, even years later. It is a major achievement . . ."
—*Science Fiction Chronicle*

"A rich and complex work . . ."
—*Publishers Weekly*

"This dark fantasy combines beauty and violence in a tale about humanity's heights and depths."
—*Library Journal*

"In the subtle distorted mirror of the Kiteworld, we can find reflections of our own superstitions, dreams, and desires." —*Locus*

KEITH ROBERTS

KITEWORLD

ACE BOOKS, NEW YORK

This Ace book contains the complete
text of the original hardcover edition.
It has been completely reset in a
typeface designed for easy reading
and was printed from new film.

KITEWORLD

An Ace Book/published by arrangement with
Victor Gollancz, Ltd.

PRINTING HISTORY
Victor Gollancz edition published 1985
Arbor House edition / May 1986
Ace edition/May 1988

Cover art by Blas.

ISBN: 0-441-44851-8

Ace Books are published by The Berkley Publishing Group,
200 Madison Avenue, New York, NY 10016.

PRINTED IN THE UNITED STATES OF AMERICA

10 9 8 7 6 5 4 3 2 1

To Peter and Anita Pearce,
for many years of loyal friendship;
to Keith Clark, for advice and help
on subjects ranging from philosophy to photocopying;
and to Gabriella, who I never met.

CONTENTS

1 kitemaster

THE GROUND CREW had all but finished their litany. They stood in line, heads bowed, silhouetted against the last dull flaring from the west; below me the Launch Vehicle seethed gently to itself, water sizzling round a rusted boiler rivet. A gust of warmth blew up toward the gantry, bringing scents of steam and oil to mingle with the ever-present smell of dope. At my side the Kitecaptain snorted, it seemed impatiently; shuffled his feet, sank his bull head even further between his shoulders.

I glanced round the darkening hangar, taking in the remembered scene; the spools of cable, head-high on their trolleys, bright blades of the anchor rigs, fathom on fathom of the complex lifting train. In the centre of the place, above the Observer's wickerwork basket, the mellow light of oil lamps grew to stealthy prominence; it showed the spidery crisscrossings of girders, the faces of the windspeed telltales, each hanging from its jumble of struts. The black needles vibrated, edging erratically up and down the scales; beyond, scarcely visible in the gloom, was the complex bulk of the Manlifter itself, its dark, spread wings jutting to either side.

The young priest turned a page of his book, half glanced toward the gantry. He wore the full purple of a Base Chaplain; but his worried face looked very young. I guessed him to be not long from his novitiate; the presence of a Kitemaster was a heavy weight to bear. His voice reached up to me, a thread of sound mixed with the blustering of the wind outside. "*Therefore we beseech thee, Lord, to add Thy vigilance to ours throughout the coming night; that the Land may be preserved, according to Thy covenant. . . .*" The final response was muttered; and he stepped back, closing the breviary with evident relief.

I descended the metal-latticed steps to the hangar floor, paced unhurriedly to the wicker basket. As yet there was no sign of Canwen, the Observer; but that was to be expected. A Flier of his seniority knows, as the Church herself knows, the value of the proper form of things. He would present himself upon his cue; but not before. I sprinkled oil and earth as the ritual dictates, murmured my blessing, clamped the Great Seal of the Church Variant to the basket rim and stepped away. I said, "Let the Watching begin."

At once the hangar became a scene of ordered confusion. Tungsten arcs came to buzzing life, casting their harsher and less sympathetic glare; orders were shouted, and Cadets ran to the high end doors, began to roll them back. The wind roared in at once, causing the canvas sides of the structure to boom and crack; the arc globes swung, sending shadows leaping on the curving walls. The valve gear of the truck set up its fussing; I climbed back to the gantry as the heavy vehicle nosed into the open air. I restored the sacred vessels to their valise, clicked the lock and straightened.

The Kitecaptain glanced at me sidelong, and back to the telltales. "Windspeed's too high, by eight or ten knots," he growled. "And mark that gusting. It's no night for flying."

I inclined my head. "The Observer will decide," I said.

He snorted. "Canwen will fly," he said. "Canwen will always fly. . . ." He turned on his heel. "Come into the office," he said. "You'll observe as well from there. In any case, there's little to see as yet." I took a last glance through the line of rain-spattered windows, and followed him.

The room in which I found myself was small, and as spartan as the rest of the establishment. An oil lamp burned in a niche; a shelf held manuals and dogeared textbooks, another was piled with bulky box files. A wall radiator provided the semblance at least of comfort; there was a square steel strongbox, beside it a battered metal desk. On it stood a silver-mounted photograph; a line of youths stood stiffly before a massive, old-pattern Launch Vehicle.

The Captain glanced at it and laughed, without particular humour. "Graduation day," he said. "I don't know why I keep it. All the rest have been dead and gone for years. I'm the last; but I was the lucky one of course." He limped to a corner cabinet, opened it and took down glasses and a bottle. He poured, looked over his shoulder. He said, "It's been a long time, Helman."

I considered. Kitecaptains, by tradition, are a strangely-tempered breed of men. Spending the best part of their lives on the Frontier as they do, they come to have scant regard for the social niceties most of us would take for granted; yet the safety of the Realm depends on their vigilance, and that they know full well. It gives them, if not a real, at least a moral superiority; and he seemed determined to use, or abuse, his position to the hilt. However if he chose to ignore our relative status, there was little I could do. In public, I might rebuke him; in private, I would merely risk a further loss of face. I accordingly remained impassive, and took the glass he proffered. "Yes," I agreed calmly, "it has, as you say, been a very long time."

He was still watching me narrowly. "Well at least," he said, "one of us did all right for himself. I've little enough to show for twenty years' service; save one leg two inches shorter than the other." He nodded at my robes. "They reckon," he said, "you'll be in line for the Grand Mastership one day. Oh yes, we hear the chat; even stuck out in a rotting hole like this."

"All things," I said, "are within the will of God." I sipped, cautiously. Outback liquor has never been renowned for subtlety, and this was no exception; raw spirit as near as I could judge, probably brewed in one of the tumbledown villages through which I had lately passed.

He gave his short, barking laugh once more. "Plus a little help from Variant politics," he said. "But you always had a smooth tongue when it suited. And knew how to make the proper friends."

"We are not all Called," I said sharply. There are limits in all things; and he was pushing me perilously close to mine. It came to me that he was already more than a little drunk. I walked forward to the window, peered; but nothing was visible. The glass gave me back an image of a bright Cap of Maintenance, the great clasp at my throat, my own sombre and preoccupied face.

I sensed him shrug. "We aren't all touched in the head," he said bitterly. "You won't believe it, I find it hard myself; but I once had a chance at the scarlet as well. And I turned it down. Do you know, there was actually a time when I believed in all of this?" He paused. "What I'd give, for my life back just once more," he said. "I wouldn't make the same mistakes again. A palace on the Middlemarch, that's what I'd have; servants round me, and decent wine to drink. Not the rotgut we get here. . . ."

I frowned. Rough though his manner was, he had a way with him that tugged at memory; laughter and scents of other years, touches of hands. We all have our sacrifices to make; it's the Lord's way to demand them. There was a summer palace certainly, with flowering trees around it in the spring; but it was a palace that was empty.

I turned back. "What do you mean?" I said. "Believed in all of what?"

He waved a hand. "The Corps," he said. "The sort of crap you teach. I thought the Realm really needed us. It seems crazy now. Even to me." He drained the glass at a swallow, and refilled it. "You're not drinking," he said.

I set my cup aside. "I think," I said, "I'd best watch from the outer gallery."

"No need," he said. "No need, I'll shade the lamp." He swung down before the light a species of burlap screen; then arcs flared on the apron down below, and all was once more clear as day. Anchors, I saw, had been run out in a half circle from the rear of the Launch Vehicle. "We've never needed them yet," said the Kitecaptain at my elbow. "But on a night like this, who can tell?"

A ball of bright fire sailed into the air, arced swiftly to the east. At the signal Cadets surged forward, bearing the first of the Kites shoulder-high. They flung it from them; and the line tightened and strummed. The thing hung trembling, a few feet above their heads; then insensibly began to rise. Steerable arc lamps followed it; within seconds it was lost in the scudding overcast. The shafts of light showed nothing but sparkling drifts of rain.

"The Pilot," said the Captain curtly; then glanced sidelong once more. "But I needn't tell a Kitemaster a thing like that," he said.

I clasped my hands behind me. I said, "Refresh my memory."

He considered for a while; then it seemed he came to a decision. "Flying a Cody rig isn't an easy business," he snapped. "Those bloody fools back home think it's like an afternoon in Middle Park." He rubbed his face, the iron-grey stubble of beard. "The Pilot takes up five hundred foot of line," he said. "Less, if we can find stable air. The Lifter Kites come next. Three on a good day, four; though at a need we can mount more. The Lifter's job is to carry the main cable; the cable's job is to steady the Lifters. It's all to do with balance. Everything's to do with balance." He glanced sidelong once more; but if he expected a comment on his truism, he was disappointed.

Steam jetted from the Launch Vehicle, to be instantly whirled away. The Launchmaster squatted atop the big, hunched shape, one hand to the straining thread of cable, the other gesturing swiftly to the Winchman; paying out, drawing in, as the Pilot clawed for altitude. Others of the team stood ready to clamp the bronze cones to the Trace. The cone diameters increase progressively, allowing the Lifters to ride each to its proper station; and therein lies the skill. All must be judged beforehand; there is no room for error, no time for second thoughts.

An extra-heavy buffet shook the hangar's sides, set the Kitecaptain once more to scowling. Mixed with the hollow boom I thought I heard a growl of thunder. The Trace paid out steadily though, checked for the addition of the first of the vital cones. A second followed, and a third; and the Kitecaptain unconsciously gripped my arm. "They're bringing the Lifters," he said, and pointed.

How they controlled the monstrous, flapping things at all was a mystery to me; but control them they did, hauling at the boxlike structures that seemed at any moment about to fling the men themselves into the air. The tail ring of the first was clipped about the line; orders echoed across the field, the Kite sailed up smoothly into the murk. Its sisters followed it without a hitch; and the Captain visibly relaxed. "Good," he said. "That was neatly done. You'll find no better team this side of the Salient." He poured more spirit from the bottle, swallowed. "Arms and legs enough have been broken at that game," he said. "Aye, and necks; in gentler blows than this."

I restrained a smile. Despite his sourness, the quality of the man showed clear in the remark; the pride he still felt, justifiably, in a job well done. The Rigs might look well enough in high summer, the lines of them floating lazy against the blue, as far as the eye could reach; or at the Air Fairs of the Middle Lands, flying, beribboned, for the delectation of the Master and his aides. It was here though, in the blustering dark, that the mettle of the Captains and their crews was truly tested.

All now depended on the Launchmaster atop the Launcher. I saw him turn, straining his eyes up into the night, stretch a gauntleted hand to the Trace. Five hundred feet and more above, the Pilot flew invisible; below, the Lifters spread out in their line, straining at their bridles of steel rope. The Rig was aloft; but the slightest failure, the parting of a shackle, the slipping of an ill-secured clamp, could still spell disaster. All was well however; the Launchmaster pulled at the Trace again, gauging the angle and tension of the cable, and the final signal was given. I craned forward, intrigued despite myself, brushed with a glove at the cloudy glass.

Quite suddenly, or so it seemed, the Observer was on the apron. A white-robed acolyte, his fair hair streaming, took from his shoulders his brilliant cloak of office. Beneath it he was dressed from head to foot in stout black leather; kneeboots, tunic and trews, close-fitting helmet. He turned once to stare up at the hangar front. I made out the pale blur of his face, the hard, high cheekbones; his eyes though were invisible, protected by massive goggles. He saluted, formally yet it seemed with an indefinable air of derision, turned on his heel and strode toward the Launch Vehicle. I doubt though that he could have made out either the Kitecaptain or myself.

The Ground Crew scurried again. Moving with practised, almost military precision, they wheeled the basket forward; the Observer climbed aboard, and the rest was a matter of skilled, split-second timing. The Manlifter, shielded at first by the hangar from the full force of the wind, swayed wildly, wrenching at its restraining ropes. Men ran back across the grass; the steam winch clattered and the whole equipage was rising into the night, the Observer already working at the tail-down tackle that would give him extra height. The winch settled to a steady, gentle clanking; and the Captain wiped his face. I turned to him. "Congratulations," I said. "A splendid launch."

Somewhere, distantly, a bell began to clang.

"They're all launched," he said. "Right up to the high G numbers; and south, down through the Easthold. The whole Sector's flying; for what good it'll serve." He glowered at me. "You understand, of course, the principles involved?" he said sarcastically.

"Assuredly," I said. "Air flows above the Manlifter's surfaces faster than beneath them, thus becoming rarefied. The good Lord abhors a vacuum; so any wing may be induced to rise."

He seemed determined not to be mollified. "Excellent," he said. "I see you've swallowed a textbook or two. There's a bit more to it than that though. If you'd ever flown yourself, you wouldn't be so glib."

I lowered my eyes. I knew, well enough, the dip and surge of a Cody basket; but it was no part of my intention to engage him in a game of apologetics. Instead I said, "Tell me about Canwen."

He stared at me, then nodded to the valise. He said, "You've got his file."

"Files don't say everything," I said. "I asked you, Kitecaptain."

He turned away, stood hands on hips and stared down at the Launcher. "He's a Flier," he said at length. "The finest we've got left. What else is there to say?"

I persisted. "You've known him long?"

"Since I first joined the Corps," he said. "We were Cadets together." He swung back, suddenly. "Where's all this leading, Helman?"

"Who knows?" I said. "Perhaps to understanding."

He brought his palm down flat upon the desk. "Understanding?" he shouted. "Who in all the Hells needs understanding? It's explanations we're after, man. . . ."

"Me too," I said pointedly. "That's why I'm here."

He flung an arm out. "Up In G7," he said, "an Observer slipped his own Trace one fine night, floated off into the Badlands. I knew him too; and they don't come any better. Another sawed his wrists apart, up there on his own; and he'd been flying thirty years. Last week we lost three more; while you and all the rest sit trying to understand. . . ."

A tapping sounded at the door. It opened to his shout; a nervous-looking Cadet stood framed, his eyes on the floor. "The Quartermaster sends his compliments," he stammered, "and begs to know if the Kitemaster—I mean My Lord—wishes some refreshment. . . ."

I shook my head; but the Captain picked the bottle up, tossed it across the room. "Yes," he said, "get me some more of this muck. Break it out of stores, if you have to; I'll sign the chitty later." The lad scurried away on his errand; the other stood silent and brooding till he returned. Below, on the apron, the ratchet of the winch clattered suddenly; a pause, and the smooth upward flight was continued. The Captain stared out moodily, screwed the cap from the fresh bottle and drank. "You'll be telling me next," he said, "they've fallen foul of Demons."

I turned, sharply. For a moment I wondered if he had taken leave of his senses; he seemed however fully in command of himself. "Yes," he said, "you heard me right first time." He filled the glass again. "How long has it really been," he said, "since the Corps was formed? Since the very first Kite flew?"

"The Corps has always been," I said, "and always will be. It is the Way. . . ."

He waved a hand dismissively. "Save it for those who need it," he said brutally. "Don't start preaching your sermons in here." He leaned on the desk. "Tell me," he said, "what was the real idea? Who dreamed it up?"

I suppose I could have remained silent, or quit his company; but it seemed that beneath the bluster there lay something else. A questioning, almost a species of appeal. It was as if something in him yet needed confirmation of his heresy; the confirmation, perhaps, of argument. Certainly I understood his dilemma, in part at least; it was a predicament that in truth was by no means new to me. "The Corps was formed," I said, "to guard the Realm, and keep its borders safe."

"From Demons," he said bitterly. "From Demons and night walkers, all spirits that bring harm. . . ." He quoted, savagely, from the Litany. *"Some plunge, invisible, from highest realms of air; some have the shapes of fishes, flying; some, and these be hardest to descry, cling close upon the hills and very treetops. . . ."* I raised a hand, but he rushed on regardless. *"These last be deadliest of all,"* he snarled. *"For to these the Evil One hath given semblance of a Will, to seek out and destroy their prey* . . . Crap!" He pounded the desk again. "All crap," he said. "Every last syllable. The Corps fell for it though, every man jack of us. You crook your little fingers, and we run; we float up there like fools, with a pistol in one hand and a prayerbook in the other, waiting to shoot down bogles, while you live off the fat of the land. . . ."

I turned away from the window and sat down. "Enough," I said tiredly. "Enough, I pray you. . . ."

"We're not the only ones of course," he said. He struck an attitude. *"Some burst from the salt ocean,"* he mocked, *"clad overall in living flame* . . . So the Seaguard ride out there by night and day, with magic potions ready to stop the storms. . . ." He choked, and steadied himself. "Now I'll tell you, Helman," he said, breathing hard. "I'll tell you, and you'll listen. There are no Demons; not in the sky, not on the land, not in the sea. . . ."

I looked away. "I envy," I said slowly, "the sureness of your knowledge."

He walked up to me. "Is that all you've got to say?" he shouted. "You hypocritical bastard. . . ." He leaned forward. "Good men have died in plenty," he said, "to keep the folk in fear, and you in your proper state. Twenty years I flew, till I got this; and I'll say it again, as loud and clear as you like. *There are no Demons. . . .*" He swung away. "There's something for your report," he said. "There's a titbit for you. . . ."

I am not readily moved to anger. Enraged, we lose awareness; and awareness is our only gift from God. His last remark though irritated me beyond measure. He'd already said more than enough to be relieved of his command; enough, indeed, to warrant a court martial in Middlemarch itself. And a conviction, were I to place the information before the proper authorities. The sneer reduced me to the level of a Variant spy, peeping at keyholes, prying into ledgers. "You fool," I said. "You arrogant, unreasoning fool."

He stared, fists clenched. "Arrogant?" he said. "You call me arrogant? *You . . . ?*"

I stood up, paced back to the window. "Aye, arrogant," I said. "Beyond all measure, and beyond all sense." I swung back. "Will you be chastised," I said bitterly, "like a first year Chaplain, stumbling in the Litany? If that's the height of your desire, it can readily be accomplished . . ."

He sat back at the desk, spread his hands on its dull-painted top. "What do you want of me?" he said.

"The courtesy with which you're being used," I said. "For the sake of Heaven, man, act your age. . . ."

He drained the glass slowly, and set it down. He stretched his hand toward the bottle, changed his mind. Finally he looked up, under lowering brows. "You take a lot on yourself, Helman," he said. "If any other spoke to me like that, I'd kill him."

"Another easy option," I said shortly. "You're fuller of them than a beggar's dog of fleas." I shook my head. "You alone, of all the Lord's creation," I said. "You alone, beg leave to doubt your faith. And claim it as a novel sentiment. . . ."

He frowned again. "If you'd ever flown. . . ."

"I've flown," I said.

He looked up. "You've seen the Badlands?" he asked sharply.

I nodded. "Yes," I said. "I have."

He took the bottle anyway, poured another drink. "It changes you," he said. "For all time." He picked the glass up, toyed with it. "Folk reckon nothing lives out there," he said grimly. "Only Demons. I could wish they were right." He paused. "Sometimes of a clear day, flying low, you see . . . more than a man should see. But they're not Demons. I think once, they were folk as well. Like us. . . ."

I folded my arms. I too was seeing the Badlands, in my mind; the shining vista of them spread by night, as far as the eye could reach. The hills and valleys twinkling, like a bed of coals; but all a ghastly blue.

It seemed he read my thoughts. "Yes," he said, "it's

something to look at all right. . . ." He drank, suddenly, as if to erase the memory. "It's strange," he said. "But over the years, I wonder if a Flier doesn't get to see with more than his normal eyes." He rubbed his face. "Sometimes," he said, "I'd see them stretching out farther and farther, all round the world; and nothing left at all, except the Realm. One little corner of a little land. That wasn't Demons either though. I think men did it, to each other." He laughed. "But I'm forgetting, aren't I?" he said bitterly. "While the Watching goes on, it can never happen here. . . ."

I touched my lip. I wasn't going to be drawn back into an area of barren cant. "I sometimes wonder," I said carefully, "if it's not all merely a form of words. Does it matter, finally, how we describe an agent of Hell? Does it make it any more real? Or less?"

"Why, there you go," he cried, with a return to something of his former manner. "Can't beat a good Church training, that's what I always say. A little bit here, a little bit there, clawing back the ground you've lost. Nothing ever alters for you, does it? Face you with reality though; that's when you start to wriggle. . . ."

"And why not?" I said calmly. "It's all that's left to do. Reality is the strangest thing any of us will ever encounter; the one thing, certainly, that we'll never understand. Wriggle though we may."

He waved his glass. "I tell you what I'll do," he said. "I'll propose a small experiment. You say the Watching keeps us from all harm. . . ."

I shook my head. "I say the Realm is healthy, and that its fields are green."

He narrowed his eyes for a moment. "Well then," he said. "For a month, we'll ground the Cody rigs. And call in all the Seaguard. That would prove it, wouldn't it? One way or the other. . . ."

"Perhaps," I said. "You might pay dearly for the knowledge though."

He slammed the glass down. "And what," he said, "if your precious fields stayed green? Would you concede the point?"

"I would concede," I said gently, "that Hell had been inactive for a span."

He flung his head back and guffawed. The laughter was not altogether of a pleasant kind. "Helman," he said, "you're bloody priceless." He uncapped the bottle, poured. "I'll tell you a little story," he said. "We were well off, when I was a youngster. Big place out in the Westmarch; you'd better believe it. Only we lost the lot. My father went off his head. Not in a nasty way, you understand; he never hurt a fly, right through his life. But every hour on the hour, for the last ten years, he waved a kerchief from the tower window, to scare off little green men. And you know what? We never saw a sign of one, not all the time he lived." He sat back. "What do you say to that?"

I smiled. "I'd say that he had rediscovered Innocence. And taught you all a lesson; though at the time, maybe you didn't see."

He swore, with some violence. "Lesson?" he cried. "What lesson lies in that?"

"That logic may have circular propensities," I said. "Or approach the condition of a sphere; the ultimate, incompressible form."

He pushed the bottle away, staring; and I burst out laughing at the expression on his face. "Man," I said, "you can't put Faith into a test tube, prove it with a piece of litmus paper. . . ."

A flash of brilliance burst in through the windows. It was followed by a long and velvet growl. A bell began to sound, closer than before. I glanced across to the Kitecaptain; but he shook his head. He said harshly, "Observation altitude. . . ."

I lifted the valise on to the desk edge, unlocked it once more. I assembled the receiver, set up the shallow repeater cone with its delicate central reed. The other stared, eyes widening. "What're you doing?" he croaked.

"My function is to listen," I said curtly. "And as I told you, maybe to understand. I've heard you; now we'll see what Canwen has to say." I advanced the probe to the crystal; the cone vibrated instantly, filling the room with the rushing of the wind, the high, musical thrumming of the Cody rig.

The Captain sprang away, face working. "Necromancy," he said hoarsely. "I'll not have it; not on my Base. . . ."

"Be quiet," I snapped. "You impress me not at all; you

have more wit than that." I touched a control; and the Observer roared with laughter. "The tail-down rig of course," he said. "New since your day. . . ."

The other stared at the receiver; then through the window at the Launch Vehicle, the thread of cable stretching into the dark. "Who's he talking to?" he whispered.

I glanced up. "His father was a Flier, was he not?"

The Kitecaptain moistened his lips. "His father died over the Salient," he said. "Twenty years ago."

I nodded. "Yes," I said, "I know." Rain spattered sudden against the panes; I adjusted the control and the wind shrilled again, louder than before. Mixed as it was with the singing of the cables, there was an eerie quality to the sound; almost it was as if a voice called, thin and distant at first then circling closer. Canwen's answer was a great shout of joy. "Quickly, Pater, help me," he cried urgently. "Don't let her go again. . . ." Gasps sounded; the basketwork creaked in protest and there was a close thump, as if some person, or some thing, had indeed been hauled aboard. The Observer began to laugh. "Melissa," he said. "Melissa, oh my love. . . ."

"His wife," I supplied. "A most beautiful and gracious lady. Died of childbed fever, ten years ago in Middlemarch. . . ."

"What?" cried Canwen. *"What?"* Then, "Yes, I see it. . . ." A snapping sounded, as he tore the Great Seal from the basket; and he began to laugh again. "They honour us, beloved," he cried. "The Church employs thaumaturgy against us. . . ."

The Kitecaptain gave a wild shout. "No," he cried, "I'll hear no more of it. . . ." I wrestled with him, but I was too late. He snatched the receiver, held it on high and dashed it to the floor. The delicate components shattered; and the room fell silent, but for the close sound of the wind.

The pause was of brief duration. Lightning flared again; then instantly the storm was all around us. Crash succeeded crash, shaking the very floor on which I stood; the purple flaring became continuous.

The Captain started convulsively; then it seemed he collected himself. "Down rig," he shouted hoarsely. "We must fetch him down. . . ."

"No," I cried. "No. . . ." I barred his way; for a moment my upflung arm, the sudden glitter of the Master's Staff, served to check him, then he had barged me aside. I tripped and fell, heavily. His feet clattered on the gantry steps; by the time I had regained my own his thick voice was already echoing through the hangar. *"Down rig . . . Down rig, for your lives. . . ."*

I followed a little dazedly, ran across the cluttered floor of the place. The great end doors had been closed; I groped for the wicket, and the wind snatched it from my hand. My robes flogged round me; I pressed my back to the high metal, offered up a brief and fervent prayer. Before me the main winch of the Launcher already screamed, the great drum spun; smoke or steam rose from where the wildly-driven cable snaked through its fairleads. Men ran to the threatened points with water buckets, white-robed Medics scurried; Cadets, hair streaming, stood by with hatchets in their hands, to cut the rigging at a need. I stared up, shielding my face against the glaring arcs; and a cry of *"View-ho"* arose. Although I could not myself descry it, sharper eyes than mine had made out the descending basket. I started forward; next instant the field was lit by an immense white flash.

For a moment, it was as if Time itself was slowed. I saw a man, his arms flung out, hurled headlong from the Launcher; fragments of superstructure, blown outward by the force of the concussion, arced into the air; the vehicle's cab, its wheels, the tautened anchor cables, each seemed lit with individual fire. The lightning bolt sped upward, haloing the main Trace with its vivid glare; then it was as if the breath had been snatched from my lungs. I crashed to the ground again half-stunned, saw through floating spots of colour how a young Cadet, blood on his face, ran forward to the winch gear. He flung his weight against the tallest of the levers, and the screaming stopped. The manlifter, arrested within its last few feet of travel, crashed sideways, spilling the Observer unceremoniously on to the grass. A shackle parted somewhere, dimly heard through the ringing in my ears; the axes flashed, a cable end lashed viciously above my head. The Lifter train whirled off into the dark, and was gone.

I got to my feet, staggered toward Canwen. By the time I reached him, the Medics were already busy. They raised him on to the stretcher they wheeled forward; his head lolled, but at sight of me he rallied. He raised an arm, eyes blazing, made as if to speak; then he collapsed, lying still as death, and was borne rapidly away.

The eastern sky was lightening as I packed the valise for the final time. I closed the lock hasp, clicked it shut; and the door was tapped. A fair-haired Cadet entered, bearing steaming mugs on a tray. I smiled at him. A fresh white bandage circled his brow, and he was a little pale; but he looked uncommon proud.

I turned to the Base Medic, a square-set, ruddy-faced man. I said, ''So you think Canwen will live?''

''Good God, yes,'' he said cheerfully. ''Be up and about in a day or two at the latest. He's survived half a dozen calls like that already; I think this gives him the record. . . .'' The door closed behind him.

I sipped. The brew was dark and bitter; but at least it was hot. ''Well,'' I said, ''I must be on my way. Thank you for your hospitality, Kitecaptain; and my compliments to all concerned for their handling of last night's emergency.''

He rubbed his face uncertainly. ''Will you not stay,'' he said, ''and break your fast with us properly?''

I shook my head. ''Out of the question I'm afraid,'' I said. ''I'm due at G15 by zero nine hundred. But I thank you all the same.'' I hefted the valise, and smiled again. ''Its Captain, I've no doubt, will have had too much to drink,'' I said. ''I shall probably hear some very interesting heresy.''

He preceded me through the now-silent hangar. To one side a group of men was engaged in laying out long wire traces; but there were few other signs of activity. Outside, the air struck chill and sweet after the storm; by the main gate my transport waited, in charge of a smartly uniformed chauffeur/acolyte. I began to walk toward it; the Captain paced beside me, his chin sunk on his chest, still it seemed deep in thought. ''What's your conclusion?'' he asked abruptly.

''About the recent loss rate?'' I said. I shook my head. ''An all round lessening of morale, leading to a certain slackness; all except here of course,'' I added as his mouth began to open. It's a lonely and thankless life for all the Cody teams; nobody is more aware of it than I.

He stopped, and turned toward me. ''What's to do about it then?'' he said.

''Do?'' I shrugged. ''Send Canwen to have a chat with

them. He'll tell them he's seen the face of God. If he doesn't, go yourself. . . ."

He frowned. "About the thaumaturgy. The things we heard. . . ."

I began to walk again. "I've heard them often enough before," I said. "I don't place all that much importance on them. It's a strange world, in the sky; we must all come to terms with it as best we may." Which is true enough; sometimes, to preserve one's sanity, it's best to become just a little mad.

He frowned again. "Then the report. . . ."

"Has already been made," I said. "You gave it yourself, last night. I don't think I really have very much to add." I glanced across to him. "You'd have been best advised," I said, "to leave him flying, not draw him down through the eye of the storm. But you'd have seen that for yourself, had you not been under a certain strain at the time."

"You mean if I hadn't been drunk," he said bluntly "And all the time I thought. . . ." He squared his shoulders. "It won't happen again, Kitemaster; I'll guarantee you that."

"No," I said softly, "I don't suppose it will."

He shook his head. "I thought for a moment," he said, "it was a judgement on me. I'd certainly been asking for it. . . ."

This time I hid the smile behind my hand. That's the whole trouble, of course, with your amateur theologians. Always expecting God to peer down from the height, His fingers to His nose, for their especial benefit.

We had reached the vehicle. The acolyte saluted briskly, opened the rear door with its brightly blazoned crest. I stooped inside, and turned to button down the window. "Goodbye, Kitecaptain," I said.

He stuck his hand out. "God go with you," he said gruffly. He hesitated. "Someday," he said, "I'll come and visit you. At that bloody summer palace. . . ."

"Do," I said. "You'll be honourably received; as is your due. And Captain. . . ."

He leaned close.

"Do something for me in the meantime," I said. "Keep the Codys flying; till something better comes along. . . ."

He stepped back, saluting stiffly; then put his hands on his hips, stared after the vehicle. He was still staring when a bend of the green, rutted track took it from sight.

I leaned back against the cushioning, squeezed the bridge of my nose and closed my eyes. I felt oddly cheered. On the morrow, my tour of duty would be ended. They would crown a new May Queen, in Middlemarch; children would run to me, their hair bedecked with flowers, and I would touch their hands.

I sat up, opened the file on Kitebase G15. A mile or so farther on though I tapped the glass screen in front of me and the chauffeur drew obediently to a halt. I watched back to where, above the shoulders of the hills, a Cody rig rose slowly, etched against the flaring yellow dawn.

2 kitecadet

HE HAD BEEN up before first light, as had all the leavemen. Now the long, barrel-vaulted bath house echoed as usual with the shouts and high jinks of his classmates. He stood at the urinal, naked as the rest; the ritual created in him its usual strange sensation, half floating, half exhilarated. Olsen, as ever, was noisily displaying his morning excitement to all and sundry. Something warm splashed his ankle; he swore, would perhaps have lashed out, but the other's mouthing was lost suddenly in the huge banging of the steam pipes. The yelps redoubled; he grabbed for soap, the semester's last issue, ran for the shower stalls. He had no intention of being caught for long behind a giggling, shoving queue.

Despite the brightening days, the big stoves in the barrack blocks had been allowed alight; beside each stood a blank-faced Sector servant, fanning warmth up steadily from the glowing grille. He fetched the spare towel hoarded in his locker, and was hailed. "Hey, Raoul, after you . . . !" He grinned and shook his head, already busy. He was proud of his hair; it was long and thick, the colour of dark corn. He snapped at the Centre man, relaxed, preened himself in warmth.

The breakfast hooter took him by surprise; he was barely halfway through. He hesitated, then drew his hair up quickly into the double ponytail that had recently become the rage. Others he knew, would do the same; on this morning of mornings, such minor affectations were invariably winked at. It looked well, he decided; nonetheless he felt a vague unease. Almost a guilt. He kept a sharp lookout for the omnipresent Olsen. On Feast Days, a certain ebullience was likewise tolerated; it was time, he had decided, for the other to receive a small memento of his displeasure, possibly in the form of a well-blacked eye. But the stocky youth averted his gaze, seeming mightily preoccupied with the texture of the lime-washed refectory wall. Which Raoul decided was just possibly a point to him.

By zero eight hundred he was through. His uniform, fresh-pressed by the Sector domestics—Base Rats they called them, though never to their faces—felt warm and comfortable; his tunic buttons had been polished till they gleamed. He adjusted the new brassard lovingly; the loop of silver cord, worn over the shoulder, that represents the main Trace of a Cody rig. In strict truth, he had no right to it as yet; he'd done his training flights, all ten of them, but that had been over the flat fields surrounding Base Camp, well behind the lines. He'd missed out on his first Operational, one of the vicious little fevers that stalk the low ground of the Salient had laid him low; but the T.O. in charge of Cadet messes, in most respects a hard and uncompromising man, had shown an unexpected flash of charity. His term's work had been good; and not all Frontier men go strictly by the book. So when the lists of Cadet Fliers had gone up on the noticeboards his name had been with the rest. He drew the new badge gleefully from Stores, and laughed at Kil Olsen's face; because for some reason the other had been pegged.

One duty remained to be performed, before leave properly began. He flicked a final time at his boots, hefted his duffel and presented himself at the office of Warrantman Keaning. He was kept waiting a considerable while; but that was part of the ritual, and accepted. He stood arms folded, staring out across the Base. The sky was bright now, on that mild spring morning; the early sun gleamed on the low lines of barrack blocks, the taller, gaunt shapes of the Kitehangars. G15, biggest of all the Stations on the Salient, would be working for the next few days at much reduced capacity; she would still man four Cody rigs though, round the clock.

The Night Observers (Blackbirds they called them, in Base slang) were coming in; he watched with approval the neat handling of the rigs, Lifter after Lifter sailing down to be detached by the ground crews, hurried into the safety of the great canvas-sided sheds. He'd heard that in the low Gs, up round Streanling way, they didn't even draw a String for shiftchange; the Observers simply swapped places in the basket, and up she went again. He curled his lip. They were all bog-happy up there anyway. At G15 each rig was drawn for checking, every time, and a new Trace flown. But G15 was the showplace of the Frontier; the best Station, he thought privately, in the Corps.

The Launch Vehicles jetted their plumes of steam; and he touched his arm again. Very soon now, he'd be a full-fledged Flier; one of the *élite*. The thought served to straighten his shoulders fractionally. He was tall, taller by a head than the Salient lads from whom the Corps was mostly staffed; and though Olsen had jeered often enough, asking how many extra Lifters he'd need for a Force Three Stable, awareness of physical superiority still brought a degree of pleasure.

The opening of the door behind him interrupted the train of thought. He turned, saluted. Warrantman Keaning was a grey haired, seamed-faced man; the longest serving of all the Base personnel, if the tale was true. His eyes flicked, from the habit of a lifetime, over the young Cadet's uniform; finally it seemed he was satisfied. He gestured, briefly; Raoul followed him into the inner sanctum, stood stiffly before the desk.

"At ease," said the other mildly. He took from his uniform a pair of curious half-round glasses, adjusted them on his nose. He said, "Ready for the off? You'll have a fine day for it."

Raoul suppressed a smile. Expecting some such comment, he'd taken careful note of the telltales on Hangar Six. "Force Three and a Half sir, gusting Four," he said. "Sou-sou-west, steady. I'd rather be flying."

"*Hmmph,*" said the other. He spread papers on the desk, studied them. He said, "Seen your family recently?"

"No, sir. Not this term."

"I see. You didn't think of travelling up to Hyeway then?"

Raoul swallowed. The thought of the little Northland farmhouse didn't appeal; his mother clattering in the kitchen baking the dry May cakes, his father sway-backed from the years he'd spent trudging his land. "Sower's arse," they called it, and there was no cure. Though they had machine spreaders now for the horse-drawn rigs, there was even talk of investing in an old tractor. A Kitecadet might not earn much, by Middle Lands standards; but in the economy of the Salient, the wages he sent home were critical. "I've never been to Middlemarch," he said. "I felt it was too good a chance to miss."

The Warrantman grunted again. "So when will you be thinking of going?"

Raoul opened his mouth, and closed it quickly. The words "First Air Leave" had all but slipped out; but at least he'd avoided the trap. You don't count those sort of chickens, if you're wise, at least not while you're still a Cadet. He said formally, "At the next opportunity, sir." The affair of the brassard rankled with Keaning, he knew; the old man at least was a stickler for regulations. He'd been expecting some sort of grilling; it was a small enough price to pay though.

It seemed the other still had not finished. "I see you were in line for a Church scholarship once," he said. "What made you change your mind?"

Raoul thought quickly. The Corps paperwork he could handle well enough, the trig, met and all the rest; but theology was another matter. The other knew that well enough of course; but he wasn't going to make the admission. Not at least till it was forced out of him. He raised his head. "It was my mother's ambition really," he said. "I didn't feel I had a vocation; I thought I might perhaps be more use here."

Keaning stared over his glasses. "Probably just as well," he said. "They don't give too many of those things out. Not in the Salient at least." So the point was made anyway; but he wasn't a long term Warrantman for nothing. He stared at the papers a final time, and shuffled them together. "Very good," he said. "These seem to be in order." He handed them over. Base Pass and ID, security clearances, the little wallet of credits; exchangeable, Raoul knew, at any counting house of the Church Variant. Or at Main Bank, in Middlemarch. He took them, saluted again smartly. The other removed his glasses, tucked them back in his pocket. "Enjoy your leave, Cadet," he said. "And keep your nose clean, won't you? You know what I mean."

The Warrantman sat for a while after the door had closed, staring into space. He wondered how many boys like that he'd seen come and go now, over the years. He glanced through the long, metal-framed windows at the Rigs; bright sails of the Lifters steady in the high blue, thin cobweb-lines of Traces. He sighed, rubbed his face and busied himself with other tasks.

The Transports were waiting, up by Main Gate; most of the other leavemen and Cadets had already clustered round them. Raoul took deep breaths of suddenly wine-sweet air, and resisted the temptation to break into a run. Good enough for a First Year maybe, or one of the Base Rats; but not when you'd got your Trace up. He strode out smartly instead, saluting the Controllers on Three and Four Rigs as he passed. Then two pilots soared simultaneously ahead, and he stopped to watch. He'd wondered vaguely why the shiftchange had been delayed; now it became clear. Hangars One and Two were racing, for the benefit of the assembled crowd.

The little kites rose swiftly, dragging their light lines, clawing for altitude; and the singing of the winch gears checked for the addition of the first trace cones. The Lifters followed, climbing each to its appointed place as the winches paid out again; in what seemed a startlingly short time the black manlifters were run out from the hangars. The Observers appeared, goggled and helmeted even on that bright day. The handlers stepped back; and the Rigs were climbing once more, steadily, into the blue. He stared up, shading his eyes. The pilots were all but invisible now, mere dots against the glowing sky; and still the lines paid out. The traces angled, steadied; altitude bells pealed faintly from the hangars, and the winches were locked at last. The Rigs hung, watchful, over the low hills of the Frontier.

Orderly Meggs was jubilant. "Five fifty two," he said. "Five bloody fifty two, we cracked six minutes. Beat that, for a Force Three launch. . . ." The G15 Cadets cheered lustily; the lads from Twelve and Fourteen, who'd be travelling with them, looked more glum. Raoul smiled. It was a smart enough stringup, certainly; but by the normal standards of the Base, the Launchers had been double-manned.

He climbed aboard the first of the gaunt, high-sided vehicles, slung his duffel in the baggage net and hurried for the back. He was long-legged, the seating centres fixed for Salient personnel; he had no intention of suffering the best part of a day of bruised kneecaps. The rest piled after him, with much pushing and shoving; the old hands grabbed the front compartment, set up a card game almost at once. Meggs checked his clipboard, yelling for quiet; and at last they were away, jolting down the rugged track that led to the first of the ramshackle Salient villages. He stared back at the Base, the Kitestrings tiny already against the eastern sky. He felt again the rise of an intense pleasure. The pleasure was anticipation. Quite what to expect, he had no idea. But he was looking good, his uniform looked good; and this was his first real furlough.

Two hours later, he was feeling bemused. He'd received an impression, his first, of the sheer size of the land the Corps protected. The Transports shook and clattered, solid tyres bouncing over potholes; and this was still the Salient, the country he'd known from a child. Dotted with little farms, the occasional small hamlet; broken here and there by the low rise of a hill, but for the most part deadly flat. Little traffic either, and few signs of life; just the odd cart, sometimes a peasant leaning at the wayside, scowling suspiciously at the small convoy. Though once they passed through a slightly bigger settlement; nearly large enough, he supposed, to be called a town. In its centre, placed at the crossing of four roads, were the twin buildings he'd come to expect from his odd trips to the Easthold; the arrogant, thrusting spire of the Church Variant, fronting the whitewashed barn of the milder Middle Doctrine.

His fellow Cadets had fallen quiet as well. Once Olsen, typically, had begun to bawl a vulgar ditty; something about how far you could get up, with a fifty-lifter string. Meggs snarled at him finally to shut up, and Raoul was vaguely glad. There was a sombreness about the place that matched his altered mood.

A brief stop, at an inn that looked as decrepit as the rest, and the land finally began to change. They were climbing now, into lush green hills. The road surface was better too; the wheels of the Transports crunched on fresh-laid gravel. This country was prosperous, more prosperous than any he'd seen; there were well-stocked fields, neatly fenced paddocks in which fine horses ran. He essayed a question, and Meggs nodded. "Yes," he said. "It's the Middle Lands."

They rounded a bend; and Raoul gasped. Ahead lay the biggest house he'd ever seen. It dominated a tree-lined combe; a high stone frontage, embellished with corner towers, set with line on line of elegant windows. Above it, over the low-pitched roofs, flew massive Kitestrings. The streamers flapped, gaudy and graceful; on them he made out the cabalistic signs that protected the Realm from harm. The Seeing Eye, the clenched fist of the Church; and the Vestibule, the ancient leaf-shape that forever distracts the attention of the Evil One. He remembered the shock he had received as a small child, when its use and meaning were first explained to him.

Stev Marden called a question; and once again the Orderly was ready with an answer. "Kitemaster," he said, and sniffed.

Raoul pondered. Kitemasters were the high churchmen who controlled the Corps itself, shaped its policies, ran each detail of its daily functioning. Always, to him, they'd been semi-legendary beings; now he understood why, if they lived in palaces fit for kings. But his attention was rapidly distracted. Ahead, and closing fast, was a private transport vehicle, one of the very few he had seen. Its sides were blazoned with the insignia of the Church Variant; so it was bound, perhaps, for the great place they had passed. Beyond it was another, and another; soon the road was dotted with them. There were more of the fine buildings too, glimpsed briefly; though none, he thought, as grand as the very first of all.

The hills rose steeper now, coated with heather and gorse. At the highest point of all the rock of which they were formed broke through the grass, showing in weathered outcrops, in rounded domes like the old, patched skulls of giants. A final wheezing climb, and the view ahead abruptly opened out.

Even Olsen, it seemed, was momentarily stunned to silence. Far off, the mountains of the Westguard loomed in silhouette, like pale holes knocked in the sky. To right and left, as far as the eye could reach, the land rose to other heights; while below, dwarfed by the vast bowl in which it lay yet still it seemed stretching endlessly, lay Middlemarch, greatest city in all the Realm.

Somebody whooped; and abruptly the spell was broken. The Cadets fell to chattering like magpies as the Transports began their slow, cautious descent. Raoul joined in, pointing to this and that wonder; the Middle Lake, the great central parkland where on the morrow the Air Fair would begin, the pale needle-spires of Godpath, Metropolitan Cathedral of the Variants. The sprawling building beside it, he knew from his books and lectures, was the Corps headquarters; beyond was the Mercy Hospital, the Middle Doctrine's chief establishment. Beyond again loomed other towers, too numerous to count; while in every direction, spreading into distance, were the squares and avenues, the baths and libraries and palaces of that amazing town. To the south Holand, the industrial suburb, spread a faint, polluting haze, but all the rest was sparkling; clear and white, like a place seen in a dream.

The road, the ribbon of gravel, decreased its slope by slow degrees; perspectives became more normal. Middlemarch sank from sight behind the curtain of its own outlying trees. Half an hour later the Transports were bowling along a wide boulevard, fringed with fine houses. From each, for this greatest Festival of the year, flew the strings of sacred Kites; and the Orderly prodded Raoul in the ribs. "Nice number, that," he said, nodding. "If you ever get tired of the Codys. Kiteman to one of the Masters; you'd be made for life."

The Cadet dragged his mind back from distance. He was bemused, it seemed, by the giddying whirl of traffic. "Yes," he said. "Yes, I suppose I would." He'd been a million miles from the Base; from the stink of dope in the hangars, the scents of oil and steam, harsh roar of the roof arcs on winter nights of wind. But leave the Codys? The thought was insupportable. The great Rigs were his life; they would be his life for ever.

They passed the massive pile of the Cathedral, folk thronging its steps already for the pre-Feast service; and the Transports swung right, and right again. Then left, beneath a high stone arch. They drew up in a courtyard, windows staring down all round; and the throbbing of the engines stopped at last. "All right, lads," said Meggs, swinging himself to his feet. "Get your gear together. Reception on the right. . . ."

The hostel was a massive, echoing place; but the room into which he was finally decanted was sufficiently like his old dorm on the Base to make him feel almost at home. The same brown, highly-polished floor; the same identically-spaced beds, each with its blanket cube deposited neatly at the foot; even the same tall, potbellied stoves, surrounded by their thin, well-polished rails. He slung his kit down next to Stev Marden, and grinned. "Well," he said, "we made it." Suddenly, the words seemed curiously trite; but the other didn't seem to notice. "At least," he said, "we got rid of that little fucker Olsen. I can't wait to get out on the town."

Raoul grinned again. "Me too," he said. "Thank Heaven for small mercies." He started laying out his gear.

Passes were issued; but the curfew was at twenty-two hundred. Lights Out twenty-two thirty. Stev moaned a little; privately, the other was pleased. The long day, the excitement, had taken more out of him than he'd realized. He was glad to hit the sack; he was asleep almost as soon as his head touched the pillow.

It seemed he had barely closed his eyes before the reveille hooters were blaring. The Cadets rose, grumbling noisily; but Raoul for one ran to the high windows, stared up anxiously. Light clouds were scudding, but the day was fine.

The Section was herded to Ablutions, then to Early Service. It seemed the chaplain droned on for an age; but at last they were free to leave. A hasty breakfast, an even hastier Dorm Fatigue; and they debouched in threes and fours, on to the city streets.

Middlemarch, that brilliant morning, presented a spectacle Raoul thought he would never forget. The hordes of people, hooting of the flower-decked Transporters; here, he decided, must be all the folk in the world. Everywhere, the dark blue of the Corps; and priests in plenty, grey and sage green of the Middle Doctrine, white, black and purple of the Church Variant. Even, here and there, the vivid scarlet of a Master and his aides. There were startling girls too, in robes the like of which he'd never seen. They too had decked themselves with flowers; they passed in chattering, laughing groups, down with all the rest. Toward the park, the great Air Fair.

He'd been separated from Stev and the others; but finding

his way presented no difficulty. It seemed he was swept along, as by a tide. Within minutes, he saw the place ahead; the tall stands erected for the visiting dignitaries, the hangars that housed the score on score of Show Strings. Decorative Kite trains already flew, outlining the whole ground with spots of vivid colour.

The proceedings were opened by the Grand Master himself, from a dais higher than all the rest. Raoul wasn't near enough to catch the words; he doubted privately though if anybody heard much. The cheering was too intense. The Master raised his arms, in a final blessing; and the first of the Launch Vehicles swept on to the field. A gust of vapour whirled above the crowd; the stink of hot oil mingled with the sweetness of crushed grass. Raoul grinned, in pure excitement; and his arm was caught.

He turned. It was a boy a year or two older than himself, a tall lad in the pale blue of a Middlemarch Cadet. He took in the other's uniform, eyes twinkling, glanced at the shoulder tags. "G15," he said. "You're a long way from home. Well, Outlander, have you come to find out how to fly a Rig?"

Raoul hesitated; but there was no malice in the words. He grinned again. "I doubt I shall learn very much," he said, and turned back to the field.

Five pilots soared together; within seconds it seemed, their Lifters were airborne too. Privately, he was amazed. He'd seen some fast stringing up, but never anything like this. "There's a trick to it of course," said the other. "They strip the fairleads, the cones are ready-spaced."

"We wouldn't have that, not where I come from," growled Raoul. "Cable warp on the drums." But the other laughed outright. "New cables," he said. "They're only used the once. No expense spared, in Middlemarch."

The Fliers worked their tail-down tackles; the Strings swung dangerously together, lapped somehow each over each. Three hundred feet above, the baskets all but touched; and from them burst a storm of pink and yellow petals. The crowd roared its delight; and Raoul's new friend grabbed his sleeve again. "That's it for half an hour," he said. "Come on, quick. I've got a pal in the cider tent; get a move on, or we shall never get a drink."

It was the start of a hectic, exhilarating week. There were

formal tours of the hangar complexes, a banquet for all the Cadets presided over by no less a personage than Kitemaster Helman himself. By accident or design, G15 drew the top table; the preparatory spitting and polishing went on for most of the day. It promised to be a prickly affair; but by the end of the evening Raoul had all but lost his awe. The old man sat beaming happily, surrounded by Variant children in their new Confirmation robes; later he shook hands, it seemed with everyone in the hall. Meanwhile, the displays went on. Girls in tiny costumes performed feats of aerial daring; Raoul gasped, but only partly at their skill. There was even a demonstration of the new-fangled hydrogen balloons; the city had been buzzing with the news for days. Research had been known to be proceeding, but the Church had hitherto released the slimmest of details. Raoul attended with the rest; he was however curiously unimpressed. The silver blimps rose slowly, above the gaggle of gas bowsers; and he shook his head. They would never replace the elegance and flexibility of the Codys.

The Festival reached its climax. On the final afternoon Canwen, senior Flier of the Salient, was to attempt a new height record. Stev was enthusiastic; but Raoul once more pulled a face. A Cody basket at three thousand feet? There'd be no air to breathe, no air at all. He'd seen the Rig designed for the attempt; the Traces looked no thicker than a pilot line, even the Lifter frames were of some new lightweight alloy. The Lifters themselves were massive, twice the span of anything they had at Base. He brooded. There were Fliers and Fliers of course; but there had only ever been, there would only ever be, one Canwen.

The day closed with a massed display. Again, he knew he was seeing something he would probably never see again; fifty Rigs, all taking to the air at once. He stared up. The Lifter strings glowed oddly bright against the clouds massing overhead; the hissing of the wind through the forest of struts was deep in his skull, like tinnitus. The crowd roared; and from every basket shot trails and loops of fire, white and scarlet and green. Aerial bombs exploded, a cannonade; as if in answer, the heavens finally opened. He ran, laughing, with the rest. It was for all the world as if the good Lord had deliberately stayed His hand; that was probably Canwen's doing though. "He's always been like it," puffed a fat priest, jogging at his side. "Born in God's arse pocket. . . ."

He realized there were two Festivals in Middlemarch; the second was just beginning. Great bands of folk, young men and girls, pranced through the streets regardless of the deluge; every window blazed, the city's many inns and taverns roared. Tonight, it seemed nobody would sleep.

He tacked from pub to pub, drank cup after cup of the rich yellow wine, juice of the miles of orchards for which the Middle Lands were famed. His pockets jingled with cash; but nowhere would they take his money. For a Kiteman, everything was free. He laughed, his arm round the waist of a serving girl. She swung to peck his cheek, her hair brushed at him; he thought it was her scent that made him giddy.

Where he found the other, he could never afterwards remember. Nor could he recall with clarity whether she first spoke to him, or he to her. She was small and neat and rounded, and her skin was brown; he thought he'd never seen so many freckles. She was barefooted, in the short skirt of a serving maid; but that was all to the good. He admired her slim legs, her sturdy little knees. She curled on his lap, feather-light, in a room where a band played jigs, where waitresses circled between the many tables with more decanters of the vivid wine. She reached up, stroked his hair; he bent his head to kiss. "It must be marvellous," she said. "What's it really like? To be a Flier?"

He pulled a face. Much sooner concentrate on rubbing her behind. "It's all right," he said. He nuzzled at her again; but she chuckled, pushed away. "Tell me," she said. "I want to know it all. You must have an awful lot to learn. Who teaches you, the Kitecaptains?"

"No," he said, "they'd never. . . ." He stopped. To a Kitecaptain, Cadets were the lowest form of life; but it wouldn't do to admit that. "They're usually pretty busy," he said. "So we have special people. We call them T.O.s. Training Officers."

She toyed with the brassard on his shoulder. "You've really flown," she said. "Right out across the Frontier. Weren't you very scared?"

He hesitated. He'd have liked to turn the conversation, but there seemed to be no way. "A bit," he said modestly. "But everybody is of course. The first time."

"The first time," she said. "How many times have you done it then?"

"Oh," he said, "a few."

Her eyes were very big and dark. "Are the Badlands really like they say? Do they really shine at night?"

He checked again; but the lie must be maintained now, he'd gone too far to stop. He launched into a description, of a place he'd never seen. He'd heard about it though, often enough; the hills and ridges of that drear expanse, treeless and desolate, stretching as far as the eye could reach, twinkling in darkness with their own blue fire.

"Gosh," she said. "Gosh, you're so brave. I'd never dare. . . ." She shivered, deliciously. "And are there people there as well? People like us?"

"There are people," he said. "You don't see much of them as a rule. They're not like us though."

"What . . . are they like?"

He touched the little curl beside her ear. "You wouldn't want to know."

She glanced up quickly. "Have you ever seen a Demon?"

"Ah," he said. "Now that would be telling."

"No, honestly. . . ."

He frowned. "No," he said after a moment. "No, I haven't."

"Some of you have though."

"Yes," he said. "I expect some of us have."

She frowned in turn. "I've never understood about them," she said. "What do they look like? Really?"

"You know the Litany."

"Yes," she said. "But it's never seemed to make much sense. I mean, it's difficult to believe in them. All that about fishes, flying in the air. And the flames all coming out. Fish can't fly."

He said, "They made the Badlands though." He smiled. "Don't worry, perhaps there aren't any left. But we've still got to be ready. In case they ever come back."

"What would you do if you saw one?"

He said easily, "Get rid of it, of course."

She looked at him solemnly. "Would it work?" she said. "Just saying words? What do you call it, exorcising . . . Would it really turn round and fly away?"

He made a face. Once more he seemed to be getting out of

his depth. He said, "That's what we're there for." He signalled to one of the waitresses. The girl grabbed the cup from him, drank. Wine trickled on her chin, ran down inside her dress. He said, "Messy thing." He kissed her. The sweetness of the drink was on her mouth.

The street door opened abruptly. "Oh, no," he said. "Oh, no. . . ." It seemed he'd been tracked down by his entire Mess. They set up a cheer at the sight of him, and Stev Marden called across. "Save some for me. . . ."

They crowded round. Olsen was drunker than the rest. He crashed against a table, wine was spilled. A Middlemarcher shouted; Stev said anxiously, "Cool it. . . ."

The girl had tensed. Olsen grabbed for her wrist. She snatched it back, and Raoul said, "That's enough."

"Enough?" said the other thickly. "Wha' y' mean, enough? Wha's she then, private property?" He pawed at her again; she jumped up, eeled away, and Raoul was on his feet. *"I said pack in. . . ."*

The other's mood changed instantly. "An' who the Hell are you?" he said. "Jus' who the Hell are you?" He snatched at the brassard. "You don' even have the ri—" He got no further; because Raoul hit him in the mouth.

He was off balance; and the blow had been delivered with all the other's strength. He reeled back, sprawled across two tables. Uproar arose; instantly he was up, arms flailing.

To Raoul, it was as if events were curiously slowed. There was time for regret, even horror, at what he had done; also for fear to grow, because it seemed he was fighting a madman. The air was full of flying fists; his lips split, numbingly, a blow on the cheek sent him crashing against the wall. He all but fell; then suddenly the objects round about seemed oddly tinged with red. He launched himself at his opponent, in a berserk rage.

There was no memory, later, of physical contact; and certainly none of pain. He was aware, dimly, of the blows he rained, of the other's contorted face; then it seemed his sight was wholly swamped. He wrestled with the arms that held him back; and Stev's voice reached him faintly. "For God's sake," he said, "you'll bloody kill him. . . ."

His vision cleared, abruptly. Olsen had rolled on to his side; he lay whimpering, hands to his reddened face. A dozen separate scuffles had already broken out; and the girl was tugging desperately at his arm. "Quick," she said, "quick. Before the Vars get here. . . ."

It registered, dimly. He'd seen the Variant police in action once or twice before. He ran with her, half-leaning. He felt giddy now and sick, disoriented. "Come on," she said. "Come on. It isn't far. . . ."

The street outside was crowded still. They turned and twisted, desperate; and there was an archway, closed off by iron-studded doors. She pushed at a wicket, ducked through, slammed. He saw treegrown grounds, a drive; beyond, lines of tall lit windows. She turned aside though, to a stable block. "Up here," she said, "up here. You'll be all right. . . ."

He negotiated, with difficulty, a steep wooden ladder. Round about was a powerful, sweet scent that in his dazed condition he couldn't place. A match flared, in the dark; by the light of the lamp she lit he saw they were in a hayloft. He sat down, shakily. His cheek was stinging now; he put his fingers to it. They came away red. He stared at them, surprised.

"It's all right," she said again. "It isn't much, I'll get some things." She swung quickly down the ladder.

She was back in minutes with a bowl and cloths, a towel. She knelt beside him, wiping gently. She said, "He caught you an awful whack," and he said dully, "I nearly killed him didn't I?" She paused then in what she was doing. She said, "I wish you had." She finished finally, sat back. "There," she said, "it's not too bad at all. How do you feel?"

"Fine," he said. "I'm all right now, honestly."

She drew her knees up, linked her arms around them. In the dim light, her eyes were unfathomable. He watched back; and suddenly he knew why he was there, what the end of it must be. His heart gave a great leap and bound; like the surge of a Cody basket almost, caught in a squall.

She saw he'd understood; she rose, unhurriedly, undid her frock and let it fall. He thought he'd never seen anything as beautiful. She knelt before him again, began to work at his tunic. He licked his lips; and when his voice came it was little more than a croak. He said, "What about the others?" and she smiled. "They'll be out all night," she said serenely. "Nobody will come here." She pressed her mouth to his, twined fingers behind his neck. He tasted salt again, and didn't care.

It was over far too quickly, the first time. "Sorry," he said, "I didn't mean. . . ." But she merely chuckled. "You should have played with me first," she said. "Don't worry, it'll be better soon." Later, he fell into a deep and dreamless sleep.

She roused him at first light. He was disoriented for a moment; then memory returned. He lay blinking sleepily. He said, "I've been to Heaven," and she smiled. She said, "Where's Heaven?" and he said, "Between your legs." She rolled on to him then, bottom pumping rhythmically, thrusting sweetness at him.

Zero nine-thirty was Departure Time. Walking back through the city, he had leisure to feel scared. He needn't have worried though. Most of the Mess had failed to make the previous night's curfew; they were still staggering in, in bedraggled twos and threes. It was well after ten hundred before they finally got on the road.

Stev greeted him enthusiastically. It seemed he'd had quite a night as well. One eye was decorated in festive green and purple, and there was an angry-looking weal across his forehead. That was nothing though, or so he proclaimed. "You should see Olsen, K.," he said. "We really ought to get a picture. Before the swelling goes."

Raoul said nervously, "Is he . . . was he badly hurt?" But the other shook his head. "Take more than that to kill the little bastard," he said. "More's the pity. . . ." He nodded at the broken brassard. "Anyway, that's a Charge to start with. If you wanted to make it stick. And we'd all back you. . . ."

Raoul was silent, while the Transports ground through the city. As they climbed the long road to the hills, he found himself staring back. Middlemarch lay as he had seen it first, basking in mild sunlight; but infinitely, secretly, more lovely now. He touched his tunic pocket, where he'd tucked the locket she'd given him. In it a scrap of paper, with her name and Postcode; and a tiny curl of hair.

"What's that?" he said. "I'm sorry," and Meggs laughed. "I know what's wrong with him," he said. "He found himself a groupie. What was she, Landy Street? They mostly hang out there. Work in the big houses." He dug Raoul in the ribs. "First one was it, youngster?" He grinned. "Nothing like the first time, eh? Nearly makes me wish I was your age again. . . ."

Raoul smiled. For a moment, there'd been a flash of rage; but it was quickly gone. In its place was almost a species of compassion. Because the other had got it so wrong; nobody could know what he'd known, or share. He lay back, felt himself sliding toward sleep; and the Transports turned due east, to the high and glowing pass.

He opened his eyes. The city still stretched into haze, the sun still shone; but lacking now in warmth. The land was altered, subtly; the leaves of trees hung still and golden, or stirred uneasy in the puffs of western wind, harbingers of the first gales. Bad weather, for the Kitemen; soon, winter would be here.

He stared round the Transport. No faces he knew, this trip; not a single one. Secretly, he was glad. He'd no desire to chatter; too much was still going on, in his mind.

He checked in at the hostel. He thought they looked at him a little oddly. He shouldn't be here of course; he should have been in the Northlands. But that was his affair, not theirs.

He walked to Middle Park. The place was deserted, in the early dusk. The stands still stood, skeletally. From one hung tatters of cloth; fragments of banners that had flown there, half a life ago.

The lamplighters were about, when he got back to city centre; tramping the streets, giving their high, yodelling cries. He tipped one, absently, and found himself a bar. A woman came to him, and smiled. He looked at her, and she went away.

The city quietened, by degrees. At twenty-two hundred, he paid up and left. He walked to Landy Street. He found the remembered archway; beyond it, strands of some creeper swayed from the high wall. He tapped the wicket softly, and it opened. She drew him inside quickly, kissed him with all her body. She said, "I didn't think you'd come. I didn't think I'd ever see you again." He stroked her hair, smelling the fragrance of her. He said, "I promised."

No lights showing, from the big house; the shadows by the stable block were velvet-dark. She took his hand. "Careful," she said. "There's a step there. And another."

She lit the lamp, stood looking at him. The place seemed oddly cold. She said, "You've grown, Raoul." He shook his head. She smiled a little quirky smile. She said, "A bit different from last time." He said, "Yes."

She took his hands. Her eyes were troubled. Dark. She said, "Have you eaten? I could get you something." But he shook his head again. He said, "It's all right."

"Raoul," she said, "what's the matter?"

"Nothing," he said. "It's nothing."

She was still unsure. She stared up again, eyes moving in little shifts and changes of direction. She said, "Do you still want me?" and suddenly his own eyes stung. "You don't know how much," he said. "God, you don't know how much." He clung to her; and she drew him down, into the hay. She said, "Undress me."

He felt self-conscious, walking for the first time in a Flier's stiff red cloak. Stev Marden drew it from him, face carefully expressionless; though as he stooped to lay the thing aside he took the chance to mutter, "Good luck, Raoul."

He stared round the field. He'd been up two hours or more; but he still felt curiously lightheaded. It took a moment for details to sink in. There was the Launcher of course with its battered, maroon-painted sides, streaked here and there with rust; beside it stood Warrantman Keaning, and both Adjutants. A little farther back was Captain Goldensoul himself; hands as ever clasped behind him, feet a little apart on the tarmac of the apron. That was an honour he certainly hadn't expected.

He squared his shoulders consciously, stepped out. Zero eight hundred, on a fine June morning; and the Rig already streamed of course, angled up steady into the blue. He saw they'd flown five Lifters; so Olsen's jibe had in part come true. Olsen himself, pilotrigger for the day, stared down from the top of the high truck. His face was as inscrutable as the rest.

The Launchmaster nodded curtly. "Your Uptime will be one hour," he said. "You shouldn't have any problems. Wind's Three, gusting Four; stable barometer." Raoul nodded in turn. He said, "Thank you, sir."

The Manlifter rocked slightly, restrained still by half a dozen Cadets. He climbed into the creaking wicker basket, checked his pistol, the breviary he carried, checked the angle of the tail gear. He remembered at the last instant to turn, salute the Base Commander. Goldensoul acknowledged, it seemed absently; and the Launchmaster snapped, "Clear Rig. . . ."

As ever, there was no sensation of leaving the ground. The briefest of bumps, a lurching of the cradle; and he was rising smoothly, drawn behind the immense string of Kites. He stared back, and down. Already, the hangar roofs had changed perspective; the big numbers painted on them showed clear, white against corrugated grey. The group round the Launcher had spread out, foreshortened on the grass. The peri fence slid underneath, swayed gently as he gained in altitude; ahead lay the border, the low hills of the Badlands.

At three hundred feet he primed the pistol, slipped the copper cap over the nipple. He checked his harness, the snap-releases that held him to the basket. The rule had only just come in, he'd heard a lot of the older Fliers wouldn't use them. He tugged them anyway, conscientiously. Because rules are rules, they're there to be obeyed. And this was his first Op.

The wind was keen already, slicing at him; he was glad of the protection of the leather suit. "The Breath of God" they called it, in those endless early sermons. On the ground, the words seemed trite; up here though, as ever, they made sense. He marvelled, as he had marvelled before, at the sheer silent power of a Cody rig. He peered up at the String. The trace snaked, gracefully, gave him a glimpse of his first Lifter; beyond, the vivid dot that was the pilot. The wind-flaw caught the basket; he lost altitude, worked at the tail-down tackle. The train steadied again.

He guessed he was at operational height. Downstairs the hangar bells would be pealing, the Launchmaster setting the safeties on the big winch. He looked back, to the grey rectangles of sheds. Westward the land stretched into haze. Somewhere beyond the bright horizon lay Middlemarch. He stared straight down. High though he was, the low, humped bushes showed clear; it seemed he could have numbered the individual blades of grass.

There was a ringing snap. The thrill lashed back through the train; instantly the Rig began to snake again, more wildly than before. He stared up, appalled. He had lost his pilot.

The Cody was now hopelessly unbalanced. The basket dipped sickeningly, soared; he grabbed for the main trace, felt the vibration of the winch. Below, he knew, binoculars would have been trained; they'd have seen, at the same instant. A Lifter boomed and flapped; at once, the line tension eased. Somewhere, a deadly calculation was going on. Too slow, and his lift was gone; too fast, and they'd crack a strut. Then he'd be done for good.

He glared back at the boundary fence; the long thin line of it, stretching into distance. So near, and yet so far. Then there was time, it seemed, for one strange thought. He remembered Olsen's face, the lack of expression there. One slip, a badly-adjusted tackle; but accident or design, it made no difference now. Olsen was through. He stared at the fence again, regauged his height. He'd realized he had more pressing problems; he'd just received an aerial lesson in trigonometry.

The basket struck, rebounded. Had it not been for the harness he'd have been thrown out, on to the sick grass of the Badlands. He worked the tail-down tackle; and the wind gusted suddenly. It made him another hundred yards; but the fence looked as far away as ever.

The shouts carried to him. "*The basket, the basket. . . .*" He understood, at last; it was tilted to one side, carrying far too much weight. He grabbed the pistol from its wicker holster, but he was too late; the thing that had boarded him already had his wrist. It was no bigger, perhaps, than a three or four years child, and its skin was an odd, almost translucent blue. It was mature though, evidently; he saw that it was female. Dreadfully, appallingly female.

The gun went off, wildly; then it was jerked from his hand. The basket rebounded again; but the other didn't relax its grip. He stared, in terror. What he saw now in the eyes was not the hate he'd read about, but love; a horrifying, eternal love. She stroked his arm, and gurgled; gurgled and pleaded, even while he took the line axe, and struck, and struck, and struck. . . .

He flung the girl away from him. She fell back, panting, in the hay. "Raoul," she said, "what is it? What have I done. . . ." He couldn't answer though; he was grabbing for his clothes. He ran, for the tall ladder; and she screamed again. "Raoul, no . . . no, please. . . ."

The city was round about him. He ran again, through Landy Street, into Main Drag, past the huge bulk of Godpath. The Middle Park was ahead; his breath was labouring, lungs burning, but he knew he would never stop now. "I'm sorry," he screamed, to the sky that didn't care. *"I'm sorry, I'm sorry, I'm sorry. . . ."*

3 kitemistress

THE ROOM WAS as spartan as the rest of the camp buildings; bare walls, a radiator, the statutory filing cabinets. The only touch of elegance was the broad, polished desk. Its top was bare save for a blotting pad and inkwell. Beside the inkwell lay a pearl-handled quill sharpener.

He stood stiffly to attention while Captain Goldensoul re-read the paper in his hands. Finally he laid it down. A brief silence; then he took off his *pince-nez,* slipped the little lenses into a case of soft leather. He said, "I see." He looked up. He said, "Why do you wish to leave the Corps, Cadet?"

He swallowed. He said, "It's in the resignation, sir."

Goldensoul smiled faintly. He said, "The resignation tells me very little. You merely state you no longer wish to fly the Codys. I think I deserve a fraction more than that."

The other didn't answer. Goldensoul glanced up at him again. He'd seen the Kites break enough men in his time; Fliers of many years' seniority sometimes. The strain, the endless danger, finally became too much. But this boy's nerve hadn't broken. Not if he was any judge. He pursed his lips. He said, "Stand easy, Cadet."

He turned back to the little sheaf of reports. In the main, an excellent record. The odd small escapade certainly; but those he both expected and allowed for. As did any Base Commander worth his salt. What mattered, finally, were the Codys. And his flew well. It had always been his belief that good Kitemen were born, not made. And this lad was a Flier. He drummed his fingers. He said, "It has cost the Corps, and therefore the Realm, a great deal to train you, Josen. A great deal of money, and a great deal of time. Have you considered that?"

"Yes, sir. I'm sorry."

He pushed the papers together. "You say you no longer wish to fly the Codys. Have you thought about switching to Ground Duties? These things can be arranged, you know."

The boy was still staring past him. He said, "Yes, sir."

"And your decision?"

Raoul swallowed. He said, "I wish to leave the Corps." He couldn't explain; but to see the Codys, to be close, and not to fly. . . . The thought was insupportable. He said, "I've thought about it a long time, sir. I've thought about it all."

The other nodded. He said, "I'm sure you have."

He rose, stared through the windows; at the neat grass of the outfield, the Kites flying in their immaculate line. He knew well enough what was troubling the youngster; he'd presided perforce at the court martial that had followed the wretched affair. One Cadet dismissed with ignominy was bad enough; but he hadn't thought at the time it would lead to this. But what boy, or indeed what man, ever did stop to consider where jealousy and hatred might lead? "Cadet," he said, "you saved both yourself and your String. You showed coolness, and considerable courage." He paused. "You are here, we are all here, to protect the Realm. You did your duty. I see no shame in that."

But he'd been neither cool nor courageous. He'd been terrified. He'd seized the first weapon that came to hand, killed a defenceless creature with it. He said, "Have you ever cut a baby's head off with a hatchet?" His back stiffened instantly. He said, "Sorry, sir. Beg pardon."

The Captain waved a hand, mildly. He stared a moment longer, then sat back at the desk. He said, "You didn't kill a baby. You killed nothing human. You destroyed an alien. An enemy of the Realm."

Raoul moistened his lips with his tongue. "It was human," he said. "And it wasn't our enemy."

Goldensoul nodded. He said, "So you see yourself as a murderer." He steepled his fingers, looked pensive. "Your concern does you credit," he said. "I can share neither your sentiments nor your conclusions; but I respect them." He considered. "An attempt was made on your life," he said. "What motives the wretched young man had, I neither know nor care. He failed; but ask yourself this. Are you now going to allow him to ruin your career by proxy?"

No answer; and the Captain shrugged. "Very well," he said. "At the end, the decision can only be yours." He tapped the papers. "I'm not forwarding your resignation," he said. "Instead I'm giving you a conditional discharge. It's a privilege allowed me under certain circumstances. In view of your past conduct, and your excellent service record, I judge these warrant it. In effect, you're on twelve months unpaid leave. If at the end of that time you've reconsidered, come back and see me." He glanced at the papers again. He said, "Your people are in Hyeway, are they not?"

Raoul said, "Yes, sir."

"There's a Transport leaving in the morning," said Goldensoul. "It should pass quite close. I can arrange travel, if you choose."

He stood to attention again. "No thank you, sir," he said.

"Then where will you go?"

"I don't know, sir."

"What will you do?"

"I'm sorry," said the Cadet again. "I don't know."

The Captain sighed. He said, "I see." He rose, and held his hand out. He said, "Good luck, Raoul."

He said, "Thank you, sir." He unclipped the silver Trace from his shoulder, laid it on the desk. He stepped back, saluted smartly. He closed the door behind him.

The Captain Goldensoul put his hands on his knees. Difficult to recall the passions and emotions of one so young. Easy to remember, but difficult to recall. One thing only was certain; the Corps had lost a good man. He unlocked one of the desk drawers, slipped the papers away. He supposed over the years he'd done a fairish job. Certainly he'd done his best; nobody could do more.

It was a shallow comfort.

Raoul strode across the Base. He ignored the Codys. There was no longer any need to salute; his Trace was down. Once he knuckled his eyes, furious with himself. Because he knew once clear, he would never come back. Nobody saw though.

It was evening already, the sun setting in long swathes of crimson. He'd put the resignation in at zero nine hundred, after yet another sleepless night; but Goldensoul had been off Base, he'd had to kick his heels most of the day.

He headed for the refectory block. Seventeen thirty; the bar should be open by now. He walked into the long, high room, with its chequered flooring of black and white tiles. As ever, it was cool. The Fliers used it; to a man, they professed to dislike warmth. He paid for a pint of beer, downed it and ordered a second. It seemed like an evening for getting drunk.

A harsh, quiet voice said, "Kitecadet. . . ."

He started. He hadn't even seen the man sitting in the far corner. He turned, and swallowed. Canwen, senior Flier on the Salient; and one of the most respected in the Corps. He said, "Good evening, Master."

The other gestured, curtly. Raoul hesitated, walked across to join him. Canwen had never spoken to him before; never, it seemed, deigned to notice his existence. Despite himself, he felt the rise of awe.

The Flier produced a black, stubby pipe. He lit it, unhurriedly. He smoked a while in silence; then he said, "So you've resigned the Corps."

He looked back; at the hard, high-cheekboned face, the icy, almost colourless eyes. He said reluctantly, "Yes, sir." He wondered how he had known. But Canwen, it seemed, knew everything.

The Flier lit the pipe again. "Good," he said. "Then perhaps your training will begin."

He frowned. He said, "I'm sorry, sir?"

"Like all young men," said Canwen, "you wish to run before you can walk. You wish to fly before you can crawl. You wish to rise, before you have known the depths."

He shook his head. "I'm sorry, sir," he said again. "I don't understand."

Canwen looked vague. He said, "I don't suppose you do." He laid the pipe down. "What do you think of?" he said. "When you're aloft?"

"I . . . nothing," he said. "Well, the job I suppose."

The other shook his head. "You don't," he said. "You think how fine the String looks. You think how fine you look yourself. You think of the yarns you'll spin, later on. You think of how you'll boast, next time you lay a Middle Lands tart."

He lowered his eyes. The words were uncomfortably near the truth.

Canwen sipped ale. "I consider the Void," he said. "I enter it, become a part of it. And the Void becomes a part of me. I join a third State, in which there is no scale. No large and small, no life and death. The reflection of a greater, perhaps. But that State may not be gained by idle wishing. It must be earned, with pain and sacrifice." He set his glass down. "Wallow in mud, and then the stars come close," he said. "Because you have earned the right to see their glory." He nodded, curtly. He said, "Drink."

He obeyed, wonderingly.

The other waved his hand at the bar. The steward served him, quickly. Canwen took a pad and stylus from his jerkin pocket. "Go to the Middle Lands," he said. "Go to Barida. Do you know the town?"

He shook his head. "No, sir," he said. "Only Middlemarch."

Canwen smiled, thinly. He said, "You soon will." He scribbled. "Go and see this man," he said. "The Master Halpert. My name will open his door. He'll find you a position."

He said, "A position?"

Canwen nodded impatiently. "He supplies household Kitemen to most of the Middle Lands," he said. "The Salient too." He rose abruptly. He said, "You must find the Way."

Raoul had half-risen himself. He called after the Flier, falteringly. "Master," he said, "What is the Way?"

Canwen turned back. "That is for each of us to discover," he said sardonically. "To each of us it presents a different face. Which is why some claim, there is no Way at all." He pushed through the door, and was gone.

Raoul woke next morning fuzzy-headed. The evening had turned into a party after all. His fellow Cadets had been reticent at first, unsure how to react; for the rumour had spread round the camp like wildfire. "Wish I could do the same," said one, a freckle-faced lad called Hanti. "Fuck the

Codys, I say. Only I need the money. . . ." There was a general laugh. He joined in, but he still felt pained. He wished Stev Marden could have been there. He'd have understood. Possibly guessed his real reason for quitting. But Stev, to his intense disgust, had been posted to the Easthold only a week before.

He breakfasted—the final time on a Kitebase—checked the last of his kit back into Stores. He collected his arrears of pay, withdrew his savings from the Adjutant's Fund; by midday he was free. He shouldered his duffel bag, tramped toward the gates. The Duty Corporal opened them for him, silently. He nodded curtly, feeling his eyes sting again. A few yards down the lane he turned, defiantly. He saluted the Codys, one final time.

He had no illusions as to the size of the Salient. He trudged steadily, across the featureless land. Though it was still early in the year, the day was warm. He pulled his jerkin undone, later devised a strap to hang it from the duffel. He saw no vehicles, not even a farm cart. No signs of life at all. But this was the Empty Quarter; sparsely inhabited even by Salient standards. He walked a further hour. For a time the G15 Kites, and those of the flanking Stations, had been visible, tiny dots against the eastern horizon; but when he finally turned again they were out of sight.

He swung the duffel bag down. He sat on the grassy bank and stared at nothing. The full enormity of what he'd done hit him quite suddenly. He put his face in his hands and cried. He got up finally, tramped on.

The old green lane turned north. Which wasn't the direction he wanted. But it soon met up with a broader, gravelled road. There, he had more luck. A farm lad overtook him, on a tractor. He thumbed experimentally, and the other slowed. He called down. "Where do you want?"

He said, "Barida," and the driver grinned. "Bit out of my way," he said. "I can take you a mile or two though." He jerked his thumb. The tractor was hauling a cart loaded with swedes. But of course the grass wasn't rich enough yet, the spring flush had hardly begun; they'd still be opening the clamps for cattle feed. Raoul said, "Thanks a lot." He scrambled up.

The other dropped him a few miles farther on. He dusted himself down, shouldered the bag again. He walked till nightfall. By then his feet were aching abominably. He reached a village; one of the tumbledown hamlets in which the Salient seemed to specialize. There was an inn of sorts. He shrugged, and stepped through the doorway. With luck, the beds would be merely flea-ridden. He had a horror of lice.

He was on the road early next morning. To his surprise, the linen had been tolerably clean; though the refreshment offered had left much to be desired.

It seemed his luck had changed. Within a couple of minutes a private vehicle drew up beside him. It was mudstained and elderly, but still one of the very few in the Salient. The driver, obviously a farmer of some means, asked where he was headed. He said, "Barida," and his benefactor jerked his head. "Hop in," he said. "I can take you part the way. I'm going down to Crossways."

In fact he took him the best part of forty miles. Raoul stood and waved as the vehicle lurched off to the south. He started walking again.

At least the land was more populous here; and what villages he passed through looked better kept. In one though he was threatened by a pack of scrawny dogs. He caught the leader a smart kick in the chest, more by luck than judgement. The animal yelped, and fled. The others followed it. Nobody came to his aid; but then, the Salient had never been overfond of strangers. A mile or so on he came across a pile of ash poles, dumped on the side of the road awaiting collection. He selected the stoutest, spent an hour haggling it to a usable length. At first he felt faintly ridiculous, stumping along like some Middle Way pilgrim; but the staff came in useful on more than one occasion.

The good fortune of the morning wasn't repeated. Night found him seemingly miles from anywhere. He climbed on to a partly demolished hayrick. He emptied the duffel, spread the contents as some sort of covering. He pulled the bag up round his legs. He still thought he'd never been so cold. He slept finally, woke frozen and stiff. Also he'd made up for the night before, he'd been bitten from head to foot. What the creatures had been he had no idea; but his back felt as if it had been peppered with shot. He wondered if it was the beginning of the penance the Master Canwen had ordained.

The day that followed was much the same; and the day after that. Though at least he managed to find himself accommodation. On the fifth morning he was overtaken by a Corps Transport. He flagged it, but it rattled past unconcerned. He set his mouth. Of course, he was a civilian now; and scruffy to boot, he had no doubt. He rubbed his stubble of beard, and hefted the stick. He tramped on again.

He neared the Salient boundary, finally. The ground trended steadily upward; ahead were the hills that fringed the Middle Lands.

The villages were more frequent now, and inns relatively numerous. But the better-looking refused him at a glance; he had to make do with their less salubrious counterparts. At least he managed a shave, and a change of clothes. After which he was picked up by a lorry loaded with milk churns. It rattled through the hills, decanted him some twenty miles from his destination.

He was fortunate again. A private vehicle pulled up almost at once. He stared. He thought he'd never seen such a resplendent motor. Its coachwork glittered, coats of arms were emblazoned on its doorpanels; on its wings pennants displayed the Vestibule, gold thread against a scarlet ground. The private carriage of a Master, evidently. The chauffeur buttoned down the window on his side. He leaned across. He said, "Where you want, lad?"

He said, "Barida."

The other grinned. "You're in luck," he said. "I'm going through." He nodded. "Get rid of that thing though. You look like a mendicant bloody friar." Raoul threw the ashplant regretfully into the hedge. He'd become quite fond of it.

He leaned back, against luxurious upholstery. He was still amazed that the thing had stopped at all. He said curiously, "Who are you with?"

The other said, "I serve the Master Helman." There was a species of pride in his voice.

He frowned. He still didn't understand. He said, "But why did you stop for me?"

The driver glanced across. He said, "The Master would have." He lapsed into silence.

He nodded. It explained a lot.

He sniffed, appreciatively. Even the air of the Middle Lands smelled different. Softer somehow, and warm. In summer he knew it was heavy with the scent of flowers. He looked round. They were passing a big stone-built house, set back from the road on a little rise of ground. Codys were streamed, the first he'd seen for days. He said, "Do you know the Master Halpert?"

The other glanced at him again. "Sure," he said. "Bishop of Barida. What are you after, a Kiteman's job?"

He nodded, and the driver chuckled. "You'll need a deep pocket then," he said. "Even if he condescends to see you. I've known people wait months, just for the chance to grease his palm."

He said, "Canwen sent me," and the other whistled. "Nice one," he said. "Nice one indeed."

Barida reminded him very much of Easthope; he'd spent the odd furlough there. The same smart lines of shops, same bustling, well-dressed crowds. But of course this was the Middle Lands. He should have expected nothing else.

The big car dropped him at the crossroads in the centre of town. There was the Variant church, with its soaring spire; as ever, the white barn of the Middle Men faced it calmly. He walked into the church. An altarservant told him the Bishop was at the Palace. He chuckled. "He don't see the likes o' you though," he said. "You've got no chance."

He walked up the gravelled drive of the place, with little hope. The Official Residence was smaller than he'd expected, but excellently maintained. Above it flew a spectacular Cody String; round it, velvet-smooth lawns were dotted with bushes sculpted into the shapes of animals and birds. He raised the knocker of the big, iron-studded door, and again. His rappings finally produced a response. A small grille opened; a servant peered out suspiciously.

It seemed the name of Canwen was magic. A wait; then bolts were shot back, he was ushered into the Bishop's study.

In fact the great man was small and somewhat gnomelike. His eyes flickered constantly, never dwelling on his face for long. There was almost a furtiveness about him. Raoul decided he didn't care for him overmuch; but he hadn't come here to make bosom pals of Churchmen. He showed him Canwen's note, and the other beamed. "Well, well, young man," he said, "we must see what we can do. Yes, indeed. . . ." He rubbed his hands. "Have you broken your fast today?"

Two hours later he was feeling almost human again. He'd bathed and washed his hair, changed into his one clean suit. It had been rumpled from the travelling; but a kitchenmaid had pressed it for him. The cook, a sturdy girl with a mass of auburn ringlets, served him an excellent lunch; and he felt his spirits rise a little, for the first time in many days. He glanced at the address the Bishop had given him. He said, "Who is this Master Kerosin?"

The cook sniffed. "Big place out on the Middlemarch road," she said. "About a mile. Richest bloke in the Realm, some reckons. Ain't a tractor nowhere what don't run on 'is fuel." She banged a big metal heater. "These things an' all," she said. "We gets through gallons of it, there's a big tank out the back. Lorry comes every week, in winter." She sniffed. "Ain't 'im you gotta watch though," she said. "It's 'er Ladyship."

He said, "Her Ladyship?"

She said, "The Lady Kerosina."

"What's wrong with her?"

She began to scrape plates. She said, "You'll find out soon enough." She would add nothing more.

He walked down in the afternoon. His first sight of the place took his breath. It was big; as big, he decided, as the Palace of a Master. Its stone front, hung in parts with some bright creeper, was crenellated in the Middle Lands style. Cody Strings flew to either side, but not from the roof; there were custom-built towers, as impressive as the house and topping it by a storey. On their fronts and sides leafshaped embrasures repeated the motif of the Vestibule. They were edged with bright red mosaic; the tops of the towers were similarly decorated. He realized with a species of faint shock that each was a multiple phallic emblem. He shrugged. After all, it was sound Var theology. Perhaps this was an extra-religious household. Somehow though he doubted it.

The Master Kerosin was a slim, balding man, brownskinned and bland-faced. He too wore a pair of gold-rimmed *pince-nez*. He was poring over a ledger when Raoul was shown in; he didn't trouble to rise. He presented his credentials; but it seemed the name of Canwen carried less weight here. The Master shrugged. His voice was flat, with a hint of sibilance, and as expressionless as his face. "These seem to be in order," he said. "But you must see the Mistress Kerosina. She has to do with the housefolk."

He said, "Thank you, Master." He inclined his head; but the other had again immersed himself in his work.

The Lady Kerosina was lounging in a chair of silvery Holand fibre. Behind her, long glass doors gave a view of landscaped grounds. A glass was at her side, and a bowl of some confection. He stared. Her hair was dark, shot with bronze highlights. It tumbled to her shoulders and below. Her cheekbones were high and perfectly modelled, her eyes huge and of no definable colour, her nose delicately tip-tilted. She wore a simple white dress; the neckline plunged deeply at the front. She wore ankle-high sandals, again of some silvery material. He saw they were uppers only; the soles of her feet were bare.

She inclined her head, graciously. "Good afternoon, Mr. Josen," she said. "Sit down, and tell me about yourself."

He took a chair, hesitantly. She crossed her knees. Her skirt was split to the top of her thigh. Her legs were long, and exquisite. He blinked. He'd seen some daring fashions in Middlemarch odd times, but nothing to compare with that. He rested his eyes carefully on the middle distance. He was aware she smiled.

He began to talk, haltingly at first, about his training, early career; but she interrupted him. "Who," she said in her well-modulated, slightly husky voice, "was your Captain, in the Salient?"

"Goldensoul, Mistress," he said. "He gave me an excellent testimonial."

"Dear old Goldensoul," she said. "Always the do-gooder." She selected a sweet, bit into it deliberately. Displayed even, pearly teeth. "And what brought you to Barida?"

He swallowed. He said, "I was sent by the Master Canwen."

"Ah," she said, "I begin to understand. I was wondering how you breached our good Bishop's defences. Tell me, is the Master still as mad as ever?"

He frowned. He said. "He's one of the most respected Fliers in the Realm."

She looked amused. She said, "No doubt."

He risked another glance at her. She wore no jewellery of any kind; but round her neck was a slender leather collar. The sort of thing you might put on a dog. It seemed oddly out of sorts with the rest of her *ensemble;* he wondered what its purpose could be. He hesitated, held out the papers he carried. He said, "If the Mistress would care to see. . . ."

She waved a hand. She said, "I'm sure they're perfectly adequate." She selected another of the little comfits. "You must see the tailor," she said. "I like my housefolk to be liveried. Can you drive a motor vehicle?"

"I'm sorry, Mistress," he said. "I'm afraid I can't."

She shrugged. She said, "It's of no importance." She picked a book up, began to turn the pages.

The interview seemed to be over. He rose. He said, "Thank you, Mistress. Thank you very much." He walked toward the door; but as he opened it she looked up. She said, "I hope you'll be happy with us."

He said, "I'm sure I shall." He walked off feeling in some way reprieved.

He found the retiring Kiteman. He was a grizzled, time-expired Corps Sergeant; he'd been putting in a few more years before, as he said, finally taking to the rocking chair. He showed Raoul over the Towers. They were immaculately kept, and seemed to be well equipped. But at that the Kiteman shook his head. "We're all right for cable," he said. "Should last you a season or two at least. Bit low on frames and fabric. No point me stocking up; every Kiteman has his own ideas."

Raoul took a tracecone from a rack, looked at it ruefully. It was a toy compared to what he'd trained on. He shook his head. He said, "I'm new to this game I'm afraid. Have to learn as I go."

The Sergeant shrugged. "It's a piece of cake," he said. "Nothing to it really." He glanced sidelong. He said, "Better than eight hour watches over the Badlands, eh?"

"Yes," he said. "Better than that."

They climbed to the roof. He was surprised to see a small hand winch. The Codys were deceptive though. Even this size of String could develop considerable lift; streaming by hand could be hazardous, particularly in a blow.

The Kiteman chuckled. "No expense spared," he said. "Nothing but the best, for Kerosin." He glanced at Raoul quickly. He said, "I assume you've met the Mistress."

"Yes," he said. He paused. He said, "A very beautiful lady."

The other chuckled again. "She's all of that," he said. "Even give me ideas, if I was a decade or two younger. As it is, it's just as well I'm not. She's not interested in old stagers."

He frowned. Surely it couldn't be as bad as that. Not with her husband home.

It seemed the other read his thoughts. "Old Kerosin ain't here once in a blue moon," he said. "Too busy making his fortune. He don't give a damn what she does. She's window-dressing for him. Same as these." He patted the little winch. "Watch yourself with her, boy," he said. "Just watch yourself."

He set his lips. "I fly Kites," he said. "Nothing more."

"Yes," said the other grimly. "So does she."

He picked his kit up from the Palace, stowed it in the room allotted to him and went in search of the tailor. His little workroom was on the ground floor at the back. He sat crosslegged, stitching away contentedly. He was surrounded by ceiling-high bolts of material. Raoul narrowed his eyes. He said, "That's Kitecloth."

The other jumped down, got busy with a tape. "That's right," he said. "Dresses all her housepeople in it."

He frowned. "I didn't think that was allowed."

The tailor looked up. He was a smallish man; baldheaded and with thick, hornrimmed glasses. "If you're a Kerosin, anything's allowed," he said. "Dress on the left, sir?"

He said, "Er . . . yes." He frowned again. This was a standard of tailoring he likewise hadn't seen.

The uniform—for uniform it was—was ready in a couple of days. He reported to the Mistress Kerosina. She was sitting in a little summerhouse. It faced the south, the distant pale blue hills that ringed Middlemarch. She eyed him critically, told him to turn round. "Yes, excellent," she said. "Where's your Trace?"

"I'm sorry, Mistress," he said. "I may not wear a Trace. I've rejected Flier status."

She glanced at him with her great, tilted eyes. "How very honourable," she said. "Kneel down."

"I beg your pardon, Madam?"

"Kneel down, Kiteman," she said. "Just here."

He did as he was told; and she ran her fingers through his hair. "What a mane," she said. "There's girls who would be proud of it. If I were younger, I'd probably be bowled over." She lifted it, bunched it into the double ponytail favoured by the Cadets. She turned his head, considered. "Yes," she said, "it suits you. Wear it like that." She patted the chair beside her. "Sit with me awhile," she said, "and have a glass of wine."

"By your leave, Mistress," he said, "I have urgent work to do." He hesitated. He said, "Permission to draw Strings?"

She raised her eyebrows. "Do what you like," she said. "You're in charge now." She watched him walk away, again with an amused expression.

He met the household, over the next few days. In the main they seemed friendly enough. The cook, around whom so many establishments seemed to revolve, was a cheerful, bustling person in her fifties. It was said in season, her apple pies were the finest in the Midlands. There were numerous dairy and chamber maids, a cobbler; the Mistress even retained the services of a full time dressmaker, though most of her creations she designed herself. Sometimes, as he had seen, with startling effect. There was also a considerable stable, though the horses seemed to be kept solely for the amusement of guests. The Kerosins owned most of the land around them, but they didn't farm; it was all rented out. When Kerosina went abroad it was invariably in a closed carriage, drawn by a pair of highstepping greys. The coachman, he discovered, was from the Salient; as a boy, he'd known Raoul's father. He even kept some of the dreadful Northland spirit. Raoul took to dropping into the coachhouse occasionally for a chat; but when the dark brown bottle was produced he always smilingly declined.

The only sour note was struck by the head horseman. Aine Martland was a swarthy, bow-legged man; a head shorter than Raoul, but powerfully built. His face too was powerful rather than handsome; broad across the cheekbones, with a thick-lipped mouth and brilliant light-green eyes. His thatch of dark blond hair was tousled and unkempt; he wore ruffed, old-fashioned shirts, usually stained from the horses, knee breeches of heavy corduroy. His hose were as suspect as the rest. The household were more than a little afraid of him. It was rumoured he had the Frog's Bone; certainly at his touch the most nervous horse was calmed, the unruly instantly became manageable. Perhaps that was why he was tolerated.

To Raoul's surprise he was often to be seen about the house itself. Once a young boy was with him; once he had the arm of a nervous, pixie-like girl. She couldn't have been more than nine. Raoul frowned; but after all, it wasn't his affair. His job was to fly the Kites.

At first downhaul he saw what the Sergeant had told him was true. The fabric of the Lifters was stained, beginning to fray; a refurbishing was called for, through both Strings. For that he went to Middlemarch. He requisitioned a horse from the stables. If he couldn't drive, he'd been riding since before he could walk. Martland offered him a wall-eyed bay; but he shook his head. "No thanks," he said. "I'll take her." He indicated a fine, big-boned chestnut. The other growled—his habitual mode of communication—but made no further demur. He saddled the creature; an hour later Raoul trotted through the yard gates, turned the mare south on the Middlemarch road.

He found himself enjoying the ride. The weather was fine, trees bursting into their first spring green; and after all he was travelling in style. A bit different from the way he arrived. Also he found the flashes on his shoulders, the Kerosina insignia, commanded great respect. They ensured good service, the choicest rooms, the best place at table. He took his time, rode into Middlemarch early on the morning of the third day.

He hadn't approached the town from this direction. At first everything looked strange; but then he was on Main Drag, the great bulk of Godpath rearing ahead. He was surprised at the pang it brought; riding past Landy Street, he looked the other way. He stabled the horse at the "Cap of Maintenance," the best hotel in town. He booked a room and freshened up, walked round to the big shop that had supplied all College wants. To his surprise, one of the assistants recognized him. He outlined his requirements, and the other nodded. "Yes," he said, "we can supply all that. How will you get it back?"

He frowned. That was the one point he hadn't been sure of. He'd supposed the spares would have to come by carrier; he'd been hoping his sails would last till they arrived. But the other shook his head. "We can supply a packhorse," he said. "No extra charge. You can return it when you next come down." He was surprised, momentarily; then he remembered again. Now, he wore the livery of the House of Kerosin.

The other looked thoughtful. "I was wondering, sir," he said. "Have you considered fantailing your Traces?"

He frowned again. He said, "Sorry?"

"They've only just come out," said the assistant. "But we've had considerable success with them. Would you come with me?'' He led the way into a back room, almost as big as the shop itself. A dozen men were hard at work repairing Pilots, building Lifter frames. The assistant showed him a complicated Kite. Its span was eight feet or more, but it was obviously feather-light. He said, ''How does it work?''

The assistant set the thing back on the table. ''Rather like a taildown tackle,'' he said. ''You fly a double Trace. The second cable's very light of course.'' He waggled a control. The tail of the Kite moved obediently up and down. ''Runs through fairleads on the Main,'' he said. ''Bit of a nuisance when you're downing; but then, you shouldn't have to very much. They come rather expensive at the moment, but. . . .'' He left the rest unsaid.

He narrowed his eyes. He said, ''Can you give me a demonstration?

''Certainly,'' said the other. ''One moment.'' He called, and two lads appeared. They dismantled the assembly quickly. He followed them up the stairs.

There was a Tower, bolted centrally to the flat roof. A Pilot was already flying, on a light line. They paid out, released the fantail. It sailed up to its cone, and the assistant took the thin wire trace it had trailed. ''We find we can vary up to five degrees each side of Force Three Norm,'' he said. ''A considerable gaining in flexibility.''

He tried for himself. He found it was true. It was a fascinating toy.

He made his mind up. ''Right,'' he said, ''can you supply three? Two operational, and a spare.''

''No problem,'' said the other urbanely.

He had one other commission to fulfil. There was a little studio, behind the Mercy Hospital. The Mistress Kerosina also designed her own Godkites. Some of the symbols were startlingly explicit; but he was growing used to them already. The studio kept the tracings; he ordered fresh paintings prepared, went back to the hotel. He ate well, got an early night. For once, his sleep was undisturbed.

Leaving Middlemarch, he found himself heaving a sigh of relief. There was a certain person he hadn't wished to see. The thought of her brought the pang afresh; but for him women were ended. They ended with a Cody basket bumping over Badlands grass. He clicked to the packhorse, urged the mare into a trot. Climbing the first of the hills, he looked at the city spread beneath him. "Rye," he whispered. "Rye. . . ."

Rounding the last bend before the Kerosin mansion, he held his breath a little. After all, this was his first big test as Kiteman to the household; the Codys had been flying unattended for five days. They'd come through well though; both Strings were still streamed, at not far short of optimum angle.

He set to that same evening; downhauled from the western Tower, got to work on the Lifters. He reskinned the first, and doped it. At twenty-one hundred though a message came for him. The Mistress Kerosina required his presence in the dining room.

He swore, and washed his hands. He put his tunic on, hurried to the house. She was seated in solitary state, at the end of the long table. The candlelight made her eyes seem very dark. She said, "Good evening, Kiteman. You've worked well; so I've invited you to dinner."

"Thank you, Mistress," he said. "But I've already eaten."

She looked at him. She said, "Then you'll eat again."

He sat. There seemed nothing else to do.

She poured wine, handed the glass across. She rang a little bell. She said, "How was Middlemarch?"

He answered, as best he could. Her dress top was diaphanous; her breasts with their high, firm buds showed clearly. She might as well have been naked to the waist. He stared at the wine; and the first course was produced. She applied herself to it, delicately. She said, "Why did you leave the Kites?"

"I haven't, Mistress," he said. "Not exactly."

She said, "You know what I mean."

He hesitated. He said, "It's difficult to explain."

"Was it to do with a woman?"

"No," he said. "It wasn't." You couldn't call it a woman, could you? Two feet long, translucent and blue?

She looked up at him. She said, "Don't you have girlfriends? A fine young man like you?"

He said, "I had one once."

"And where was that?"

He said, "In Middlemarch."

She smiled. "You're a very secretive young man as well," she said. "I think you have hidden depths." She poured more wine. She said, "Did you see her the last trip?"

He shook his head. He said, "I didn't look for her."

"Did you fall out?"

"No, Mistress," he said. "We didn't fall out."

She rang the bell again, for the first plates to be cleared. "Sometimes," she said, "I could be angry with you, Raoul. Would you like me to be angry?"

He looked at his hands. He said, "I hope I have given the Mistress no cause."

She laughed. "Always so formal," she said. "Always so very correct. Don't you ever relax?"

He said, "It's hardly my place to."

"What do you mean?"

He said, "My father was a farmer."

She stared at him. "And what do you think mine was?" she said. "I know about Sower's Arse as well."

He didn't answer; and she drank, refilled the glasses yet again. "Raoul," she said, "I decided one thing, a long time ago. That we only have one life. I know the Church says this and that, but I've got no proof." She linked her fingers under her chin. "We must live each day as fully as we can," she said. "Ideally, they should be filled with love. But if that's not possible, there are compensations. Why did you leave the Kites?"

He said, "It's a long story." He looked back at her. Her fingers gleamed with rings. The candlelight woke fire from them; blue, and gold, and red. She saw the direction of his glance. "I often decorate myself," she said. "Or perhaps you hadn't noticed."

It must have been the wine. He said, "The Mistress needs no ornament."

"You say the nicest things," she said. "You are the sweetest boy." She addressed herself to her plate. "I'll tell you why you left," she said. "Your eyes are the wrong colour." She waved a hand. "They should be the blue of the midsummer zenith," she said. "But they're not. They're a sort of muddy green."

He didn't look up. He said, "I'm sorry they displease you."

She said, "They don't displease me." She reached to touch his wrist. "I'm putting too much pressure on you," she said. "I'll take it off." Amazingly, she did.

Later—the plates had been cleared away—she said, "What did the Master Canwen say?"

"What about, Mistress?"

"About you leaving."

Again, he didn't answer; and she laughed. "Young men wish to run before they can walk," she said. "They wish to fly, before they have known the depths." He looked up, startled; and she laughed again. She said, "I've known him a very long while." She gestured; and a serving girl came forward. She proffered a polished, inlaid box; the Mistress Kerosina selected a long black cheroot. "I always like to smoke after a meal," she said. "It's the only time I really enjoy it." She bit the end off the cigar, spat it across the room. She said, "I really do have some disgusting habits."

The girl offered the box to him. He shook his head. He said, "No thank you, Mistress."

Kerosina raised her eyebrows. "Mistress?" she said. "She's not your Mistress. I am." He didn't answer; and she stroked ash into a tray. She said, "Don't you ever smoke?"

He shook his head. He said, "Not very often." He glanced at the chronometer on his wrist. He said, "Will you excuse me, Madam?"

"For what reason?"

"We're only streaming from the eastern Tower," he said. "I have to check the String."

"Of course," she said. "Otherwise the Demons might get in." She nodded. She said, "Go and fly your Kites." She sat a long time after the door had closed, staring at nothing in the dim-lit room.

He found he couldn't sleep. He dozed from time to time; but images of her intruded constantly. Her eyes, her hair; her breasts, her long, slim legs. He groaned and tossed, restlessly. He was angry with himself; but that didn't help the case. He sat up finally, clasped his arms round his knees. How could someone like her have sprung from the background she claimed? From earth? He shrugged. All folk sprang from earth. As they returned to it. Where was the difference then?

He rose, and lit the lamp. It was zero two hundred. He let himself out by the servants' door, locked it behind him. He climbed the stairs of the western Tower to the workshop. He got busy on the Lifters. By dawn, the String was aloft again.

Summer came, the ripening of the crops. He was amazed at

them. Never had he seen wheat grow so tall. But the soil was black, and rich. He began to see why the Middle Lands were wealthy.

Kerosina drew up fresh designs; Godkites to be flown for Harvest Home. At least they were more conventional than the last. He rode to Middlemarch with them, took the first week of his leave. He'd learned to trust his fantails. Barring a Force Ten, they would fly. He walked the streets more boldly now. At first, he'd been afraid of meeting her; but he'd realized he wouldn't. Because people never come back. He walked to Middle Park, sat half a day watching gangs of workmen prepare the stands. The big Air Show was due; he'd miss it by two days. He was glad. The basket Codys were no longer his concern; he was a private Kiteman now.

He wondered why Kerosina haunted him so. He was beyond emotion, beyond love; yet day and night he couldn't rid himself of her image. Each turn of the head, each nuance of her voice; her hair, her hands, her feet. He imagined kissing her; privately, as he had once kissed Rye. The Vestibule had gaped then, leafshaped as the Kites. Demanding, and pathetic. He stared up at the Codys. The answer was there, the answer was in the sky; but the Strings were mute.

He rode back, when the new designs were finished. The studio lent him a horse as well. Aine Martland wasn't pleased. He walked round it, hands on hips. "What?" he said. "You expect me to feed a spavined nag like that?"

He shrugged. He said, "Take it up with the Lady Kerosina."

The other mimicked him. *"Take it up with the Lady Kerosina,"* he said. He picked up a short hayfork. "Take it up with her yourself," he said. "You're more qualified than me, you longhaired pretty." He turned, and lunged.

Raoul was appalled. He'd been standing by the stable wall; now he was pinned to it, the tines each side of his neck. He realized he'd missed death by half an inch. His knees were shaking; but the rage still boiled and bubbled. "I saw you driving Charm the other day," he said. "I know where you put your hands to keep them warm."

Expressions chased themselves across the Horseman's face. Finally he wrenched the tines from the wood. He flung the implement away, walked off. He looked back once; then he clicked to the horse. He said, "Come on, girl." The old mare whickered, and followed him.

The Master Kerosin was home. He was surprised at the pang of disappointment he felt. Two days later though she sent for him. She was sitting alone as ever, at one end of the great dining room. This time he took his place without argument. She said, "Wine?" and he shook his head. He said, "As a matter of fact I prefer beer."

She rang the bell. A serving girl appeared. She said, "Beer for the Kiteman." The other curtsied, reappeared with a foaming tankard. He said, "Thank you."

The Mistress Kerosina followed the girl with her eyes. She said, "You'd prefer her to me, wouldn't you?"

"I beg your pardon, Madam?"

"For fucking," she said irritably. "She's younger."

He looked at the table. So much to say; yet there was nothing to say at all. He said, "The Mistress realizes I cannot answer."

"Of course you can," she said. "It's very simple. Yes or no."

He looked up. He said, "If there is no answer, there cannot be a question."

"So you're Middle Doctrine," she said. "I wouldn't have believed it." She shook her head. "Now I shall never know," she said. "It's such an unfair world. But then, you're still living in it. So you wouldn't understand." She toyed with a richly-decorated coaster. "What I'd like," she said. "But there's so many things I'd like. I'd like to be you. Then I could run after Maia, and catch her in the kitchen. I'd screw her arse off for her." She smiled, crookedly. "I'll tell you what I'd like," she said. "I'd like to see a little Cody rig. About so long." She spread her arms. "I'd like to see it anchored that end of the table," she said. "And I'd like to see it streamed. So the Demons in the room couldn't spoil the food. Could you fix that for me?"

He set his lips. He said, "No, Madam."

"No," she said. "I didn't expect you could. It's still a nice idea though." She considered. "What would have happened, if I'd been born rich?" she said. "Would I have been satisfied then? I know I'm beautiful; but it doesn't seem to matter."

He said, "I don't understand you, Mistress."

She shook her head. "Raoul," she said, "sometimes you disappoint me." She drank wine. "I've got servants by the score," she said. "I snap my fingers, and they run. But it doesn't really give me any pleasure." She brightened. She said, "Will you be my servant?"

He said, "I am your servant, Mistress."

"In a way," she said. "Should I make you my body servant though? You'd have to stand behind me. Massage my neck, every time it got sore. And move my chair, whenever I wanted to get up. Would you do that for me?"

He knew, meltingly, that he would do it all. But he still shook his head. He said, "I fly her Ladyship's kites."

The weather broke, with wind and floods of rain. He drew both Strings, spent time on more refurbishing. He reorganized the stores, made a complete inventory. After that there was little else to do. He sat in the eastern Tower day after day, staring through one of the leafshaped apertures. Out there, somewhere beyond the veils of grey, was the Salient. The Salient, and all his folk. He felt he should write; but his father could scarcely read, and his mother wouldn't try. It would just embarrass them. He wrote to Stev Marden instead. He hardly expected an answer; nonetheless, one came. He deciphered the scrawl, with difficulty.

"Ray, you old bastard. How crafty can you get? Here's me stuck down on an F Base, and you living off the fat of the land. How do you manage it?

"They double-man the Codys here. Which means eight Lifters, even for a Five. The local Vars were sure we were in for an invasion. Haven't seen any signs of it yet though. . . .

"How's that little girl of yours in Middlemarch? You still scoring with her? There's not much talent down this way. Mostly, they're broader than they're tall . . . .

"We've got these new six-shooters. It gives you a better chance. I can't shoot worth fuck, I never could. But I reckon I could just about get the Adj. . . ."

He sniffed the envelope. It was absurd of course, it was all in his mind; but it seemed even the paper smelled of Cody hangars. The oil and dope and steam. He shook his head. "If only you knew," he said. "Stev, if only you knew. . . ."

The skies cleared. He streamed his Kites instantly. The following day a letter came from his folks. Ill-spelled, but at least they'd made the effort. Which was more than he had done. There was another communication with it. On Corps notepaper. It was from Goldensoul. Stev Marden had been lost, from F16. The Captain tendered his condolences.

He showed it to the Mistress Kerosina. She read it quickly, shrugged. She said, "You'd better have a drink."

For once, he felt like it. It led to several more. She matched him glass for glass. She was lounging on a settle in the drawing room, the room in which he'd first been interviewed. Her dress was negligently buttoned; from time to time he saw the quick flash of a nipple. He said, "He was a good friend."

"Yes," she said. "I'm sure he was. Come on." She took his hand. It was a major shock. He'd forgotten how warm a woman's fingers are.

He followed her. Things were spinning, he was no longer sure of his surroundings. She led him down a flight of steps, unlocked a door.

It was a part of the house he'd never seen before. A basement, lit by the electric light. She pushed a further door. She said, "Are you fussy about smells?" He shook his head.

She clicked a switch. He was surprised to see the little room was ankle deep in mud. Thick, and blue-black. The sort of harbour sludge he'd seen once in the Southold. She said, "My private beauty parlour." She slipped out of the dress. She wore nothing beneath it. "I told you I'd make you my body servant," she said. "Massage me. Don't get your uniform dirty though." She walked into the mud, lay on her back. She grabbed a handful, smoothed it between her legs. "It's wonderful for the skin," she said. "It tones it up like nothing else."

The world collapsed. He took her twice, harsh and desperate. Finally he staggered to his feet. He said, "I've got to go somewhere." He'd seen a further chamber; a shower, and a loo. She said, "No. . . ."

"Kero," he said, "I must." He wasn't really conscious of the words. He said, "I've got to have a pee. . . ."

She clung to his knees, and kissed him. She tightened her grip. She said, *"I'm not stopping you. . . ."*

• • •

He woke at first light. The shame woke with him. He packed his clothes carefully, shouldered the duffel. Walking down the drive, he glanced back at the Towers. No need for checking though; both Rigs streamed at optimum angle. Both would fly, his fantails would fly; until they found themselves another Kiteman.

He turned south. Life, he supposed, was a series of ups and downs. Like the switchbacks he'd seen odd times, at Middle Lands fairs. He wondered which direction he was headed in right now. Hard to decide; but then, nothing was ever simple. He wondered how many people actually lived inside each human skin. The boy who'd known Rye in Middlemarch, the boy who'd used the hatchet, the boy who'd tendered his resignation from the Corps; none of them were him. Last night's ravening creature hadn't been him. She'd trapped him of course, he realized that vaguely. Chosen her moment well. To him, Stev Marden had still been flying, high up in the blue. To her though it had been vital to win. By any means at hand. He frowned. Were there other people inside her too? Was there a little child, who wanted model Codys streamed above the table?

He eased the strap of the duffel bag. He'd caught himself trying to blame her. No use in that though. He'd been in love with her, he realized now. In love from day one. Had a part of her been in love with him? The words of the Master Canwen returned, with almost shocking force. *"Wallow in mud, and then the stars come close. Because you have earned the right to see their glory. . . ."* He shook his head. How could he have known? How could he possibly have told? At least he knew now where his own star hung. There was a tart, in Middlemarch; freckled and short-skirted, with sturdy little knees. She loved him without question, without demand; and that was good enough. He said, "I'm doing it for her." He meant the Lady Kerosina.

The sun rose, steadily. He'd entered an area of scrubland. He'd marked it briefly, on his rides to town; now though it seemed endless.

He walked two hours; finally he turned. There was a horseman behind him, moving fast. He recognized the chestnut. He flung the bag away, ran on to the heath. It was useless of course, the other rode him down. He rose, tried to run again; but Martland had already launched himself from the horse. He tackled him round the knees, fetched him headlong. "Well, my pretty," he said. "Here's a different tale. Well now, my pretty. . . ."

He tried to defend himself; but it was equally vain. For a time, he thought Martland had been sent by Kerosina; but after the first few blows it seemed Raoul entered a new state of awareness. The Mistress wouldn't do a thing like that; she'd been in love with him. This was a private revenge. The horseman might procure for her; but he would never know her favours.

He rolled on to his side finally, raised his arms to cover his face. So Aine Martland used his boots. When he had finished he stood over him. "I shan't kill you, my pretty," he said. "I'll leave that to the Land. It'll be slower." He whistled to the mare. She trotted to him; he mounted, and rode away.

Raoul began to crawl, on hands and knees. Once he rose to his feet; but the pain in his side was too intense, he soon returned to the proper mode of locomotion. He reached a brooklet, finally. He slithered down the bank and bathed his face. He traced the damage with his fingertips. One thing was certain; he'd never be pretty again. So if that had been his only crime, he'd been well paid. He crawled back to the grass, and fainted.

He woke some hours later, pushed himself up on his hands. The sky was dark, which meant it was the night. He must go on though. He had to get to Middlemarch. He tried to stand; but the world spun, he collapsed again.

There were many voices in his brain. Rye, the Mistress Kerosina. One seemed more persistent. It was thick and bubbling; it sounded very close. *"Man thtay to water,"* it lisped. *"Man not go away."*

"What?" he said vaguely. "What?"

"Man thtay to water," said the voice again. *"Water good. . . ."* He sensed a rustling round him, in the dark. *"No-man help Man,"* gurgled the voice. *"No-man hand poithon. But no-man not touch food. Food good. . . ."*

"Food?" he said. "What food?" There was no answer. The creatures, whatever they had been, had fled.

He collapsed again. He woke at dawn. For a time, the things round about were shadowy. Then they returned to focus. In front of him, a couple of feet away, lay an old cracked plate. It had blue flowers round the edges. On it were what looked like rabbit haunches. A small, mouselike creature was working at one of them; nibbling nervously, scrabbling at the food with its paws. It stared at him a moment, with huge black eyes; then it turned, and bolted.

He overcame his revulsion. He crammed the food at his mouth, regardless of the pain. Later he drank again, from the brook. He crawled into a stand of bushes, went to sleep.

They brought him food again; and again the third night. By then his brain was clearer. He thought, "So they're even here. In the Middle Lands." So much for the Kites then. Once he thought he saw one of the creatures humping away. On all fours; smaller than a dog, and blue. He pushed himself up on his hands. "Come back," he called. "Come back, I want to talk to you. . . ." But the bushes stayed still.

He wiped his cheeks. He'd met its sister once, and killed her. This was how they were repaying him. With Life.

On the fifth morning there was no food. He understood that he was better. He got up, staggered off toward the road.

He was still lightheaded. Sometime in the day he saw a Cody string. He intoned to it. *"For that our brother in God hath felt the call; for that he, in answering the Most High, hath taken to himself the sacred duty. . . .*

"For that he hath from henceforth pledged his life . . . to the protection of the Realm, of all that we hold dear. . . .

"From the authority vested in us, we do appoint him . . . Kitecadet, and Guardian of the Way. . . ."

He was appalled. As he'd been appalled lying in the mud. The things he'd done, and said. He decided he was going mad. Later, it seemed a fresh awareness was vouchsafed him. The Demons, Badlanders; all were irrelevancies. He'd flown the Kites simply because he loved them. He built a Cody string, in his mind. He streamed the Pilot, on its slender line; he attached the cones, and saw the Lifters rise. He climbed atop the Launch Vehicle, felt the great Trace thrill. She lay under the Kites. The Mistress Kerosina. But they all lay under the Kites. Even the Badlanders.

The sky flickered again. "Kitecadet," he said. He rolled into the ditch.

He came round toward evening. A group of folk were moving up the road. Tinkers, if he was any judge. Dammakers. They haunted the Middle Lands as well. But there was no harm in them. They mended pots and pans, and paid no tax. They were the Free Folk; free as the Fliers. He got to his knees. He said, "How far to Middlemarch?"

They clustered round him, stood staring down. Then one of them pulled at his jerkin. He resisted, feebly. It was no use of course. It was dragged from him; and another grabbed his shirt. It tore.

"Look at that," said the Tink disgustedly. "Bad times, we're livin' in. No use even robbin' beggars." He put his foot against Raoul's chest, and shoved. He rolled back, into the muddy water.

The great Air Show had come and gone; the visitors had left; Middlemarch was settling down, preparing for the winter. Though the streets were still crowded, the inns doing a good trade. Better to collect while you could though; these were the last pickings.

All steered clear of the creature on the path. It was ragged, and dirty; it veered from side to side, seemingly half blind. "*Innocent,*" said one woman. She made a certain sign, and hurried on. Later, a child said, "Mummy, what's *wrong* with him?"

"He's drunk," said the other. "I'll tell you when you're older. You wouldn't understand, not yet." She steered well clear. "Come on,' she said. The child stared back, wide-eyed.

The Vars strode purposefully across Main Drag. "We got another one," said the Sergeant. "Must be the season for 'em." He approached the derelict, dragged at his hair. He said, "Where you from, my friend?"

The other whispered something. He leaned closer. "Sorry," he said. "Din' quite catch it, sir. . . ."

The scarecrow whispered again.

"Kiteman," said the policeman. "Kiteman. The things you people do get in your heads." He hauled the other to his feet, and hit him. He fell down again.

"Oh, look," said the Constable. "Run straight into your hand. What clumsy blokes they are."

"Yes," said the other, "aren't they? Comes from all the booze." He unslung the automatic from his shoulder, administered a few desultory whacks. The derelict got to his hands and knees, eventually; but there was no more fun in him. He hung his head and panted, dropped bloodspots on the path.

"Don't be here in the morning," said the Sergeant. "You might be in trouble else." He nodded to his partner; and they strolled away.

It seemed his life had focused to a point. He staggered on, reached his objective finally. The Church of the Moving Clouds. The steps proved an obstacle; he climbed them on hands and knees. There was an iron-studded door; in its centre, a great bronze ring. He grabbed it. It moved downward, slightly; and a bell tolled, deep within the building. "Sanctuary," he said. "Sanctuary. . . ."

There was a Var patrolman. He sauntered up. He was already unslinging his gun. He said, "What?"

"Sanctuary," whispered the fugitive. "Give me peace. . . ."

"I'll give you peace," said the Var. "All the peace you could want." He swung the weapon by the barrel; and his wrist was caught.

He looked round, startled. The priest was tall, and gaunt; he was dressed, of course, in the sage green of the Middlers. His face was calm; but the deepset eyes were blazing. "Sanctuary has been claimed," he said. "Sanctuary is granted." He relaxed his grip. He said, "About your business, Master."

The other's face mottled. He opened his mouth; and the priest held a great looped cross before his eyes. Golden, and plain; the Life Symbol of the Middle Church. "By all Laws, this is just," he said. "Uphold the Law. . . ."

The Var backed off, unwillingly. He shouldered the gun. He said, "You're welcome. We need more garbage collectors anyway." He adjusted the sling, walked huffily away along the path.

The priest looked down pityingly. "Sanctuary has been claimed," he said. "It is yours, my son. Come . . ." He reached to raise the other's arm; but the derelict shoved him away. He snatched something from round his neck. A locket, on a thin gold chain. "Her name is Rye," he said. "Her name is Rye. . . ." He lost his grip on the door, rolled down the steps. He landed on the pavement, lay on his back unmoving.

The girl walked swiftly. A shawl was across her shoulders, a scarf over her head. She reached the steps of the Mercy Hospital, hesitated. She made her mind up finally, and entered. Inside, she was once more bemused; at the noise and bustle, clattering of utensils, trolleys. The air had a faint, sharp tang; young women scurried in long white robes, neat caps. She stepped back, all but ran away. "The Master Trenchingham," she said. "The Master Trenchingham. He sent for me. Where is he?"

"I am here," he said. "Have no fear, sister. Come with me." He proffered his arm; she took it, sensed the strength in him.

There was a side ward. A little room, one-bedded. She ran to him. Saw the poor, broken face. She dropped to her knees. "Why?" she whispered. "Why, Raoul? Was it because of me?"

He brushed her cheeks, feebly. "You mustn't blame yourself," he said. "It wasn't to do with you." He stroked her hair. "Rye," he said. "Rye of Middlemarch." He took her hand.

4 kitecaptain

THE BAWLING NOISE he made was that of an animal in pain. He ran from the house, hands clutched to his head, and reeled across the yard. "Ruined," he moaned. Then, "Why . . why her. . . ." Then, "No. . . ." And again, in desperation *"No, no, no. . . ."*

Although so early, little after zero four hundred, the long house and the buildings clustered round it were already astir Folk hurried, attracted by the din; all stopped at sight of him They backed away; and a buttery maid bit her wrist and began to whimper. This was a Justin Manning they'd never seen before.

He wrenched at the doors of the barn, dragged them back Their iron-shod leading edges screeched on cobbles. The early sunlight shafted on to the motor inside; gleamed from the coachwork that had been his pride and joy, the smart brass rad. He advanced the spark, twisted the hand throttle desperate, scarcely aware of what he did. He swung the handle, and again. The engine sputtered, caught. "Why her," he moaned. *"Why. . . ."* The pain was acute now, torturing like a poison swallowed, burning at his vitals.

A hand was on his shoulder. Rik Butard, his Manager. He was unaware of what was shouted, what he answered; but the other's face changed abruptly. He set off toward the house, at a run.

Quickly, because of the poison. The pain. The air would blow it away. *Must.* He careered across the stackyard, past the tall, glinting silos. He couldn't see them for the tears that starred his vision. *"Tan,"* he whispered. *"Tan, my little Tanny. Tan, Tan, Tan. . . ."*

He jolted down the lane. A mile to the main road; he swung left, still unaware. The road beyond was rutted too, rank grass growing between the wheel tracks, weeds showing through the hardcore with which it was sporadically patched. But metalled roads were rare, throughout the Eastern Sector; in the Salient, they were almost nonexistent.

His foot was to the boards. The Swallow whined and crashed, protesting. Old when he bought her, she'd always been cosseted; he'd never punished her like this. But what came of cosseting? Blood came from cosseting. Blood, and agony. The pain he felt now.

His hands were slippery on the wheelrim. He looked at them. Over the right knuckles, thick caps of skin stood on edge. He didn't know how that had happened. It was fitting though. His blood mingled with hers.

There was a village. Better kept than the rest of the Salient hamlets; neat cottages in pink and white and blue. And garden fences, the occasional patch of flowers. But the Manning Estate had always cared for the welfare of its tenants; as three generations had taken pride in the great farm. Grandfather Manning it was who'd really built up the spread, laid the foundations of the family fortune. But he'd left the money entailed. His own mother would have spent it; as a Landy Street groupie would, it had once been whispered. But she'd never had the chance. Middlemarch held the purse strings, his grandfather's solicitors; and they held them tight. An implement, an outbuilding, a machine part; wire for a broken fence, the silos of which they'd been so proud; all had to be fought for, justified. So she'd worked instead; at the scrubbing and mending and baking and buttermaking, the thousand and one tasks of a farmer's wife. It had aged her prematurely; helped her to an early grave perhaps. Partially, it was seeing that happen that had made him break away; that and the burning ambition he'd owned for as long as he could remember. He would be a Kiteman; there was nothing else in the world.

Through the village, up the long slope beyond; the big car wheezing now, complaining. But her use was almost done. As everything was done. The sun shone; but there was no light. Only the pain.

He crested the rise, racketed down the farther hill. One of the few hilly parts of the Salient; for the most part it was deadly flat. G9 to his right, two Codys streamed; and the dawn wind blowing stronger, as it always did. A part of his mind realized the Launchers would be paying out as the Observers clawed for altitude. The gateman saluted him, surprised. He didn't respond.

Another Cody, tiny in the distance. That was G7; the others in the chain were out of sight. They crawled out in a great curve, protecting the huge bight of land. Winter and summer, day and night; untiring, loyal and useless. He groaned, tears coursing down his face. He said, "The Demons are already here."

Another hamlet, straggling this time and sullen. Coldmarsh. He scattered chickens; they squawked, erupting. One flew into the screen, left excrement and feathers. He didn't use the washers. He could see enough for his needs. He'd seen enough already.

A villager shouted, a dog ran yapping after the car. He swung right. The lane narrowed at once. Tall hedges, thick with the lush weeds of summer; poppy and speedwell, foolflowers with their stinking creamy heads. He stamped the brake, hauled right again. G8 gatehouse flashed by. The guard, equally taken aback, hurried to salute; but he was too late.

He left the car door swinging, ran across the compound. The single string was being drawn; he waved his arms, crossed them above his head. "Belay," he shouted hoarsely. "Belay. . . ." The Launchmaster hesitated, surprised. Stared up at the Observer's basket. It hung at sixty feet, rocking and vibrating. He snapped an order. Steam jetted; the clanking of the winch ceased abruptly. The Rig began to climb again, into safer air.

He ran into the hangar, stared at the wind telltales. "Sergeant," he said. "Rig for high flight."

If the other was surprised he didn't show it. It's the privilege of any Base Captain to schedule Stringups as he chooses; and he knew Manning for a conscientious Commander. He'd high-flown enough before, on hunches; and doubled, sometimes even trebled the Watching. But the enemy had never been found. The Sergeant saluted, briskly. He said, "Three cables, sir?"

"Six," said the other. "Six. . . ."

This time, the shock registered. Nobody, except the great Canwen himself, had ever flown six cables. And those height trials had been in Middlemarch, in air more stable than any to be found here. In the Salient the manoeuvre was unheard of. He wondered for an instant if his ears weren't playing him tricks.

Vital to leave the Earth. Fly far, far off. He shouted again, "*Six* . . ." and the Sergeant jumped. He said, "Six cables, sir." He ran off, bellowing orders. Whistles blew; within seconds Manning heard the bugles from the gatehouse. The call for All Personnel.

He couldn't wait; he grabbed the first of the spools, began to heave it forward. Gashing his already lacerated hands. Some fragment of remaining sense made him pause, snatch up a pair of the ground crew's heavy gauntlets. Nobody can man a Cody with fingers cut to the bone.

The place was filling now. Cadets scurried, half of them still bleary with sleep; two Corporals were hastily assembling the extra Lifters they would need while the Riggingmaster, with a set face of disgust, was laying out the great bronze spliceblocks that would link the cables end to end. Riggingmasters as a breed detested altitude flying. Fine if you could bring the Cody back in steady, detach each union, clamp off and respool; but in practice that seldom happened. Height meant danger, emergencies; reel in fast, lump the spliceblocks on to the drum, and you were in trouble. Five blocks meant six warped cables; and that meant a report to Middlemarch.

The Launchmaster was at his elbow. He said, "Permission to draw the String, sir?" He glanced at his wrist. "Well overdue," he said. "Forty-five minutes."

Justin nodded, vaguely. Eight hours in a Cody basket, even on a summer night, is enough for the most hardened Observer. And he was a kindly man; or had been, in other times. "Yes," he said. "Bring him in."

His ears were buzzing; and the pain coming again in waves.

He could barely hear the voices round him, although they shouted close. He said, "Prepare Launcher Two." No, wait. That would take time; and time was running out. "Belay," he said. "I'll fly from No. 1." Heads turned sharply at that. Within seconds the news would be across the Base; a Captain flying watch? That was unheard-of too.

The bowser was already bumping across the field. Hoses were slung; men scrambled to turn the massive stopcocks. Water splashed; the Launcher replenished herself as she worked.

The Manlifter was grounded, on the back of the huge truck; two Cadets were holding it, wrestling with the struts as the wind gusts tried to lift the great black wings. "Sergeant," he said again, "belay. Don't draw the String. Just give me two more Lifters."

This time the other looked aghast. The Launchmaster had turned too, was staring down as if unable to credit his ears. He glanced at the hangar, back to his Commander. It was contrary to every rule in the book. Once only had he heard of such a thing; in G12, on a wild night of storm. But he'd never expected, in all his life, to receive such an order himself.

For a moment, sanity returned to Manning. He understood the other's dilemma well enough. The splicedrums must be hoisted in sequence to the Launcher's back; to do that she would use her own steam derrick. The operation was simple enough; back tail-first into the hangar entrance, re-anchor there. But she'd have to down rig first. To move a Launcher with a Cody streamed was tantamount to heresy. Then the roaring was back, threatening to block out sense entirely. "Do it," he groaned. "Do it, in the name of God. . . ."

The Sergeant waited no longer. He picked up one of the electric megaphones just coming into use. *"Clear anchor tackles,"* he said. *"Secure basket."* He swung the trumpet-mouth of the machine toward the hangar. *"Attention,"* he said. *"Launcher movement. Live String."* The disgust was patent, even in the distorted metal voice.

The machine thundered, began to edge cautiously back. The Sergeant walked beside it, one hand to the maroon side, the other signalling the driver. Down left, and straighten; right. The Launcher clattered steadily; above it the Kitestring flapped and dipped. The cable thrummed; and the Sergeant dropped his hand, palm flat. A hissing; and the brake was set. He said with evident relief, "Re-anchor." Cables were run out smartly to the mooring rings halfway down the bay; and the tension eased a little. The Captain leaned against the truck's side, rubbed a hand over his eyes. He said, *"Why? Why?"*

The Base Medic was touching his arm. He said anxiously, "You all right sir?" Don't look too good to me."

He opened his mouth to send the man packing; but the words were lost anyway. The Launcher's donkey engine clattered, deafening in the confined space. More steam gusted; the first of the spare drums was slung aboard, spindle already rigged. Cadets guided it to its sockets, snapped the keepers shut.

"Two Lifters," said the Sergeant. "Unship basket." Cable paid out; the first of the extra trace cones was attached. He said, *"Hurry. Hurry. . . ."* The wind telltales vibrated, rose again and steadied.

"Lifter clear," said the Launchmaster. "Pay out." The great Kite sailed up the line to join its sisters; the angle of the Trace altered at once.

The Base Chaplain was there, with his stole and book. He handed across the breviary and pistol. He said, *"For those who watch as for those who wait we pray; honouring Thee, Lord, begging our vigilance receive reward. . . ."*

"Enough of that," he said. *"Enough. . . ."* The other glanced at him keenly, pursed his lips. He turned and walked away.

The second Lifter flew. The Launchmaster said, "Clear fairleads." His face was set as well. The fairleads with their curving arms were geared to the main winch drive; through downhaul they moved from side to side, disposing the cable neatly on the drum. But the spliceblocks wouldn't pass them. The cable would rise now straight from the drum itself; and to the drum return. It was an offence to his tidy mind.

The Manlifter was reattached. He climbed in, clicked the harness straps. He said, "Clear basket," and at last he was rising smoothly, up into the wide blue sky. The din behind him faded, replaced by the singing of the wind. A wave of sickness came, and passed.

He slipped the pistol into the holster in the basket side, tucked the book into the pouch by his left hand. He stared at his fingers. The blood had dried now, in ragged brown stripes. Her blood, that had been so vivid. It was as if she herself had faded, become already a creature of the long-dead past. He felt true madness flicker at the thought.

He looked around him. The horizon was half lost in pearly haze. Somewhere to the southwest, miles away, lay Mannings; Mannings, and everything he loved. Had loved, he told himself. Because nothing remained. A knife had been drawn, across memory. Across his brain and heart. He stared up, past the great wings of the Lifters. The Pilot was a tiny dot, against the deeper blue of zenith. He rubbed his face.

Flying had always calmed him. He felt its influence, even in his present desperate state. The tumbling thoughts had slowed, allowing him at least to put them in order. An old fantasy had come to him. The Kites were in some way conscious, sentient. Knowing his need, they drew him upward smoothly; away from the realm of despair, to where he needed to be. The sky was unsullied, spotless. The sky could not bleed.

Operational height; the climb continued through it. Five minutes, and he sensed that he had checked. He stared down. Already the buildings of the Base, the hangar from which he had flown, seemed small as matchboxes. They lay almost in plan; he could see the big numbers painted on the roofs, white against corrugated grey. G8, and SAL for Salient. Down there they would be attaching the first of the big splices, tightening the cable nuts, checking and double-checking; the Riggingmaster fuming no doubt, the launch crew watching impassive. He could imagine the excitement among the Cadets, the whispers and flutterings; for they were seeing something they'd never seen before. Would probably never see again.

The faintest of jerks; and the upward flight continued. He stared at the String again, shading his eyes. The Lifters pulled steady, barely rocking. He'd found stable air, as he'd known he must. The sun, climbing now and strengthening, struck thin reflections from the distant dural spars. Some of the Salient Stations were still rigged with wood; but he'd insisted, years back now, that G8 receive the up-to-date equipment. Pestered and pestered till Middlemarch had given in; more in self defence he'd thought, than out of special love for him. After all, G8 wasn't a showplace. Not like Middlemarch, or even G15. Just a cluster of huts, the hangars and workshops, little parade ground where the Cadets worked out each morning under the eagle eye of an irascible PTI. A workaday Salient Station.

He squared his shoulders fractionally. Workaday or not, the safety of his men had always come first. They'd had a bad blow a year or two ago, the worst in memory. G10 had lost an Observer, G11 two. All for the same reason; collapse of the wood-framed Lifters. His people, mercifully, had escaped; but that had been when the barrage of letters had started. And continued, until he got his way. He'd known he must finally win; because he'd always had recourse to a second threat. Unspoken, but still real. If a Captain could order the flying of all Traces, he could also order their grounding, for the safety of his men; and that would leave a gap in the defences through which the enemy might swarm. So Middlemarch acceded, gracefully; though he'd had no doubt Admin had damned him black. He'd shrugged. He'd done his best for the people he commanded; as he'd tried to do his best by everybody. Though that had still ended in ruin and failure.

He checked the pistol. One of the new-fangled revolving arms; something else he'd badgered Middlemarch into supplying. Copper caps in place over the nipples, fronts of the chambers smeared with grease to ward off flashround. G8 carried no armourer, none of the smaller Bases did; but priests were usually experts. Previss certainly was an old hand, and a crack shot as well; he would have allowed no-one else to arm him. A pyrotechnic expert too. He'd granted Previss a weekly firework levy from the pay of all personnel; and though there'd been some grumblings here and there, come Foundation Day no Station on the Frontier boasted a better show. He'd wondered with amusement, in the old life when he'd been sane, if all priests just liked bangs, if that was the true attraction of the Cloth.

A Lifter flapped slightly in a flaw of wind. Dipped, steadied again. He watched it; but the String was stable, balanced. He had a good team. It ought to be; he'd trained most of them himself. Cadets had asked often enough to transfer back after their tours; to volunteer for the Salient was no small accolade to him. So he couldn't in the main have done too bad a job. A hard man certainly, when need arose; because you couldn't run a Cody station on softness. Fair though. He'd always tried to be fair.

The notion of sentience remained. The Codys had been a part of his life now for more years than he cared to count; but their fascination had never faded. He remembered, vividly, the first time he'd ever seen a streamed Trace. He'd been a tiny child, little more than a babe in arms. He'd forgotten the occasion; some Fair or other in the Middle Lands, he supposed. Certainly it had been his first long trip away from home, in the old carriage his father had owned. And his father before him. It still rested in the carthouse; a beautiful wagonette with curving strakes and deep-dished yellow wheels. Varnished and lined with gold, the name of the farm displayed proudly on the sides. It had been drawn by two high-stepping greys, their harness agleam with brass; and he and his mother, the housefolk, sitting high, well muffled against the winds that swept in clear from Southguard. That had all been exciting enough; but when they'd rounded a bend he'd seen the great Kites rise majestically, strung half across the sky, and all else had faded. He'd held his arms out; as if he could catch the bright wings, draw them down to him. "What are they?" he'd said, again and again. *"What are they?"* They'd answered as best they could; in the main the country folk knew little, and truth to tell cared less, about the Corps that guarded the land. His mother knew, for she had lived in Middlemarch; later she came to regret the knowledge she imparted. It would have made no difference though had she held her peace. He'd stared behind, as the strange, lovely things receded; but soon of course there were more. Many more. Their sisters, he decided; sisters of green and blue, orange and scarlet and bronze. For it was a Feast Day; every Station they passed—and there were many, along the route they took—was dressed overall. He'd chattered about them the rest of the day, and all the long drive home, till his family no doubt got sick and tired of hearing. They humoured him, expecting the fad to dissipate; but it did no such thing. He badgered and badgered; till on one glorious, never-to-be-forgotten day his father had put him into the car—they owned a little automobile by then, an almost unheard-of thing in the Salient—and driven him off, to a secret destination. They jolted down a lane, rounded a bend; and before him was the neat white fencing, the small square guardhouse just inside the gate. He could read and letter well enough by then—his family had never stinted on tutors—he had no difficulty making out the letters on the big white board. G8.

They'd passed through unhindered—the name of Manning carried weight, even with the Corps—into a magic world. He saw a Launcher close up for the first time; the great truck with its high maroon sides, its drums and winches and derricks, its hoses and big, spoked wheels. Cables ran back from it to anchor points in the grass; and a rig was flying high, almost invisible in the blue. He stared and stared, squinting, till when he walked into the hangar he could see nothing at all for the spots of colour floating before his eyes. His other senses though seemed preternaturally acute. He heard the talk and laughter of the Cadets, smelled the scents of steam and oil, heavier sweetness of dope from where they repaired and refurbished the great wings of a Lifter. Up close, he was amazed by the sheer size of the Kites. Though here were no gaudy colours. This was a working Station, an outpost of the Realm; its rigs were sober, matching its sober task.

He was lifted into an Observer's basket, stood on tiptoe to peer over the edge. He crouched in the bottom of it; and in imagination he was already flying, the keen air round him and the endless, flawless blue. He watched a String drawn, saw the new Trace streamed; and his ambition, already fixed, became unalterable. There was only one thing to do, in all the world; he would be a Kiteman.

His father at first had been inclined to scoff. Certainly his mother shook her head. The life was dangerous, hard and thankless. None knew better than she; her father had been a Flier, two of her brothers had joined the Corps. Only to be lost together, in the same disaster; a Southguard Kiteship dragged her anchors, swept helpless onto the murderous lee shore. She chided, telling him his place was here, working at his books, learning to run the farm that would one day be his; but the words had no effect. She saw in his eyes that he would never change; she wept, privately, but after that she let him be.

Things might not have fared so well had it not been for his grandfather. Curt Manning was ailing then, well into his eighties and long past useful work; but his mind was as sharp as ever, he was still a force to be reckoned with. Justin remembered being summoned to his presence, one day in early autumn. The old man regarded him sternly, hands clasped round the head of his great gnarled stick. His hands were gnarled as well; the skin brown and wrinkled, marked with the frecklings of age. He considered for a while before he spoke; then he began. He questioned Justin in detail on his knowledge of the Codys, of the Corps, the Church to whom they owed allegiance. He answered, stammering a little; the old man's eyes were still a piercing blue, their gaze unnerved him. But he didn't falter. Sensing real interest, tutor after tutor had brought him books; he had his own library upstairs, well thumbed, and knew them from cover to cover. He could reel off the Stations of the Salient, their complements, supply depots, even their duty rosters. While as for the Kites, he knew the different patterns of Lifter, height and endurance records, configurations for each windforce. He'd flown a Cody trace so often, in his mind, he felt he could do it blindfold. The old man nodded finally, sat quiet again awhile. He watched down at the carpet, still unsure, listened to the faint crackle of the fire in the grate. Then the other nodded. "Well, Jus," he said—he seldom used his forename, even less often its diminutive—"I think I can probably help you. As you know, we're by no means badly connected. I know a couple of Masters; I think old Helman would probably be the one. If you're going to do it, and it seems you've made your mind up, there's nothing like starting at the top."

There'd been a sudden great leap in his chest; but he'd shaken his head. "Please, sir," he said falteringly. "If you please . . . I'd like to do it like everybody else. Start as an Apprentice. Then I'd know. . . ." He stopped. He didn't know how to finish the thought.

Surprisingly, the old man chuckled. Then he reached out, slapped him on the shoulder. "Hoped you'd say that," he said. "Spoken like a Manning. That's the way it will be then." He leaned back. "You've a year or two to wait of course," he said. "Work as hard as you can. Remember you can't ever learn enough. The Kites aren't the only thing in the world. But you'll find that out from the Corps, soon enough."

Next year, Tan was born.

The Trace had checked again. He peered down. He was well over the Badlands now, the Station buildings all but vanished in the haze. Below and behind was the cobweb line of the Boundary, the broader scar of the ditch they'd dug to keep at bay the crawling things that lived there. Not that they'd attempted infiltration for years now; perhaps they'd all died off. He himself only remembered one attack; that had been in the Easthold, miles away, when he'd been a mere Cadet. The Border Guards intercepted rapidly enough. One they shot dead; the others fled, wailing and splashing what passed with them for blood. Curiosity—the curiosity of the young and brash—had made him peer close at the thing on the grass. He'd shuddered, and wished he hadn't. He'd walked away, and been very sick. In the morning, there'd been no sign of the invaders; save that where the body fluids had touched it, the grass was yellow and dying.

Time enough now for them to have fixed the splice. Time and to spare. He leaned from the basket, held out the signal pistol all Observers carried. A bright green ball arced upwards, drifted down slowly toward the half-visible ground. The flight was resumed.

He'd resented her birth, as an only child will. At first, when his mother had told him formally she was carrying, he'd been confused. He'd said, "Carrying what?" and looked round him. She'd laughed then, and patted her body. "A child," she said. "A brother for you, Justin. Or a sister."

"Oh, no," he said. "You can't, mother, you *can't*. . . ." He'd fled to his room and cried, thrown himself on the bed, kicked out in sheer frustration. This was the end of it then. The end of it all. He hated babies; nasty, sticky things that crawled about and spoiled your books and stole all the attention so you sat in the corner and sulked, because nobody had any time for you any more. He'd seen it happen often enough, or thought he had. He was silent for a week; then, slowly, it seemed acceptance grew. And with it a certain curiosity. He thought how strange it was that one human being should make themselves inside another; and how they managed to pop out. On that matter he was wholly unsure, and far too shy to ask. He wondered if the other thing was true after all, that they were found under certain bushes or that the fairies brought them. It had always seemed far more likely.

His tutor helped him, gently. He supposed with hindsight it had been at his parents' suggestion. He sat frowning. The facts seemed bizarre. Later he began to worry. He was a dutiful child, and loved his folk; but especially his mother.

What he had learned seemed painful and dangerous. He found resentment of the unborn child beginning to rise again. Nor would it go away. His mother was worried, his father downright vexed. Finally he tearfully confessed his fears to her; and she laughed, and hugged him. "Jus, don't be so silly," she said. "Hundreds of women have babies, every day. In the Salient, and Middlemarch, and Southguard; all over the Realm. There's nothing to it at all, you'll see." She smoothed his hair. "Think how nice it will be," she said. "Someone for you to play with, and talk to. Your father and I have wanted another child for years; but we were thinking of you as well."

He stuck his lip out. He wouldn't be consoled. He said, "You can't talk to *babies.*"

She sighed. "I know," she said. "You're being one yourself. Now run along, and find something to do. And put a better face on at dinner, young man; you're getting your father really annoyed."

He went and read his Kitebooks; but for once, they brought no comfort.

A midwife was hired, and a wetnurse—he had to have that explained as well—and the great day finally arrived. He hadn't seen his mother for nearly a week; she'd taken to her bed, and there were whispers in the household that things weren't as they should be. Cook had definite information, and the parlourmaids went round with knowing looks in their eyes. He tried to pump them of course, but it was no use. He felt more shut away than ever.

He was allowed to see her briefly, the last morning. He'd wondered how on earth she could tell just when the baby would come; but that was a mystery as well. He puzzled over it for a while and gave it up; he'd become tired of the inexplicable.

He was shocked at how white and tired she looked; but by that time he'd learned just a little. He held his tears back, talked cheerfully till the nurse rose to usher him from the room. Mav took his hand then. "Go and see your father," she said. "I think he's got a surprise for you. Then you can come back later."

"Yes, mother," he said. "I will." He leaned over and kissed her. Her forehead was dry and hot.

His father was genial; in a better mood than he'd seen him for days. "Now, young man," he said, "come with me." He followed, puzzled, to one of the outhouses, stared at the big flat packing crate. The lid had been prized up; he rummaged in the woodwool that filled it, gave a cry. For a moment, words failed him. "It's," he said. "It's . . . I. . . ." He rushed to his father. There were tears in his eyes again; but they were tears of gratitude. "Thank you," he said.

"It's not just for you," said Tange Manning. "It's for the house. I'm putting you in charge though; you're the expert." He smiled. "I'll lend you Aniken for the day," he said. "We shall want a good strong anchor point. Where would you suggest?"

"Middle of the west front," he said instantly. "There's access from both boxrooms. Good liftpath too. No obstructions." Which was true of course. The great main stacks were toward each end of Mannings; the Trace could fly between.

His father grinned again. "You're the boss," he said once more. "I'll leave you to it. Tell Ani when you're ready."

Left to himself, he lifted out the great bright Kites with reverence. A personal Cody rig; wealthy families often bought air rights from the Church, streamed them to ensure protection and prosperity. Some, he knew, even had their own Kiteman; and certainly all the Masters. They were respected members of the household staff. He assembled the String, almost with the ease of practice; his books, pored over for so long, made actions nearly automatic. Then he hared in search of Aniken. The old man left his work grumbling. No Manning had ever flown a Cody; he'd never thought he'd live to see the day. In his opinion, it was downright superstition.

He bullied him. "It isn't, Ani," he said. "It *isn't*. It's vital. . . ."

He'd realized that every second was precious. His mother lay in labour, in an unprotected house; his scalp crawled at the thought of what might happen. "Aniken," he said, "hurry. Please, hurry. . . ."

The old man grumbled more at all the stairs; while the final spidery ladder all but defeated him. He hauled himself through eventually; stood blinking, looking round.

The roof was steep-pitched; but round the edge ran a narrow walkway. Flat-bottomed, lined with lead, protected by a waist-high parapet. Justin ran to the spot selected. He held up a streamer—supplied with the pack—saw he had chosen rightly. The little ribbon fluttered bravely, marking the wind direction. So if the fixing was *here,* just by his hand, the Trace would fly up well, above the houses and the stack-yards, straight toward the Badlands. A warning and a threat, to every Demon that flew. They'd veer aside, invisible, and leave the place in peace. "Quick, Ani," he said again. "Just *here*. . . ." The old man sniffed; but he set to work.

The job took longer than he'd realized. Much longer. Aniken was thorough, nobody more thorough on the farm; but he was slow. It was lunchtime and past before he pronounced himself satisfied.

Justin went back to the boxroom. He cleated the Pilot to the line, measured and marked the cable at the recommended intervals. He frowned. He realized he could have been doing this while the old man fixed the mooring. Somehow though he hadn't been able to tear himself away. It seemed he had to see every part of the procedure; make sure in his own mind it was good. Now, he had to hurry.

You couldn't hurry though. That was the first rule of any Kiteman. Hurry, and you made mistakes. That would be disaster. He went back to the booklet, reread parts to make sure he'd got it right.

He positioned the little bronze cones, checking their diameters with care. The fixings were strange to him. Instead of heads, the bolts had octagonal indents; and there weren't any spanners. Instead there were little metal rods, right-angled at one end. He supposed they'd just come in; some of the books he'd read had been quite old. He took care not to over-tighten; he knew about stripping threads. Then he remembered he was only a boy, and gave all the bolts another half turn. He sat back. He was sure that would be right.

One of the housemaids called, from the corridor outside. "Justin . . . Master Justin. . . ." He frowned. Hoped she wouldn't open the door. He couldn't stop to *eat*. She didn't. She gave a little snort of exasperation, went away.

He coiled the line, carried the Pilot to the roof. It began to flap and pluck, a live thing already. He slipped the line through the upper mooring ring, and then the lower. He held the little Kite above his head, released it. He paid out, heart in his mouth. It hung uncertain for a moment, then began to climb. Sure, and sweet. He whooped.

He tied off with a hitch he'd learned, went back for the first of the Lifters. He paid out till all cones were clear, clipped the tail ring to the line, released. The Lifter climbed sweetly as well, checking and clicking, to its proper place. So did the rest.

The Trace angle looked good. He tested its power, tying off carefully first. He was surprised at the generated lift. Pull back on the tautness and it was as if you held a live thing, trembling and shaking, tugging at your arm. The rig would certainly fly a rabbit, or a small dog. Perhaps even him.

He fetched the Godkite, the big pale oval with its Seeing Eye and the other symbols he couldn't understand. Bold and black, but picked out beautifully in gold. He streamed it, and paid out. Tied the fall off with a jamming hitch. Then another, to make sure. The Trace hung proudly, far out over the pastures, shimmering in sunlight; he put his hands on his hips, and smiled with joy.

There was a distant noise. He stared round, puzzled. People were cheering; from the barns, the stackyard, everywhere. His father among them. He waved; and they waved back.

There was a closer sound. Muffled, but coming from inside the house. He frowned, cocking his head; and it came again. A scream.

He dropped to his knees, started confusedly to pray. He prayed to God, to Father Andri, to the Cody trace. It dipped at once, and swung. As if it understood.

The rig had checked. He waited, frowning. Had they come for him already? He leaned from the basket, fired the pistol. The ascent was resumed.

First thing next morning he rushed outside. He was appalled. The Trace was at negative angle, all but brushing the farmland. He pelted upstairs and drew the Rig. He squatted, puzzling. Breeze lighter, and a little flawed; but it shouldn't be doing that. He rebalanced the Lifters. Present more face to the wind, that was the answer.

He frowned, biting his lip. No. It wasn't the answer. Windspeed was the answer. Create more flow, more vacuum. . . . He rebalanced the other way. He streamed the Cody, again with trepidation.

He couldn't believe his eyes. Even in that light breeze, it rose and rose. Why, it must be . . . it must be making more than forty degrees! He shouted with joy. He felt it was the best moment of his life. Then he remembered his mother, and felt instantly guilty.

It was a week before he saw her again. And much longer than that before she was allowed to get up. When she finally came downstairs she looked if possible even more pale and haggard than before. Her hair was lustreless, and there were great dark marks under her eyes. He ran to her, appalled; but she pushed him gently away. "Don't be silly, Justin," she said. "I'm better now. I shall get stronger every day." She wasn't better though; she paused frequently as she walked, and sometimes had to hold on to the backs of chairs.

He stared curiously at the tiny thing in the cot; the cot they always kept by the sitting room hearth, where a fire burned night and day. Its skin, he saw, was red and wrinkled-looking, its eyes a strange pale colour he could not determine. It lay solemnly, staring up; but there seemed to be no focus in the gaze. He said, "It's funny," and his mother smiled. "Not "it," Jus," she said. "She's your baby sister."

He returned again and again, to stare. It didn't cry, like other babies do; nor did it move about much, wave its legs and arms. It seemed content to lie there, and be still. Though sometimes it made little mewing noises. Like a kitten, he thought. Or a very young puppy. The wetnurse would come then, and shoo him from the room; once as he closed the door he saw her unfastening the top of her dress. He understood better by then; he knew the damp patches he sometimes saw on her clothes were milk.

He shook his head, in the privacy of his own room. He thought, with one of those strange flashes of wisdom that often come to children, "At least there'll be no more babies."

Nor were there of course; and as his mother promised, she gained in strength. Though she was never quite the same again. His earliest memories were of her working with the maids or buttery girls; swabbing the stone-flagged floors, turning the handles of the great wooden churns. Now she sat quietly by the fire, and was easily tired.

A winter came and went. Another summer. Tan lay in her cot and didn't move. He thought his mother sometimes looked at her with worried eyes. He streamed his Kites, and prayed; early, in the high green dawns, last thing when the rain was falling, snow and sleet flurries swirled about the big house. He mended the spars the buffeting spring winds snapped—he learned the skills from the village carpenter—replaced the fabric as it wore and rotted. He learned to know when a Lifter could be spared, without endangering the Trace; because at all times the Cody must stay flying. His former notion seemed strengthened. The Kites had saved his mother, of that he had no doubt; so they were sacred things.

Eighteen months after her birth, Grandfather Manning sent for the child. Justin of course was banned from the discussion; he heard about it later, from a chambermaid. Though how she knew so much he was never sure; perhaps his mother had confided in her. The old man took the silent little bundle, stared long and carefully into its face; the eyes that focused now, but in which there was no awareness. He was silent for a while, as was his wont; then he shook his head. He handed Tan back, gently. "There is no spirit," he said. "Give her to the Church."

Mav had started up, appalled. "No," she said. "No, *no*. . . . She is a creature of God."

The old man looked at her pityingly. "Then to God she must return," he said. "For she is no Manning. She is no human child."

He'd winced, as the girl prattled on; because for once he'd known precisely what was meant. Though "euphemism" had not been part of his vocabulary then. Fear stalked the Realm; it always had. Year in, year out, the westerlies blew; but just occasionally, they failed. Then the Codys streamed backward, into the Salient, the Easthold; and the people quailed, slammed their windows and doors. Because the Badlands were exhaling, and their breath was doom. The churches closed, field beasts were hurried into their byres. Let man or woman breathe the vapours, or a mother big with child; the results could not be guessed. Or dreamed of, save in nightmare.

Mav shook her head, violently. "No," she said again. "No, *no*. . . ." She cradled the little bundle, rocking and crooning. She knew as well as the other what the priest would do. He would examine his conscience, commend himself to God; then he would take a small, leaf-bladed knife, and with it gently sever the baby's head. "It wasn't the Badlands," she cried. "No winds blew from them, the Kites streamed every day. Justin saw to it. He is my loyal son; and she my daughter, grandfather."

Curt Manning shook his head. "It may not be," he said. "My decision is made."

The eyes were burning, in her wasted face. "Then I will leave this house," she said. "Barefoot if needs be, no coat to my back. Or die myself, by the same priestly blade. She is my own, old man; nobody takes her from me."

A silence, that lengthened. Her husband stepped forward, alarmed. He touched her shoulder, and she pulled away. Then she relented, reached to grip his hand. She spoke more quietly. "Under the Kites we live," she said. "Under the Kites she was born. No Dark Thing reached to her; so if she is afflicted, and I do not own she is, then the affliction comes from God. Not from a Demon."

Silence again; then suddenly the old man lay back. "No joy will come of it," he said tiredly. "Let my words be heard. Let them be written down."

"No curses, grandfather," she said. "Grant me the one boon."

He closed his eyes. "So be it," he said faintly. He waved his hand, in a gesture of dismissal.

Curt Manning died in the autumn of that year; and a great entourage arrived to take him to the dour Variant church that stood apart from the village on a knoll of ground. The cars and traps, the carriages, drove back to the house, passing the silent knots of fieldpeople; and Justin worked with the kitchen staff, circulating through the big old rooms, handing out food and beer. His mother told him afterwards how good he had been; but it hadn't been like that. It was the first death he had known; he hadn't realized what the effect on him would be. It seemed he still heard the old man's deep, slow voice, the rap of his stick as he called to the kitchen to bring him ale. Or for the nurse to come, adjust the pillow behind his head. His shape still occupied the old chair in the morning room; nonexistent, and yet visible. It was many months before it began to fade.

At four years old, Tan suddenly began to walk. Her first efforts were extraordinary; wild, blundering rushes, accompanied by much flailing of her arms. She fell continuously, cutting herself, bruising her face; but once aroused her will seemed indomitable. Always she would get up, stagger on; only to collide with something else, a chair, a table, a wall.

She never cried; instead would come the little mewings that were the only sounds she ever made, and that he realized—though he didn't formulate the thought at the time—were expressions of frustration. Or despair. He ran to help a hundred times; but she would shove him away, and her face would flush with rage. This was something she would conquer on her own, or die.

She'd changed by then. Her hair and eyes had darkened, to a wonderful browny-gold. He saw that she was well-named Tan. She was still tiny, almost frail-looking, and for a long time she was insecure. But she rapidly gained in confidence. It almost proved her undoing. Once she fell headlong, from top to bottom of the great main flight of stairs; he rushed to her appalled, but she was already struggling up. She pushed him off, again with her mewing cry. He thought her unhurt; then he saw the blood welling from the long gash on her arm. He carried her to the kitchen despite her struggles, and Cook helped him to bind it. Tan watched the process carefully, making no demur. When they had finished she looked at the bandage, touched it. She turned to him, looked back again at her arm. His heart leaped, because he thought for a moment she was aware; but there was still nothing at the backs of the great eyes. Nothing, at least, that he could understand.

Cook told his mother; and she said how well he'd done. He frowned, staring at the fire. Something he needed to say; but he couldn't find the words. "I didn't really," he said. "She was hurt. I tried to help." He bit his lip, fell silent. How explain further? The pain he'd felt, seeing the blood stream from her skin, was a new experience to him.

She smiled. "You're a good boy, Justin," she said. "You've learned to look after her so well. Better than I do sometimes. I saw you in the garden yesterday. She'd fallen asleep; and you fixed a sunshade for her. So she wouldn't be burned."

He looked at the carpet, embarrassed. He hadn't thought anyone had noticed. "That wasn't anything," he said. "You would have done the same. Or father."

She shook her head. "Tange wouldn't have thought of it," she said. "He's a fine man, I've got so much to thank him for; but he wouldn't have done that." She smiled again. "Do you remember how angry you were?" she said. "When I told you I was pregnant again?"

He frowned. The word was newly-learned; he still felt

faintly embarrassed by it. He said, "I'm sorry. I was only small then."

She said, "And now you're a grown-up man." She saw the hurt in his eyes, saw him tense; and laid a hand quickly on his arm. "I'm only joking, Jus," she said. "A man can take a joke. One day I shall be very proud of you."

He worked hard at his lessons. It seemed one year blended with the next. The leaves fell, grew again fresh and new; the days lengthened and closed in. There were trips with his father, on business for the farm; to Easthold, the Middle Lands, on one occasion Middlemarch itself. He learned the complex affairs of Mannings; the sowing and harvesting and ploughing, building of ricks and clamps, ordering of cattlecake and seedcorn, the endless accounts and bills. In between he studied; maths and history, what history of the Realm was known, logic, theology. It seemed his brain was a sponge, soaking up knowledge almost despite itself. He realized dimly it was a time that would never come again.

He was sixteen when the revelation finally came. Master Holand, who he'd never cared for overmuch, had been cramming him without mercy. He sat in the morning room, in the big old chair his grandfather once used, and rapped out answers to the dominie as fast as he could fire the questions. In just a week he would travel to Middlemarch, sit his exams for entrance to the Kitecorps College; he was beginning to feel supremely confident of the result.

The door opened, and Tan ran in. She was lithe now, and brown. She wore a dress that left her slim legs bare, and there were flowers in her hair. He guessed her mother had put them there, or one of the maids. She would never have thought of such a thing for herself. She crossed to him, ignoring the dominie. She put her arms round his neck, and kissed. Her lips were frank, and sweet.

He disengaged her, gently. He said, "Not now, Tan. Go and see Meri. Or find one of the Trandon boys, I bet they're in the cartshed. I'll be finished soon." He ushered her to the door, closed it. From the corridor came one of her mewing wails.

He rose again instantly, and the dominie looked annoyed. "Let the wretched child be," he said. "I'm tired of hearing her."

Justin knew his face had darkened. He was quite unable to

explain the sudden gust of rage. He looked down. He'd broadened a lot; and he was tall for his age, he all but topped his father. He didn't speak; instead he walked to the door, opened it. He scooped her up, walked back. "It's all right, Tan," he said. "Hush now." He brushed her cheek with his finger; and she snuggled contentedly.

It was like a burst of light. He thought, "I love her. And she loves me." It came as a considerable shock; he wondered why it had taken so long to understand.

He thought about it later, sitting in his room. He hadn't thought himself capable of the emotion; or rather, it had never crossed his mind. He tried to analyze his feelings. Was it because of her beauty? Or because she needed him? Or was it both? He frowned. There was no answer; least, none that he could see. He wished there was someone he could ask. Someone cleverer. Older perhaps. But there was not. His last thought, just before he slept, was strange. Maybe there would be, in Middlemarch.

The Corps ran coaches to the College. One picked up round the southern Salient, passed almost by his door. He could have taken a horse, his father would have loaned him one, and ridden there in style; but he didn't ask. He had no doubt it would be frowned on. Horses were for the gentry; there was propriety to be observed in all things. He was going as a tyro, as a tyro he would arrive. And prosper, the good Lord willing.

He streamed a new Trace, early on the day he left. He thought vaguely it was for himself as well. He watched the Cody critically, as it climbed in the light puffs of breeze. The angle was good; it would fly awhile. He said softly, "Look after Tan for me." As ever, the Kites seemed to curtsey an acknowledgement.

He made his farewells to his parents and the housepeople. He saw there had been a reversal of roles; now the tears stood in his mother's eyes. His father too was gruff; but in any case he had few words now. He seemed to have sunk further into himself since the birth of his second child. Justin sometimes vaguely wondered why.

Lastly he ran to find his sister. She was in the little orchard behind the house, sitting on a swing. He whirled her for a while, till she mewed with pleasure. He was sure now he could detect the different meanings in the cries. He stopped the swing finally, knelt on the grass in front of her. "Tan," he said, "I've got to go away."

She frowned. Joggled hopefully, trying to make him swing her again. He touched her knees, shook gently. "No, Tan," he said. "Please listen."

At least her eyes returned to his face. Though whether she could actually hear words he'd never quite decided. He said again, "I've got to go away. I'm going to learn to be a Kiteman. Do you understand?"

She watched him. Then suddenly flung her arms about his neck. She began to sob. He'd never ever heard her cry before.

"Tan," he said. "Oh, Tan. Don't make it worse." He rubbed her back; then gently pushed her away. He took her hands. "Listen," he said. "And try to understand. I've got to go, but it won't be very long. I'm going to Middlemarch. There are trees there and Kites, and a park with a great big lake." He pointed, over the roof of the house. "That's a Kite," he said. "Only they're bigger, and they fly much higher. You can go right up in the sky. Do you understand?" He shook her again. "Listen," he said. "When I've been to College, and learned to be very clever, and got to be a Captain, I'll take you there as well. I'll buy you lovely clothes, and look after you. That's all I'm going for really. So I shall be able to look after you. And it won't be very long. Will you wait for me? And be good?" Strange words; he wondered why he was saying them at all.

She put her arms round his neck again, and solemnly kissed him.

He stared round, from the basket. Four Traces; higher than he'd ever flown before. The sun was a white-hot ball; he could feel its heat even through the searing of the wind. He looked down. The horizon was clearer now, the dawn mist boiling away. The Badlands showed in stark detail; outcrops of rock, vast scarrings where it seemed the land itself had flowed, frozen into ripples like glass or burning iron. The occasional stunted trees, clinging precariously to life; and far off on the horizon, still cloud-dim, a hitherto-unsuspected range of hills. He worked the tail downtackle, felt the basket begin to rise again. The movement was all but undetectable; it was only his Kiteman's senses, developed over many years, that told him it was taking place at all.

His awareness had seemed sharpened. Tan rode with him, on the coach. He remembered a time she'd pirouetted across the lawn. Spinning and twirling, poising on her toes. He thought he'd never seen anything so lovely. He clapped his hands. She paid no heed; so he clapped again, in front of her face, and finally drew her eyes. "That's dancing, Tan," he said. "It's beautiful. Do it again." She still paid no attention; so he imitated, clumsily. "Dancing," he said. "Dancing. . . ." She'd already lost interest though. Her eyes were blank again; she walked off, back into the house.

Another time he'd tried to take her on a trip. Down to the Easthold, with his father. Tange had hummed and hawed; Justin had realized he was unwilling. He'd persisted, and finally the other had given in. She'd climbed into the motor obediently enough. He sat her on his lap; he'd thought it would please her. Before they reached the main road though she'd begun to writhe, emit the mewing cries. They became more piercing; and his father looked across grimly. "It's no use, Jus," he said. "Not when she's in this mood. I knew it was wrong from the start." He pulled on to the rough, bumped round in a circle. Headed back the way he had come.

He'd been blackly disappointed. He said, "What's wrong with her, father? What's *wrong*?" But the other merely shrugged. "You tell me, son," he said. "You see more of her than I do."

The mood had persisted. That evening though she'd come to sit by his feet. She put her chin in her hands, stared up. She didn't take her eyes off him all night. He'd tried to ignore her at first; finally, he stroked her hair. He couldn't be angry with her. He wondered if she knew it as well.

The Transport slowed for a bend. One of the brakes made a funny little sound. Like a kitten. He wondered where he'd heard it before.

Middlemarch nearly defeated him. His first view of the town took his breath, as it had the time before; the avenues, the buildings, stately lines of houses, palaces of the Masters in their elegant landscaped grounds. The coach was old and ramshackle; but at least its slabsided height gave him a good view. He was decanted with a dozen more into an annexe of the Central College; and then of course the round of fatigues began. He'd thought, with critical exams coming up, they'd be given a breathing space at least; but not a bit of it. He polished and scrubbed with the rest; and slowly the anger built. He realized, or thought he realized, they were testing him; testing his will, to see if he would break. Though there were times when he even doubted that. These Corporals and Lancejacks, jumped-up Orderlies; they seemed to take real pleasure in the infliction of indignity, the handing out of pointless and banal tasks. He bore it nonetheless. He scraped and painted, black-leaded already gleaming stoves, washed windows by the yard; first light till dusk, for the best part of a fortnight. Finally, when he was thoroughly jaded, when everything he'd thought he had by heart had vanished from his mind, they sat him in a hall with half a hundred more. A dour Kitecaptain saw to the issuing of papers, and the examination began. He dashed his answers off with contempt, disinterested in whether he gained admittance or not; and was mortified to see, a week or ten days later, how close he had come to failing. He steadied down—a conscious effort, his temper still tended to get the better of him—and wrote to his folks. To Tan, he sent a line of big red crosses. Knowing she wouldn't understand. He still found the exercise oddly comforting.

The mortification continued. His work was wrong he discovered, from first to last; his maths suspect, his theology gravely wanting. He studied in a species of cold fury, and over the first term his marks began to improve. It was then he received his greatest shock to date. Term breaks existed, he'd been counting off the days; but not for First Years. No let-ups for them; it would be winter before he saw his folks again.

His group protested, in no uncertain terms. Their tutor was unimpressed. "What?" he said mildly. "A year in Middlemarch? Folk pay good money for that. You're getting it for nothing."

Somebody said sullenly, "It isn't fair."

"Fair?" said the tutor. "You'll be telling me life's fair next." He shook his head. "So you want to be Kitemen," he said. "But you can't stand a semester in the biggest city in the world. How'd you get on with a twelve month posting to the Salient?"

He said abruptly, "I was born there."

The other turned to him. "Then perhaps you'd better go back," he said. "Nobody's stopping you. There's just one thing. Don't try to come back here."

He set his mouth. He didn't understand, they'd none of them understand. Tan wouldn't have expected this. She'd think he'd let her down. Or forget him altogether. But perhaps she had already.

He wished he hadn't had the thought. But it was too late. It was there, and nothing would drive it away. He experienced a time of desolation. He was sure that it was ended, he would leave. He wondered what Curt Manning would have thought.

She came to him in the night, and mewed. She said, *"I haven't forgotten. I shall never forget."* But that was just the dream.

He opened his eyes. It was still pitch dark. He started to cry. The sobs got louder, he couldn't control them. Later he was appalled. What if they had heard? But the dorm snored on, regardless. Maybe they were used to it.

His other trial came in the second term. He'd worked hard, topped his set in logic and science. Then he encountered Master Atwill.

For the first time, the syllabus included theology. But he'd never heard theology like Master Atwill taught. His questions were illogical, his choice of topics baffling in the extreme. Demons existed; of that there was no doubt. Very well. Granted their reality, could one deny the presence of angels? Excellent. Granted then their co-existence, how big were they? How many might one pile into the basket of a Cody? He suggested various formulae by which an answer could be reached, and left them to it.

He answered, as best he could; yet it was his paper on which the dominie chose to heap his scorn. What, and he a logic First? Come now, an error surely had been made. The little man rubbed his hands. He would take the matter up with the Master Geen, at the first available chance. Meanwhile, would he condescend to try again?

His temper snapped. He said deliberately, "I know nothing of angels, Master. But I have been flying Codys since I was ten."

"Flying Codys," said the other. "Hmm. . . ." He looked up, over his little half-spectacles. "Repeat your statement," he said.

He sensed another trap. But he was unsure in which direction it lay. He said, "I've been flying Codys since I was ten."

"Hmm," said the other again. He seemed lost in thought. "Come out here a moment, will you?"

He rose, puzzled. Walked up to the desk. It was placed on a low dais. Master Atwill perused a pile of exercise books. "Closer," he said. "Closer, Mr. Manning. A strange thing."

"What?" he said. He leaned forward, thinking his attention drawn; and the other's fist flashed out. The blow took him in the ear.

It wasn't the force of it; it was little more than a push. It was the unexpectedness. He was off balance; he ended sitting on the floor. The set rocked with laughter, then was suddenly still.

He got up, slowly. He was seeing the world through a thin haze of red. Nobody—not his father, not anyone else—had ever struck him. Not since he had been a tiny child. He took a step forward, fists bunched; then suddenly a strange thing happened. He was icy cold.

"That's better," said the dominie. He regarded him mildly over his glasses. "You come here to learn, young man," he said. "Not to boast. You may sit down."

He returned to his place in silence. He should have felt humiliated, less than an inch high; and yet he didn't. An image had come to him, in that frozen moment; Tan, swinging in her little orchard. He felt her arms, almost with physical strength, felt the pressure of her lips. He'd told her once, he was doing it all for her; and he'd forgotten. Now, she'd reminded him.

He walked the town, when he was finally released. Stared at the troops of folk thronging Main Drag and Centre Parade, stared into the bright-lit windows of shops. He bought her a dress; pretty, beribboned, the sort of thing a child would wear in Middlemarch. He'd never done such a thing before; but again, there was no embarrassment. He discussed her measurements solemnly with the assistant; he found her most helpful. He had it packed, walked on and found a carter who admitted trading with the Salient. He haggled, came to an agreement. He paid the man—the whole transaction would leave him short for a time, but that was of no importance—and wandered back to his dorm. He took supper with the rest, washed his plate and cup with care. Later, after Lights Out, Dav Sollen—one of the few friends he'd made—spoke thoughtfully. "Why didn't you kill the little runt?" he said. "I would have."

He shrugged, in the darkness. He said, "I'm here to learn the Codys. He doesn't really matter."

The other didn't speak again; but Justin sensed his bafflement.

The basket was halted again, he assumed for the addition of the fifth trace. At this height even his Kiteman's sense was becoming confused. The shocks and little thrills that normally ran through a cable were absent; also the sag and droop of it, the extra trailing weight, induced strange behaviour in the train. Despite the extra Lifters. The tail-down tackle, semi-automatic, adopted unexpected angles; also a swaying motion had begun, a libration for which he was unable to account. He trimmed the tackle fractionally. The motion eased.

He stared back and down. Far off, in the grey smudge that was G8, keen glasses would be trained. He doubted he was visible at all; he fired a green regardless, and another. Later he detected further movement by the slow creep of the land beneath. He trimmed the tackle again. This time his Kite senses once more aided him. He'd doubted further lift was possible; but he was rising again. Quite fast. He swallowed to equalize pressure. He'd heard it claimed, with all solemnity, that above three hundred feet there was no air to breathe. In that case he was dead; he'd already entered God's realm. It was an eerie place. Round him, above, below, nothing but blue. Blue, and an intense silence; a silence almost of expectancy. He rubbed his face. It was as if the air itself was becoming visible; an azure fluid, seeping to fill the basket, flowing and ebbing through the interstices of its sides. Though that was absurd of course; the defect was in his sight.

He swallowed again. He'd thought, for a whirling instant, he might see God Himself; a great calm figure, seated on His glowing throne. What would he beg Him, from his earth-bound speck of a Cody? To turn the clock back by a day? Two hours? It seemed such a little thing to ask, for the world to live again. His world; after all, He'd made it.

He groaned. It wasn't for him, a sinner, to ask favours. Pray then that his crimes be visited on him? "It was me," he cried to the empty sky. "It was me. *Why. . . .*" The punishment had been visited on another. It had been monstrous.

That first year at College was bad. The Corps didn't believe in leaving its Apprentices any illusions. The life of a Kiteman, as his mother had warned, was hard and thankless. A few, the favoured ones, would be posted to Middlemarch itself; there, their duties would be largely ceremonial. Though the spitting and polishing would be awesome. For the rest it would be the Salient, the bleak lands of the Easthold; or the Kiteships of the south, the barren northwest coast. Three weeks or so of journeying, just to reach their Station. He shrugged. He didn't want the Middle Lands, they weren't why he'd joined. The folk were fat and prosperous, their Stations a mere second defence. In case the Salient failed. He no longer cared where he was posted. After all, his job was to fly the Codys. Nothing more. He gave no further thought to quitting; though many of his fellows did in fact give up. Even his hatred of Atwill ebbed in time, settled to a cold and steady contempt. The little man didn't brave him again; though had he done so the result would have been the same. To strike a dominie, even to raise a hand, was instant dismissal. It would take more than Atwill to destroy what he had planned.

There were girls of course, girls in plenty; the bright cloaks of the Apprentices drew them like moths to candles. Though for his part he could never see what they hoped to gain. He was hard-put to make ends meet; and the bulk of the students were much worse off than he. He sampled the high life occasionally, when his allowance had come through; worked the city centre pubs with Dav, sometimes the others. But after the first experiments it seemed his interest waned. See one of the squawking creatures and you'd seen them all. He'd have liked to say there was nothing behind their eyes; but there was far too much. Dav pulled his leg a bit, once chided outright; but Justin merely smiled. He bought a pair of summer sandals for Tan; tiny white things, held by a single strap between the toes. Despatched them by the carrier.

A letter came from home; an ill-spelled note from of all people, Aniken. They'd had a storm; three Kitestruts had been snapped, he was running short of spares. Also the fabric of the Lifters stood in need of repair, he urgently needed more. "*Bleu,*" he suggested, or "*grin.*" Nearest supply was in Easthope, two days' journey away; and at this time of year no-one could be spared for the ride.

Tange had increased his allowance; he had more than enough for present needs. He bought the supplies on Main, in the big shop that catered for the College; and the carter was pressed into service again. "*Keep the Trace flying, Ani,*" he wrote. "*As you love Mannings, and me, never let it fail. May God bless everyone; but most of all, may He bless you. . . .*"

His mother's letter he opened with more care. "*All is well,*" she had written. "*Mannings looks lovely now. The crops are good, the best I've ever known. We shall get fat, this wintertide.*

"*Tan is growing fast. When you come home you'll hardly recognize her. She's very brown. She should be; she spends all day in the garden. Except when it rains of course. She'd even go out then, we have to stop her. She made a fuss at first; but she's much better now. It's just as well, because she's got so strong. I can hardly hold her any more. When she's naughty, I tell her you'll be cross. I read your letters to her, and say your name. Over and over. It always quietens her; I'm sure she understands.*

"*It's strange, but she spends most of her time in the orchard. Where you left her that last day. I'm sure she thinks if she waits, you'll come back to her there.*

"*Thank you for sending the shoes. She hasn't worn them yet, though she keeps them in her room. She won't wear shoes any more, she hasn't since you left. Father Andri says it's a sort of penance; but I don't know.*

"*He's come round a lot. You know he wanted to take her when your grandfather Condemned her. But he visits regularly now to see that she's all right. I think everyone loves her. I'd like to think Grandfather would too, if he could see her now. She'll be a beautiful woman one day.*

"*Keep well my dear, and all my love. I'm sending you some warm things by the carrier. You'll need them, with the winter coming on. I know Main Drag in leaf-fall; only too well. . . .*"

She didn't mention the dress.

Autumn was another trying time. After the Air Show, the lure of the great Kites redoubled; but no First Year would ever touch a Cody. Or even be allowed nearby. Instead he was seconded for duty in Godpath, the great Cathedral of the

Variants. He spent his days in purple-carpeted gloom, serving at the altar, swinging a censer while they chanted the endless prayers. At first, bored, he would allow his attention to wander; float in the clouds, at the end of a mighty Trace. It took several cuffs from the Master of Novices—himself a one-time Flier, and no man to be trifled with—to remind him of his duties. Later, there were compensations to the hum-drum days. As he learned its secrets, the building came to intrigue him. The endless dim-lit corridors, the shuffling monks that thronged them; the plaques and statuary, busts of old Fliers draped with more purple for the Festival to come; the lines of lancet windows admitting their dull, rich light. The great East Window in particular fascinated. It showed Cody rigs, train after train of them in complex, crossing patterns. They flew above a town, or city, that had surely never existed; plain square buildings, flat-roofed, jumbled on a hillside. Beyond were towers, topped by curious domes; onion-shaped, and pointed. Above them, the sky was a rich and jewel-like blue. Master Anton assured him there had indeed been such a place; in the Old Time, before the Demons came. But its name had been forgotten.

The Demons were his study subject now; their habits, their natures, their infinite maliciousness. He'd learned the Litany of course, as a good Variant child; here though were complexities undreamed of. The bodies of some were striped, he learned, others were chequered. Some were blind; others had eyes in their foreheads, many eyes, and spinning brains behind them bent on death. Some swam wholly beneath water, striking at ships. The wounds they made tore outwards, in some way he couldn't grasp, so that their victims sank swiftly. Some spawned in midair, tearing themselves apart; the children they released in swarms were deadly too. There had even once on a time been friendly Demons, whose very glance would eat up all the others; but the art of controlling them had been lost. Justin wrestled with the complexities; but for each fact learned there seemed to be half a hundred more. He committed it all to memory, grimly, as he had committed the rest; and his winter paper earned top marks in his intake. It even carried a prize; a model of a Cody rig in silver and gold, flying from a base of polished wood. There was a plaque, inscribed with the names of winners from previous years. He could keep it for a twelvemonth; after which his name would be added to the list, and it would be awarded to another. He asked to be allowed to take it home with him for the holiday, and permission was granted. He packed the tiny thing with care, locked it away.

The last week was one of continual services, dawn to dusk. He'd discovered a fairly pleasant tenor voice. He'd never make a soloist or cantor; but it passed muster well enough with the rest. He sang in the clerestory choir; at least it saved him from the chore of incense-swinging.

Candles were lit, for the last service of all; Godpath discovered a new, ethereal beauty. Then it was over, and the drudgery of the first year finally ended. Next term he would start his proper training. A bus had been laid on, thirteen hundred tomorrow; in just a day he would see Mannings again. His parents, the staff, old Ani. He would see Tan. The rush of feeling the thought brought in its train left him nearly giddy.

He felt giddier later. He drank wine, with Dav Sollen and a dozen more, in one of the city centre taverns; legally at last, though they'd drunk wine enough through the year. They smuggled it into the dorms for late night parties; the practice was known to go on, but it was generally winked at. Unless of course there was too much noise, or a boy was late on parade, or a tunic button was dirty; then, all Hell would break loose. He'd thought odd times a full scale visitation of Demons could scarcely have been worse. Tonight was different though. This one night of the year, there were no rules.

He left the others carousing finally, slipped away. He had his packing to finish; and he wanted a clear head for the morning. He laid out his parade tunic and slacks, buffed shoes that already gleamed; by that time the rest of the dorm had begun to drift, or stagger, in. The talk was desultory, soon ended; after a very few minutes the place resounded with snores.

He had one surprise. After refectory next morning. He bumped into Master Atwill. He bowed, as the rules of the place dictated, stepped to one side; but the other also stopped. He regarded Justin brightly, head on one side. "Ah, Manning," he said. "You've worked and studied well. I've made a good report on you to the Master Devine; and I have seen your other assessments. They are uniformly excellent. Congratulations."

He inclined his head again. He said formally, "Thank you, Master." He wondered what the other could be getting at. There was something else, he was sure.

Atwill was still watching him thoughtfully. He said, "There are some things I would like to discuss with you. Can you spare me a few minutes of your time?"

He havered. He half-glanced at the big clock on the corridor wall; and the dominie smiled. "Your Transport is not for three hours," he said. He touched Justin's arm. "Come," he said. "I shan't keep you long."

He followed, wondering. The little Master led the way out of the College, stepping briskly. They emerged into bright winter sunlight. Atwill turned right and left, into Main Drag, crossed the wide road in front of Godpath. Beside it stood a smaller building; squarish, and as plain as Godpath was ornate. The Church of the Moving Clouds.

He hesitated again. He'd known for a long time of course that Atwill was of the Middle Doctrine; but he'd never set foot in one of their places of worship. Though his mother had told him a little, his father had always been strict Variant; and he was nothing if not loyal. But the other urged him, still with a faint smile. "Come," he said. "You are not here to pray." He led the way. Inside the big street door was another, lined with thick green cloth. He stepped through. It swished to gently behind him.

The inside of the place was as spartan as the exterior. No statuary, no inscriptions; just limewashed walls, relieved at intervals by the slim grey shafts of pillars. Only in the roof was there complexity; curved wooden beams supported others that rose in tiers below the high gable. The glass too was plain; lamps burned here and there in coloured bowls, although the day was bright. In the pews were scattered groups of people, heads bent in meditation. He saw Brothers of the Order, some of the female priests that only the Middle Doctrine allowed. He frowned, would have spoken; but the dominie touched his arm again. He said, "Come with me."

He led the way quietly, down a side aisle, toward the rear of the place. He pushed open another door. He said, "My little hidey-hole. A sanctum the Brothers allow me to maintain. I sometimes think it preserves my sanity."

Justin looked round. He saw a desk and chair, a bunk bed, a leather-padded easy. Above the desk hung a complex model;

a six lift Cody rig, in flight. The other followed the direction of his glance and nodded. "Yes," he said. "I had my dreams too, once. I wanted to be a Flier. But I was never thought robust enough. I was prone to a nervous disability, a stammer I later managed to cure; and my eyesight was too weak. In short, I was a failure; you will achieve what I could not." He crossed to a wall cupboard, took down a decanter and glasses. He said. "Wine?"

He nodded, wondering. He said, "Thank you, Master."

"Be seated," said the old man. "Be at ease." He handed one of the glasses to him. Justin took it. Delicately cut crystal. The wine inside, a Middle Lands vintage, seemed to glow with its own yellow fire.

Atwill scotched down at the desk. Flicked his cloak across his knees. He said, "This will perhaps sound unusual. But I feel I owe you an explanation. Maybe even an apology."

He looked up, sharply. He said, "That is not necessary, Master."

"I think it is," said the dominie. He pursed his lips. "I have seen many Apprentices come and go," he said. "I know their minds; to a certain extent, their dreams. I knew your father, many years ago; and your mother, when she came to Middlemarch. She was a member of this congregation." He shook his head. "We take the Middle Way," he said. "Punishment forms no part of our doctrine. Though we can be stern when occasion demands." He smiled, fleetingly. "As stern as our brothers of Godpath. Sometimes I think sterner." He swirled the wine in his glass. "A building is a concept," he said. "To decorate it with spires and pinnacles, to grace it with rich fabrics and many-coloured glass; that is to make it gorgeous to the eye. But to say, 'This is a roof,' and, 'These are walls. This is a doorway; these are windows, by which light may enter.' I sometimes wonder if that does not take more courage."

Atwill set the glass down. "It was necessary," he said. "Not as a corrective, but to focus your attention. You had become complacent; from complacency springs arrogance. You had embellished a simple fact—your desire to be a Flier—with figures of your own conceit. And so your mind had wandered and become vague; although at the time you were unaware of it. You would have failed."

He picked the glass up, sipped. "By the mercy of the

Lord, I was saved from your anger,'' he said. ''For which I thank Him. I am in no sense a brave man. You were saved from the ruination of your life; by self denial, and your own intelligence. That very moment, my hopes for you began. Now you must go on. There will be distractions; tragedies perhaps, disasters. You must see them for what they are, and not allow yourself to become diverted again. That way you will perhaps become a fine Flier. As fine as the Master Canwen; who can say?'' He considered again. ''Who is the girl,'' he said, ''who so fills your waking thoughts?''

Justin jerked, startled. All but dropped the glass. For a moment he couldn't speak; he was almost sure his jaw had sagged. Then, quickly, anger flared. So they rifled student lockers. He'd thought better of the College.

It seemed Atwill read his mind. He raised a hand, gently. ''No,'' he said. ''Your privacy has been respected. The Corps does not employ spies.''

He said slowly, ''Then how did you know?''

The other said simply, ''Because I saw her, reflected in your eyes. I saw her on the day of the rebuke. I think her hands reached out, to comfort you.''

He said impulsively, ''It's not as you think, Master. It's not like that at all.''

''Nothing is quite as one thinks,'' said the dominie. ''No life is like the next. Even the lives of the dullest people have secrets.'' He drank again. He said, ''Would you like to tell me about her?''

He hesitated; then it all came, with a rush. How his mother had saved her from the knife; how she'd grown and changed, how she'd become a person. Real, somehow, to him; more real than the five-sensed folk who talked and prattled everywhere. Atwill heard him through, not interrupting; when he finally stopped, he smiled. ''There is much love in you, Justin,'' he said. ''And it is strong and true. But be counselled by me. All things have their other side; as a coin must bear two faces. And if one of those is bright, the other must needs be dark. There must be night; else how could we know the splendour of the day? There must be winter; or how could we cleave to the spring? This is a belief we hold, that the Variants abhor.

''Go to your little girl, who I've no doubt loves you too. Though she cannot in our terms express that love. She is a child in a cage; a cage not of her making, but the Lord's. Why these things must be, we cannot tell; nor may we question His will. Once, He allowed Demons to punish all the world. Another Mystery; the answer lies beyond our little understandings. Go to her, pour out your love; it does you naught but credit. Stint not, nor fear; for love, true love, is the only well that never can be drained. But at the same time, tread with caution. There are pits in every pathway; this pathway most of all. They are deep; and their bottoms are cruel-lined with spikes."

He frowned. He said, "What are they, Master? These pits?"

The other shook his head. "That I cannot tell," he said. "It is not given to me to know the future. Any more than to you."

There was more. The dominie talked of his own young life, in the Middle Lands. His Ordination, his first ministry; a mission for seamen, far off in the Southguard. He questioned Justin about the farm; its running, maintenance, the number of servants and field folk it employed. Justin tended to lose track of time. He felt wholly at rest; more at rest than he'd been in years. He realized for the first time in his life he'd talked about the matters closest to his heart; and in the process he had made a friend.

The little man rose finally. "Consider this refuge yours as well," he said. "When things become too much. As they sometimes do for us all. I make no claim to wisdom; but a sympathetic listener is perhaps worth more. Talking, we hold a mirror to ourselves; discover our own natures." He held his hand out. "Go with God," he said. "Tread boldly, but with care. Remember we must all walk down a street; but every street has sides. We may choose the sunshine, or the shadows."

Justin felt his eyes sting, suddenly. He dropped to his knees. "It's I who must apologize to you," he said. "Give me your blessing, Master."

The dominie laid a hand lightly on his head. "You have it already," he said. "It has never been withheld." He gripped his arm, gently. "Come, Justin," he said. "Your friends will all be waiting."

The restlessness returned, on the long coach journey home. The others laughed and chattered, roared out bawdy songs, engaged in rumbustious games of cards. He sat apart, turning over in his mind what the dominie had said. Was it then possible to decorate a concept? Pile spires and pinnacles on it, till it towered in the mind as Godpath towered over Middlemarch? And a simple, obvious truth was lost? There seemed to be some relevance to him; to his feelings for Mannings, for the Kites. For Tan. But the link, if link there was, eluded him. He grappled with the notion; but try as he might, it endlessly slipped away.

The Transport, even older than the one on which he had arrived, wheezed and rattled, pulled in time after time to cool its overheated engine. Night had fallen long before he reached the Salient; and still two hours to run. His mind outpaced the ancient vehicle, time and again; seeing the old house decked with solstice greenery, hearing the chattering and laughter, seeing the blazing hearths, the great range sizzling in the stone-flagged kitchen. Cook would be bellowing instructions, ordering this, countermanding that, setting the parlourmaids and spitboys scampering; rolling out pastries with her sturdy, powerful hands, setting the puddings boiling, drawing the trays out golden and smoking from the stoves. And old Ani swearing under his breath, staggering in with the baskets of logs, almost certainly a little the worse for wear. He had his own private liquor store in the house, he'd had it for years; the raw spirit brewed in the local villages, that only he could drink. Justin's mother knew about it he was sure, probably his father too; but nothing had ever been said. Nor would it be. He was their oldest and most loyal retainer; he had served them well, and his father's folk before that. Ani would never change.

He debussed finally, waved to the few Apprentices remaining. He hefted his duffel bag, set out to walk the two miles to the farm. A hundred yards on he was hailed. He stopped, made out the dim shape of a pony and trap. He said uncertainly, "Ani?"

He scrambled up. He said, "It's good to see you, Ani. Have you been waiting long?"

"Not long, Master," said the old man; but he was blowing his hands with the cold.

"You are a fool," he said. "You could have caught your death. Then where would we have been?" He leaned to light the sidelamps. "Move across," he said. "Get yourself under a rug. I'll drive." He grinned. "Best get that bottle out as well. I'll join you."

The other hesitated, then groped under the seat. He took a swig, wiped the neck and handed it across. For once Justin took a mouthful. It was even more vile than he remembered. He managed not to spit it out, swallowed it somehow. It left his mouth and throat feeling they were on fire. "Good stuff," he said, when he could get his breath. Later though the warmth spread stealthily right through him.

He thought his mother looked frailer than before; though she greeted him happily enough. His father too was greying; it was as if much more than a year had passed. There was awkwardness for a while; then Tange fetched drinks, set bottles and glasses on the table. The gesture was a silent one; but it warmed him as the spirit had done. It meant, subtly, that he'd matured; now, he could drink like a man. He knew his progress had been reported to them; and that they were pleased. Later he fetched the trophy from his pack, set it on the sideboard. His mother touched it, wonderingly. She said, "What a beautiful thing."

Tan was the only disappointment. He ran to her, when she walked into the room. He would have hugged her; he tried to take her hands, but she snatched them back. Her eyes were dead, expressionless. She stared as if she looked right through him; as if he were glass, invisible. He experienced a moment of desolation. "Tan," he said. "Tan, please. . . ."

Mav touched his arm, gently. "Leave her," she said. "She'll come round; but it will take a little time." She smiled. "Come and sit down," she said. "Tell me about College."

The girl walked away. She sat in the far corner of the room, her back turned to him. He saw she wore no shoes. The words of Master Atwill, still so fresh, came back with doubled force. *"There are pits. They are deep; and their bottoms cruel-lined with spikes. . . ."* He said, "Did she like the dress I sent?"

Mav glanced at his father, set her lips. "She tore it," she said. "I did my best; but it will never be the same." She touched his wrist. "Don't blame her," she said. "She was very upset."

"I don't blame her," he said. "I don't blame her at all."

He sat with Tange until the early hours, discussing this and that; his schooling, Middlemarch, the running of the farm. The executors had finally agreed to the erection of two of the new-fangled silos; the senior Manning hoped to ensile for neighbouring farms as well, sell to the millers in bulk. It would be a handy source of extra income. Also he had at long last bought a tractor. Elderly perhaps, and a little decrepit; but a tractor nonetheless, something he'd set his heart on years ago. It seemed the lawyers had finally relented a little; but so they should of course, the profits from last year alone would more than cover the outlay. Ani had complained loud and long at its arrival, and still took every opportunity to revile these modern methods; but it had become his secret pride and joy. Nobody could handle it as he could; he'd talk to it on cold mornings like a recalcitrant horse, and somehow it always started. Tange smiled, poured more of the Middle Lands brandy. He touched on the possibility of increasing Justin's allowance, but he shook his head. "I can get by," he said. "You've done enough already. Wait till I've earned it."

He got to bed eventually; lay and tossed for a while and thought about Tan. He slept finally, only to be haunted by dreams. She came to him, with her little mewing cries; knelt before him, tried to kiss his hands. The image shocked him; he jerked awake, saw grey light was already in the room. He rose hastily, began to dress.

His first act was to climb to the roof, check the Godkite and its Lifters. He drew the String—easier now than for the child who had first flown it—but the Cody was in fine shape. He streamed it again, stared round him in the biting wind. He saw the tractor move faroff across a dark hogback of land; a gaunt, skeletal machine, Ani perched on high like a well-muffled doll. Justin examined it later in the shed, admiring the massive frame, the great rear wheels with their spiked iron rims. Ani shrugged, said it was all right for them as liked new ways; but he grinned. The brightwork, what little it possessed, was gleaming; and the engine had that sleek, well cared-for look that only constant attention will achieve. The old man was in his element.

Tan took a week to forgive him. He ignored her, following Mav's advice, though it was a constant pain to do so. Finally, her mood changed. She ran to him; he heard the mewing again. She glanced down, drawing his attention; and he saw she was wearing the shoes he'd sent. The summer sandals, with their pretty thongs. Absurd of course, on an icy winter day; but not for worlds would he have tried to make her change them. He hugged her and she cried, dabbing her eyes. He saw she'd learned to blow her nose as well. She did it clumsily, left a wet smear on her lip. He wiped it for her, gently. At least the effort was there. She sat by him afterwards, her hands in her lap. He knew her eyes were seeing him again. ''Tan,'' he said, ''I've got to go back to College. Not yet, but in a little while. I'm learning to fly the Kites. The Codys, like we have on the roof. Do you understand?''

No response.

''The Kites,'' he said. ''The Kites that keep us safe. The Codys.'' He crossed to the sideboard, picked the trophy up. ''These,'' he said.

She mewed. For a moment he feared she would snatch at it, but the hand she extended was gentle. She touched it with a finger, as she touched everything that interested her. Stroked the slender golden Trace, the spread wings of the Lifters. She mewed again, it seemed with pleasure.

He returned the prize to its place of safety. He sat down, took her hands. ''Tan,'' he said, ''you must promise. You mustn't be unhappy again. Because this time I shan't be long. We get term breaks now, do you understand? It's only the first year you have to stay away.''

She looked worried; and he rubbed her fingers. Raised them gently, and kissed. ''You understand,'' he said. He stared into the blank, lovely eyes. They were tilted, almond-shaped, the lashes long and dark. ''What do you think about, Tan?'' he said. ''What goes on, inside you?'' The worry increased; and he hugged her instantly, laughing. ''It doesn't matter,'' he said. ''Because you're Tan; and I love you. At least you know that much. I sometimes wonder if the rest matters anyway.'' Later, in the quiet of his room, he shook his head. The answer had made itself; perhaps it had always been there. It didn't matter. Nothing else mattered at all.

She sat with him at dinner, refused to be parted again. Later she curled up by him, on the settle. Snuggled. He let her. It was good to feel the closeness of her again, even to smell her. The freshness of her linen, faint scent of her hair. She was clean, clean as one of the cats that sat blinking sleepily by the hearth. Though there had been a time when the reverse was true. He'd taught her patiently, over the years; by persuasion, by example. He'd taught her the use of a potty, later the privy. Blushing furiously, hating himself, biting his lip till it bled. And that was something not even his mother knew. It had been a desperate, last-ditch attempt. But he'd persevered. Because it seemed wrong; wrong that she lived in worse state than an animal. She who was so beautiful. He'd come close to despair; then suddenly, when hope had all but gone, she'd understood. And life for the household had changed. It had changed for him.

He looked up, caught his mother's eyes. She was smiling. She knew how much he'd done for Tan. Most of it anyway. Maybe she'd even guessed the rest.

The Rig was stationary again, in its world of biting blue. A part of him realized he was chilled to the bone. It didn't seem to matter.

Strange that he was still tethered to G8. Almost impossible to believe it any more. There was no Kitestation, no Salient. No Earth. He brought his mind to bear, with difficulty. Down there, in that world he had left for ever, he knew what they would be doing. The line clamped off, over the great drum; and the derrick chuffing, lifting the last spool into place. The Riggingmaster would be waiting, to fix the final splice; and the Launchman standing anxious, gauntleted hand to the cable, feeling the throb and thrill. The tension. They'd have doubled up the anchors; because with that weight aloft there was a chance the Trace could drag even a Launch Truck. A chance, but that was all; none of them could tell. Because nobody, not the Riggingmaster, not the oldest hand on Base, had ever flown such a string. Nor would they again.

He frowned. Because climb as he might, he could not escape. The link, though tenuous, was real. Soon, the last cable streamed, they would begin to draw him down. To the world he knew he could no longer bear. If orders didn't reach them before. He glanced above him, to the Trace. He could sever it, sail off into the blue for ever. The cutters were there, part of the emergency gear every Cody carried. He shook his head. That wasn't the way. Do that, and every man on Base would feel the consequences; because the enquiries would be endless. He'd no intention of allowing the innocent to suffer; there'd been enough of that already. He lowered his eyes to the horizon. There were other heights beyond the first. Mountains, infinitely distant; like pale holes knocked in the sky. He thought he saw on one the gleam of snow. He thought how she would have liked them.

He shook his head again. He knew, with a strange certainty, that he would not return. One of Master Atwill's pits would open; but it would reach upward. Into the sun.

Clouds were sailing. The puffy white clouds of summer. One passed around him; the others floated beneath. When the sky cleared, the Rig was rising again.

He experienced a hope, as faint as it was fleeting. Maybe the air would thin, eventually. He would sleep then. Sleep, and not wake up. He knew in his heart though, that was not going to happen.

The Lifters pulled steadily, climbing even higher.

That holiday, the first, had passed swiftly. Far too swiftly for his liking. It seemed impossible; but the last morning arrived, and the packing of his bags. He folded the new clothes carefully, the clothes they'd given him, stowed them in the duffel. Then it was goodbye time; and Ani waiting with the trap, to take him to the Transport. He made his farewells quickly, kissed Mav, shook his father's hand. Lastly he turned to Tan. She was standing empty-faced, still wearing the shoes. She hugged him. He kissed her, and was startled. She opened her mouth as wide as it would go, pushed her tongue between his teeth. He stepped back instantly. "Tan," he said, "that's wrong. It's very naughty. You must never do it again." She stared at him, uncomprehending; and he took her shoulders. "Tan," he said, "do you remember what I told you? You mustn't be unhappy. It upsets Mummy and Daddy. I shan't be away long. Not this time. I shall come back to see you as soon as I ever can." He kissed her again, trying to be gentle; but that was one lesson she would never learn. He shook his head, and turned away. As he walked through the doors, she deliberately kicked off her shoes.

He reflected wryly, as the coach rolled west, that any Middle Lands tart could learn from his kid sister. But what they learned they could never put into effect. One cannot copy Innocence; either it exists, or it is gone.

The year that followed was bad. The worst, he decided, of his life. Spring term was bearable, even enjoyable in parts; but early in the summer came horrendous news. He slit the flap of the envelope with foreboding, recognizing his father's hand. Tange Manning was a reluctant correspondent; it was a serious matter that could induce him to put pen to paper.

There had been an accident, at Mannings. The tractor had run away; and Aniken, who'd served it well and loyally, had been its victim. Nobody seemed too sure how it had happened. The headland had been steep, the brake had failed; or maybe the old man, for the first and only time, had neglected to set it properly. He'd been in front; and he had had no chance.

Justin applied for, and was granted, compassion leave. He made the long haul back once more. It bit into his savings; the trip was unofficial, the College made him pay. His father reimbursed him. For once he accepted the gift.

He talked to a fieldman who'd seen it happen. Seen it, but been helpless to intervene. The front wheels veered evilly, caught in a rut; so one of the great spiked rims. . . . The body had been whirled, he said. Again and again. Under the high mudguard, passing back to earth. Till the machine had come to rest, a hundred yards away. Displaying its trophy for all the world to see. It had been sold for scrap, and what was left of Ani buried; but the farm would never be the same again.

He walked, past the big shiny silos. He stared up at them. The sunlight reflected from their silver sides. He was confused; appalled at the shortness of life, its inconsequentiality. He wondered why they flew the Codys; day after day, night after night, year after year. What were they protecting? A fragileness, that was doomed as it was born.

Tan came to him shyly, took his hand. He touched her cheek with one finger. "I'm protecting you, Tan," he said. "Do you understand? You're all that matters. I don't know why; but there isn't anything else." She mewed, and pressed herself to him.

He talked to his father, late that night. "I don't know," he said. "I haven't graduated; but I think I've lost my faith already."

The other took his time about answering. Just as his grandfather had done. "You're not thinking straight, Just," he said finally. "He was an old man. He'd had his life; a good one. And it was quick; I don't suppose he knew a thing about it. Better than lying for years, wasting away from some disease or other. You know him; he'd have preferred it the way it was."

Justin shook his head. "It isn't that," he said. "He loved that damned machine. Kept it going when nobody else would have bothered. And see what it did to him."

His father poured more of the rich, dark brandy. "You think it knew what it was doing then?" he said. "You believe that machines are alive?"

He looked up under his brows. Recognized the trap, and refused to be drawn. "All I shall ever do is fly big Kites," he said. "You can't help questioning, sometimes."

The other didn't answer.

"It's pointless," he said irritably. "I'll come and work the farm. Work for you. It's what you always wanted anyway."

Tange sipped the brandy, carefully. Set the glass down. "Listen," he said. "I'm going to tell you something you don't know. Remember that day you streamed the Cody? The first day of all?"

He put his hands round the glass. He said, "I was a little child."

"That's not the point," said his father. He leaned forward. "The midwife saw the Trace through the bedroom window," he said. "She raised Mav to look. She told me later she'd just about given up hope. It was all it needed. Her faith is very strong."

He looked up again, sharply. "But she screamed," he said. "I heard it. She screamed. . . ."

"She screamed because it was over," said Tange Manning. "It happens like that sometimes." He looked down at the table. "I don't want to get drawn in," he said. "I know as much theology as you could write on the head of a pin. But if you hadn't flown that Trace, I wouldn't have a wife. And you wouldn't have Tan." He reached across, gripped his arm briefly. "She's all right, Justin," he said. "She understands. I don't know how, but she understands. And you've gone too far to pull out now. Go and fly your Kites."

Only he wasn't flying Kites. That magic was still to come. He was learning the intricacies of the Launchers, spending long days in the classroom, others elbow-deep in blackened grease. Crossheads and cylinder cocks, water lifts and steam outlets, valve chests, differentials. His notebooks filled, became a half-inch thick apiece; and still there was more to know. Some nights he got to bed dogtired; but he was grateful for that. It took his mind from a careering tractor, a tattered body whirled on a great wheel.

The other news came the day before he was due to break up for summer. Brought by a Variant policeman. The black-edged envelope had arrived by special courier; so he knew the worst had happened. He read it, uncomprehending. Then again. Mav Manning had passed away; peacefully, in her sleep. Her health had been failing for months; years probably, though she'd never complained. In its way, it had been a merciful release.

No chance of transport, so near end of term. He had to wait for the morning. He went to Middle Park, sat staring at the lake, the big stands round the Air Show ground. He flicked stones at the water. And thought of nothing at all.

Dav Sollen found him. He squatted beside him for a while, not speaking. Then he said, "Come and have a drink."

"No, thanks," said Justin. His mind was far away. Now, if ever, he needed Master Atwill. But the old man had retired last term, on a sudden whim. Gone to the little cottage he'd bought, in Southguard. Where he could see the sea. "I'll be okay," he said.

The other put a hand on his arm. "You won't," he said. "It's all right, I shan't talk. I shan't say a word." So he'd gone with him, sat in a pub off Landy Street, listened to the din; watched the tarts working the leavemen, barmaidens circling with their trays of wine. Later, as he'd lain sleepless, one horrendous thought had come. He tried to block it; but it was useless, it was already there. As he read the letter, his heart had given a bound. He'd thought it might be Tan.

She came with him, to the funeral. She wore a summer dress; white, with embroidery of roses and pretty leaves. And the white sandals. He'd tried at the last minute to persuade her into something more suitable; but she'd begun to squall and cry. And so he'd let her be. She clung to his arm, stared down at the raw hole in the earth. He wondered if she understood. She mewed once, and pointed. But it wasn't at the grave; it was a Cody rig, rising tiny above a distant line of hills.

The summer was long, and hot. He studied the books he'd brought home with him, talked to Tan. Played with her; for sometimes she would play. Once she threw a ball to him, for nearly a whole hour. Her aim wasn't very good; but he sensed she was trying hard. Was it to make up? Usually though she sat and watched him solemnly. And sucked her thumb.

Her favourite place was still the little orchard. She'd swing there half the day, she never seemed to tire. Once she mewed, and took her shoes off; he looked alarmed, and she smiled. She put them back on.

His father engaged a full time nurse for her. She seemed pleasant enough; a bustling, homely woman from the village, widow of one of his tenants. Tan seemed to like her, as far as he could tell; which was the most important thing. Mav, of course, would always be a part of him; but his concern now was for the living. He sensed that she agreed. She came to him one night, and blessed him. He had heard of such things before.

He flew, and graduated. Looking down from the swaying basket, his sole thoughts were of Tan. He wondered if she'd like to ride a Cody. He forgot to be afraid; but he didn't forget his drill.

He wrote to Master Atwill, telling him the news. He felt he already knew what the old man would say. *"A coin must bear two faces. And if one of them is bright, the other must needs be dark. There must be night; else how could we know the splendour of the day?"* He wasn't far wrong.

He put the letter down, smiling. Tan was the day, to him; the dark had gone.

He received his first posting. As he'd feared, it was to the far northwest. A six month tour. He wrote a long letter to his father, another to be read to Tan. Stupid perhaps; but she would know it was from him. He sent her clothes, even a picture book. Horses and ships, the lazy Middle Lands cattle. She kept it in her room, even learned to turn the pages; but she never understood it. As often as not, she would hold it upside down.

The years passed. One day he realized with a shock she was sixteen. He'd made Lancejack a long time back, then Corporal; served his time on the Southguard ships, done a tour of the Easthold. He'd been faced with a choice then. Go for full Flier status, or switch to Ground Duties. Sergeant, then try for his commission.

Once, the decision would have been easy. Now, it wasn't. He talked it over with his skipper, a grizzled Major on the point of retiring. He'd seen too many good men lost in his time; to squalls, to fatigued rigs, to Groundcrew error. The sky was a dangerous place to be. Even Dav Sollen came a cropper, high over the Salient. Smashed a leg so badly it had taken months to heal; there was still some doubt if he would continue in the service.

The Major agreed. "It's a young man's game," he said, pulling at a tankard of beer. "We can't all be Canwen. . . ." So the choice was made. Justin hadn't told the other the whole truth though. Tugging the other way, and mewing, had been a slender, bronze-haired wraith. Tan needed him; and she had won.

Always, during and between his tours, he'd taken every chance to travel back to Mannings. Always, the big house welcomed him; it was still his home. He'd sit with Tange far into the night; puff his pipe and sip his brandy, pore over the books. Father Andri would visit or the local medic, bigwigs sometimes from the Easthold, the Middle Lands. Always, Tan would be there. Suggestions were made of course, insinuations that her presence was less than helpful to the smooth transaction of business; but that was just too bad. Try to shut her out and she'd mew and kick. And that he would not bide. So Tange gave in; and the rest could take their choice.

She ran to him wailing, when he came from Easthold. Tugged his arm in distress. "Tan," he said, "what is it? You can tell me. Tell me now. . . ." She wouldn't though; just pulled him even harder. He gave in, followed her. He knew, with a strange certainty, where she'd head. Toward the orchard. "All right," he said. "What is it?"

She mewed, glared right and left. Grabbed her frock hem, hauled it to her waist.

He stared. Then he slowly shook his head. "Poor little creature," he said. "So it's only just happened. It took you a long time to walk as well." He pushed her shoulders gently, made her sit on the swing. "Tan," he said, "it's not your fault, you haven't done anything wrong. It happens all the while, to everyone." He fetched towels, a bowl. He cleaned her, gently; showed her what she had to do next time. "Change dress," he said. He gestured. "Change your dress. Then we can go out. Would you like to go out?"

She smiled. She was comfortable again, and reassured. She flitted into the house.

He sat on the swing himself. Pushed with his toes, made it move in little arcs. He thought, not for the first time, that it was a strange relationship. It wasn't really though. Things like that don't matter. Because love is a bottomless well.

They strolled nearly to the village. On the way he gathered posies for her; buttercups and scabious, dandelions with shaggy sunburst heads. She didn't seem interested; so he threw them away again. "I agree," he said. "They're not half as lovely as you."

His father was away, on business in the Easthold. He sat her in the study, fetched her food. May cakes—she seemed to prefer them to anything else, though he'd always found them dry—a carafe of Cook's rich, biting lemonade. Later he shook his head. "You poor little creature," he said again. "They thought you couldn't understand. Even Mother, sometimes. She was wrong though. You were so afraid, you daren't even show Nurse." He took her hands. "You needn't be scared," he said. "Not any more. It's just you're grown-up now. So nothing else will happen." He looked her up and down. The lovely, vacant eyes, the mane of hair from which the sun woke long bronze streaks; the perfect breasts, slight under the thin white dress, long legs that tapered to the slender ankles. "Tan," he said. He sighed. "Will you ever know how beautiful you are?"

Later, in his bunk, he lay and tossed sleepless. Because another thought had come, unwanted but not to be driven away. He wasn't sorry, he'd never been sorry. Because her beauty belonged to him. To him and no-one else. Master Atwill had counselled once against the onset of pride. There were worse sins though. Dishonesty, hypocrisy. . . . He wasn't sorry. Did that mean he was glad?

He whispered to the dark, "I'm sorry, Master. . . ."

The years seemed crowded on him. Posting after posting; the Southguard again, Middlemarch, the North, even a stint in the mansion of a Master. A part of him still longed for the dip and surge of a Cody; he supposed it always would. He performed his duties conscientiously, and in time diligence was rewarded. He was commissioned in Middlemarch, received the precious *bulla* from the hands of the Kitemaster Helman himself. The old man smiled as he slipped the silver chain round Justin's neck. "Go with God," he murmured conventionally, "and fly for Him. Congratulations, Captain."

For a moment, he couldn't believe his ears. They'd skipped two ranks; he hadn't realized they valued him so highly. Bad form though, to let elation show. He stepped back, saluted stiffly. He said, "Thank you, My Lord." He strode out feeling he was walking on air. He wished Dav Sollen could be with him, right this minute. Because he knew exactly what the other would say. "Well done, old boy. Tell you what, let's go out on the toot. . . ."

There were women of course; older now and more responsible. Some he loved dearly; one he sat with all one warm spring night, in a big house on the outskirts of Kiteport, the great town in the Southguard. But with the dawn she smiled, and shook her head. "It's no use," she said. "I've just been fooling myself. You don't want me, do you? I don't think you want anybody."

He shook his head. It seemed he was already in thrall. To a pair of tilted, longlashed eyes, a mane of bronzy hair. A girl who could never be his; yet could never belong to anyone else. "I don't know," he said. "I just don't know, Shani." He rose, abruptly. He said, "Forgive me. . . ."

He wangled himself a three day pass, commandeered Base Transport. He drove to the Salient; and Mannings, the great stone house on its hill. Again he felt himself tugged in differing directions. His father was far from well; the weight was dropping off him, he was unable any longer to work the fields with his men. It distressed him; he saw it as a failing of his duty. Justin tried to reassure him; but Tange Manning shook his head. Hair white now, eyes tired behind his steel-framed specs. "It isn't right, son," he said. "It isn't right. I'd like to have seen you settled."

"I am settled," he said. "I've got Mannings. And you."

The other looked up sharply. His lips parted; but whatever he'd meant to say was left unspoken. He carried the secret to his grave.

Justin's career thrived. Staff Officer at G12; then a Section at G15. Where he might have gone, with singlemindedness, was an open question; because his loyalties were still divided. He travelled home time and again; spent long hours in his father's study, poring over his accounts. Increasingly it seemed, the running of the estate devolved on him. He saw to the hiring of extra hands for harvest, motored to the Easthold to haggle with the millers for the ensiled grain. He whirled Tan on the orchard swing, and brooded. She was twenty-two, coming twenty-three. She still looked a bare sixteen.

It was his father's last year at Mannings. He died in the autumn, as Grandad Curt had done; and once more Tan watched empty-faced. The horses came, black-plumed; and the motors with their sombre bonnet ribbons, their railed toploads of flowers. He took her back to the house, sat down to take some sort of stock.

The Corps were good to him. Six months' leave of absence, with full pay. The pay he refused; he had no need of cash. It could go to the Fliers' Fund; God knew there were enough deserving cases. He summoned the executors from Middlemarch. Later he travelled there himself, in the old Swallow he'd bought. Bought with his own cash; the entailment of Estate funds still caused irritating problems. He took Tan with him, packed her things himself. Her nurse fretted, worried for her charge; but he merely smiled. If he couldn't look after her by now, it was time he learned.

There were harnesses fitted to the front seats of the Swallow. Most newer vehicles had dispensed with them, but these old motors still had built-in luxuries. He slipped the straps over her shoulders, clicked the belt round her waist. She looked alarmed at once, began to pluck and complain. "It's all right," he said. "Tan, it's only so you'll be safe. I don't want you to be hurt. Please trust me." She frowned, but made no further protest.

He drove down the track from Mannings, pointed the bonnet west. "It's funny, Tan," he said. "Do you remember, years ago? I said when I was very clever, I'd be a Captain. Well, I did it. I said I'd take you to Middlemarch then, and buy you pretty things. We're doing that as well. I didn't really believe it when I said it. But it's all come true."

She glanced at him sidelong with her tilted eyes. Pulled at the straps again.

He drove past Station after Station. Always with a faint but definite pang. Sometimes she smiled, pointing to the Codys; once clapped her hands and laughed, seemingly with pleasure. At other times her eyes became opaque. Blank, yet with a quality of wariness. He wondered if new impressions were flooding in.

It was a long run. Even in the Swallow. He stopped halfway, at an inn deep in the Middle Lands. He knew its owners to be kindly folk. The landlady took Tan under her wing at once. She trotted after her happily enough. Later though she ran back into the bar, flung herself wailing into his arms. Mistress Lanting followed at once, apologetically. "I'm sorry," she said. "I think it was the horse. We rented the paddock, she didn't know it was there."

"She's seen enough horses," he said. "She's just being silly. Aren't you, Tan? You're just showing off a bit. New people to impress."

The other diners were watching the scene curiously. He glanced at them, and they instantly dropped their eyes. The tinkle of cutlery was resumed.

Driving into Middlemarch, down the long slope of the eastern hill, he waved a hand. "We're here, Tan," he said. "Isn't it a big place? Don't you think it's beautiful?" But the great vista failed to evoke a response.

There was an inn he knew. A little way from the Drag. A quiet place, unpretentious but clean. He left her in the car, hoping she wouldn't panic. But she didn't seem concerned. She'd brought the picture book with her, she was looking at it. The right way up for once.

He knew they had a double room. He hoped it was free. He was in luck. He put her in the little inner chamber. To reach the landing she would have to pass his bed. She didn't try.

He got a good night's sleep. When he woke she was already up and dressed. She was sitting on the bed, trying to comb her hair.

"Here," he said. "Let me. Your fingers are all thumbs." He took the comb away. Once she would have mewed indignantly; but now she seemed content.

He took her to the outfitters the College people used. They had a lady's section. He knew the manageress; she was the wife of one of his old tutors. She clucked at sight of Tan.

"Fix her a wardrobe," he said. "It doesn't matter what it costs." He paused. He said, "Her mother's dead."

She clucked again. "Poor soul," she said. "You'll be all right with me. It's all right, Daddy won't go away." Tan went, not without a backward glance.

He rubbed his face, a little ruefully. So she'd forgotten him. Or had he changed that much?

They were gone a considerable time. There were no problems though. When they came back their arms were full of clothes. Tan was mewing continuously, with pleasure or excitement. He said, "Was it all right?" and the older woman smiled. She said, "She was as good as gold." He thought there were tears in her eyes.

Tan demurred when the other started to pack the things. He had to take her wrists, shake gently to make her attend. "It's just to keep them clean," he said. "They still belong to you. We're taking them with us, Tan. Look, here's the first."

She gave him a fashion show in his room. Dashing through each time to change. She'd never done a thing like that before. He lay on the bed, a pillow at his back, and applauded each appearance. Strangely, despite his father, he felt at peace.

The last dress was the prettiest of all. Plain white, with a skirt slit to the thigh. And a deep vee neckline, closed by a little lace. "Tan," he said, "that's naughty. Really naughty. . . ."

She smiled at him.

She wore the dress at dinner. Despite his protests. She turned heads, in the dining room. She was unaware. He tucked a napkin round her carefully; but no disasters ensued. Later they walked, down to Middle Park. Codys were flying, gay streamers fluttering from each Lifter and strings of little coloured lamps. She tucked her arm in his. She was lissome, elegant. He felt the defocused happiness again. He decided it was sheer pleasure in her. Perfection of face and figure, hair, the flawless amber skin. She *was* perfection, he realized it quite suddenly. The First Woman of the myth, from whom sprang all the world.

Apogee. The Lifters hung unmoving, in an endless dream of blue. He leaned back in the basket, wearily. Clenched and unclenched his clumsy, numbed fingers. There can only be perfection once. It can never come again.

Somewhere, the faintest of jolts. The basket swayed fractionally. He glanced down, unwilling, and the drifting clouds were closer. They were reeling him in, like a bulky skyborne fish.

A Staff Major visited, to discuss his future prospects. Justin sat in the morning room, long unoccupied, and talked. Waving his hands to the windows, the rolling spread of farmland. Tan curled on the corner settle, watching with her gold-brown eyes. More than once the other's glance strayed to her worriedly. He said, "So you're leaving the Corps."

He'd shaken his head. "I don't want to," he said. "It's the last thing I want to do. I've made it my life." He offered more brandy; the Kiteman declined, with a smile.

Justin's glance strayed to the corner too. "You can see the responsibilities," he said. "I can't evade those either. It's the hardest decision I ever had to make."

The Major said, "Hmm." He riffled papers, thoughtfully. He drummed his knee, stroked at his little clipped moustache. Then it seemed he came to a decision. "I'm maybe overreaching myself," he said, "and I certainly don't want to raise false hopes. But . . . between you and me, G8 is coming up. Old Lowndes is retiring at last. I could put in a recommendation. How would that appeal?"

It was like a burst of light. G8, the Station he'd first seen as a tiny boy. It had always been a special place to him. "Could you?" he said. "Could you do that for me?"

"Don't see why not," said the other. "Have to go to Middlemarch of course. So don't rely on a thing. But they have started a local staffing policy; and with a record like yours I'd say you stand as good a chance as the next." He slipped the papers into a briefcase. "Consider it done," he said. He pulled a face, and rose. "Got to get on the road," he said. "Due in the Easthold at some ghastly hour tomorrow. Court martial. Some fool of a Lancejack slugged a Sergeant Rigger. . . ." He shook hands. "Good luck, Captain," he said.

The posting came through. There followed the happiest time of his life. He put in a Farm Manager, fetched him from the Middle Lands. Later he installed a housekeeper; a greying, hardfaced woman, Mrs. Brand. He didn't care for her overmuch; but there was no doubting her efficiency. And her references were irreproachable. He gave her very special instructions, particularly with regard to Tan. She smiled thinly, clipped the keys to her belt. She said, "I shall try to give every satisfaction, sir."

He said, "I'm sure you will."

Tan disliked the new arrangement at first. Twice she wandered, searching for him perhaps, got nearly as far as the village; but she was brought back gently enough. Finally she seemed to grow accustomed to the routine. Off at zero nine hundred, generally back by seventeen hundred latest. The evenings he spent with her were long and rich. Particularly in summer. She could go to her beloved orchard, swing and suck her thumb.

Straightforwardly, G8 was in a mess. Lowndes had been long past retirement, things had been let to slide badly. The Corps had let him stay on out of kindness; but it was obvious nobody at Headquarters had known the true state of affairs. Justin got rid of a couple of Corporals, had them posted. Then a new contingent of Cadets arrived, and things began to look up. He started out with them the way he meant to go on. Kantmer the Rigger and Holbeck the Launchmaster were old hands of course. Stalwarts. He had the beginnings of a team.

He bullied Middlemarch for the new Lifters. Then the special pistols. There was less hassle over them; they were getting used to his stubbornness. There followed a spot inspection. The brass descended in droves; but he merely smiled. He'd known it would come; his people had been spitting and polishing for days. Even a kerchief rubbed on the guardroom floor disclosed no speck of dirt. Three Rigs were streamed; his maximum capacity. The launch times compared quite well with G15. And they had a double manning capacity. After that he was left in peace.

Mannings prospered. Beyond his father's dreams. He added a third silo, took on four more men. The Salient folk were pleased. Work had always been scarce; traditionally, it was a depressed area. They'd been suspicious of him at first; he sensed his stock had risen considerably.

Dav Sollen visited. At first Justin barely recognized him. He was burly now and bearded, sporting a wife and a brace of fair-haired kids. He carried a stick, and walked with a heavy limp. The leg had healed better than the medics had thought; though it still gave him Hell in wet weather. He'd left the service; he was a civilian contractor now, supplying anything from cable drums to logbooks and tide tables. So he was still in touch with the world of the great Kites.

Tan charmed them all. The children in particular took to her. She showed them her toys, one after the next, winding up the little, squeaking dogs, the green tin frogs that hopped along the carpet. Later she even let them use her swing; a signal honour, that.

His first harvest in, the work piled up again. He couldn't expect Butard the Manager to cope with the wholesale/retail side as well. There just weren't enough hours in the day. He needed an outside man, somebody free to travel, make the contacts for him. He found one in Easthope, courtesy of an acquaintance of his father's. He'd been a stocktaker once, worked for the Corps. Mal Trander. He looked to be in his thirties. Rakishly handsome, curly chestnut hair. He said he'd been married once, given it up as the bad job. Which was all to the good. Nothing to distract him.

He rolled his head from side to side, and groaned. "How could I have known?" he whispered. "How could I have guessed. . . ."

As ever, he studied Tan's reaction carefully. He'd hired and fired accordingly, and never been wrong. She'd become his voiceless partner, though nobody else knew that. Sometimes it took her a while to make up her mind; but this time she seemed to have no doubts. She ran to the stocktaker at once, giving her little mewing cry. Within the hour she brought him her picture book. She held it out to him, upside down. He turned it round for her. "That way, my love," he said, eyes twinkling. "Gee-gees aren't very good at standing on their heads." He looked at her appraisingly. She was wearing denims, figure-hugging, and a new top Justin had bought; stripy, and with a wide scooped collar. They'd told him the style was called boat-necked. Later Mal Trander said, "What a pretty kid. Nice with it too."

The Captain glanced up briefly. "Yes," he said. "She's sweet." He consulted the notes he'd made. "What say we start with Ransams in Condar Street? I've never sold to them yet; they'd be a good outlet to have."

He'd never have known anything was wrong. Never suspected. Had it not been for a stray whisper, overheard on Base. He brooded about it; then he sent for Kantmer. He havered a bit, staring through the long windows of the office while the Riggingmaster waited. He'd never been one for confiding in inferiors. It was a weakness; led to slackness, indiscipline. But Kantmer was an old hand. And anyway, a Lineman of his experience could scarcely be termined inferior to a Captain of three years' seniority. He turned from contemplation of his No. 1 String, hanging steady against the blue. "This character Mal Trander," he said. "What do you know about him, Bend?"

The other was ready with his answers. His marriage, reasons for breaking with the Corps; he was terse, and to the point. Justin felt his mouth set in a harder line. Finally he nodded. "Thank you, Riggingmaster," he said. "Thank you very much." He inclined his head toward the cupboard, "Drink?"

"No thank you, sir," said Kantmer steadily. "Got to get that shackle fixed on Three. She's due to stream at seventeen hundred. . . ."

When the other had gone he sat and brooded again. Drummed his fingers on the desk top. Certainly Trander had worked well enough for him. He'd no cause for complaint; the contrary in fact. And his past was his own affair. To an extent at least.

By fifteen-thirty he'd made his mind up. The other was due back that afternoon, from a trip to the Middle Lands. Best face him with what he'd heard. Give him a chance to put his side of things. He left the Base abruptly, drove the Swallow home.

The stackyard was wide; he knew the engine sound would be inaudible from the house. He left the car by the silos anyway, walked the last two hundred yards. Trander's old jalopy was parked beside the main door.

He let himself in, silently. The place seemed oddly quiet. He checked the lower rooms. Nobody. But of course the nurse was having one of her rare days off. The rest would be in the dairy, Mrs Brand taking her afternoon nap.

He walked upstairs. The door of Tan's room was ajar. He pushed it with his foot, walked in.

Her skirt was round her waist, her ankles locked about Trander's hips. He was panting, driving into her hard; and there was blood. A lot of blood, spattering the sheet. So it was the first time. She was clawing at him, giving the little mewing cries.

He put his hand to the other's shoulder, heaved. He was a

powerful man; but he'd never used his strength in anger before. The stocktaker landed on the floor. He tried to scuttle away; and Justin caught him, hauled him up by the shirt. He slammed him against the wall. The room shook. He used his knees and boots. Then started with his hands. When the other fell he picked him up. He knocked him down again. His vision had narrowed; what sight remained was tinged with red.

He stepped back. Trander was on his hands and knees. His breathing sounded harsh. He retched; and there were teeth, bright spatterings. He hauled himself up by the doorframe, staggered. He began to work his way along the landing; gripping the banister, his other hand to his groin. He didn't turn. From somewhere came a scream. Mrs. Brand would give her notice now. Refuse to work in an unruly house.

She'd pulled her skirt down. She was huddled in the corner of the bed, her knuckles to her mouth. He yanked her toward him, hit her across the face. Then again. She whimpered, tried to cling to him. He flung her away. She rolled over, lay face down. He tugged at his belt buckle. He beat her with all his strength, across her back, her thighs, her bottom. In time the mewings stopped. She lay silent, shaking. He walked out, closed the door. He went downstairs. Walked into the morning room, opened the drinks cabinet. He took down brandy and a glass.

The house seemed muted still. There were shufflings, whisperings; but nobody came near him. He drank, and watched the light begin to fade. He'd never beaten a living thing like that before. Not a human, not an animal.

He lost track of time. The afterglow was flaring when there was a scratching at the door. She opened it. She stared a moment; then she dropped to her knees. She worked her way toward him slowly, skirt brushing the polished parquet. She reached the chair, stared up. He saw the swollen lips, the teartracks on her poor bruised face. He thought, "If I touch her now, I know what the end will be. At last, I understand." There was a sense of doom, the yawning of a pit; but also a curious rightness. Who but himself anyway? He who knew her every cry, the meaning of each whimper. He stared a moment longer; then reached out gently, began to stroke her hair.

• • •

He'd entered cloud again. As he'd entered cloud before. The greyness swirled, obscuring. He wondered why he'd never understood.

He supposed in a way he had. He'd crowned a simple Fact with pinnacles and spires, not wanting to see it as it was. *"This is a roof . . . and these are walls, and windows. . . ."* The meaning of the parable came clear at last.

The moral issues ceased to trouble him. It was right to hold her, right to love. Right to bathe her, comb her beautiful hair. He encircled her; as she encircled him. She was Dawn Woman; and she needed him. As surely woman never needed man before. He was complete; he existed in her aura.

Days came and went; the seasons followed their course. He trimmed her nails; an hour of chuckling, playing, for each hand and foot. Her fingernails were shell-pink, shapely. When they showed signs of splitting he varnished them, with dope from the Lifter sheds. He sent for dresses; from the Southguard, Easthope, Middlemarch. Each one she greeted now with cries of delight. She'd pull open the tall doors of her wardrobe; run her fingers along the hangers, make a wooden clatter. "Yours," he'd say. "All yours," and she would crow and chuckle. She'd try them on, one after the next, and prance and pirouette; and then she'd take them off. Sometimes she'd dance in the stackyards, in the garden; shake fruit from the orchard trees, the blossoms in their season. She was destructive, mischievous; like a bird, a squirrel. Other times the mewings would return. She'd huddle close then, in his great bed; draw herself down beneath the covers, into dark. He'd huddle with her, rub till she was warm, the tremblings stopped. She'd kiss him then and whisper; tiny broken sounds that were nearly words. He undestood in time what each breath intake meant. "Tan," he'd say. "Oh, Tan. . . ." By day, the Codys flew.

Mrs. Brand didn't leave. He should have been warned; but he was deaf and blind. She went about her duties, calmly and efficiently. Checking the household lists, supervising the laundry that bubbled in the great brick coppers. She announced his visitors, as and when they came. One morning—he was taking a rare day's leave—she ushered in the village priest.

He was working in his study at the time. "Father Andri," he said. "You're welcome. Please be seated." Then came the shock, the dreadful pang. The other was in his formal robes; the blazing scarlet, Cap of Maintenance, of the great Church Variant itself.

The Father waited till the housekeeper had rustled from the room. And closed the door behind her. He said without preamble, "You know why I am here."

His throat had dried; for a moment his vision flickered. "No," he said. "No, I don't."

"Captain," said the priest, "Don't make it harder for yourself. Harder than it has to be." He still waited; and finally the other sighed. "A sin has been committed," he said. "A vile and grievous crime, for which there can be neither pity nor forgiveness."

Justin looked through the window, to where Tan kicked high on the orchard swing. Crowing, showing her legs. Her little yelps of pleasure sounded through the glass. He put his face in his hands. They were shaking. "Father," he said, "tell me one thing. If there is no awareness, where is sin?"

"Awareness?" said the other "The Demons sinned, by wasting all the world. Were they aware?"

He said, "She is a child."

"She is a woman," said the priest. "And with a woman's parts. Chop me no logic, Captain."

He laid his hands flat on the desk top. He already saw, dimly, the way the thing must go. He wondered how he could have shut it from his mind. The consequences of actions. It had been madness. And yet . . . mad? Mad to love beauty, wherever it is found? Mad to love the Ultimate? He said, "She's everything. Mother, daughter, wife. A child of God. But you wouldn't understand that, would you?"

The other looked up, under his brows. "A child of God?" he said. "She was Condemned once. As you know very well."

He was finding it difficult to make words. He said, "But she has done no harm." The other's expression didn't change.

He raised his hands, the fingers crooked. "She is an Innocent," he said. "Can you not understand? Will you not try?"

"She was Condemned once," said the priest. "It can be done again. There are larger knives. For tougher little necks."

Justin found he could no longer see. Also his hearing was impaired. There was a buzzing, roaring. When vision returned he was standing over the Father, fingers still crooked. And the other watching him calmly. "Kill me then," he said. "Do you suppose your secret will be safe? Do you imagine I'm the sole repository?"

Once before, he had experienced an icy calm. He experienced it now. He walked away, stood staring through the window. Watching Tan on the swing. He said, "It's hatred, isn't it? Hatred of beauty. Freedom. Hatred of love. You, who profess to peddle love of God." He turned back. Nodded toward the farther wall. "Out there," he said, "is a place they call the Badlands. Have you seen them? Have you seen the things they spawn?"

Father Andri didn't answer.

"Their flesh is blue," he said. "Their lips are made of blubber. Their inner workings can be seen quite plain; and you cannot meet their eyes. Once they were men. And women."

He sat back at the desk. "We were spared," he said. "This one little Realm. We praised God for it. For His mercy. Then what did we do? We spawned you. To sit among us, dispense burning fluids. When your blood drops on to grass, it dies." He pointed. "Leave this house," he said. "Leave, while you can walk."

The Father didn't move.

He rose again; but it was useless. The rage had gone, as quickly as it had arisen. He remembered the hold the Church had on the land. Every city, village, town; always the Scarlet, always needle-pointed spires. Nowhere would she be safe. They would find her; and out would come a shining, leafshaped knife.

He'd seen, just once, the ruin of a Cody string. Snapping of struts, the sagging of the Trace; then the other Lifters, folding under too much stress. Till what had been proud and lovely lay a shambles on the grass. He knew he was destroyed himself. He turned back to the window. The swing still moved; but empty. She had run away. He said dully, "Can you save her?"

The priest said, "Yes."

He moistened his lips. He said, "I suppose you have conditions."

The other nodded. He said, "You know what they are."

"Yes," he said. "Of course."

The door opened. Tan came in. She hesitated when she saw the priest. Then she ran forward with a little mew. Tried to grasp his robe. He twitched it away. She stood back, puzzled and a little hurt.

Justin stood up. He said, "I shall do as you require."

Father Andri rose in turn. "See to it, Captain," he said. "For her sake, if not for yours." He paused at the door. "If you love her as you claim," he said, "then it should be a joy." The door closed behind him.

She was still looking concerned. He smiled. "It's nothing, Tan," he said. "Come out and play."

He swung her, the rest of the afternoon. Later they sat on the grass. "Tan," he said, "I want to talk to you. Very seriously indeed."

She linked her arms round her knees, put her head on one side. He pushed her legs down, gently. She smiled a little, troubled smile.

"Tan," he said, "I love you more than all the world. Because you are the world. That's why I have to go away."

He pulled a stem of grass. "You see," he said, "there are certain things that are wrong. I don't think they are, not really. Not with someone like you. But other people think they are. And we've been doing them." He looked up at the sky. "Some people think that everything is wrong," he said. "I think they believe it's wrong to love at all."

She didn't respond.

"You see," he said, "It's not us. You and I. That isn't what matters. It's the Church."

She frowned, looked partly over her shoulder.

"Yes," he said. "That's right. People like Father Andri. Maybe they think what they're doing is right. I don't know any more. I think we made our own Church. Just the two of us."

She reached out, grasped his hand. He pushed her away, gently. "Tan," he said, "if I go on loving you, they'll cut your head off."

She put her fingers slowly to her neck.

"Yes," he said again. "That's right." He looked at the grass stem, tossed it away. "It's all a question of priorities," he said. "Getting things in order. The most important first, and then the rest." He thought a moment. "I was told that once,'' he said, ''by a very wise old man. That was when I was at College, learning to be clever. Only I didn't learn. Not properly. I'm still learning now.'' He looked round. ''I shall have to sell this place,'' he said. ''Father Andri wouldn't want me to stay. But that will be all right. I shall be able to find you a really lovely home. In the Middle Lands, perhaps. He'll help, if he knows we're both sincere.''

She looked round the orchard, troubled. He smiled; he almost took her hands. Then he remembered. ''Don't worry,'' he said. ''There are trees all over the Realm. I can buy you swings. And send you letters, and more dresses.'' He swallowed. ''That's the way it's got to be,'' he said. ''There isn't another answer. I've known it for a long time now.''

He glanced round him again. ''I did it all for you,'' he said. ''Learned to fly the Codys. So you would be safe. Well, this is for you too. You can be safe again.'' He stared at his hands. ''A lovely home,'' he said. ''There'll be others just like you. You'll be able to talk to them, and play. And you'll be safe for ever.''

No response. He tried another tack. ''Do you remember, all that time ago?'' he said. ''I beat you, dreadfully. You should never hurt anyone like that. Whatever they've done. Well, this is my punishment. Because when you do something bad you have to pay for it sooner or later. And I've been bad to you. You see I'm not really a very nice person at all. I love the Kites; there isn't room for anything else. No room for you; not a teeny little place.'' He swallowed again. ''You think I'm being hard,'' he said. ''Well, that's the way it is. You see, life is hard. Flying the Codys is hard. You can't let feelings get in the way of that.''

She stared at him; then for the first time in her life she slowly nodded.

''My angel,'' he said gently. He leaned forward, kissed her carefully on the forehead.

He'd thought she'd understood. But at bedtime she began to squall. She clung to him, desperate; and he pushed her away. ''No,'' he said, ''it's over. Tan, *it's over. . . .*''

There was a rustling, at the door of the room. Mrs. Brand glided forward, lamp in hand. ''You may leave her, Captain Manning,'' she said calmly. ''I will see to her.''

He ran for the door, slammed it behind him blindly.

• • •

Blind? He was no longer blind. He was below the clouds, Earth taking shape again. Sunlight struck from above; made ragged silver edges, dazzling against the blue. He fell back in the basket. "No," he groaned. "Please, no. . . ."

There was brandy in the morning room. He finished one bottle, started on another. He lost track of time. Perhaps he slept; if he did, he was roused by the chirpings of birds. It seemed her voice mixed with it; the trilling, and the mewing.

Always, the rustling of that dress. She shook his shoulder. He started, stared round wildly. "Captain," she said, "you must come with me."

"What is it?" he said hoarsely. "What is it, Mrs. Brand? Is it Tan?" She didn't answer directly. She said, "You must come with me."

He followed, reeling on the stairs. The bedroom door was open. He ran in. She lay head turned, hair wild on the pillows. He'd thought she was asleep; but she wasn't. Because her teeth were clenched. "Tan," he said again. "Tan, what is it. . . ." But the housekeeper forestalled him, snatched back the covers with a quick, contemptuous flick. His eyes dilated. He saw the dreadful brightness of the sheets, the lake that was her blood; the knife still gripped, her leg vibrating with shock. On it from knee to ankle, crudely carved in quarter inch vee gouges, was his own name; JUSTIN. He'd always known, one day she'd speak to him. She'd spoken now.

The bawling noise he made was that of an animal in pain. He ran from the house, hands clutched to his head, and reeled across the yard. *"Ruined,"* he moaned. His lovely temple ruined. Then, *"Why . . . Why her. . . ."* Then, "No. . . ." And again, in desperation, *"No, no, no. . . ."*

The noise in his ears was thunderous, drowning the wind. He sat up, stared. He rose, stood in the rocking basket. He gripped the Cody sides, while the colour left his face.

It moved forward slowly, sharp-cut against the silver clouds above. And it was big, bigger than he could have dreamed. He saw the sun glint from its silver flanks. He saw the fins, the markings on its sides. He saw the scarlet rings that tipped its nose.

He grabbed for the pistol, cocked. *"Accursed Demon,"* he said. *"Messenger from Hell. Thou sooty spirit, get thee gone. Avaunt. . . ."* He fired; and the thing vanished, in a dazzling burst of light.

There was another, and another. He fired, and fired again. Pushed at the barrel release, flung the smoking cylinder away. He grabbed a second, rammed it home.

They were flying beneath him now. They had the shapes of fishes, just as in the Litany. Below were others and still more; the Cunning Ones, clinging to the land. None passed; because his aim was true. Spots swam before his eyes; he grabbed for the third cylinder, the fourth. Skin tore from his fingers; but still he rammed the red-hot barrel home. He laughed; because his life had been fulfilled. This was the point toward which all had been directed. At last he was protecting her; really protecting her. His lovely, wounded angel. The Demon-shoal scattered, panic-stricken, diving. Flicking their vile shadows on the land. The yellow fins, the black, the red. They turned back, angry, desperate, roared at the Rig. Those too he atomized; and suddenly, the sky was clear.

He dropped to his knees. He knew now—why had he not seen before—that all had not been lost. It was so easy; he would go back, he would take her away. Far away. And heal and minister, till she was whole again.

The gun fell from his hand. He hung his head. The roaring was back; but louder than before. He coughed, desperately; then darkness overtook him.

They'd heard the fusillade of shots. Coming it seemed from miles away. The winch was yelling; atop the Launcher Cadets stood in pairs, steel crowbars in their hands, guiding the snaking cable on to the drum. A desperate manoeuvre; hands had been lost and arms, playing that game. The Winchman yelled; and at last the cable, sloping impossibly into the blue, became the cable of a Cody rig. They saw the swaying basket, beyond it the great train of wings. Snaking and dipping from the crazy speed.

The Winchman threw his lever. Squeals from the brake-blocks, and the Trace was close. The Cadets flung themselves away. He worked the lever again, head turned, gentling the train in. The Launchmaster raised an arm; suddenly the Observer's basket filled the sky. A dozen pairs of hands grabbed, lowered down; and silence fell, broken only by the seething of the truck.

Slowly, the Base personnel crowded round. They peered into the basket; and more than one Apprentice blenched. Their Captain lay curled up in the bottom of the Cody. The blood he had voided soaked his chin and tunic, spattered the wicker sides. His hands were clenched; and his eyes still glared at the sky. In triumph or in terror, none could tell. Lastly the Chaplain approached. He stared down calmly; then reached with a finger and thumb to close the lids.

Across the field stood a massive scarlet vehicle. Almost the size of a Launcher, but totally enclosed; and with a vicious ram jutting from between its wheels. By it stood a little knot of men, also robed in red. To one side, Rik Butard still sat a lathered horse. The priests paced forward; and their leader folded his arms. "So die all heretics," he said. "All sinners, who seek to evade the Lord."

The Chaplain faced him mildly. "Perhaps," he said, "he didn't choose to escape. He flew to meet Him."

The Hunter-Bishop waved a hand dismissively. "We will take the corpse," he said. "It will be disposed of, in a fitting manner."

"You will not," said the other, still quiet. "Last rites are for the Corps to organize."

The Bishop's colour flared immediately. "Out of my way," he said. "His goods and property are forfeit. Also there is another sinner to attend." He pointed. "Clear that Rig."

An axe flashed, contemptuously. The Trace leaped, snaked up into the sky. Whirled out over the Badlands, and was lost from sight.

The Bishop stared, as if unable to credit the evidence of his senses. "For that," he said, "your head will roll, Launchmaster." He groped beneath his robes; and behind him there was a click. He froze, turned slowly. He and his group were surrounded by a ring of armed men.

He swallowed, and the flush faded quick as it had risen. Was replaced by pallor. "This," he said, "is heresy. Heresy, and insurrection."

The Chaplain shook his head. "No," he said, "it is justice. The Corps ministers its own. For all your trumpeting."

The other opened his mouth, and closed it.

"Where is your authority?" said the Chaplain. "Where is your warrant, from Middlemarch? Your power wears thin, my friend."

The other felt, cautiously, under his robes. "This is my power," he said. He held out a Staff of Office.

"And this is mine," said the slim man. He held out in turn a small looped cross; the symbol of the Middle Doctrine. He jerked his head. "Hold them, during my pleasure," he said. "Later, they will answer to their own." The Variants were hustled away; and he turned to the great rig. "Launchmaster," he said, "you are in command. Secure the Base; post guards, until another authority comes." He turned again. Glanced at the scarlet truck, back to the Launcher. He smiled, thinly. Because the Base was angry at last; angry at useless sacrifice. The Variants had stirred a hornets' nest; and found that hornets can sting. "Doctor," he said, "a hurt child needs your urgent skill. Will you come with us?" But the Medic was already there, carrying his black tin box. He swung into the Launcher's cab; armed Cadets ran forward at once, clustered the top of the great truck, its running boards. The Chaplain followed; and the cables snaked away. The massive machine bellowed, lurched toward the gate. The last the others heard was the roaring of its engine, building speed along the lane.

5 kiteservant

HE'D BEEN AWAKE by zero three-thirty, on the road by four hundred. Though that hadn't been much of a trick of course. His things were laid out for the morning, and his bags all packed; the two big grips he'd bought the day before, the valise Rone had lent him for allegedly important papers. Though it contained little of significance at the moment.

He glanced behind him, into the body of the Buckley. Two oval windows in the rear doors, giving light; and the dark red paint, same as the outside. The doors would never shut properly, however he tried to pad them. They'd always squeaked. They were squeaking now.

Rand looked round him. At first the morning had been misty, cool; great shapes of trees hanging to either side of the road, each a still shadow of bluey-green. By Garnord though the heat of the day had been beginning to make itself felt. Sky clearing to a vivid blue, the dust starting to rise. The little van trailed a whitish cloud behind it; a cloud that dissipated slowly in the almost windless air.

At Garnord he encountered a metalled road; one of the very few, in truth, he'd ever seen. Streanling, where he'd been born and where he'd lived his first quarter century, was the acknowledged capital of the Northwest; and though Garnordians—Garnordites some called them, though that was an invitation to instant battle—were traditionally fond of quibbling the fact there'd never been much doubt in his mind. After all, it was in Streanling the Variants held greatest sway; apart from Middlemarch itself of course. There was Skyway, second Cathedral of the Realm; and the Civil College, at which he'd toiled four long and sometimes wearisome years. But Streanling still didn't have paved roads. Somehow they'd never felt the need of them.

Though he had heard rumours the Vars were losing ground even in Middlemarch. Why, he'd never been too sure. The Middle Doctrine that opposed them had always seemed to his mind vague and bumbling by comparison; while those of its priests he'd met had an irritating habit of answering questions with others. Thus:

"What is the Middle Way?"

"The Middle Way is what you decide it is."

"Is it a religion?"

"If you wish it to be."

"But all religions are Ways."

"Perhaps. Then are all Ways religions?"

That had been years ago though, with Father Alkin; when he'd had an argumentative, perhaps more enquiring mind.

He glanced at his fuel gauge. Then the bright new chronometer on his wrist. That last a present from Rone; unexpected, and to tell the truth unwanted. The fuel gauge was of little help either. As with all these old Buckleys, the needle flickered continually across the little yellow dial; full to empty, empty to full. Dipping the tank was the only real answer; but even that was difficult. Somebody had rebuilt the Buck from a pair of wrecks. Overall he'd done a fairish job; but he'd neglected to allow for a proper fall in the gas hose. It made filling a slight difficulty too.

He remembered an incident up in Seahold, on the ragged Northwest coast. One of the first trips he'd taken when he'd acquired the van. A little filling station, set on its own beside a dusty track that seemed to lead to nowhere; and a striking girl, elegant and tall, with a mane of tumbling auburn hair. He'd already put a notice on the Buckley's side; CAUTION, SLOW FILLER. She'd been impatient though. Maybe there'd been a reason; her beautiful and miles from anywhere, the day too hot. But three pulls on the big old handpump and the nozzle had still blown back, left her soaked to the knees and the tarmac of the little forecourt glistening. She'd abused him roundly; old crocks on the road, wasting her time and his own. The words stung; after all the Buckley was a new possession. He paid her, curtly, told her to keep the change; and then she'd tried to walk away. He'd seen the soles of her smart new shoes had glued themselves to the matrix of gravel. He'd laughed, and started up the little van. Later though he'd streamed a new train for her, from the house roof. The Godkite carried a vestibule in gold; cost him a fortune in the Skyways shop. He wondered why he'd bothered. That night the wind got up; and the whole thing blew away. So maybe the Lord had noticed too.

He set his lips. He'd realized deep inside him he was scared.

He set himself to analyze the feeling, with some care. So he was taking up his first appointment as a Servant. Internal audits on the Easthold Bases, later a tour into the Salient. His first long trip from home; and in the first motor vehicle he'd ever owned. New experiences all; but were they in themselves a cause for fear? Emotion was burned from him; so he could know neither joy nor apprehension. He grimaced. Because he knew, or could guess, what the Master Sprinling would have said. *"Fear, like pain, is a gift from God. Both have a purpose, as all things in life have a purpose. Against them we test ourselves. As the Church has been tested, and will be tested again. We must not be found wanting. . . ."*

He shook his head. It didn't really help. Because Father Alkin was in his mind as well.

"What is fear, Father?"

"Fear is what you decide it is."

"Why does it come?"

"That, my son, you must discover for yourself."

"Is there a reason for it?"

"Perhaps, perhaps not. One day, you will decide . . ."

He rubbed his face. He was remembering a time when he cowered in the corner of his room all night and whimpered, wanting the impossible; that all the folk he knew, all the folk he'd ever met in the world, could somehow be with him, crowding round, holding back the dark. The dark that seemed to crawl, encroach, flood through him. Because he'd realized for the first time, he was mortal too. He wondered why it had taken so long. But of course that was after Janni.

He pushed the thought away, as he'd pushed it away before. He'd risen from where he crouched, walked to the window. The simple act had taken all his willpower. He sat and watched a green dawn brighten round the spires of Skyway. He'd washed and shaved then, changed as required into the robes of an acolyte; and walked to College, to sit the first of his finals.

He looked at his wrist again. He'd made good time, better than he'd hoped for; coming zero six-thirty, and the rounded hills that encircled Garnord already behind him. The Buckley had chuffed a little, climbing them; he'd pulled in twice to rest her and cool the little engine, but she hadn't boiled. Which had been the first blessing of the day; he'd been afraid of the rad leak starting up again. He'd cured it two days before, with the additive Master Bone had supplied him; but he'd been warned the respite would only be temporary. He'd have liked to install a new core, but funds were scarce; and in any case such things had to come from Middlemarch, there'd been no time to order. So here he was, with a suspect cooling system and a diff that as ever bonked and clattered, crossing the Realm from one side to the other.

He wondered why he'd set himself the task. After all he could have made it easily enough by College coach; first stage to Middlemarch, second to the Crossways, third curving down into Easthold. He suspected it had to do with Janni; though what the exact connection was eluded him. One certain fact was that whether he succeeded or failed, she wouldn't care. Why should she? She'd already made her views plain, on that and other matters.

Rone then, or Shand, his sister? She would have been no help either though. The dark eyes would have watched, from the slim brown face; she'd have stroked ash sideways, from one of the rank-smelling tubes she always insisted on smoking, and shrugged. He could even hear her voice. "You'll have to make your own mind up. I can't live your life for you. Nobody can."

No. He'd never tried to live hers. Despite the accusation she once made.

He took a bend. There was a further vista of trees. More, he imagined, than you'd find in the whole of Northguard. He supposed he'd entered the Middle Lands; though there'd been nothing to announce the fact. The rest of the country looked the same as the land he'd been driving through the last hour or so. Low, rolling hills fringeing the horizon; broad fields yellow with crops, others under grass. Fat cattle grazed the pastures, the occasional donkey or horse. No people moving, no other vehicles; and a good half hour since he'd passed as much as a village. He was beginning to appreciate, if he hadn't known before, the sheer size of the Realm.

He narrowed his eyes. Ahead, far off, was the bright string of a Cody. That was also the first Rig he'd seen since Garnord. In the town the Kites, even the great string on the Tower that was their pride and joy, had all been trailing; at negative angle in the nearly windless air. He saw the new train was no exception.

He changed gear, more to relieve boredom than for any real reason. He allowed the Buckley to build up speed a little. The clanking from the rear warned him at once; he returned to his former sedate pace.

He thought about the Master Bone. How he'd have laughed at Rand's new-found excess of caution. He supposed he'd been a bit headstrong then, when he first started working for him; though he'd known plenty worse. The job still supported him most of the way through College, supplemented the pittance that was all the Church allowed. Evenings and week-ends, in the little tin-roofed shed at the back of the manse, the shed that reeked of oil and gasoline and hand cleaner, that was baking hot in summer, burning cold in the long North-west winters. He supposed the old man had taught him a lot, one way and another. He remembered one occasion vividly. Wrestling overhead in the half-dark trying to dismantle the spring assembly of an ancient, rusty Swallow; sweat running into his eyes, the wrench slipping, grease stinging the cuts on his knuckles. He'd lost his temper finally, beat at the thing; and instantly a hand was on his shoulder. He turned, and caught the old mechanic's eyes. The Master gestured curtly; Rand thought for the first time since he'd known him he looked angry. He wriggled aside; the other stared again, and took the adjustable. He showed him, silently, how the thing should be done. The nut turned sweetly; the Master handed the spanner back, and walked away. The silent rebuke had more effect than a volume of abuse.

Later, in the little pub they sometimes used after work, the Master condescended to discuss the matter. "A vehicle, any vehicle, is a machine," he said. "A machine assembled by men. What has been assembled can be disassembled." He puffed at his old, stubby pipe. "Never let me see you lose your temper again," he said. "If you do, you know where the yard gate is. Walk through it, and don't come back. . . ." He smiled, glanced across with his vivid blue eyes. "Tip up, young Rand," he said. "Your turn for a round. . . ." He bought the drinks, thoughtfully. He was wondering, not for the first time, if the Master was of the Middle Doctrine too.

He supposed he'd learned more than engineering. He'd thought about it sometimes, when the hot nights made him restless. A human being, he decided finally, was a machine assembled by God. Any human being. So they too were to be gentled, understood; not abused, coerced by bad Mechanics. He'd thought his feet were on the Way; though finally he'd been disabused of that as well. Once more, he'd failed.

The land was flatter now, the vistas wider. Also the road was trending upward steadily. Which meant he was closing with the place he privately dreaded. He'd been cocky enough, making his farewells to the few chums he'd made during his twelve month stint in Streanling Supply. But over the horizon, not too far off now, lay Middlemarch, greatest city of the Realm. His first and sternest test of driving skill. Roads existed to the south and north, the maps he carried showed them well enough; but he'd elected, again for obscure reasons, to route himself through the city. He wondered what Father Alkin would have thought. Applauded his courage, determination? Or merely raised his eyebrows, shaken his head a little?

Father Alkin. He'd gone to him the night of the great shock. When he'd finally realized what Shand had done. How long ago had that been? He winded as he remembered. Nine years. Long years, and for the most part full of pain. And Father Alkin had smiled, and made no comment. He'd given him a glass of wine—it had made his head spin a little, you're not used to such things at sixteen—and sat and talked. About animals and people, the Northwest and the Kites and cars; he'd known already they were a passion with Rand. He'd been appalled; he'd thought the old man didn't know what drove him, what he had come to say. He nearly interrupted, blurted out the angry words; then he saw the priest's eyes. What Father Alkin was doing he couldn't understand; not at the time at least. But he'd held his peace; and when he finally rose to leave the other smiled again. "Life is long, Rand," he said gently. "It consists of many lessons; one follows hard upon the next. As for you, so for us all. You are still learning; so am I. Never will the whole truth become clear. Knowledge is for the One we worship; He of the Kites. So make no judgements; hold yourself in peace. Judging, we betray ourselves; against the day the Lord will judge us too."

Walking home he'd felt uplifted, almost cheerful. He'd thought again it was the beginning of maturity; but the road, like all roads, was long and hard. What he'd felt was not forgiveness, but the rising of contempt.

He'd gone to the old man's cottage many times after that; the cottage that winter and summer he managed to surround with colour. Flowers, or bright-leaved shrubs. But that of course was part of Alkin's special magic. He loved Life and the folk who lived it; fervently, and with candour. Always there would be Middle Lands wine for him; and the Maycakes the Father embellished, even on Holy Days, with helpings of cream and fragrant homemade jam. Cherry, and wild strawberry. He'd questioned him once on that, greatly daring; but the priest had merely shrugged. "God made them," he said gently. "As He made the flowers of the field. Who are we to refuse His gifts? It would be ingratitude. . . ." He'd realized then the old man took the sternest view of all; he saw things for what they were. Sweetmeats were for the eating, wine was to be drunk. A spring shackle wasn't to be shed blood on, to be cursed and hammered; it was an assembly, to be dismantled.

He shook his head. He'd wondered, often enough, what Rone had thought; but his stepfather, wisely perhaps, had remained silent. The peace wrought by the Father was real enough; but it was tenuous. A volcano still seethed, waiting to erupt; the Variant disciplines they had all professed sat ill now on the house.

A Kitestation was on his right. One of the first big Stations of the Middleguard. He'd seen it coming up ahead for a mile or more; long shapes of the hangars, the stubby control tower, cluster of low huts that he knew would be the barracks, workshops, refectories. He stared as he passed, through gaps in the boundary hedge. He saw a Cody string had grounded. The basket was tethered safely enough atop the Launcher; beside the big maroon truck a group of men stood disgustedly. The Observer was among them; goggles pushed up to his forehead, hands on hips. Others were running, across the open ground in front; he saw two Cadets heft a massive Lifter, stagger back towards the sheds with it. He shook his head. There'd be bills to the Church for sure; for flattened crops, damage to boundary hedges. He should know; he'd served his time in Accounts. There'd be a reprimand for the Captain too; loss of pay increments, perhaps the pegging of his career. God's vagaries were one thing; but the Vars had never acknowledged human error.

All the same, there was something disquieting in the sight. Shocking almost. He'd never thought himself particularly devout; but an image had come to him, unbidden. All across the Realm, on this stifling, airless day, the Codys would be grounded; lying like bright confetti across the pastures, hills. So the sky, the empty, burning vault, was open to anything that might choose to come. He shivered, despite the heat. He'd wondered, as a tiny child, just what a Demon looked like. The answer had come in the form of a recurring dream. It was always tiny at first; he'd see it winging from the distance, an inkblot against just such an infinity of blue. It would land and fold its wings, spread its long talons on the grass; and somehow in the dream he always found his voice. He'd speak to it, ask its name and what it wanted; and it would turn. Then the screaming would start. Because it had no form; it was a black shape merely, a hole in reality through which one might see the ultimate Void. It had no eyes; but he always knew it stared.

He shuddered again, briskly. He was giving himself the horrors; as if there hadn't already been horrors enough. He wiped the wheelrim with the cloth he carried in the dash. He topped the rise; and Middlemarch was spread before him, detailed in the brilliant light, seeming to stretch for ever. He swallowed, made a conscious effort to clear his mind.

An hour later, he was feeling slightly better. The traffic of course had been heavy, even at that still-early time. Coaches and lorries, the private cars of the wealthy—more than once he saw, flying from a high mudguard, the scarlet and gold pennant of a Master—even the odd jalopy like his own. Plus horses and carts of course, dashing two-wheelers drawn by high-stepping greys, the closed carriages of ladies, lumbering waggons piled with the rich produce of the Middle Lands. At each junction stood a Var policeman, resplendent in white and gold. Pistols were strapped to their hips; they blew whistles from their little railed podiums, waved and gestured imperiously, made half-comprehensible signs. He observed them carefully, trying to give no offence; he'd heard a little about their methods from the Middlemarchers at College. A couple of bad moments, when he felt himself hopelessly lost; but in the main the road ran straight and true. He oriented himself on the great bulk of Godpath, daunting with its immensity, saw beside it the square white barn of the Middlemen. Leastways that was what his Variant colleagues always dubbed them. It nestled close, almost companionably, by the side of its vast companion; arrogance, it seemed, was answered by quiet assurance. He'd liked to have stopped and entered; but there was no chance, no chance at all. He drove on instead, following a battered grey coach routed for the Salient; lads waved through the high rear window, one brandishing a bottle. Corps Apprentices no doubt, fresh from a Central College course. They at least didn't seem concerned at the grounding of the Codys. Or maybe they hadn't noticed.

Another swirling confusion of traffic; and it seemed the worst was finally behind him. He drove along a wide boulevard, straight and tree-lined. To his left he saw the Palaces of the Masters. Each massive building stood in its own grounds; and beside each rose a high, latticed Tower. But no Codys flew.

He nodded. The Strings would have been drawn. Disaster to let a Pilot touch the grass; but far worse, loss of face. The population, even in Middlemarch, were by no means universally convinced of the efficacy of Faith. Less so than ever, as the years went on. The Kiteman of each household would have been up since before dawn; if he'd gone to bed at all. He'd heard that *in extremis* some of them would even wet the Lifter sails, to catch what fragment of breeze remained; but tricks like that wouldn't avail today. Windspeed was zero.

Climbing the great hill to the east of the city he fancied the air lightened fractionally. But the engine still began to overheat. The Buckley carried no temperature gauge of course;

but some sixth sense still warned him. A change of note perhaps, harder rattle of the splash-fed bearings. He pulled in and switched off. The engine clanked awhile before condescending to stop. He set his lips, prepared himself for a long wait. He wiped his face, sat in the shade of the van and stared back at the city.

An hour later he saw how lucky he'd been. The rubber filler cap had jolted from the tube atop the block, lodged by some miracle in the inlet manifold. He frowned, and checked the sump. The dipstick barely touched oil. He got a gallon from the back, poured in three pints. He checked the water; but curiously that seemed fine. He swung the crank by hand. It turned freely enough. He got in, pulled the starter. The engine caught first time.

Over the hill, the treelined vistas returned. Here though the land was more populous. He passed cart after cart, each drawn by a burly shire. Some of the drivers sat stolidly, staring ahead; but mostly they waved. He acknowledged them curtly, checked the chronometer again. Not midday yet; and the trip already nearly half done. He wished now for one of the devices the Variants used, the little machines the commoners thought devil-possessed but that he knew were wireless telegraphs. Then he could call Streanling, speak to his home. Tell them he was on course, that the Buck was running sweet, that Middlemarch was behind him.

His face clouded at once. Tell them? Tell whom? Rone, and Shand? What would they say, would they truly care? Yes, he decided sourly. They'd care, and they'd rejoice. Because of the miles between. Now, perhaps, they were safe.

Stupid too to feel a yearning for the place. After all, it wasn't his home. Not any more. It hadn't been for years. In a way he'd known that all along. He'd been a supernumerary, surplus to requirements. An embarrassment perhaps. He frowned again. It was still the house he'd been brought up in. Most of his life at least. He'd known every brick of it, every bough of the orchard trees. In part, it had seemed to belong to him. Stupid of course, nothing belonged to him. But maybe the notion was unavoidable.

He pulled in to consult the map. Realized he was a bare ten miles from Crossways. He decided he'd earned a break. So had the Buckley of course. He drove on, keeping an eye open for a likely-looking inn.

He saw one almost at once; a pleasant, white-walled building, low and thatched, set back a little from the main road. Obviously it served some local village; he could see a scatter of house roofs, lost among further trees. He pulled in, tyres scrunching on gravel, turned the key. This time the engine stopped without complaint.

Rand stretched, took his glasses off and rubbed his face. Normally he didn't wear the spectacles except for office work; some lingering trace of vanity perhaps. But on a drive like this it was better to be safe than sorry. He closed the van and locked her, walked towards the pub. He saw by its sign it was the "Kiteman." Must be a base nearby. He couldn't remember offhand; and the Civil maps were locked in his case. He ducked through the doorway, turned left into a wide, stoneflagged bar. The place was refreshingly cool; but the thick stone walls saw to that.

There was just one other customer. Launchmaster by his shoulder tags, in off-duty drab. He nodded pleasantly, gestured for Rand to join him. He bought a beer, sat down. The other produced a much-battered pipe, glanced at him keenly. He said, "Kites?"

He was vaguely surprised. He said, "To do with," and the other chuckled. He nodded to the window, answered Rand's unspoken question. "Saw you pull up," he said. "Not a farmer's truck; and the local yokels don't get round to gasoline." He puffed the pipe alight. "What are you, Civil?"

Rand nodded. "Audit," he said. "Easthold, part of the Salient."

The Launchman laughed again. He said, "They'll love you like a brother. This your first tour?"

He shook his head. "No," he said. "I did a year in Streanling."

"Dead and alive hole," said the Corps man. "Did a stint there myself. Glad when they shipped me out."

He was irritated for a moment. Then he realized how absurd that was. After all he'd knocked the Garnorders enough. He said, "You zeroed as well?"

The other nodded. He said, "With a vengeance. I got out. Before some smartarse found me a spit and polish job. Come far?"

"Yes," he said. "Streanling."

The older man glanced up again. But if he realized he'd

made a gaffe he wasn't concerned. His eyes twinkled slightly. He said, "What's it like farther over?"

"Flat," he said. "Everything down." He described the grounded String he'd seen, and the Launchmaster grinned. "That'll be West Four," he said. "Always did fancy themselves. They'll have their heads on spikes."

"You have any trouble?"

He lit the pipe again, and shook his head. "No way," he said. "We downed at zero two thirty. Skipper's like that. Doesn't take that sort of risk. He'll down for anything. Force Six and he starts getting the trots."

"Your place close?"

The other jerked his thumb. "Just through the woods. Five Stringer. Supply depot too. You'd have fun with us."

He said, "Lucky it's not my patch then."

Some other personnel came in. The Launchmaster excused himself, ambled over to join them. Rand was vaguely glad. Something about the clipped slang of the Corps always got to him. Took him back. Too far, sometimes. His father had been a Flier. One of the best in Northguard. Till a wild night of storm, nearly twenty years ago. He'd seen the squalls come lashing across the sea and shuddered, though he was still a tiny boy. He found out later his father had seen them too, and known instinctively the Cody wouldn't live. He'd given Ground a red; they'd downrigged, but they hadn't been fast enough. He'd been a year in hospital, half his bones shattered, some beyond repair; and never walked again, except with massive sticks. They pensioned him well enough; it kept his children clothed and fed, but for him life had lost meaning. He hung on till Rand was ten, his sister twelve. He'd taken to his bed then; worn out, Rand realized now. By grief, frustration, by the endless pain. Something in the boy had known he wouldn't last long; but he'd suppressed the thought. Until the night his father called him to his room. He lay propped up by pillows; cordial beside him on the table, his pipe and baccy case, a box of lucifers. He wasn't smoking though; he stayed quiet for a while, gazing through the window, blueing now with dusk. Far off a Cody flew, tiny with distance, graceful against the deepening sky. He talked then, inconsequentially it seemed; about his own young life, the many postings he'd had, the close calls he'd survived. Finally he gripped the boy's wrist. "Rand," he said, "I'm going to ask you something." He frowned, seeming to search for words. "The Codys cost me your mother," he said. "Soon after Shand was born. She couldn't stand the strain. Not any more. She gave me a clear choice; so I've got no complaint. And then they gave me this." He glanced down at the bedclothes. "I was a good Flier," he said. "One of the best. But they still gave me this. You see, it isn't a case of whether it's going to happen. It's a case of when." He looked back to the boy's face. "Don't do it, Rand," he said. "Don't be a Flier. Your life's worth more to you. And me."

For a moment the room seemed to spin. He hadn't realized his father understood his secret dream; because in all the years since the accident he'd never spoken of it. He swallowed; when he could speak again he said, "I promise. I'll get the Book."

The other shook his head. "No," he said, "I don't need any Book. Your word's good enough." He lay back tiredly, and closed his eyes.

Rand made a private pact with God, later that night; but God, it seemed, had not seen fit to listen.

So Rone had come quietly to the grieving house; Rone silver-haired and dignified, even then. But he'd been silver-haired from youth. He spoke quietly, to the aunt who was the only relative, the priest, the Corps Chaplain who had organized the service. He'd borne the children away with him, to the sprawling house on the hill; Rand and the dark, hollow-eyed girl. And there they lived till the boy became a man, and Shand a graceful woman.

The house looked down on the town. Behind it, over the orchard and the garden wall, the Codys streamed; the wind sang in their Traces. He'd watch them by the hour, in between schoolwork, the chores Rone found for him. Rone, who had become his legal guardian. Sometimes he thought he'd learned to hate the Strings; but the emotion didn't last. Only the promise held. Break it, and his father would be truly dead. He pondered, sitting alone in his room; and finally his decision was made. He knew he couldn't keep away from the Codys, not for ever; so if he couldn't be their master, he would be their servant. He broached the matter, at dinner that same evening; but Rone as ever was brusque. "Do what you choose," he said. "It's your life; only you can lead it." He wiped his mouth with a napkin, readdressed himself to his wine.

He frowned. Shand was the one of course, the apple of the old man's eye. Shand with her whisperings, her snufflings, her instant stamping tempers. He'd have slapped her; in fact he often did. She'd scurry to Rone for comfort then and he'd take her on his knee; sit and let her cry against his shoulder, soothe her, stroke her hair.

He rose, abruptly. He'd been meaning to eat; but now he couldn't face it. He strode out to the Buckley, started up and drove away.

They made Rone a Freeman, for his services to the State. He became more dignified than ever. The official scroll hung framed above the dining table; the chain and medallion he wore whenever possible. Rand frowned again. Was it petulant of him, to doubt the other's virtue? Behind Skyway loomed a high, dour building, the Northwest Hospital. Though hospital, he felt, was a misnomer. There they sent the castoffs of society; Corps men who had been broken by the Kites, the other unfortunates whom the good Lord had seen fit to bereave of wit. Rone had worked there all his life, risen from the humblest of positions to be Chief Administrator, finally Head Warden. It was his domain; there, his word was law. For the happiness of others he had given up his own; refused marriage offers, the chance of a family. His devotion was patent; and in his field he was the acknowledged master. He travelled extensively when his other duties allowed, to the Middle Lands, the Southguard; lectured in church after church, to congregations that hung on every word. Always he would tell them what they needed to hear; that the power of God was infinite, the Variant Church His one true mouthpiece; that the Law was paramount, because it meant normality. The preservation of the order of things. And after all, who was better equipped than he to preach the *status quo*? He'd seen the reverse of the Lord's coin, the horrendous results of tolerance.

Rand frowned. He'd visited the hospital just once. He'd seen the shambling oldsters, blank-eyed children, the girls with filthy, matted hair. He'd heard the howls that came from barred rooms. He saw that on their uniforms the inmates wore at front and back a florid, circled initial. "I" for Innocent.

He tackled his guardian about it the same evening. "Father," he said—he'd called him that for years, perforce, though it still irked him—"what's normality?"

The other looked surprised. He gestured with his pipestem, waved a hand at the quietly elegant surroundings. "This is," he said. "Books to read, and flowers on the table. Wine in the cellar, good silver. Sometimes I don't understand you, Rand."

He considered. He said, "But all folk don't have things like this. Some of them are poor."

"Of course," said Rone comfortably. "So what they have is normal for them."

He pursed his lips. "Then normalities are different," he said. "Perhaps there's a different one for everybody."

The other narrowed his eyes, looked suddenly cautious. "Normality is normality," he said. "That's plain and obvious."

"But you've just said it varies."

Rone glared at him. "I gave my life to that place. My life and more. Don't presume to question me, young man. . . ."

He shouted back. "Then what are they doing there? Who decides they have to be locked up?"

The other shook his head. "It had to come," he said wearily. "I suppose it was inevitable." He slung his napkin away. "Have you ever gone hungry?" he said. "Have you ever been ill-clothed? Have the Realm, the ideals it stands for, not supported you? Have I failed so badly? Answer me, my son."

He looked up, under his brows. He said, "I am not your son."

Rone Dalgeth sighed. "That too I should have expected," he said. "The ingratitude of the young. Perhaps it was no more than my due."

He said, "You pompous charlatan."

The other nodded. "I know you aspire to the Middle Faith," he said. "And so I try to understand it. Difficult though it might be. It preaches logic. Or pretends to. So we should burn this house. What would that achieve? How would it help those wretches down in Skyway?"

It was no use though. The volcano was bubbling, forcing at its cone. He said, "Tell me, why do they cry?"

"Why do who cry?"

"The inmates. The ones you lock in cells."

His guardian shook his head. He said, "They are not cells."

"They looked like it to me."

"They are placed there for their own protection," said the Warden. He sighed. "Very well. They see them as a prison."

"Why are they put into prison? Because they cry?"

The other said, "I am becoming tired of this conversation."

Rand ignored him. He rubbed the dark wood of the dining table, almost wonderingly. "I think," he said, "this should be made of bones. The bones of other people."

Rone Dalgeth rose, stood leaning on his knuckles. He said, "Go to your room."

He'd risen in his turn. His face was white; but a red anger-spot glowed on either cheek. "So you're the arbiter," he said. "You choose normality for all the rest. That rather lets you off the hook, doesn't it?" He smiled. "She's my sister," he said gently. "Tell me, does she call you Father too?"

The old man's hand flashed out. The blow was heavy; but he made no attempt to avoid it. He felt a trickle of blood start, run to his chin. He bowed his head. "I could kill you of course," he said. "But I won't. I want my hands to stay clean."

Rone was breathing heavily. "You will leave this house," he said. "As soon as possible tomorrow. You will beg my forgiveness before you ever return."

He shook his head. "Not tomorrow," he said. "I'll go tonight." He turned and walked from the room.

He was startled, momentarily. Ahead was a great intersection. More vehicles moving on it, more of the lumbering carts. Crossways; he hadn't realized his attention had wandered so far. He'd driven the last few miles automatically.

He slowed behind the little line of waiting traffic. A heavy private car, probably a farmer's, two smartly turned out traps; one of the big, gaunt tractors he'd heard were coming into use. He edged forward, slowed again. Finally his turn came. He glanced to either side. The other road ran southwest to northeast; Southguard to the Salient. His route lay straight across; later it would curve down, into the Easthold. He waited for a farm cart, another private carriage, eased the Buckley carefully across. He built up speed again.

He'd stayed that night with friends. He lay a long time

sleepless, trying to make the anger drain away. He remembered that first dread revelation. He'd been sleepless then as well; turning and tossing, sheets sticky with the summer heat. At zero four hundred he'd given up the attempt. He rose and dressed, padded to the kitchen for a drink of water. On his way back up the stairs he froze. He'd heard, quite clearly, the click of a bedroom door. His guardian's. It was followed by the creak of a floorboard. He'd heard such things before, in waking dreams; but his mind, half-dazed, had refused to understand.

He stood in shadow, in an angle of the stair. He saw her clearly though. Her flimsy night-things shimmered in dawn dusk; through them her body gleamed pale. He took her wrist, heard the quick intake of breath. Her eyes blazed with fear, became opaque again. She said, "Let go my arm."

For a moment he couldn't speak. Finally he whispered, "Why? Why, Shand, why. . . ."

She snatched free quickly, drew the little shawl she wore closer about her shoulders. "My life is my own," she said. "I do with it as I choose. Find your own solace, brother." She raised her chin, stared at him a final time; moved away, and was gone.

He couldn't remember how he got through the next few days. Or weeks. He visited the Father, ate May cakes and drank his wine. Walked aimlessly through Streanling, out to the Northern Road, sat for hours at a time and stared at distant hills. It seemed his world was shattered. That she, that she . . . His mind balked, circling, refused even to finish the thought. He'd felt his life foursquare; rooted to rock, well-bastioned and safe. Now a cornerstone had suddenly been wrenched away. Sometimes the rage came; rage such as he wouldn't have believed. Because each night he lay on her and grunted. *Her* . . . He realized, belatedly, he'd loved her. As had her own father. The thought brought floods of hot and bitter tears. He'd wipe his eyes, stare up; and the Cody rigs were flying all around. Keeping the Realm from harm.

The Codys haunted him; by day, and in his dreams. Sometimes they bore symbols he couldn't understand; sometimes the Godkites had faces of people on them. Some were folk he thought he knew; but they changed and melted even as he stared. Others were people he'd never seen before; so maybe the future had its ghosts as well.

He was saved, finally, by something Father Alkin said. "Actions are actions, Rand. Each has its purpose, each its allotted place. Though purposes are things we cannot grasp. But if you are dressing, you are dressing. If you are brushing your shoes, you are brushing your shoes. Perform each as is proper; and do not search for meanings. In that way, meanings will one day become plain. . . ." So he began; and in time he found the doctrine easier. Breakfasts were breakfasts, school was school; the night time was for sleeping. He discovered courtesy, as a secondary effect; he was grave and quiet, till even Shand began to look at him with puzzled eyes. He affected not to notice, finally took pride. Though pride had its own dangers, as he realized later.

The land was changing, with surprising speed. The hills had gone; round him flat country stretched to the horizon. The villages were more numerous; he passed through half a dozen in as many miles, each visible from the next. In the last he found a little gasoline station. He filled up, pulled two wheels of the Buckley on to the kerb to ease the flow to the tank. The attendant seemed amused at the manoeuvre.

More of the flat emptiness, through which the road ran for the most part arrow-straight. Finally he came to a great arch of rusted iron. It spanned the carriageway; in its centre it bore a medallion, once gilded. He couldn't make out the device. Below though were the ragged letters EASTHOLD. He pulled in for a while, sat staring. For some reason he found it an oddly touching sight.

He started up again, drove through. It seemed with the simple act he put his life behind him, began afresh.

Today, the day of the grounded Kites, seemed a time for introspection. He found himself remembering the pumpmaid, with curious vividness. Her slimness, lovely legs in their blue cloth, the sunlight sparking from her hair. He wondered what she was doing, at this exact time. What everyone was doing, all the folk he'd ever known. And what about the others, the ones he would one day meet? The notion of future ghosts returned to him. After all, if the past had its shades it stood to reason the future must own them too. He felt a curious thrill, almost of anticipation.

He'd moved into College accommodation, the first available

chance. The Church cavilled, cautious as ever of its funds. Eventually, Middlemarch grudgingly agreed. He expected letters had been exchanged with Rone Dalgeth. He wondered what had been said.

His studies came hard at first. He attended to them assiduously; Father Alkin's advice was once more a blessing. The opening of a folder, the closing of a textbook, became small Actions in themselves. He thought his tutors looked on him with favour; though at least once the Master Sprinling frowned. He wondered if the Middle Teaching was discernible from acts as well.

In time the work began to pall. He realized just what he was committed to; the endless totting of figures, counting of parts, spares, supplies. Cable drums and spliceblocks, Lifter stays and cones, crossheads and valve assemblies, grommets, bolts and screws. Cane for the baskets; though "cane" was a word he hadn't come across. The substance was manufactured by extrusion in the industrial suburb of Middlemarch; in fact there was a move afoot to call it Holand fibre.

He struggled nonetheless, toiling at his books, huddled in blankets sometimes when his stipend wouldn't run to coal. He scraped his grades the first two years, groaned at the thought of the rest. He would have given up at any time; but he'd burned his boats. Or had them burned for him. He set his lip. He would succeed because he had to. And then get out of Northguard. For good.

Janni Nesson changed his life. In more ways than one. Though at first she was a greater distraction than the rest. He'd known girls enough of course. He cultivated them, when he got the chance; and found that skill became easier too. In fact Brad Hoyland, one of the few chums he'd made, commented on it one night. They were sitting in a bar—one of his rare binges, his grant had just come through—and the other shook his head. "Wish I knew how you did it," he said dolefully. "Round you like flies, they are; and you don't even put any effort into it."

He was genuinely puzzled. "I just talk to them," he said. "I don't know anything about the rest."

"That's just the point," said the other. "I try that, they want to see my grant statements. . . ."

Janni was different though. To start with she'd applied for, and won, college entrance. An almost unheard-of thing for the Vars; the Church had fixed views about the role of women. It didn't seem to trouble her though. She buckled down, worked hard; by the end of that first term she was heading her section. He'd noticed her of course, in refectory and elsewhere; you couldn't really miss her. The mane of dark hair, the broad-cheekboned face, the candid violet eyes. She wasn't particularly tall; but then she didn't need to be. The students danced attendance to a man; but she didn't seem impressed. She'd treat each one the same, gravely and politely. She'd come to study Civil Administration; and that was what she was going to do. There were rumours naturally, whisperings; stirrings of jealousy, even the odd dormitory fight. He was glad, not for the first time, he wasn't living in. He'd seen the results of that sort of thing before. An iron wall existed, in his mind.

One day she sat opposite him at table. The long Refectory was more than usually full. It was about the last vacant place. She said, "Mind?" and he shook his head. He said, "Of course not." He passed the condiments.

She talked as she ate. As if she'd known him for years. Who had done what in class, who had said that or this. Student chatter, inconsequential enough; but he still found himself intrigued. Her voice was low, with a trace of huskiness; but beautifully modulated. She'd had a good education; but that was a matter of common knowledge. Her folk were well-to-do, farmers in the Middle Lands who ran a livery stable on the side. He found himself watching her hands. They were sinewy, slim-fingered but broad across the knuckles; more like the hands of a boy. There was a preciseness too, an economy of movement. He wondered if it came from the years of training.

It seemed she divined his thoughts. She said, "Do you ride?"

He shook his head. "The original ignoramus," he said. "Don't know one end of a horse from the other."

Janni grinned. "That's easy," she said. "One end kicks." She pulled her sleeve up, showed him a big scar on her arm. Curving, and deep. He said, "Good Lord. You mean it didn't put you off?"

She shrugged. She said, "These things happen." She glanced up again. She said, "You're Rone Dalgeth's son, aren't you?"

Rand looked at his plate. "No," he said. "I'm not."

She waved a hand. "Oh, I know about that," she said. She considered. "My father knew yours," she said. "There was a big Station near us. On our land in fact. Shame when they pulled out. Nice little source of income."

He steered the conversation on to safer ground. She chuckled at his tales, once wrinkled her nose at a mention of Master Sprinling. He found the gesture enchanting. Finally she pushed her plate away. He said, "Like a sweet?" but she shook her head. "Sorry," she said, "got to dash." She grinned. "In any case, they reckon I'm sweet enough already. See you around."

On the way out another student nudged him in the ribs. "Hands off, Rand," he said. "She's spoken for."

"Who by?" he said. "You?" He put his hands in his pockets, and sauntered away.

He thought about her a lot after that. Behind the banter there was high intelligence; of that he had no doubt. But in any case it wasn't in dispute. Something extraordinary must have induced the Vars to admit a girl student; social influence existed of course, but there were limits to what it could achieve. Also there was something he hadn't met before; an openness, a candour he found intriguing. She could have pulled rank on him, boasted about her family, their holdings; any other Midlander would. But she'd done no such thing.

He grimaced, faintly. She was also very lovely. He grudged the thought at first, later admitted it more freely. He wondered what Father Alkin would have said. He remembered the jam and cream on Holy Days, and had little doubt.

The engine of the Buckley died. He swore, and steered on to the rough. Though he needn't have bothered; the long straight road ahead was empty. He opened the bonnet, tapped the little fuel pump with the handle of the jack. Nothing. He frowned. Then reached into the cab, turned the ignition switch he'd cancelled. The pump began to tick at once. He drove on again.

Mid-afternoon; and the heat at its most intense. Mirages floated over the road ahead. Each silver lake dissipated as he approached. The blue sky was still unmarked. No Cody strings; but of course there were no Stations here. The Easthold was much like the Salient. There, they fringed the Badlands;

here, they ringed the coast. The inland folk weren't rich enough to matter.

He passed through another village. Bigger this time, but curiously deserted. Maybe they were all sleeping through the heat. A tractor stood outside a filling station. So there was at least one wealthy farmer round about. Hard to credit, seeing the barren fields. Even the livestock seemed scarce.

Gaven was the first town of any note. Then Killbeggar, and Fishgard. His destination. Though there was little enough fishing these days. In this Sector at least. Sometimes the sea was bad. "Urination of Demons," the Master Sprinling had said; and he'd frowned. The image wouldn't form; it didn't sort with his view of physics. He shrugged. The Master was the College's top theologian; so he ought to know. It hadn't troubled him overmuch. He'd been deep into duplex book-keeping at the time.

In Gaven he noticed something he'd seen before. To the right of the High Street rose the thin spire of a Variant church; facing it, opposing almost, was the square barn of the Middlemen. The juxtaposition recurred on the eastern edge of the town; and again in the hamlet beyond. It was visual proof of what he had felt before; in the Salient, the Easthold, the power of the Vars was challenged. Gently, peacefully; but challenged nonetheless. He frowned. The Demons, in their squabblings with God, once ruined all the world. Would the last Men one day finish their task for them?

Beyond Killbeggar the road surface deteriorated sharply. The Buckley slewed and bounced, wheels dropping into pot-holes. He was vaguely surprised. After all, Fishgard was the capital of Easthold. But then, Streanling had never found a use for paving either.

His thirst was rising, his mind running on thoughts of a glass of ale. An inn showed to the right; before it was a parking area lined by stunted, dusty bushes. He almost pulled across; but the place had a shabby, ramshackle look. And even if he could rouse them, they'd be grumpy; they'd certainly be having their siesta. He drove on.

She did see him around. Quite a lot in fact. He resisted for a while the notion that she was seeking him out; finally it became patent. It didn't improve his stock with his fellow students; once he thought he was in for a major fight. She laughed when he mentioned it to her. "Oh, Giggleguts," she said—she meant an urbane youth called Giller. "He thinks whenever he whistles, the girls should come running. It doesn't work with me though."

He frowned. Somehow it seemed she'd become a special person to him. "I don't whistle," he said.

She looked at him. "I know," she said. "That's why I'm here." Unexpectedly, she tucked her arm through his. "Come on," she said. "Let's go and have a drink."

She had strange views about the role of women. Heretical at first, to his mind. He pondered them. If a woman did a man's job, she should get a man's pay. He supposed that was morally right. Indeed, it couldn't be gainsaid. But women *didn't* do men's jobs. Janni did though. Or would one day.

Her views on marriage were even more bizarre. Women should have the right to choose their partners, the same as men. After all, marriage was a business like any other; it should be run on business lines.

"Fair enough," he said. "But every firm still has to have a boss."

She punched him. "Yes," she said. "And that's you, isn't it?" She was only being playful; but he still rubbed his arm. He hadn't realized just how strong she was. He reflected ruefully that he wouldn't want her to hit at him in anger. There was more in this equality of the sexes than he'd realized.

The evenings with her ate into his slender reserve. Her notions of equality, it seemed, didn't extend to the sharing of bills. Not at first anyway. He examined his finances carefully, considered. He went to see the Master Bone. Things were a little easier after, though keeping abreast of his College work meant studying far into the night; till zero four hundred sometimes. He'd stagger to bed dog-tired, catch a bare three hours sleep; because First Session started at zero eight.

Surprisingly, the College work didn't suffer. In fact his grades steadily improved. He topped his set in his third year, again in the early fourth. It seemed she'd become a source of inspiration to him. Certainly a source of energy. She drained it from him; but always it was mysteriously replaced. The emptiness he'd felt before had gone. Life had a purpose again; though what that purpose was he didn't for a time admit.

Vacations were more difficult. He'd see her to the coach, watch it set out on the long drive to her home; and subtly the world would change. He'd wander aimlessly, on those days when Master Bone had no need of him, scuffing at pebbles, staring up at the high, bright shapes of the Codys. The old fantasies returned. He decided he'd like to fly one, higher and higher, till he could see the Middle Lands themselves. He was sure the place she lived in would have a glow to it. An aura. He decided he was in love. He'd wonder what she was doing, every minute of the day; riding perhaps, or mucking out the stables, cleaning tack. Or out with friends; she had a lot of friends, she'd chattered about them often enough. Perhaps of course there was a special friend. One she hadn't mentioned.

The thought was like a dagger in the heart. He was faintly ashamed of himself; but it was no use trying to deny what had flashed through his mind. Perhaps she was just using him, whiling away the evenings of the long terms; so when she had finished College. . . .

He shook his head. There were plenty of students better off than he; she could have chosen from a hundred. He reminded himself he was a lucky man, told himself not to question the Lord's bounty. After all he had been tested, tested to the hilt; and he had not broken. Could it be she was his reward?

It seemed the question was answered instantly. Almost as if she had known. There was a letter waiting for him when he got home. He recognized the strong, sloping hand; unfeminine, yet so typical of her. He tore the flap, his fingers trembling with excitement.

It's been beautiful here, she'd written. *The weather's perfect, there hasn't been rain for weeks. How has it been with you?*

Centus is coming on wonderfully. I think he's the best horse we've bred. I take him out nearly every day. Daddy says he's going to enter him for the Yearling Stakes in Middlemarch. He's absolutely sure he'll win. Isn't it marvellous?

I think of you a lot, working on those greasy old cars. Do you think of me? I bet you've got a girlfriend I don't know about. Probably loads. I'm sure you could take your pick. . . .

I'm going to the races myself tomorrow, we're all going down. Daddy has got a fortune on a horse called Blue Equality. It's going to be Blue Murder if he loses; but I think he'll still be running when we get back home.

What I want to know is, why can't there be women jockeys? I'd beat any of the boys I know; sidesaddle too. I think I shall have to start a campaign. . . .

'Bye for now, Rand. Write if you get a minute, I'd love to hear from you. If not, I'll see you next term. I'm looking forward to it.

Much love,

Janni

PS. We had a Cody land here yesterday. All the way from Streanling. I looked to see if there was a message from you on it. I could imagine you dashing about with a hacksaw. . . .

He tucked the note under his pillow that night. He got the best sleep he'd had in weeks.

He met the coach when it jolted in, the day before the start of summer term. She ran to him at once, and kissed. Put her arms round his neck. He swung her, laughing, set her back on her feet; to the envy of some, and the fury of quite a few. That didn't matter though; nothing mattered, except that she was back. He walked her to her digs, she chattering all the way; about the races, and the farm, and the new foal. She insisted he come in and wait while she bathed and changed. "I'm all grot," she said. "Dead yucky. Look at this." She pulled her skirt hem up, exposing a vista of bronzed thigh, frowned at the dirt that marked the creases. "Those coaches are filthy," she said. "I'm going to write to College. Suggest they clean them at least once a year. Maybe Foundation Day. Shan't be long." She dashed for the stairs.

In fact she was gone an hour or more. He didn't mind. He sat and sipped at the wine she'd left him and pondered. There was a change in her, something he couldn't place. She had always been vivacious; now she was electric. Poised somehow, like a dancer. As if some inner excitement was about to burst through.

She came back looking radiant in white. Twirled to make the skirt fly out again. He said, "How do you get so brown?"

"There's this barn," she said. "You can get out on the roof. I lie up there all day with nothing on."

He thought his heart was going into spasm.

She grinned at him. "Where shall we go?" she said.

He kissed her. "I don't mind," he said. "As long as it's with you."

She took his hand. "Let's go and have something to eat," she said. "Then I feel like getting drunk. Just to celebrate." She waved a wad of notes. "Don't worry, Daddy put my allowance up. It's all on me. . . ." For once, he didn't argue.

They walked past Master Bone's on the way into town. She glanced through the gates and turned her nose up. "You can chuck that grotty old place soon," she said. "You won't need it any more. Anyway you'll have to when you get your posting."

Again the little pang; and once more it seemed she read his thoughts. "Don't worry," she said. "It's still a term away. And a term's a lifetime. I should know: I have to live through them too."

"Perhaps I might fail the Finals," he said. "Deliberately, just to stay with you."

She looked solemn. She said, "You say the nicest things." She took his arm. "How about the 'Twisted Trace'?" she said. "Then we can go on to the 'Master of Streanling.' The lobster there's divine. . . ."

She did get drunk. Not raucously so, it wouldn't have been her style. But very definitely tipsy. He walked back with her finally, saw her to the door of the little cottage. She kissed, in the shadow of the porch; and he all but gasped. She'd kissed often enough before; but never like that. Mouth opened wide, tongue pushing. He reacted; and his hand, instinctively it seemed, cupped her breast. Began to squeeze and fondle.

She pushed away. "Not here," she said. "Not here. . . ." He thought for a desolate moment she was dismissing him. He stepped back; and she instantly took his wrist. "Don't be a clot," she said. She fiddled in her handbag, still swaying a little, found the key. Climbing the stairs, she took his wrist again. "Careful," she whispered. "That one creaks a bit."

They kissed again, in her room. She touched him between the legs, and chuckled. She said, "You are a naughty boy." She reached behind her. The dress slid down without fuss. She said, "You can take the rest off. Part of your job."

She twitched the covers aside, lay back on the bed. She

sighed; then she sat up again, took something from a little jar. She popped it into herself; the movement of her hand was almost too quick to follow. "Sweetie," she said. "The sort I like the best."

He was fumbling with his shirt. "Janni" he said. Or croaked. "Janni, are you sure? Are you really sure?"

"Why?" she said. "Don't I look as if I am? Come on, slowcoach. . . ."

Ahead, unexpectedly, was a low range of hills. The road angled toward them. He changed down, tackled the first incline. He glanced at his rear view mirror. He'd thought a haze was spreading from the west; now he saw for the first time a blue-grey edge of cloud.

Another bend; he changed gear again, breasted the final slope. Beyond was a straggling village. He saw the style of architecture had changed. The houses were of stone, narrow-windowed and dour. He stared. Jutting from each chimney stack was a narrow ledge. A Demon seat. Night horrors could rest there before flying on. They'd be grateful, and not trouble the folk beneath. He shook his head. He'd heard of such things, but never quite believed them.

He stared again. Ahead was a second range of hills; above them, faint but unmistakable, a pearly glower. The reflection of the sea.

He qualified, passed out in the top ten. His posting came with commendable speed. He read the flimsy twice; the first time he hadn't believed his eyes. His first tour was in Streanling.

He took Janni out, to celebrate. Events tended to repeat themselves. He was more skilled by now of course. He tucked his forearms under the pillow. That way he could kiss her, and not muss her hair. They slept awhile; he woke in the wee small, saw she was awake too. She sighed. She said, "It's such a pity."

"What do you mean?"

"That you have to go. I'd like to wake up in the morning with you. Then we could do it again."

"You," he said, "are without doubt the sexiest girl I know."

She eyed him sleepily. "I was the first, wasn't I?" she said.

"The first what?"

She refused to be drawn. "You can always tell," she said. "Don't go for a minute."

He cuddled her again. Finally he pushed himself away. "Janni," he said, "I *must.*" He swung his legs from the bed, started to dress. "We may have a place of our own," he said. "One day. . . ."

No answer; and he turned. She had drifted back to sleep. He covered her, gently, and tiptoed from the room.

He rented a little flat. It left him short; but the first year with the Corps was traditionally difficult. In time he found he could supplement his income by private jobs; stocktaking for the local shopkeepers and such. The work bored him; but money was money. By careful budgeting he found he could even save a little each week. A few months later he went to see the Master Bone. The Buckley was standing in the corner of the workshop. The other eyed her appraisingly. "Not much to look at I grant," he said. "In need of a little love. But I've checked her through, basically she's sound. She'll do you a turn for a year or two." He twinkled at him. "No racetrack stuff though," he said. "Or you'll soon regret it. She's not a young lady any more."

Rand glanced up sharply. He wondered if the other had heard rumours. But the old engineer's face remained bland.

He started the little van up. She rattled. But she was dirt cheap. He paid the Master on the spot, and drove her home. He stripped her interior, scrubbed through. He paid special attention to the seats; because she would be carrying a queen.

Janni came round in the evening. He stared. She was wearing a pair of the figure-hugging blue trousers favoured by working girls. He kissed her, rubbed her bottom; and she grinned. She said, "You like them?" and he smiled back. He said, "I like what's inside better."

She pushed him away. "Later," she said. "We've got work to do."

They carried on till nightfall. He managed to get the first coat of paint on. He stood back finally, hands on his hips. The Buckley was already starting to look spick and span. He said. "She really is a pretty little motor."

She turned her nose up. She said, "I'm jealous."

"Why?"

"I think you love her more than me."

He said, "We can work that out tonight."

He took her to his local pub. Over glasses of beer he said, "How did you manage to get those things so tight?"

"What things?"

"Those things you're nearly wearing."

She glanced down, smoothed at her thighs. "Sat in the bath," she said. "Then let them dry on me."

He'd never heard anything like it. He said, "That's immoral!"

"Yes," she said. "Nice, isn't it?"

She should have gone down at the end of the summer term. But she was taking a postgrad course, she'd already booked for it. She'd finish up better qualified than him. She sat her Finals, came through with flying colours.

She invited him to the Middle Lands, to her parents' home. "Come the last week of the hols," she said. "Then you can bring me back. Save me going on that ghastly coach."

He havered. Unsure of the reception he would get. After all, they were way out of his class. But the prospect of a whole week with her was irresistible. He said, "I'd love to. . . ."

She'd been pestering him to get in touch with Rone Dalgeth. He'd set his mouth at first, refused to discuss the matter. She didn't know of course what the cause of the quarrel had been; nor would he tell her. But she could be winsome when she chose. "I know it must have been bad," she said, time and again. "But whatever it was, you're big enough to take it. We're a long time dead; and anyway, he could be useful to you one day." She'd dimple at him then. "Won't you?" she'd say. "Not even for me?"

He gave in, finally. He couldn't refuse her; and anyway, guardian or not, they weren't of the same blood. So no crime had been committed. Except perhaps the omission of the banns. Also—and here of course was the nub of the whole thing—he'd got Janni now. The Lord had been good to him; it was time he gave a little on his side.

He hardly expected an answer to his letter. Nonetheless one came, couched in stiffly formal terms. It invited him and his young friend to dinner in two days time.

It was end of term; Janni was a little sloshed from the breaking-up party. He wondered what the old man would make of that. He held the van door for her. She climbed in, albeit unsteadily. But in sight of the house she clapped her hands with delight. "It's beautiful," she said. "It's beautiful. You never said. . . ."

"Yes," he said. "It is rather fine, isn't it?"

He'd asked her once, what he ought to call the Buckley. She'd been ready with an answer. "Janni," she said. "I'm not having any competition."

He stroked the wheel rim. "Janni," he whispered. "Janni. . . ."

Strange to walk into his old home after so long. See the furniture still in the same positions, nothing changed. He paused in the hall, half-involuntarily; and she instantly took his hand. Gave it a little squeeze. His heart leaped, for sheer pleasure of her. She understood.

The dining room looked smaller somehow than memory painted it. Smaller, and darker. But Rone Dalgeth was the same; sitting in the highbacked chair beside the empty fireplace. Shand hovered uncertainly at his elbow. She'd filled out, matured; but she was still a beautiful woman. She came forward, unsure; and he took her hands. He said, "It's good to see you."

She said, "Me too." She pecked him on the cheek. He returned the gesture, carefully. She hugged him then, with something like a sob. She said, "It's been a long time."

"Yes," he said. "It has."

The conversation was stilted to begin with. He spoke carefully, avoiding delicate topics. He talked about the Kites, his career so far, his chances of promotion. Janni kept her side going with skill and tact. He wondered how he'd have fared without her.

At least the meal was excellent. But Shand had always been a superb cook. Janni greeted the main dish with cries of delight. Middle Land venison, marinated to perfection and served with simple vegetables. "It's wonderful," she said. "Nobody—sorry—can grow it like us."

He smiled. In excitement, she often spoke with her mouth too full. In another, it would have been an annoyance; with her, tiny blemishes merely underlined perfection. Like the scar on her arm, the mole an inch below her navel. The thought sent a thrill through him at once.

Rone Dalgeth seemed intrigued by her. He listened attentively to her descriptions of her parents' home. But then, property had always been a major interest. Or why would he have acquired so much, scattered throughout Streanling? And for all Rand knew, the rest of the Northguard.

The meal over, Janni was borne off to see the house. It was obviously prearranged. Silence fell for a moment; then his guardian coughed. He said, "A very lovely girl. You're most fortunate."

He swilled the wine in his glass. "I know what you're waiting for, Father," he said. He hesitated, set his lips. "I apologize for speaking harshly," he said. "No-one should speak harshly, whatever the circumstances. But my opinions are my own. They have not changed."

The other rose, stood staring through the window at the tree-grown grounds, blueing now with dusk. Finally he turned. "That must suffice then," he said. "You're of an age now to make your own judgements. For right or wrong." His manner seemed to soften fractionally. "There's still a room here for you," he said, "If you choose. Pour yourself some more wine."

"Thanks," he said, "It's appreciated. But I think I'll stay where I am for the moment. I shall have a posting coming through in a month or two anyway."

The other nodded curtly. He said again, "As you choose." Later though, when he and Janni were leaving, he shook his hand. "Visit us again," he said. "Don't leave it too long this time. None of us are getting younger you know." He smiled. "And bring your young lady with you. Or this time you won't be forgiven. . . ."

Janni left for home. Walking back to the flat he felt better than he had in years. At last, everything in his world seemed to be coming right. He was overdue for leave. He booked a fortnight of it, got into the Buckley and just drove. He quartered the Northguard, stopping off at inns, wandering the little hill villages as fancy took him. He called at most of the Kitestations he passed, and sent his card in. Each time he took care to write across the bottom ON LEAVE. He was made welcome at them all; he began to wonder if the horror stories he'd heard about audit tours really were just that. He learned a lot about the manning of the Frontier Codys; more, he thought, than he'd learned in all his studying. Field courses had been part of training; he'd done his trips to Garnord and Settering, once Middlemarch itself. It was good to smell the hangar scents again; oil and dope, hot steam. These Stations were different though. Optimum Lifter rigs, terminal speeds for downing, all existed in the standard manuals; here he found in practice they varied widely from Base to Base. In the hills the winds could be cranky; while conditions changed with lightning speed, sometimes it seemed from minute to minute. One and all, the Launchmasters were long-service men; and a good spattering of them local. It was they, and not the Captains, who had the final say; they who really ran the Bases.

The Frontier could cause other problems too. He found out quickly what salt air could do to cable. "Look at this lot," said one dour Riggingmaster. He kicked disgustedly at a corroded pile in the corner of a hangar. "Never tell a Seabase they're carrying too many spares," he said. "You're liable to have a drum wrapped round your ears." Rand nodded thoughtfully. He felt instinctively that was a piece of advice that would prove more than useful.

At A11, set high on the cliffs above a place called Dancing Bay, they even half-jokingly offered him a flight. His heart leaped; for a moment he was minded to accept. Then he smiled, looked out to sea. Purple clouds were lowering and massing; the horizon was a brilliant, glowing band. "No thanks," he said. "I think it's coming on to rain." The Winchman looked down. "If it rains," he said, "I'll lend you my coat."

The Launchmaster, a grizzled man who must be close to retirement, glanced at him keenly. "You're old Del Panington's son, aren't you?" he said.

He nodded, surprised. "How did you know?"

"Oh," said the other, "the word gets around." He shook his head. "I knew him," he said. "One of the best. Launched for him more times than I've had hot breakfasts. It was a downright piece of luck." He glanced up at the pair of Codys already streamed, and pursed his lips. Rand wondered how much of the rest he had guessed.

He watched a Stringchange. The sea breeze was keen and capricious, gusting up over the cliffs. They still handled the great Kites smoothly, it seemed easily. He knew that last was deceptive. The fresh Trace was streamed, the Lifters sailed to their places; "*clear basket*" was ordered, and the winch ratchet began to clank as the Cody rose to operational height.

It was a big Base, the biggest he'd seen so far; they had good mess facilities and a first-rate bar. He made a night of it, got fairly tipsy in the end. They gave him a bunk in one of the ground crew huts. The place resounded with snores; but he was used to that. He slept quickly and well.

Two Cadets were going on furlough. He took them back a few miles towards Streanling, dropped them where they were sure to pick up another lift. Everybody stopped for Kitemen. He turned west again; and there came a day when he stood on the farthest promontory of the Realm. Behind him and to the south the cliffs marched into distance, ragged and grand, the sunlight on their faces; while a mile or two offshore was a low, mounded island. From it, barely visible in the haze, flew a solitary Cody rig, its wings bright against the blue-grey crawl of the sea. The Realm protected itself, at every point.

He turned for home; reached Streanling by early evening, left the Buckley with Master Bone for a check. He was pleased with her; she'd run all the way with scarcely a hiccup. He still wanted her in top condition though, for his trip to the Middle Lands.

He let himself into the flat. On the carpet was a little pile of letters. Four or five of them, all addressed in the same hand. The hand he knew so well. He took them through to the kitchen, put the kettle on. He arranged them in date order, sat and smiled at them. Finally he slit the flap of the first. He more or less knew what he would read. Janni had a way with words that would curl the hair. "Loin language," he'd called it once; and she chuckled. "Women aren't supposed to like that sort of talk," she said. "I do though, I always have. It turns me on." As it was turning him on now. "You naughty girl," he said. "Oh, you naughty little girl . . ." He smoothed the second sheet. The kettle had almost boiled dry before he remembered. He sat down later to answer. His phrasing was more careful. Quite sedate in fact. But they'd developed a private language of their own. She would know what he meant.

The visit to her folk went better than he'd dared to hope. Her mother was a bustling, friendly woman, quite different from what he'd thought, her father amiably vague; though Rand suspected the studied absentmindedness concealed a sharp enough brain. They were both considerably older than he'd realized; but then she had two married brothers, both with families of their own. He guessed she must have been lonely as a child; nobody of her age at all.

They placed him in a big, comfortable room in one of the wings of the house, itself a building of considerable extent though in typical Middle Lands style; stone-faced, the shallow-pitched roof half hidden by a decorative parapet. Driving to it, he'd seen at the south west corner an anchor point for a Cody rig; but nothing was streamed at the moment. He bathed and shaved, looked down later from the tall windows. The paddocks stretched to the horizon. He smiled. He'd decided, to his surprise, he was going to enjoy himself.

His behaviour, of course, had to be equally sedate. Though there were ways and means. On the second day she surreptitiously piled blankets and pillows into the Buckley, directed him to a place she knew on the far edge of the estate; a little wooded knoll, bright now with summer light. He nosed the van into the trees, switched off. He looked round. Not a building, not a farmworker for miles. "Nobody ever comes here," she said. "When I was small I used to call it my castle." She kissed him; then pulled with urgency, at the fastening of her skirt.

For the first time, he loved her half-clothed. He found the experience curiously exciting. When she wanted to go again though he undid her blouse. Wrong to hide her glory, even for a second. Finally she lay back with a sigh. "Nobody does it like you," she said. "It's like fireworks going off, all the time. With a great big cracker at the end." She snuggled against him. "I couldn't have waited any longer," she said. "It was terrible. I nearly got dairy elbow keeping myself going."

She slept. He lay listening for footfalls, the sound of an engine. None came. Finally he felt dozy himself. But that was dangerous. He kissed her awake and she sat up. "I told you they wouldn't," she said vaguely. She started pawing for her clothes. "Look," she said. "Somebody made these knickers back to front."

She showed him the stables, proudly, and the new young racer. Later she tried to get him on a horse; but at that he demurred. He said, "I'll leave it to the experts."

She pushed her hair back, laughing. "Coward," she said. "It's easy."

"It might be for you," he said. "I need an ignition switch. I know what I'm doing then."

He watched her ride. Even to his unpractised eye she seemed superb. There was a grace to her, a fluidness; she and the animal seemed in perfect unison. Also it was unnervingly erotic. He'd never seen a woman ride astride before. But she merely laughed. She said, "One day it will be the normal thing. Just wait and see."

He gave in to her, finally. She chose a big old gelding for him. "He's so docile," she said, "if you let him stand still too long, he goes to sleep."

He stared at the saddle. He said, "What do you call that?"

She said, "Even you know what *that* is." He said, "It's more like an armchair."

He mounted, gingerly. He didn't make too bad a first of it. In fact she said he did it quite well. "Very professional," she said. "You're facing the wrong way of course."

"This," he said firmly, "is the front. It's sharper."

"So it is," she said. "I never noticed." She led the way into the yard.

"One thing," he said. "I'm not going to jump."

She looked over her shoulder scornfully. "It's not a jumping saddle. It would kill him."

"It would kill me."

She said, "It would probably be mutual."

He found the experience more pleasant than he'd thought. In fact towards the end of the morning he was positively enjoying it. She rode to a little pub, a gnomelike building set deep among woodlands. Other horses were tethered to a rail outside. She knew all their owners of course; but they seemed friendly enough as well. "You see," she said later, "we're not all like you think. Us Midlanders."

He said, "You're not like I thought. There isn't another like you in all the Realm. That means the world of course."

She glanced across. She said, "You haven't seen the world." To his surprise, her eyes were bright with tears.

The week ended far too quickly. He drove her back to Streanling. Work came hard; she said it did for her as well. But there were still weekends and evenings. They were better than before. If that was possible.

A message came, from Middlemarch. He opened it with trepidation. He knew well enough what it contained; advance warning of his new posting. Again he had to read the thing twice. The Northguard tour was extended by six months; his new patch would be Garnord. Central was apologetic. A mixup over postings; plus a temporary shortage of trained men. He whooped; and that night they went out on the town.

He was bidden home for the winter celebrations. The invitation included Janni. She accepted with alacrity, and he frowned. He said, "But you'll be with your folks."

"As a matter of fact, I won't," she said. "I'm a big girl now, I can stay away from home if I like." She simpered. "I can stay up after twenty-four hundred too," she said.

He grabbed her. He said, "Not if I have anything to do with it." Later he said, "But what will you do, Jan? You can't stay at the cottage. College digs close down, I always had to move out."

She looked troubled. "Yes," she said, "it *is* a problem. If only I knew someone with a little flat. . . ."

He hugged her. He thought life had never been more perfect.

Shand fixed them rooms with a communicating door. So that was just right too.

He saw more of his guardian, as the year wore on. Janni came with him each time; the old man wouldn't hear to the contrary. He seemed to have taken a genuine liking to her. Sometimes, if it got too late, they'd stay the night; the twin rooms were always there. As the days lengthened once more he'd walk with her on the hill, where the great Kites swooped and rustled. A score of times he turned to her, and the question that was uppermost in his mind all but popped out; he couldn't imagine life without her now, didn't even want to try. But always for some reason he held his tongue.

The posting came through. The Easthold. He rushed to tell her; but she seemed curiously withdrawn. "You'll have to go then," she said. "After all it's a good number. You'll get Frontier allowance; it'll mean a lot more pay."

"But what will you do?"

"Finish my course I expect," she said. "It's almost finished anyway."

He felt the rise of desperation. "But Janni, it's only ten days!"

"That's all right," she said. "You'll have plenty of time to pack."

He took her shoulders. "Janni," he said, "Janni. . . ." He tried to kiss her; and for the first time ever she turned her face away. "I'm tired," she said. "Not now. . . ."

Rand left her, stunned. Sat in the flat and brooded till dawn was in the sky. Finally his decision was made. He'd realized why she'd been so cold. It should have been sorted out before. A long time ago. Despite her vaunted liberality she had her areas of reticence; he'd known that well enough. She'd been waiting for him to ask, waiting for months; and he hadn't. So she'd thought she was being taken for granted.

He rummaged in the sideboard drawer. Took out a little leather-covered box. Inside it was the ring his mother once returned to Del Panington; a delicate thing crafted in pale gold. It bore an oval plaque; on it was the leafshape of the Vestibule. Outlined in gold, carnelian against turquoise. A proper ring, the only ring for Janni; a ring for a Kiteman's bride. He put it into his pocket.

The day dragged. He thought it would never end. He hurried to the cottage, banged the door. She answered. He said, "Janni, I've got to see you. I've got something important to say."

She looked dull and pale. Defeated, somehow. She said, "I've got something to say as well. You'd better hear me first."

She led the way into the little morning room. Stood back turned for a moment. Then she clenched her fists. "I can't see you any more, Rand," she said. "I can't see you after this."

"What?" he said. "*What*?"

"I can't see you," she said. "It's as simple as that. It's over. It's been nice, but it's over. That is all there is to it. . . ."

His mind was whirling. "But," he said. "But Jan, Jan. . . ." The things they'd done, the places they'd been, how they'd mattered to each other; the horses, the farm, the driving . . . All blown away, as if they hadn't existed. It was impossible. Simply and straightforwardly impossible. He said stupidly, "But you can't mean it. You can't. Why. . . ."

She swung to face him. There were tear-tracks on her cheeks, but her face was like stone. "Because I've found somebody else," she said, "who can look after me better than you. It's as easy as that. It happens all the time."

"Janni," he said. "Jan. . . ."

She shouted at him. "Go. Just go. And never come back. . . ."

He found a pub, and drank. He drank all night as well. Somehow he got to work the following morning. Two days later he closed the audit abruptly; left a Streanling Kitecaptain whistling with surprise. And maybe heaving sighs of relief. He despatched the papers; after which he was free to drink again.

One day blended with the next. She was gone. It was over. His mind, circling, came back again and again to the single monstrous fact. Like a rudderless ship smashing into rocks. Assimilation was impossible. It couldn't have happened; and yet it had. It was like the gigantic pain of toothache. But this tooth could not be drawn.

Brad Hoyland found him. Brad on furlough, revisiting his old stamping grounds. Rand found he couldn't talk to him either. What could you say? The other went away.

He sobered a little, finally; and a notion came to him. He'd go to see his guardian. Once they'd fallen out, certainly; but the mess he'd made since of his life had left him wondering which of them was truly wise. This time the apology would be complete. Sincere. And the old man would advise him. Tell him what to do.

He got the Buckley, drove up out of town. He made a detour to avoid the place she lived. Dusk was falling by the time he reached the hill; although it was high summer. He hadn't realized how late it had got. Perhaps the Warden would be in bed.

There were lights on in the house though. As he pulled up, the front door opened. A figure slipped away. It shielded its face; but there was no mistaking. He even caught the dark sheen of her hair.

He drove again. When he finally stopped he was lost. Even the hills around him looked strange. He sat awhile and watched a Cody rise, dark against the afterglow. "One wasn't enough," he said. "One wasn't enough." He screamed, at the sky. "*One wasn't enough. . . .*" He found himself lying on the ground. His fists were bloody. Sometime, somehow, he got back to Streanling.

His room was warm. He still kindled a fire. He took everything of hers; her letters, clothes, the little trinkets she'd given, and burned them. It was as if the flames were eating along his veins. Lastly he picked up the valise. He stared at it, and put it down again. He could dispose of that later.

Dawn was in the sky by the time he finished. The early pubs round the marketplace would be open already. He got some more money, staggered from the house.

Two days from departure his brain suddenly cleared. It was as if he'd drunk himself back to a state of sanity. He'd heard of such things happening, but hadn't believed it possible. He wanted no more beer; the very thought of it made him gag. The rage had gone; in its place was an icy, deadly calm. He saw now that he existed for revenge; revenge on both of them. And sometime, somewhere, that revenge would be exacted. He piled his things into the Buckley, looked back a final time and drove away.

He topped the last rise, pulled in. For the first time in the day, a breeze was blowing. Strong and cool, steady from the west. Before him, detailed in the bright air, lay the town and port of Fishgard; huddle of stone roofs stretching into distance, darker spires of churches, bland faces of the occasional taller buildings. Beyond, silver-blue and vast, was the sea.

He started up, and let the clutch in. As he rolled down the slope he saw a Cody rise, bright against the pale shield of the water.

6 kitewaif

VELVET COULDN'T SLEEP because of the heat. She tossed and grumbled, in her little room. The room was built into the side of the great stone arch that spanned Fishgard High Street. It was cluttered with nests of old unwanted tables, folding chairs, garden furniture and the rest; because it wasn't really an arch at all, although it crossed the road. It was the sign of the "Dolphin," the biggest hotel in town; and a feature of which the owners were very proud. It was sturdily built of stone; it rose from massive buttressed pillars, pillars so broad that on the pavement side there was barely room to squeeze between the foundation and the long front of the inn. Above it was a writhing crown of carvings. At its centre rose the great fish itself; a creature of legend surely, for none existed now. There were tales of course that they had been seen sporting themselves, by mariners far out in the ocean; but nobody in their right mind gave credence to the yarns of seamen. Not at least after a night spent in the taverns with which the town abounded. There were many other oddities; serpents with pretty, waving fins, strange creatures half-fish, half-man. Some with mitres on their heads, some holding three-pronged spears. Like the fish spears Velvet remembered seeing as a tiny child. But that must have been in another part of the Realm.

One of the creatures she particularly liked. She was a girl, also with a great fish tail. Her hair was long and flowing, her breasts well-formed and slight. She was very naughty at the front, you could see the lot; but her face was sweet. In one hand she held a glass, in the other a comb; and her lips were parted, as if she was singing. Velvet would have liked to climb up and touch her, but there was no way. The arch was high, and at that point its side was smooth and sheer.

Round the rest of the sides were Demons. The inevitable Demons that clustered and crawled on nearly every roof in Fishgard. And most of the Easthold; or so she'd been told. Why they put them there she had never been sure. After all, a real Demon flying by would be more tempted to stop and look if he thought he saw a friend. They even put seats on chimneystacks for them. The priests said they were grateful for the rest, and wouldn't harm the people in the house beneath. It had always seemed dubious to her; though so far it had seemed to work. She'd certainly never seen a Demon. She wouldn't particularly want to.

One of the beasts on the arch side was particularly bad. He was clinging to a buttress right by the stair to her little room. At first the thought of him outside all night had prevented her from sleeping; also she never liked to open the door first thing, see him staring in. Till one day she had become angry, and hit him with the handle of her parasol. To her amazement his great hooked nose broke off, and flew across the street. It made him look so funny she began to laugh. Now she was quite fond of him. After all, a Demon without a nose can't hurt anybody.

She was proud of the parasol. It had been given her last year at one of the big houses on the edge of town. She'd gone there with her truck, selling cordwood for lighting fires. It had been raining, and she was very wet. The person who opened the door of the servants' wing had seemed upset to see her. She'd turned away, but the other had taken her arm. She made Velvet go inside, into a great kitchen. She'd sat her by the fire and dried her hair, given her a bowl of soup. It had been very good. Later the lady of the house bought all the wood. Gave her a good price too. After which she had made the place a regular call. They were good customers, for other things apart from kindling.

When she left, the cook had hugged her unexpectedly.

"You poor little waif," she said. "Here, take you this. And don't get wet again." She'd put the parasol into Velvet's hand, and she'd gasped. After all, people didn't give things away for nothing. It didn't make sense. She'd grabbed it and fled, before the other changed her mind. Later she'd wondered at the word she'd used. What was a waif? She was sure it was nothing to do with collecting wood.

The parasol became her prize possession. She carried it everywhere with her, winter and summer; though she seldom opened it, save in the privacy of her room. It was very gay, all white and pink stripes, and little tassels she was sure were made of gold. It was very old though, because the colours were faded. She was afraid the rain might harm it; and she wouldn't want to be without it now.

She guessed by the brightness of the sky it was zero five hundred. She couldn't understand chronometers, they'd always baffled her; but her sense of time was nonetheless acute. She got up, muttering to herself, began to put her dress on. Beneath it she wore voluminous petticoats, layer on layer. Got a bit hot in summer, but it was only sense. She always wore as many of her clothes as she could. After all, somebody might get in while her back was turned and nick them. Where would she be then?

She scuffed at her hair, in the fragment of mirror she owned. It was nice hair, it hung right down her back. She tied it with a fresh piece of string, and put her hat on. It was made of black straw, with ribbons and flowers to one side. Though they were getting faded as well now. She'd found it in a rubbish bin on the Ridge. That was where the really well-off people lived. She wondered why they threw such things away. She supposed they could afford to, being rich.

She adjusted the hat to what she thought a cheeky angle, slipped a big pin through it to keep it firm. She couldn't remember how she'd got the pin. It seemed she'd always had it. It was another of her treasures; it went everywhere with her. Which was why she always wore a hat. You couldn't just put a pin through your hair; it would look silly. Besides, it wouldn't stay put.

She picked the parasol up. Her feet she left bare. She had a pair of shoes, very smart, with pointed fronts and little inch-high heels. Though the leather was cracked a bit. She'd thought they made her look very grown-up. But the only time she'd worn them they worked big blisters on several of her toes. Now she left them behind. She didn't care if they did get nicked.

She opened the little round-topped door, grinned at the Demon outside. She padded down the flight of worn stone steps, stood staring up. It was still early; but the air felt even hotter. It was going to be a scorcher, she could tell. No breeze at all to clear it.

Which was one good thing of course. Without the wind, the Codys couldn't fly. Normally they streamed a big Trace from the Tower near the church, it flew right over the High Street. Fishgarders were proud of it, they said how fine it looked. She'd never shared their enthusiasm. She hated the idea of it hanging over her head. After all, she hadn't asked them to put it there.

Though even the Kites could be useful. She remembered finding a great String once, caught up in trees a long way from the town. A place she always went to, to get mushrooms. She'd scurried back, gone straight to the church; though the man she'd seen, when they finally let her in, had been less than sympathetic. He'd shaken her and said, "Where is it then?" And when she'd refused to tell, started to beat her. She yelled; and the other man had come, the one in bright red clothes. He'd said, "*Leave her.*" He'd sounded really angry. He'd taken her to a little side room, sat and smiled. He said, "Won't you tell me? Please?"

She'd glowered at him. She knew there was a reward. She said, "I wants my money first."

He'd sighed. "You'll get it," he said. He'd taken her in a car—the first time ever—and paid her for the find. All in a big brown envelope. She hadn't dared to open it, not then; but later on she'd gasped. More money than she'd ever seen; up to that time at least. She'd been looking for broken traces ever since. But she'd never found another.

Crows were working in the street, big shiny flocks of them. She stumped toward them. Some flew away, cawing indignantly; the rest just shuffled to one side. Carried on squabbling over gutter scraps. She swung the parasol, tapping as she walked. She'd seen rich people do that, though she didn't do it often. It tended to wear the tip away.

She paused outside the "Anchor," stared. She couldn't believe her luck. They'd left some crates of empties in the yard; and nobody was about. She hurried back to the "Dolphin," undid the small door at the foot of the arch and got her truck. She collected the spoils, watching round her cautiously. She hid them in the arch. It was one of the advantages of early rising. There was good money in bottles; and the crates as well. She'd take them to Master Lorning later on. He always paid her without argument.

She frowned a little. She had a nasty feeling he knew where they were coming from. And that when she took his crates back to the Anchor, they knew as well. It piqued her slightly. She liked to earn her keep; she'd always rather resented charity.

She thought about Master Lorning. His family had owned the "Dolphin" now for three generations. She didn't know how long that was; she supposed it must be hundreds of years. He'd been very good to her though. She'd been sleeping behind one of the houses on the Ridge, in a little hut she'd found. She'd thought it would be all right, but they chased her away. They had a dog with them too, it tore her dress. Though she'd mended it, you couldn't really see it now. She'd scampered back with the truck, sat awhile and brooded on the waste ground opposite the "Dolphin." For once, she was feelng a bit depressed. She hadn't been doing any harm. Not that she could see. She'd have gone away without the dog. She examined the torn dress mournfully. It was her best as well. Finally she had a walk about the town. She did her usual trick with the bottles, went round the back as soon as the "Dolphin" opened. She knew they didn't like her in the bars; that was where the well-off people went. After he'd paid her, Master Lorning said, "Where are you sleeping now? Haven't seen much of you this last few days."

She shrugged. She never liked to give too much away.

He'd stared at her keenly. Too keenly for her taste. He said, "What's the matter? They booted you out up top?"

She looked at the ground and pouted, scuffed her toes on the cobbles of the yard. He was a big man, huge to her, with masses of iron-grey hair.

A little silence; then he stepped out, and closed the door. He said, "Come with me, Velvet. Don't worry, you'll be all right."

He walked across the dusty, rutted road, up the steps on the far side of the arch. He unlocked the little door—she'd always wondered where it led—and ushered her inside. "I know it isn't much," he said. "But it's all I can do." He looked a bit helpless. Funny, for a grown-up. "It's the wife," he said. "She's difficult. Otherwise . . . you know what I mean."

She didn't know what he meant, she hadn't the faintest idea. Nor did she care; because she'd fallen in love with the place at once. It was like a house, a real house of her own. She couldn't believe it. She even started to cry. She knuckled her nose, furious, and he touched her shoulder. "Here," he said. "No need for that. Here. . . ." He looked helpless again. "You'll be all right," he said. "I can send some grub across. If we're busy, nobody will notice." She wondered if it would matter if they did.

She brought her things up from the truck. Lucky she'd already had it packed. But then, she'd always had a funny feeling about that shed. She spent a happy hour arranging them. The place was thick with dust. But that was normal, wasn't it? You got dust everywhere.

There was even a little cupboard at the back. She put her shoes in it, and the other bits and pieces she didn't care about. Then she arranged her driftwood. She was an experienced beachcomber, she'd been doing it for years. And driftwood fetched good value, it made pretty-looking fires. The Mistress Kerosina told her once the flames came blue and green. Some of the bits she kept though. They reminded her of things. Animals mostly, though she wasn't sure such creatures had ever existed. There was one with about twelve legs, and all sorts of eyes, and its mouth open like a cow when it was lowing. And another like the dolphin on the arch, and another like the lady with the tail. Least, if you looked at it certain ways. She placed it in the middle of the sill; stepped back, and was quite pleased. Then she set about the bed. It stood upright against the farther wall; she lugged it into position with a bit of puffing, spread the blankets she'd fetched from the truck. She lay down to try it out. She thought she'd never been so comfortable. Later in the day she took a walk about the town. Some of the harbour boys laughed at her; but she merely raised her chin. She was a lady now, she had a home of her own. Which was more than they could say.

• • •

She wandered down the High Street; but the pickings weren't too good. Even the tailors' rubbish bins were empty; she could usually find cloth scraps to sell to Tinka. Though to tell the truth she was half afraid of him. He'd always spit on the coins before he paid her. She'd take them, gingerly; but she never felt right till she'd washed them in the sea. She tried the back of the forge; old horseshoes were worth money, she sold them on the Ridge. Some nailed them with the points upright, so the luck wouldn't run out; but most put them upside down, in case the demons saw them and were annoyed. That way they attracted lightning too. Master Billings usually kept them for her; but this time he hadn't put any out. She went back, got the truck again. She squeaked down to the harbour, turned along the Quay. Beyond the mole a track led to the beach. She plodded stolidly, steering the truck through clumps of wiry grass. At the bottom of the incline she looked up and scowled. A Kiteship was lying at anchor. You could always tell them, they had a tower thing in front. She scowled again. She didn't like the Codys, though she'd never been too sure why. Something about her father, the Master Lorning said he'd had to do with them. But then, he said all sorts of things. For instance, he always reckoned she was twelve. But she knew—no way to explain it, she just knew—she was fourteen.

No driftwood; but a lot of seacoal had been washed up. Not much use this time of year; but it could always be stored. Though the bin the Master Lorning let her use was getting really full, there wouldn't be space for much more. She'd have to start storing it in her room; though somehow she didn't like the idea of that. She collected it anyway, spent an hour or more. By then it was getting really hot. She pushed the truck back up, trundled it to the "Dolphin." She unloaded it—just managed to get all the coal in—and put the truck away. She went upstairs, and bolted the door of her room. She saw she hadn't got much water left. Enough to soak the May cakes though. This lot were stale, and hard. But they were better after she'd left them for a bit. When she'd eaten, she lay back on the bed. She was feeling sleepy. She closed her eyes; her breathing steadied, and became deep. It was afternoon before she woke. She was really quite surprised.

The heat lay like a blanket on the town. It seemed it even

muffled sound as well; so that the jingle of a passing cart, the desultory clip-clop of a brewer's horse, were flattened somehow. Stray noises came from the little boatyard; clang of a hammer on metal, sudden scream of some machinery. The gulls wheeled, circling; but they were muted too. Everything endured, waiting for the dusk.

The silting had been bad, this last few years. Even fishing boats had trouble with the quay; you had to know the marks to aim for, to stand a chance at all. The big stuff—coasters, Kiteships—had to anchor offshore, or tie up to the buoys. The Church had been appealed to, times enough; but they never seemed to care. All right for the farmers well inland, over the Doomview Hills; they were looked after. But then of course, they could still pay their dues. Fishgard grumbled, discontentedly; or drooped its shoulders, settled for its lot. The place was dying. Slow maybe; but sure. Perhaps it suited Central policies.

Not that there was much fishing any more. The boats that landed catches still had to run the gauntlet of the Vars. They were always present, on the quay; day or night, the news of an offing brought them down in droves. And with a scarlet Hunter Truck to back them. They'd hold strange instruments above the fish; black, shiny things that clicked and rattled. Sometimes they'd nod, and the baskets would be hurried ashore; at others they'd shake their heads. Then, at gunpoint if needs be, livings would be thrown back to the water. Never an explanation, never a by-your-leave. The town seethed, quietly.

Between the quay and boatyard stretched a long spit of mud. On it, half submerged when the tide was in, lay the shell of an old boat. Most of her planks had gone; her ribs rose gaunt and blackened, Within her, cooled by the mix of sea and mud, lay half a dozen harbour boys, sons of the fishermen whose cottages crowded the straggling lanes above. "Littluns," they were known as; the Biguns, when they troubled to appear, used the other wreck, the hulk that lay close beside the boatyard wall. The Littluns would have resented the description; but the distinction, though undefined, was curiously precise. From time to time one of them moved lazily, flipped water on himself; but for the most part they lay eyes closed, too tired by the heat to talk.

"No Kites," said Tol Vaney indolently. He was a slender,

long-shanked lad, half a head taller than the rest. He nodded at the flawless sky.

"Fuck the Kites," said somebody succinctly.

The slim boy shook his head. "Likes to see 'em," he said. "Gets used to 'em. What if the Demons come?"

"Fuck Demons," said Rik Dru belligerently. "I ain't never seen none. An' the Kites ain't never done nothin' for me."

"They ain't supposed to."

"Then why ain't my ol" man got no work?"

"That ain't to do wi' the Kites."

"Still likes to see 'em," said Tol. "What you then, a bloody Middler?"

"I ain't nothin'," said the lad who'd spoken. "No more than you. Don't matter what we are anyway. It's only for the toffs."

"What toffs?"

"The Ridge lot. You can afford it then."

"What you know about 'em?" said a small lad who'd not yet spoken. He splashed water on his hair.

"I knows though," said Tol. "Wait till you get wi' the Biguns. Find out then."

There was a ripple of laughter.

"Oh, Kerosin's ol' sow," said Rik. "I could do 'er a turn."

"You couldn't do nobody a turn."

"Like to bet?"

Nobody seemed to want to. Silence fell again.

"I reckon we stands more chance 'ere," said Dil Hardin. He was a thoughtful boy; generally left the others standing. They all agreed, privately, he was a bit round the twist.

"More chance o' what?"

"You know."

"I don't! I don't!" A chorus of denials.

Dil leaned back. "Don't think she's what you said," he opined. "I think she's pretty."

"Garn!"

" 'Andsome is as 'andsome does," said the small boy.

"What's that mean?"

"I dunno. My Ma's always sayin' it." He scooped a handful of mud, plopped it contentedly on his head. Runnels began to trickle down his face. He stuck his tongue out. "Dirty sod," said Tol.

"She bin back 'ere in that coach of 'ers?"

"Last week, they reckoned."

"Ought to get the priests to try them Demon detectors on 'er," said Dil.

"Why's that?"

"She takes enough out the sea."

"I'm piddling'," said the small boy. "Anybody feel it?"

"Long as it ain't the other. Stinks enough already."

"Who says it ain't?"

"We'll chuck you out the boat!"

"It ain't a boat. It's a wreck."

A tussling. Water flew, and mud. The small boy vanished over the side. He climbed back, cautiously. "I was only jokin'," he said plaintively.

A Church patrol came along the quay. They cheered, derisively. The big van slowed; they tensed, ready to dive in different directions. It moved off, turned the corner out of sight. They relaxed again.

The afternoon wore on. The heat abated slightly. To the west, over the town, the sky veiled itself. Tol cocked an eye. "Won't last," he said.

Nobody argued. They were all weather-wise.

The men knocked off from the boatyard. They tramped along the quay, carrying their kit. A cloud grew, over the chimney tops. "Breeze gettin' up," said Tol.

The small boy squeezed his chest. He said, "Why do we 'ave tits?"

"Why do girls 'ave pricks?" said somebody.

"They don't!"

"My sister 'as! She let me feel it! So there!"

"Don't be stupid."

"I ain't!"

"They ain't as big as ours," said Tol magisterially. "But they do got 'em."

The Littluns pondered the information, carefully.

"What about this?" said Rik. A pink-tipped column rose, from the mud between his legs. He stroked it affectionately. " 'Ave anybody, that would," he said.

"Dirty bastard," said Tol. "Go blind, you will."

There was a clicking of heels. A small figure hove into sight along the quay. It was dumpy and foursquare, and wore a long and grubby dress. Beneath it showed the hems of several equally suspect petticoats. It wore a ribboned hat; and over its shoulder, rather like a rifle, it carried a furled parasol. Velvet, for once, had decided to wear her shoes. She observed the boatload coldly, raised her chin. Crossed to the other side, and turned the corner out of sight.

"Orlright," said the small boy. "You're all chops. Let's see 'ow you go on about that."

Rik jumped from the boat with surprising speed, ran up the steps to the quay. He mugged at them, leaped in the air. He loped across the road, vanished in pursuit. Silence for a moment; then they all distinctly heard a thwack and yelp. He came back looking dejected. There was a general laugh.

"Look," said somebody. "There's a Cody."

"Fuck the Codys," said Rik. He nursed himself, beneath the soothing water, and scowled.

A car drove across the quay. It screeched to a halt, and a tall man with black hair ran across. "Hey," he called. "Hey . . ."

There was a hasty exodus.

He sat in his room. It was a small room, square and plain. But there was a wash-stand, water in a jug; towels, and a bed. He needed nothing more.

He turned the valise in his hands. It had a cheap brass lock. In fact he hadn't realized before just how tawdry the whole thing was. There was a relationship to Rone somewhere. Though he couldn't quite see it.

He opened the case. Took out the photograph inside. The precious contents. He laid it face down on the little table. Finally he turned it over. Janni smiled at him. The eyes, the lovely hair. Across the corner she'd written, *"To Rand, with love."* There followed a line of little crosses.

He put it back in the valise. Love was what she was surrounded by now. Well, that was what she'd wanted.

He lay on the bed, stared at the ceiling. Fishgard had been a shock, there was no denying that. Even in his dulled state. He'd heard the tales of course, hadn't they all? But . . . the narrow-slitted windows, streets that crisscrossed and meandered, the endless goblins scrambling on the roofs. They clung to chimney breasts, to eaves, to cornices. They stared down as he passed; each face seemed more malevolent than the last.

The place was haunted surely, possessed. Needing a mighty blast of wind, something to blow it clean. He wondered what Janni would have said, and instantly choked off the thought. There was no Janni. She had never existed.

He'd stopped off at the big Var church. But they'd known nothing; hadn't heard of him, didn't know of the posting. And the Civil Headquarters had been locked up. His banging finally produced a grumpy caretaker. He advised him to come back at zero nine hundred, slammed the door. He drove away, feeling the anger mount. This was all he needed. He'd crossed the Realm; and this was his reward. But that was wrong of course. He'd had his reward before.

He drove through the fishermen's quarter. He was appalled by the hovels that leaned and clustered, each staying upright it seemed by the support of its neighbour; by the narrow, garbage-choked lanes, by the evidence of poverty on every hand. Groups of men lounged in doorways; they turned as the Buckley approached, watched it go by. Their faces were blank; though once an old woman, rocking under a stone-roofed porch, took a pipe from her mouth and spat.

He reached a little market, finally. The oddest he had seen. A cobbled square stretched to a low stone wall; beyond was the sea. The lines of stalls looked as ramshackle as the rest, their awnings bleached and ragged, their wooden trestles decayed. Some were selling fish. Beside each stood a red-robed priest, Counter in hand, demonstrating their harmlessness. Other stalls sold fruit and vegetables, clothing, church-ware. He saw a well-dressed woman haggling with a trader. Above his head hung a faded Vestibule.

A gaggle of boy-children dashed up from the beach. They were naked. Others, equally bare, were serving behind stalls. Nobody seemed to bother.

At least there was a Variant policeman. He asked where he could get accommodation for the night. He gave Rand complicated instructions. He tried to follow them, got lost in another maze of lanes. He gave up, headed back toward the sea.

He saw an attempted rape. At the other end of a street of leaning houses. He blew his hooter, careered toward the combatants. The girl vanished into an alley; the other—unclothed as seemed to be the norm—took to his heels in the direction of the quay.

He wasted several minutes looking for her, drove down himself. He hailed a group of children in an old, decaying boat. They ran like hares.

He drove past more of the shabby stone-roofed cottages. Interspersed with them were pubs and warehouses. He turned left, into the High Street. A stone arch spanned the road. Beneath it hung a sign. *The Dolphin Tavern.* He swung into a cobbled yard, parked the Buckley by a creeper-hung wall. And yes, they had a room. Payment would be in advance.

He walked to the window, studied the great arch with its fantastic topload. Malevolence, it seemed, was concentrated here. Above it, plumb down the High Street, flew a massive Cody string. Six lifters. He wondered why they needed them; there was no Observer's basket.

He craned his head. He saw the Trace was anchored to a Tower not unlike the Tower of Garnord. Buttressed, and castellated. He looked back to the arch. The juxtaposition seemed extraordinary. He took the valise, walked down to the quay. More folk about now, in the growing dusk; they strolled in groups and pairs, enjoying the cool of the day. The off-shore breeze blew steadily; he saw a Kiteship was anchored, a half mile from the curving bight of land. She was streaming too.

There was a sandy path. It wound to the beach, through waist-high tussocks of grass. He followed it, walked to the water's edge. He watched the wavelets cream and lap awhile; then he flung the case as far as he could, into the sea. He hunched his shoulders, climbed back to the quay. Despite himself, he hadn't been able to dispose of all of her at once. But there was nothing left now. Not even memory.

Fatigue hit him, suddenly. He walked to the "Dolphin," let himself into his room. To his surprise, he slept.

Headquarters were apologetic, next morning. Some mixup with the postings, they'd thought they were taking an Officer from the Southguard. Then when his cancellation had come through. . . .

He shrugged. It was of no significance.

An office had been made available to him. Somewhere to prepare reports. He even had the partial use of a secretary. He seemed to be a rather partial young man himself. Willowy, and languid. He waved a hand, apologetically. "Not much of a place," he said. "But remember, this *is* Fishgard. . . ."

He looked round. The building seemed as cranky as the rest of the town. Smart enough facade, stone-lined and set back from the street; but the rest was evidently much older. Walls of wavy plaster, erratic black-painted beams. Door architrave at one angle, window-frames at others. But there was a desk, and filing cabinets. Even a little loo. He said, "It'll serve."

Digs had been fixed for him. A Mistress Goldstar, just back from the quay. He picked the van up from the "Dolphin," drove it round. He was beginning to know the town a little now. The morning was bright and sunny; but the heat of the day before had gone. He pulled up briefly on the quay, glanced left and right. Four Codys streamed to the north, three visible to the south. It seemed he was in for a busy time.

Mistress Goldstar seemed a pleasant enough person, cheerful and capable; the widow of a fisherman lost in the Great Storm, the storm that had wasted half the Easthold. Later, the little boarding house he'd bought for her had been a boon. "Don't know what I'd 'a' done without it," she said. " 'E were like that though. Always thinkin' ahead." She sighed. "Trouble was, the Kites were down," she said. " 'Ad to, see? Not as I blames 'em for that. Wouldn't 'ave 'appened else though. . . ." She took a saucepan from the stove, poured. He accepted the cup, mind busy. This was a level of faith he hadn't seen in years; he certainly hadn't expected to encounter it in Easthold.

They were sitting in her little kitchen. Neat curtains, polished red-tiled floor. "We runs a decent 'ouse," she'd said as she showed him his room. "Not like some I could mention. Bawlin', comin' in all hours. . . . 'Cept for you," she added hastily. "You comes and goes as you chooses, Kites is Kites. Can't do no special meals though. You know, funny times."

He'd smiled, in spite of himself. "That won't be necessary," he said. "I don't suppose I shall be in all that much. Got a lot of work to get through. . . ."

They'd given him a schedule. He saw his first audit was the Tower. He called that afternoon, sent in his card as protocol dictated. Unembellished this time. He was shown into a pleasant little office, well lined with books. All the standard manuals plus Corps histories, biographies; even a few he hadn't seen. He took one down. And Canwen. *The Flier and his God.*

The door opened. The man who entered was tall and well set, blond hair drawn into a double ponytail. He had what he'd heard called a lived-in sort of face. A scar across his forehead, another on his cheek. Also his nose had been broken at some time, and badly reset; or not reset at all. He seemed pleasant enough though. "Raoul Josen," he said. "Controller, Fishgard Tower." He held his hand out. "Pleased to meet you, like a glass of something?"

Rand said, "I wouldn't say no." The Basket Bases, as they called them, warranted a Captain, or a Major at least. Town Stations didn't. Josen was a noncom; but Rand sensed he was a good one. After all, the noncoms were the mainstay of the Corps; he'd found that out already.

The other handed him a drink, glanced at the book he'd laid down. He said, "Ever meet him?"

"No," he said. "Did you?"

The Controller looked reflective. "Yes," he said. "Flew with him for a bit." He smiled. "He was Senior, G15," he said. "I was a singularly snotty-nosed Cadet."

Rand said, "What's he like?"

The other shrugged. "Strange man," he said. "Don't think anybody ever understood him. I certainly didn't. You know he lives round here?"

He shook his head.

"Got a place up on the Ridge," said the Controller. "Posh end of the town. You get some funny people, on the Ridge." He put the glass down. "Doubt you'll meet him though," he said. "Bit of a recluse. But then, he always was. Never used to start below a thousand feet." He riffled through the book. "You can borrow it sometime if you like," he said. "Put down the day and the date though."

"Maybe," said Rand. "Let's clear the junk first though."

They got down to work. The Tower, like most Bases of its grading, carried a standing complement of twelve. Plus Launch- and Riggingmasters, and a Painter and Apprentice. They supplied Godkites to half the Southern Sector, sometimes as far as the Salient. It was a lucrative sideline. Supply Depot F12, immediate superior F4. At which Raoul Josen pulled a face. "Watch the Skipper there," he said. "Real Taildowner. Eats Controllers regularly, on toast. Audit people too."

"Thanks a lot," he said. "That's my next trip." He made the last of his notes, and closed the folder. The Controller said, "Like a look round while you're here?"

Rand nodded. He said, "Fine." The other's manner had been guarded at first; but he'd rapidly thawed. Seemed to accept him as another Kiteman, though he couldn't really see why. He followed the blond man from floor to floor; workshops and rest areas, the Kiteflat where they refurbished the great gay Lifters; a Studio where a tall, cadaverous man in paint-smudged robes meticulously applied gold leaf to a big cartouche. They emerged finally on the launch platform, where a bored-looking Cadet leaned on the parapet and stared moodily down into the street. He saluted smartly enough though, at sight of his Controller.

"Something you haven't seen," said Raoul. "Maybe you have though. Ever come across twin stringing before?"

Rand shook his head. The fixed winch carried two drums. The cables were cinched at intervals by slim brass coupling tubes; he could see the first half dozen winking in the sunlight. He said, "What the Hell's the idea of that?"

"Search me," said the Controller. "Local regulations; overflying a built-up area. Easthold is a law unto itself."

Rand stared up at the great curve of the Trace. The Lifter wings showed one above the next; the Pilot was little more than a bright speck. "That's crazy," he said. "Wondered why you were six-flying without a basket. If one goes, the other's bound to part. You'd ditch in the sea anyway."

"Try telling 'em," said Raoul. He picked up a coupler that lay on the parapet. "Don't ask me to account for these things either. Fine on a normal down; but if you're in a hurry you don't have time to clamp. They go like snot off a doorknob. We get 'em brought back occasionally; record's three hundred yards."

A thought occurred to him. He said, "Do the Lifters override okay?"

"Sometimes," said the Controller. "Sometimes not. Depends on your luck."

He made another note. "I shan't query your cable backup then," he said. "Leaving aside corrosion."

The other glanced sidelong. He said, "You've been here before." He looked round him. "Good view, ain't it?" he said.

Rand nodded. Heightwise, they topped all but the church steeple. The grey roofs of the town, with their misshapen population, stretched in every direction. Beyond were the quays, beyond again the huge expanse of water. He saw the Kiteship still rode at anchor.

He peered down into the street. Almost directly below, a small figure ambled along. It was pushing an old wooden truck. He touched the Controller's sleeve, and pointed. He said, "Who's that?"

Raoul shrugged. "One of the local denizens. They call her Velvet. Funny little kid, don't know much about her. Asked a couple of times, but nobody seems to want to let on. Why?"

He shrugged. "No reason," he said. "Just thought I'd seen her before."

The audit went well. He prepared his report, left it for the secretary to transcribe. He walked back to the Tower, smiled at the Controller's enquiring look. "No problems," he said. "You run a tight Base, Raoul." He steepled his fingers. "Look," he said, "I can't guarantee a thing. I can only advise. We're toothless really, it's one of the hazards of the job. But I'm recommending we scrap the twinning, go to single cable. It'll nearly halve the rig costs. That should appeal to Central if nothing else does."

The other fetched a bottle and two glasses. "To that I will drink," he said solemnly. "Let's hope they see the light. . . ."

They drank again that evening, in one of the town centre pubs. Later he went on to the Controller's house, a pleasant little cottage on the outskirts of town. He met Raoul's wife, a slender, dark-haired woman, and a brace of cheerful kids. The meal she prepared was excellent. They chatted afterwards about old times; Middlemarch, the Northguard, the Salient he had yet to see. It was only later, sitting alone in his room, that the ghost returned to plague him.

He saw the girl again a few days later, stumping along the High Street. Minus her truck this time; but there was no mistaking. The rakish little hat, the dress, the froth of grubby petticoats. "Hi," he shouted. "Hi. . . ." She hesitated, turned; and he called, "Velvet. . . ." She stopped at that, appalled; then took to her heels.

It was a market day, the town was crowded. He jinked and swerved cursing; dodged round one farm cart, was almost run down by another. But by the time he reached the opposite sidewalk she had vanished again.

He raised the matter with the secretary. "Denning," he said, "that kid who goes round town. The one who pushes the truck. Know anything about her?"

The other shrugged, studying a file. "Couldn't say, I'm sure. . . ."

"But who are her folks? What's her other name?"

The secretary looked vague. "Hell," he said. "That's what they call her anyway."

"What?"

Denning said, "Hell. . . ."

Rand spread his hands on the desk. "Do you know what you just said?"

The other looked surprised. "Just told you what her name was," he said. "Sorry, I'm sure. . . ."

He gritted his teeth. He said, "Forget it." Next morning he drove to Base F4.

Velvet had had a good day. The Flaxtons were away, she'd got it from the maid. She rose at first light, pushed the truck to the Ridge. The property was surrounded by a high stone wall, topped along its length by broken glass; but there were ways and means. And the orchard was out of sight from the house. She'd equipped herself with a massive basket, woven of Holand fibre. She filled it to overflowing with cherries, spent the morning hawking the wares round town. By lunchtime she'd disposed of the lot; she repaired to the back door of the "Dolphin," tapped. She waved the bundle of grubby notes, demanded ale. But Master Lorning smiled. "I'll bring you some over in a mo'," he said. "Got a job for you."

She frowned. "Can't do it till tomorrer," she said.

He shook his head. "Customer o' mine," he said. "It's got to be tonight."

"A'right," she said. "Expect I can fit it in. Don't be too long though, will yer?"

He came over to her room in minutes, with a crate. He outlined his requirements, and she nodded. "Yeah," she said. "I can fix that up all right."

"Good," he said. "I'm relying on you. Twenty?"

She opened her mouth. It was on the tip of her tongue to say twenty-five; then she remembered he'd given her her house for free. "I don't want nothin', Master," she said. "You knows that."

"Don't be daft," he said. "I makes good money, why not you?" He rose to leave; but on the steps he paused, stared at the Demon with his smashed-off nose. "Look at that," he said. "Nothin's safe no more."

She shook her head. "Terrible, ennit?" she said. "Shockin', what some folk'll do."

She ate a handful of cherries, drank one of the beers. She hurried round to Transon, the fishermen's quarter that lay behind the boatyard. Mo Sprindri was at home; sitting in the little front parlour, sucking at his pipe. Velvet laid the deal out briskly, and he nodded. "All right," he said. "I'll send Hol round tonight."

A wild-haired child was watching, from the inner room. Sucking her thumb, staring with big smoky eyes. She wore a ragged singlet, full of holes. It stopped at her waist; the rest of her was bare. Velvet looked her up and down appraisingly. She put her age at nine. "Sorry," she said. "Send Rye."

He twitched at that, and clenched his fists. He set them on the table. *"No,"* he said hoarsely. *"No. . . ."*

She mentioned a figure, saw his face begin to crumple. After all, he hadn't worked in years. He was quiet for a while; finally he spoke. "All right," he said. "I'll see she gets cleaned up."

She shook her head. "No," she said. "Send 'er as she is." She rose to leave; and he looked up. There were tears in his eyes. "I don't blame you, Velvet," he said. "It isn't you I blame."

She hurried back into town, vaguely puzzled. She couldn't work out what he'd meant. After all, it would bring him in good money. Better than the days he'd been employed. No blame in that. Walking up the High Street, she glowered at the Codys.

She climbed the hill to the Mistress Kerosina's home. Privately she thought her the most beautiful person in the world, with her lovely clothes and her huge green eyes and her long slim legs. She wished hers were the same. She tolled the bell and waited, leaning on the parasol. She looked round at the garden. The Mistress was also very good for trade; there was no denying that. With Velvet, affection was keyed perforce to practical considerations.

The carriage was waiting, the newest one her Ladyship had bought. All curtained, just with little chinks to peep through. She changed her carriages constantly, but people always got to know. There'd even been whispers about this one, and she'd only had it a few weeks. She'd have to tell her soon, but she'd been putting it off. The Mistress Kerosina wouldn't be best pleased.

They jogged back into town, turned on to the quay. The Littluns were mudlarking as ever; her employer parted the drapes with the little fan she carried. She stared awhile, and pointed. "The tall one," she said huskily. "The tall one with the long fair hair."

Velvet waited her moment, hopped down. She ambled to the quayside, gestured. Tol Vaney came across, unwillingly. A bartering; and she held up a handful of notes. He swallowed at that, waited his chance and ran for the steps. He glanced to either side as she had done, bundled in. She followed. He crouched in the carriage shivering and dripping mud. The horses clopped away.

The Mistress Kerosina crooned at him. Her eyes were glowing. She liked them bare; because then they were wholly in her power. She pulled his head back, kissed him savagely; then she did something else. Velvet cupped her hands round the parasol. Tomorrow he'd have to go to the other boat.

It was late before she got back to the arch. Well, lateish anyway. She wondered whether to drink more beer, decided not. She settled for cherries and a damp May cake. She thought about the man who'd called to her, the tall man with the glasses and dark hair. Quite good looking, he was. He'd been there the other night as well, the night old Rikki tried it on. She'd thought he was Church at first; they always reckoned they used plainclothes Vars. But now she wasn't sure.

She reached under the bed, pulled out a black valise. She opened it, looked at the picture inside. She was really pretty, she wondered who she was. Pity the damp had spoiled it a bit. It had gone wavy now, and the writing down the side had got all smudged. Not that it would have made much difference if it hadn't. She'd watched him throw it in the sea, waited for the tide to bring it back to land. She'd known whereabouts it would drift in. She'd been disappointed at first; but she'd kept it anyway. Everything had potential.

She made her mind up. One thing was sure; he certainly

wasn't a Var. They'd never do a thing like that. She swung her legs from the bed. She grabbed the parasol and headed for the door. "Never spoil a winnin' streak," she said.

G4 was as bad as he'd been warned. They started giving him a hard time from day one. He retaliated in the only way he could. You didn't count each nut and bolt, not on Frontier audit; it was a matter of give and take. He counted them twice. Then he turned to the books. Discrepancies showed at once; they hadn't even been cleverly disguised. Nothing much in themselves; but after a while, they totalled. And they hadn't had an audit for five years. He put the fear of God into a Quartermaster and a Rigging Corporal, made an unofficial visit to a local farmer. He gave equally short shrift to him. After all, what sort of fool fences his pastures with Cody wire? He repaired to the office of Captain Helworth. He presented his views; and the other stroked his moustache. While he didn't accept the findings, he nonetheless found them interesting. Surely though an arrangement could be reached?

Rand looked up, under his brows. "Transfer them, Captain," he said. "Transfer with reprimand, pegged promotion. These things can be arranged." He saw the other's face begin to mottle, and forestalled him. "You fly the Codys," he said. "I serve them. We both serve the Corps."

The Captain blustered anyway. "You Central people," he said. "Timeservers, the pack of you. A penny here, a shilling there; why this, why that? Poking your fingers into things you don't understand, things that don't concern you. . . . We're the people who do the work, we're the ones who take the risks. To keep you folk in comfort. You and the bloody Church. . . ."

He shouted back. Stung into retaliation for once. "My father understood. He understood enough to give his life. I give what I can; and may the Lord forgive me if it's not enough." He slammed the folder on the desk and rose. "It's not wire they're selling," he said. "It's blood. Men's lives. . . ."

The other looked up, startled. A silence; then he slowly shook his head. He said, "You're a funny sort of audit clerk." He spread his hands on the desk top, frowned. He said, "Who was your father?"

He said, "Del Panington."

Helworth appeared to wrestle with himself. Then he got up, walked to a side cupboard. He took down glasses, and a bottle. He said, "I didn't know. I didn't have any idea."

"I know that, sir," said Rand. "I'm not questioning your honour. But you know now."

The other nodded tiredly. "Yes," he said. "I shall comply with your suggestion. Have you any other recommendations for me?"

He thought the matter over, on the short drive back to Fishgard. He wondered if he'd discovered a new source of strength. He decided no. After all, what had they tried to do? Frighten him with bogles; he who lived with Demons.

He took a few days break. He felt he needed them. He wandered the town, got to know it better. The quayside taverns were best avoided, at all times; but there were others, tucked away in sidestreets, where you could get a peaceful beer. He seldom went near the water anyway. Invariably, he put the mudlarks to flight; like firing a maroon into a cloud of gulls. He'd no wish to alarm them; but there seemed no cure for it. He wondered who on earth they thought he was.

Mistress Goldstar had laid supper for him in the kitchen. He often ate with her now, away from the other lodgers. He found her company pleasant, undemanding; presumably she felt the same of his. She'd talk about the old days; the hauls they'd made, the catches they'd brought in. Though that had been before the Vars had taken over. Spoiling the town's prosperity, ruining honest folk's trade. He'd frown a bit at that, though he wouldn't contradict. He knew a little about the instruments the priests carried; and though the notion of Demon piss had never suited his vocabulary he knew they'd saved the people from themselves. Time and again. The Church guarded the Realm; and the Codys were its offspring. Yet in her mind the great Kites were discrete, an entity. He began to see how complex the whole issue was.

He pushed the plate away. "Mistress, that was delicious," he said. "Thank you very much." She made to speak; and a rapping came at the door. She clicked her tongue. "Who on earth?" she said. "This time o' night, an' all . . . 'Scuse, my dear. . . ." She bustled from the room; he heard a low exchange, the sudden flurry of her voice. "That I shan't do,

Mistress Minion,'' she said. ''That I will *not.* The gentleman's at supper; an' I knows your kind. . . .'' He frowned; and she raised her voice again. ''Off you go, Miss Velvet; an' don't you not come back. I runs a decent 'ouse. . . .''

''Mistress Goldstar,'' he said. ''Please . . .'' The short figure was already receding along the path. ''Velvet,'' he called, ''Come here. . . .''

She returned, uncertainly. ''You was the gentleman what called me,'' she said. ''Come to see what you wanted.''

''I'm sorry, Mistress,'' he said. ''She is right. Do you mind?''

The other's face froze. ''I wouldn't 'ave thought it of you, sir,'' she said. ''Straight I wouldn't.'' She hesitated a moment; then she stalked away. After all, she was a Fishgarder; and the Corps were her best customers. ''No noise,'' she said over his shoulder. ''An' it's lights out twenty-four hundred.'' She slammed the kitchen door.

He looked after her; then he touched the small girl's arm. ''Come on,'' he said. ''This way.''

She sat warily on his bed, the parasol gripped between her knees. She still wore the black straw bonnet; he wondered if she slept in it as well. ''All right,'' he said. ''You wanted to see me, and you have. Now, what did you really want?''

She looked up, guardedly. Till then he hadn't realized the full beauty of her face; broad cheekbones, the great tilted eyes, the stubborn, perfect little chin. The candles woke reddish highlights from her hair; wisps hung beside her ears, the rest draggled nearly to her waist. It looked greasy though, he was sure it probably stank; the rest of her he'd already become aware of. He smiled. ''You're very lovely,'' he said. ''But God, you could use a bath.'' She turned her nose up, instantly. ''Baths is fer kids,'' she said.

He smiled again. ''And what do you think you are?''

She bridled. She said, ''I can take care o' myself.''

He said, ''That wasn't what I asked.'' He rose carefully, poured a glass of wine. He offered it to her; but she shook her head. Also the tension of her knuckles warned him she was poised for flight. He sat back, well away from the door. She seemed to relax fractionally. ''When I shouted, you ran away,'' he said. ''Why did you come back? And how did you know where I lived?''

No answer. He tried another tack. "Where do you live?" he said.

"Close," she said. "Not far."

"Close, not far," he said. "Sounds like a riddle. Only I'm not very good at them. Is Velvet your proper name?"

She stuck her lip out.

"Do you have parents? Do you live with them?"

Velvet risked another glance at him. He really was good-looking, even with his glasses. Funny way of talking as well. Sort of soft. There was something else though. She knew he wouldn't hurt her. She didn't know how, but she could tell. For a moment, strange thoughts stirred. She couldn't for the life of her have said what they were.

He was still watching. He said, "It was you that first night, wasn't it?"

"What night?"

"When I came down in the van."

Her silence was eloquent.

He said, "What was happening?"

She shrugged. She said, "That wadn't nothin'. Wadn't nothin' at all. 'Appens all the while."

"It happens all the while," he said. "I see."

She gripped the parasol afresh. She was wondering if he might be a Var after all. She looked round her. "Ain't ever bin in 'ere before," she said. "It's nice."

"Why haven't you been in?"

She shot a baleful glance at the door. "She won't never let me,' she said. "She says. . . ." But it didn't matter what she said. What anybody said. Not really.

He was still gentle. He said, "She let you in tonight."

She looked up, and away again. He realized what had been troubling him. The face was young, and tender; but he thought he'd never seen a pair of wiser eyes. She said, "That was 'cos o' you. She likes you. Gettin' on all right." She stared at her hands. The meeting wasn't going well. Not well at all. She'd thought . . . well, there were many things she'd thought. She'd thought she'd known what he wanted. When she found out he wasn't a Var. Now though she wasn't so sure. Normally, half a dozen pitches would have sprung to mind. She thought about Rye Sprindri. She'd be upset for a day or two, they always were. But they soon got over it. She'd be all right; till somebody ruined her of course. Then there were the mudlarks, if he was the other way. Rik was coming on nicely, he'd be quite useful soon. She frowned. It wasn't right, none of it was right; she knew instinctively. Everybody was the same; and yet he wasn't. It was all very puzzling.

She looked up. He was still watching her. He said, "What do you do for a living, Velvet?"

She grasped the straw. "Things," she said. "I do things fer people."

"What sort of things?"

"Anythin'," she said. "I can do anythin'."

"What do you mean?"

She waved a hand impatiently. "The usual," she said. "You know. I ain't on offer though," she said. "I ain't in the deal." She considered. "Well, p'raps fer special rates."

He said, "You poor little girl." He smiled. He said, "You should have some cards printed. What would you call yourself though? Procuress?"

She looked baffled. She said, "What's cards?"

He reached into his pocket. He said, "This is a card." She took it, frowning, stared at it. Turned it the other way, handed it back no wiser. She said, " 'Course, you needs stuff like that. You're a toff."

Rand laughed. "I'm not a toff," he said. "I work for the Kites. None of us are toffs."

Her face clouded instantly. He said, "What's the matter, Velvet? Don't you like the Codys?"

No answer.

"They're nothing really," he said. "I think they're rather fine. They keep us safe, keep all the Demons away. What's wrong with them?"

She shivered slightly. " 'Angin' over yer 'ead," she said. "There all the time. Can't never get away."

He looked quizzical. He said, "You're not afraid of them. . . ."

She blazed at him. "I ain't afraid o' nothin'. . . . !"

He'd stepped on delicate ground. He changed the subject. "What else do you do? Apart from what you said?"

"Anythin'," she said. "Anythin' that comes along." She brightened. "Bin pickin' cherries this morning. Whole lot. Flogged 'em as well."

"That was very good. Were they your cherries?"

Velvet stuck her lip out. She said, "They wadn't 'ome. Bin away fer a week."

"It still wasn't very honest."

"They wouldn't 'ave eaten 'em," she said. "They never do. There's too many."

"The Demons will get you," he said. "They'll pinch your nose."

She said, "Garn." She grinned, suddenly. It lit her face up, like a little lamp. "I knocked a Demon's nose orf once," she said. "Wi' this." She brandished the parasol.

"That wasn't very kind. Where was he?"

"Up on the arch. It went fer miles."

"What went for miles?"

She said, " 'Is nose."

"I can imagine. Why did you do it?"

"Din' like 'im," she said. " 'E was right outside my h———" She stopped dead. Realized she'd gone too far.

He said, "So you live near the arch."

No answer.

He remembered the carvings clustering the columns. He said, "*In* the arch? Are there rooms *inside* it, Velvet?"

She bit her lip. Wished she hadn't spoken. But she supposed it didn't really matter. He could have found out easy enough by asking someone else. "It was Master Lornin'," she said. " 'E was ever so good to me.'E don't charge me no money."

"No," he said. "I suppose you render services instead." He shook his head. "This town's rotten," he said. "Rotten through and through. It stinks. . . ."

She looked indignant. "It don't," she said. "Well, maybe a bit when the tide's out. . . ."

He started to laugh. "Velvet," he said, "you are priceless. Absolutely priceless. . . ."

She scowled. She thought he was laughing at her. Then she realized he wasn't. She joined in, though she didn't know what was funny; and a door slammed on the landing. She jumped up at once. "I gotta go," she said. "She's comin'. . . ."

"She's not. Anyway, you're all right. You're with me."

"I'm not," she said. "You know what she said. It's twenty-four hundred."

He looked at the chronometer. It was indeed a minute to. He said, "How did you know?" but she was already scrabbling at the door. "All right," he said, "Go steady. You'll wake the house up else. You'll need a light." He grabbed a candle, turned with his hand on the knob. "You don't have to go at all," he said. "You can stay here if you like. You'll be all right, I can sleep in the chair."

She considered. Nice to curl up for once, and just be safe. It wasn't on though, the old sow would come. He'd get in trouble as well. Also her own little house was calling. This place was all right, it was done up nice. But it wasn't like the arch. She shook her head. She said, "I gotta go. . . ." She hesitated. She said, "Thank you, sir."

"What for?" he said. "I haven't done a thing."

Velvet frowned. She supposed he hadn't. Not really, when you thought about it. She'd even forgotten what she'd come to say. There was a moment when she felt she'd like to kiss him. But that was funny too. She couldn't remember kissing anybody ever. She'd seen other people do it, but she didn't know what it was like. She supposed it must be all right. Else they wouldn't bother.

It seemed he understood. He put his hand on her shoulder. He said, "Come on, Littlun." He kept his hand there all the way down the stairs. It was nice.

He shot the front door bolts. He said, "You be all right?"

" 'Course," she said. She was always all right.

He opened the door. "My name's Rand Panington," he said. "And Velvet. . . ."

She turned.

He said, "Thanks for coming to see me. I enjoyed it."

She walked off, baffled; and he called again. Softly. "I'll be away four days," he said. "But then . . . I'll buy some cherries from you. Don't get into trouble though."

She looked over her shoulder scornfully. "I don't get inter trouble," she said. "See yer. . . ." She turned the corner, and was gone.

Rand didn't feel like going to bed. He walked down to the quay, sat on the sea wall. The tide was making; the old wreck the mudlarks used was already part-submerged. The moon was high, riding a clear sky; he watched the long reflections move and dance. Beyond was the vast horizon of the sea. He imagined he could see the curving of the earth. He shook his head. He'd thought himself beyond the realm of feeling; but it seemed it wasn't so. He set himself to analyse his mood. So she was on the game. Or worse, controlling it. He shook his head again. Despite what Mistress Goldstar had said, despite what he'd said himself, he'd been talking to a child. A child who didn't realize her own needs. He wondered what Janni would have said, and closed the thought away. Janni didn't exist; because she wasn't here. There was only the moon, and the sea.

He shrugged. Wrong to seek for meanings; stop looking, and they made themselves plain. She hadn't known herself why she had come. Because people were people; and they made demands. Sometimes they didn't know themselves what the demands were; but as long as folk existed, they would flow. If you acknowledged them, you paid. One way or another. If you didn't. . . .

If you didn't, what? Became less than human, he supposed. Though he wasn't wholly sure that mattered. One thing was certain; you'd get on a whole sight better.

He got up, walked back to the digs. On the way he watched the Codys; rig after rig receding into distance, the moonlight glinting silver from their sails.

He woke early, shaved and dressed. He considered; then he walked through to the kitchen. After all he hadn't been told not to. Breakfast was distinctly fraught. Mistress Goldstar wielded pots and pans, her lips set into a line; finally he spoke. He said, "I think there's something you need to understand."

She kept her back turned to him. She said, "I understands enough, sir."

"No," he said, "You don't. You haven't even started." He rubbed his lip. "I didn't ask her to call," he said. "That was a lie. But neither could I turn her away."

She said, "I'm sure you knows your own business best."

Things flickered for a moment. He remembered something Father Alkin said once, something from an old book. What it would have been he had no idea. *"Whosoever causeth one of these little ones to stumble. . . ."*

She banged a pot.

"It were better for him, if a millstone be hanged about his neck. . . ."

She banged another.

"And he be cast into the depths of the sea. . . ."

He stood up, leaning on his knuckles. He hadn't been as angry for a long time. "Mistress," he said, "There are many people in this Realm. Some take their pleasures one way, some another." He spoke very quietly. He said, "I do not take sexual advantage of children."

Mistress Goldstar was turning, with a saucepan. She dropped it. Soup spilled across the tiles. He rose, fetched the mop. He didn't hurry; because if you are talking to a child, you are talking to a child. And if you are swabbing the floor, you are swabbing the floor. When he looked up she was wringing her hands. He'd never actually seen that done before. "She's not a child, sir," she said. "She's not a child."

He said, "That was all I saw." He put the mop away.

She served his breakfast. Later she said, "I'm sorry, sir."

Rand looked up, vaguely surprised. He said, "Sorry for what?"

She seemed uncertain. "You knows the Kites," she said. "So you knows more than I."

He shook his head. "I know very little," he said. "I know the Kites are flying, and that the bacon is good. There's no call for apologies, Mistress."

He took himself round to the Middle Doctrine church. The big one, opposite the Tower; fronting the Vars as usual. The incumbent was pottering about replacing candles; the little lamps they kept burning night and day. "Ah, yes," he said, "the little girl. The one who pushes the truck. Lives somewhere by the 'Dolphin' I believe." He coaxed another flame alight with the long taper he carried. "A sad case," he said. "Very sad indeed. Her father was a Flier. Lost at sea, some years ago now. Her mother. . . ." He clicked his tongue. "A fickle creature," he said. "Lacking responsibility. Still, she was as the good Lord made her."

"So the child was deserted. Left to fend for herself."

"In a manner of speaking," said the priest. "Yes, I suppose that's correct."

"And nobody took her in. Nobody helped her, gave her shelter. . . ."

The other faced him blandly. "She seems to be self sufficient," he said. "Remarkably so in one so young."

"Self sufficient," he said. "Living like a rat in a skirting. What if she's taken ill? What if she dies?"

The priest smiled. "All," he said, "is within the will of the Lord."

Rand walked out. He'd realized, not for the first time, that any discipline, however noble, is only as strong as its adherents.

He drove to F5. His first sight of the place was a shock. Weeds round the guardhouse, the ill-kept buildings; paint flaking, windows unwashed. Beside the gate stood a broken-down, rusty Launcher. Bird droppings streaked its sides; and a low String was flying, on a three-lift. He stared. They had a basket aloft; but there was no Observer.

He tackled the Commander, a tired-looking middle-aged Major. The other shrugged. "No relief," he said. "Poor chap has to have a day off sometimes."

He said, "But this Section is unguarded. That's a court martial offence." The other merely shrugged. "Then break us," he said. "Central have been informed, we can't do more. You'll find the books are in order though."

Amazingly, they were. And the spares, what there were of them, well-kept. He finished sooner than he'd estimated, sat in his room and brooded. His responsibilities, after all, were clearly enough delineated. To take stock, and examine the accounts. Finally he began his report. After he'd finished he sat and drummed his fingers. He added a terse observation that morale seemed low, more positive support would be an asset. He closed the file, walked round to the local inn. He was introduced to Downstringers. He'd heard wild tales of Frontier hooch. He found they were understatements.

Velvet rose early, at first light. She pushed the truck to the beach. There wasn't much in. A few knobs of coal, not worth the picking up, the odd bit of wood. She collected them anyway, trudged on.

The path descended to the sea. Pushing the truck was hard; but she persevered, rattling over the shingle. She passed under the Strings of the first big Station, glowering at them. She found the path again.

The way curved left. There was a little inlet. She'd always thought of it as her private bay. This time she found some bottles though, strewn about on the grass. So other people knew about it as well. She was disappointed. She retrieved the rubbish anyway, put it in the truck. It would be worth a few coppers from Master Lorning.

She looked back. The town was out of sight of course, the Station hidden by a rise of ground. She edged the truck to the water. The sea-kale grew here in profusion; Master Lorning wouldn't buy it, but the "Anchor" usually gave her a good price. She collected a dozen bunches; then she sat on the beach and brooded. "Reckons I stink," she muttered. "More or less said as much. Cheek. . . ."

She looked back again. The Codys were still close; but both were well out over the sea, and rising. She hoped the Observers would have more important things to look at. She took her top off, pulled her skirt undone. The various petticoats fell one after the next. Finally she tugged at the hatpin. She half withdrew it, then set her lip. She pushed it back firmly. You had to keep some sort of decency.

She walked into the water, waded a long way. When she stopped the sea was only to her thighs. She looked down. She didn't really like herself all that much. Her breasts were coming, but they weren't like Kerosina's; she imagined they were floppy already. Also her fur was growing, downy and fine. She didn't like that either, she'd be like one of the Biguns before you knew where you were. But there didn't seem to be anything to do.

She sat down. It brought the water nearly to her shoulders. It was even colder than she'd thought. She began to rub herself desultorily. She'd never seen much point in it. If you carried on long enough you only got sore. Later though she piddled contentedly.

A long weed worked itself between her legs. Round, like dark brown grass. She was frightened for a moment, she thought it was a worm. She pulled it by the roots. It floated away.

She splashed back to the beach, used one of the petticoats to dry herself. She looked at the rest and shrugged. If she was dirty she supposed her clothes were dirty too. She didn't know what to do about that though, the problem was far too complex. She dressed, and wriggled. She wondered if she felt cleaner. She decided she did, a bit.

She headed into town. There was a hubbub on the quay. A fishing boat was in, from Mattingale; the Vars were clearing the catch. She liberated three baskets from a warehouse loading bay. She swaggered back with them, pushed into the crowd. She'd found if she swung her hips, people didn't argue with her.

She'd taken a handful of money. She disliked actually parting with it, but sometimes there was no choice. She piled the baskets on to the truck and wobbled away. The load was a bit top-heavy, but she knew she could manage. After all she'd done it often enough before. She wheeled the truck to the High Street, pushed it onto the waste ground the other side of the arch. She stopped where a stand of bushes hid her from public gaze. She scratched her head and considered. There was a new fishmonger, a Master Finling. She was sure he'd be pleased to buy the local produce; after all he probably hadn't made good contacts yet.

She fetched the cherry basket. She lined it with paper, emptied two of the creels. Big square stones were lying about; she wondered if they'd once fallen off the arch. She weighted the baskets, redisposed part of the catch. She stumped up the High, turned down toward the Transon.

Master Finling was suspicious. Unnecessarily so she thought. She was quite hurt. He insisted on tipping the contents of the first creel out, examining them in person. The price he offered wasn't good; but she supposed she could have done worse. She staggered in with the others, dumped them gratefully round the back.

He called as she was hurrying from the shop. " 'Ere. What about the baskets?"

"It's all right," she said. "I'll pick 'em up later. Ta. . . ." She wheeled the truck hastily away.

As soon as she woke next morning she knew she wasn't well. She felt dull, and had the beginnings of a headache. She lay awhile watching the sky brighten through the one pointed window. She'd have liked to stay where she was. It was no use though, the day was wasting. She sat up, and there was an instant twinge. She felt her behind, and groaned. "Oh, no," she muttered. "No" again. . . . Another boil was coming, she'd had some terrible ones lately. Lasted for weeks sometimes. So that was what came of hygiene. Limping up to Master Billings' forge, she glared at the Codys. "If you was any good," she said bitterly, "these sort o' things wouldn't 'appen. . . ."

It was worse next day, worse than ever the day after. On the fourth morning she didn't think she'd be able to walk. She had to though, there was a contract to fulfil. The Kiteman needed cherries.

On the way back from F5, his fuel pump failed again. Terminally, or so it seemed. He banged and sputtered three or four miles; finally he coasted into a village. Pleasant-looking place, stone-built and set with trees. Ducks floated on a railed-off pond; beyond, the Vars and the Middle Doctrine opposed each other across a cobbled square.

He fiddled with the pump, but it seemed beyond his skill. It clacked desultorily a few times, packed up once more. He stood back, scratched his head.

A cottage door opened. A red-haired man came out. He said, "Do you have trouble? Can I help at all?" So they weren't all surly, in the Easthold.

Rand explained the problem briefly, and the other smiled. He pointed. "Can you make it across to Aro?" he said. "He'll sort you out."

"Suppose so," he said. "Thanks a lot." The engine sputtered, and caught.

The garage reminded him of Master Bone's; a dark, junk-piled cave, smelling richly of oil. Old cars stood about and farm equipment, even one of the obsolete steam tractors. The man who met him was short and bandy-legged; brilliant-eyed, and with a great aquiline nose. Rand began to tell him what was wrong, but the other waved his arms. *"Nah,"* he said hoarsely. *"Nah. . . ."* He ran out to the Buckley, raised the bonnet. He checked the ignition, went straight to the fuel pump. *"Dia-phra,"* he said. *"Dia-phra. . . ."* He fitted a new diaphragm, quickly. The engine started at a touch. He laid fingers to the bonnet, tested the vibration and smiled. *"A-ri,"* he said.

Rand took his wallet from his pocket. He said, "Thanks a lot. How much?" But the other shook his head. *"Ki,"* he said. *"Ki. . . ."* He patted the symbol on Rand's shoulder, steepled his hands. He pointed to where, distantly, a Cody string was flying. He said again, *"A-ri. . . ."*

Rand drove away. It seemed responsibilities were loaded on to him. Whether he wished it or no.

It was lunchtime before he reached the digs. Mistress Goldstar met him. "That young gel come round," she said. "Twice, already. Got some stuff for you. Wouldn't leave it though."

He said, "Stuff?" He was vague; then he remembered the cherries. "That'll be all right," he said. "I'll sort it out." He wondered why he'd asked her to bring them. He wasn't even particularly fond of them. He decided it had probably been to help her out.

She was back at fourteen hundred. He took the basket from her. "They're the Whites," she said. "Don't look so good; but they eats better."

It seemed she had trouble with the stairs. Couldn't walk too well. He said, "Velvet, what's the matter?"

Unexpectedly, she started to cry. He held her. Had a bit of bother with her hat brim. "It's all right," he said. "Velvet, what is it?" He rubbed her back. Later he patted her bottom. She shrieked.

He moved faster than she'd have thought possible. He whipped her clouts up. The lot. She stood for a moment paralysed with shock. He stared; then he said, "Right. Come on."

She started to squall at once. It was no use though, he'd already got her wrist. He put her in the van. She had to sit sideways a bit.

They drove up the High Street. He stopped outside the Tower. She started to yell again. "No," she said. "Not there. . . ."

"Shut up," he said. "Shut up. . . ." He hauled her inside, by main force. There wasn't a Base Medic; but they had first call on one of the local doctors. Rand summoned him, in no uncertain terms.

Once through the doorway she fell curiously quiet. Compliant almost. Till the doc appeared. She started to kick up a fuss again then; but he took her hand. "It's all right," he said. "Don't worry, I'll come with you. . . ."

She lay face down, whimpering. Though whether with fright or shame he couldn't say. The doctor boiled a kettle on a little hob. He filled a wineglass, tipped it away and filled again. He said, "I thought you'd lance it," but the other shook his head. "Cause her less trouble afterwards," he said. "Old-fashioned, but effective."

He watched, with a species of fascinated horror. He'd never seen cupping before. The first application didn't work.

The doctor frowned, boiled the kettle again. He took the steaming glass, pressed it to the girl's behind.

There was a pop. Velvet shrieked. The doctor held the glass up. "Look at that," he said. "Drop of the best. We got the core as well." He pointed to something that looked like parcel string.

Rand turned away and swallowed. He was feeling very sick.

The other busied himself with dressings. Once he looked up, keenly. He said, "I didn't know she was Kites."

He hesitated. He said. "They owed her this."

"Hmmph," said the doctor. He pulled the grubby skirt down. "There you are, young lady," he said. "Feels better already, doesn't it?" Velvet didn't answer.

He shook his head. Stood up, and washed his hands. "For God's sake get her cleaned up," he said. "She gets an infection in that sore, I wouldn't like to answer. Get some proper food into her as well. Ninety per cent of this is malnutrition." He packed his bag, and left.

Raoul was hovering. "Take her up to the house," he said. "Rye will look after her."

Rand shook her shoulder. "Come on," he said. "You're all right now." She gave him a smouldering glance.

Rye clucked when she saw her. She said, "Poor love." She bore her away. He sat and drank a glass of wine. He expected ructions; but in the event none came. He thought how peaceful life had suddenly become.

Velvet did demur at first. She said, "I can't get in that. I got a dressin' on." But the dark woman merely smiled. She said, "Then I can change it for you later."

She gave up, climbed into the bath. She stuck her lip out; but in fact she thoroughly enjoyed the process. She'd never bathed in warm water before. She lay back, luxuriated. Later the other even washed her hair. The stuff she used felt soft. Quite different from washing in the sea.

She got upset when she couldn't have her clothes. Rye just smiled though. "Tough luck," she said. "They're in the copper, boiling." She held out a sort of little gown. She said, "You can wear this."

Velvet recoiled. She said, "I can't go inter town in *that,*" and Rye smiled again. "You're not going to," she said.

"You're staying here tonight. You can have your things back in the morning. Don't worry, Rand's staying too."

Raoul turned up at eighteen-thirty hours. They ate a meal. It was somewhat punctuated. The shampoo had discovered a wavy, dark red mane; and Velvet was inordinately proud. She ran to Rand several times, flung her arms round his neck. Finally she whispered, "Sorry. . . ."

"Velvet," he hissed. "Sit down. Or I am going to get extremely cross." She only chuckled though. She knew he didn't mean it.

It seemed Raoul read his mind. They escaped to the local pub. The other set the beers up, sat awhile in silence. Finally he said, "You do make problems for yourself, don't you?"

He said, "Perhaps." He glanced up. He said, "What's with the pony tails?"

The other grinned, and flicked at his hair. "Reminds Rye of her misspent youth," he said. "Little word of warning for you; never marry a fruity woman."

Rand said, "It seems to have suited you." He considered, staring at his glass. He said, "It's funny."

"What?"

"Problems," he said. "Responsibilities." He considered. "The car broke down, on the way back from F5," he said. "A deaf-mute fixed it for me. He wouldn't charge. Because we fly the Kites." He smiled, ruefully. "Least, you fly the kites," he said. "I just make myself a nuisance round the edges." He paused again. "I sometimes wonder if we're doing any good," he said. "The whole pack of us." He took a swig of beer. "They were all Grounded when I came across," he said. "We had a Zero, right across the Realm. You're still here though. So am I."

Raoul looked at him. "I tried to duck out once," he said. "It didn't work. That's why I'm doing what I'm doing." He paused. "You can only do what you're given," he said. "And do your best."

"Yes," he said. "Even though you're being taken for a sucker."

The noncom glanced up again. He said, "She isn't taking you for a sucker."

Rand said, "I wasn't talking about her."

He replenished the beers. Raoul produced a stubby pipe. He said, "How'd you go on F4?"

"So-so. F5 was worse."

The Kiteman rubbed his lip. "Yes," he said. "Poor old Silverton. Lost his wife a couple of years ago. Been trying to lose himself ever since."

He said, "I didn't know," and the other shook his head. "No," he said. "I don't expect you did."

"Raoul," he said, "it seems to be a night for getting drunk."

They did no such thing of course. They had another and then headed back. Velvet had gone to bed. Or been put there, firmly. He looked in on her. She was asleep, cuddling a big woolly toy. It had been lent to her by one of the kids. He stared for a moment. "So that's a whoremistress," he said. "Just as well they told me." He closed the door quietly, and walked away.

She was chirpy, on the drive back into town. "I wants some cards," she said.

"What sort of cards?"

"Cards. You know. Like the one you showed me."

He glanced sidelong. "What good would that be?" he said. "You can't even read 'em."

She looked indignant. "I could learn," she said. "Anyway, don't matter if I can't. Other people can."

He said, "I'll think about it." He dropped her by the arch. He said, "Will you be all right?"

" 'Course," she said. "Ta-ta. . . ."

She decided just for once it wasn't a working day. She took a stroll round town instead. Paused on the quay, and watched the mudlarks playing. She leaned on the parasol, and stuck her backside out. Rik gave her a bit of cheek; she lipped him back, and he ran for the harbour steps. She wagged the parasol, and he thought better of it. She walked back to the High, head in the air. From time to time she couldn't help sniffing her dress. Because it smelled so good.

Rand made his first tour of the Salient. Bases G4 through 7. He found a strange, green land. Humpy and hillocky in parts; yet even the hills looked wrong. As if the Lord had not created them, they were the work of lower hands. He remembered his theology. This too was where the Demons fought. Once, in the long-ago. The grass had spread, vivid and persistent; yet here and there vast patches were still bald. He shook his head. Was it true then, after all? What the Master Sprinling had said? Was this where they had voided their dirt?

He reached the Frontier, finally. Stood and gripped the wire, saw the great fence stretching into distance. He turned to the Launchmaster at his side. He said, "I can't believe there's people still out there."

The other shrugged. "Probably not," he said. "Haven't been seen for years. They weren't people anyway."

He looked at the older man curiously. "You ever see one?"

The Kiteman nodded. "Years ago," he said. "Just the once. Wouldn't want to again." He held his arm out, thumb and finger circled. Made a little tent-shape above his head. He said, "All dead and gone by now. The good Lord willing."

Rand stared at the Codys rising to either side. String after String, each at the same perfect angle. Reaching into distance, like the fence. A line from the Exorcism came to him. *"Go back. Go back into the night. Into the Blue Shining. . . ."* He said, "I don't think it was their fault."

The Launchmaster shook his head. "Nobody said it was. . . ."

He drove on to Easthope. Unusually for the Salient, it was a pleasant, bustling little town. Most of the rest were mounded, humped and sullen; eyeless to the east, in case the Bad Winds blew. In Easthope though were shops, lines and arcades of them; more, he thought, than he'd seen since Middlemarch. He sauntered past them, smiling. He'd always been bad at shopping, or so it had been alleged; but that had been when he was a tiny child. He saw what he wanted, finally; a black straw boater, trimmed with velvet roses. He went in. Once again the Kite tags on his shoulders worked their charm; the assistants were more than helpful. How old was his little girl? How tall was she? They conferred busily, finally fixed on a size. If it wasn't right of course it could be changed. They packed it for him, in a smart round box. It even had a knot of ribbons on the top. He paid them, and walked out. It had been too complex to explain; and so he hadn't tried. But the assumption they'd made stayed with him. She'd never had a father of her own; by the same token, he'd never had a daughter.

He finished at G7; wrote the last of his reports, and packed his bags. He headed back to Fishgard. The town had seemed strange at first; now there was almost a feeling of coming home.

Master Finling was incensed. After all, he was an honest trader. Like his father, and his father before him. And he'd been cheated. By this . . . whatever she was. Urchin certainly, foundling; and worse, if the tales were true. He'd been on the lookout for her for days; but she'd always given him the slip. Now though she couldn't escape. He shook her by the wrist, holding her arm high in case she tried to bite. "Wot about them fish then?" he said. "Wot about them fish?"

Velvet howled, trying ineffectually to wriggle free. "I can't 'elp it," she said. "So they picks up bits o' grit. It ain't my fault."

"Bits o' grit," he said. "You're a bit o' grit." He hit her across the face, raised his arm again.

His wrist was caught. He looked round, startled. The stranger was tall, well-built. Black, curly hair, a handsome, strong-boned face. But he thought he'd never seen a pair of colder eyes. He hadn't registered the squeal of brakes; he registered it now. He saw the shoulder tags. The other said, "What seems to be the trouble, Master?"

He embarked on an explanation; but the Kiteman cut him short. He said, "What does she owe?"

He estimated, rapidly; but again the other didn't let him finish. He flung a wad of notes on to the path. He said, "I think that should cover."

The passers-by had hesitated; now, being Fishgarders, they streamed past unconcerned. Finling retrieved the money, cautiously. "I'm sorry, sir," he said. "I didn't know. Didn't know she was under the Kites."

"We're all under the Kites," said the stranger. "Don't forget again. Now, go and run your shop."

The fishmonger made his escape. Later, when he checked the money, he whistled. Triple the value, at least; it had been a profitable transaction. And he'd still got the baskets.

Velvet was clinging to him. Rand put her into the Buckley, drove down to the march. She only spoke once. "Bin chasin' me all over," she said. "Lucky you come by." She rubbed her face, resentfully. "Belted my ear 'ole," she said. "Nasty ol' git. . . ."

He glanced sidelong. "If it had been me," he said, "I'd

have taken a strap to you." He pulled the Buckley into the kerb, and set the brake. He said, "Are you all right?"

"Yeah, fine," she said. She hesitated. Then she nodded. "Want ter come in?"

"Ah," he said. "The *maison* Velvet. At last." He considered in turn. "You don't deserve it," he said, "you naughty little girl. But all right. Just for a minute."

She tramped up the steps, flung the door wide. The last month had seen a transformation; though of course he wouldn't realize that, not having been before. She'd scrubbed through, with salt and vinegar; later she scurried all the junk into what cupboards she owned. She'd even acquired herself a bowl of flowers; though Mistress Gellern's garden wouldn't look the same for days. He still sucked his breath though, stood staring round amazed. "What's the matter?" she said. "Don' you like it?" She felt a bit disappointed.

"Of course," he said. "It's fine." But he didn't sound convinced.

She scotched on the bed, crossed her ankles under her dress. She tucked it round her toes. She'd noticed she'd got tidemarks again. This cleanliness could get to you, after a bit.

He was looking past her. She gasped. It was too late though, he'd already seen the valise. She should have put it away. He said, "Where did you get that?"

She avoided his eyes. "I seen you throw it in the sea," she said. "Sorry. . . ." She held it out to him, but he shook his head. "It's yours now," he said. "You found it."

She hesitated. "Who is it?" she said. "She's pretty."

He said, "Someone I used to know."

She fingered the brass catch. It had gone all green now; but that was the salt of course. She said, "She looks nice."

"Yes," he said. "I used to think she was."

She sensed danger. She laid the case aside, quickly. For a moment she couldn't think of what to say. It was all right though, he changed the subject for her. He nodded to the windowsill. He said, "What's that?"

"What's what? she said. "Oh, 'im." She picked the creature up. "That's Bruno," she said. " 'E's got twelve legs. Well, more or less." She hugged him. "Don't know why I calls 'im that," she said. "Just seems ter suit."

He said, "It's a bit of driftwood," but she shook her head. "No it's not," she said. "It's Bruno."

"Velvet," he said, "you are the most extraordinary girl."

She pouted slightly. She couldn't decide whether it was a compliment or not. "Where you bin?" she said. "You bin away fer ages."

"Oh," he said, "here and there." He settled back, took out a pipe and lucifers. "So what have you been doing?" he said. "Apart from cheating fishmongers?"

"Earnin' me keep," she said. She put Bruno back on the window ledge, haughtily. Sat back on the bed, and covered her feet again. She decided it was time for a bit of an attack. "More than you do," she said. "Least, that's what Master Lornin' reckons."

He nodded. "I know how he earns his," he said. "He's still probably right though." He shifted his position. He said, "Do you remember your parents, Velvet?"

Her face set at once. "A bit," she said. "I was only a kid though." She nodded at the window. "They took my Dad," she said. "The Kites. . . ."

He shook his head, gently. "They didn't take him," he said. "They don't take anybody. He gave himself to them. That's a bit different."

She brooded. Then she brightened. "I seen a Dragonfly today," she said.

"A what?"

"Dragonfly," she said. "They're always goin' about. Least, that's what people call 'em."

His attention was wholly engaged. He'd heard the stories before of course, most folk had; but he'd never talked about them. "What do they look like?" he said.

"Big," she said. "They only comes over the sea though. Big silver wings," she said. "You can see 'em miles an' miles."

He considered. It didn't make sense. Big silver animals, that used the sky. He said, "Velvet, are you pulling my leg?"

"No," she said. "Why should I?"

"Are they Kites?"

"No," she said. "They're not Kites."

"You say they don't come close."

"No," she said. "Well, not usually."

"Have you seen one close?"

"Once," she said. "Long time ago, that was."

"Do they make a noise?"

"Sometimes," she said. "It depends."

"What sort of noise?"

She shrugged. "Just a noise," she said. "Noises is noises." She was looking wary again.

"What do you think they are?"

"Dragonflies," she said. She pointed, over his shoulder. "Would you like some beer? I got a bottle or two."

There was a curtained alcove. He pushed the drape aside, looked at the head-high stack of crates. "Velvet," he said, "you haven't got a bottle or two. You've got a brewery."

He was quite whistled by the time he left. He ran down to the van, and groaned. He'd seen the hat box. He hurried back. He thought she looked startled when she opened the door. "Sorry, I forgot," he said. "Little pressie for you. Hope it'll be all right."

She crowed. Sat on the bed and stared at it, turned it in her hands. Finally the strain became too much. He said, "Well, try it on." It fitted.

She ran the big pin through it. "I'm goin' out," she said.

"That's all right," he said. "I shan't hold you up."

After he'd gone she looked up at the Codys. They didn't seem quite so menacing now. After all, a Kiteman had bought her a hat. Nobody had ever bought her a hat before.

There was a letter waiting, at the digs. He turned it over, curiously. It was faintly scented. Astringent, but haunting. The stationery was good too. He slit the flap. He was bidden forth to dinner that evening, at the home of the Mistress Kerosina.

He drove up in the Buckley. He'd seen the Ridge of course, but never visited any of the properties. The house he finally reached was spectacular. He scrunched up the drive, sat a moment and stared. At the great south-facing mullions, the battlemented eaves. Kitemasts were rigged on both wings. The western Trace was streaming. The symbols were unusually explicit; The Tower Master had enjoyed himself; or maybe his Apprentice.

Mistress Kerosina met him personally. He was surprised at that. Though the notion of surprise soon left him. He half glanced at the drive. Realized he should have left the Buckley round the back. It seemed she read his mind. With alarming accuracy too. "That's quite all right," she said. "You're not a tradesman. You're from the Kites."

She led the way into an elegant sitting room. She gave him a perfumed drink, in a tall slim glass. A transparent dragon snarled, clutching the stem. It was climbing from an egg.

On the side table was a bowl of sweets. Rose petals, coated in some way with sugar. She took one, ate it slowly. She said, "I always like to meet new people in the town."

He looked at her. Decided he'd never seen a such a startling woman. Huge tilted eyes, no colour he could define; a mane of hair; long legs, very much in evidence now. "Catlike" was a phrase he'd heard applied; he realized it occasionally had relevance. He stared carefully through the window. He said, "Is the Master Kerosin at home?"

She took another sweet, and shook her head. She said, "He very seldom is." She glanced round her. "All done on tractor fuel," she said. "Amazing isn't it?"

He set the glass down. He said, "Do you have the Kitefaith?" and she shrugged. He wished at once she hadn't. She said, "It comforts the servants."

A gong called them to dinner. He was the only guest. As he'd expected, the meal was superb. He'd thought it might be served by naked children. It wasn't though. Perhaps she kept them round the back.

She called for liqueurs, smoked a long cheroot. He was having trouble with her nipples. Either one was showing, or the other; sometimes both at once. She said, "I believe you know my little helpmate."

He brought himself back from distance. "Velvet," he said. "I think she's rather sweet." He knew why he was there of course. But then, he'd known before he arrived. For all its vagaries, Fishgard was a small town.

It seemed the remark amused her. "She's invaluable," she said. "I couldn't do without her."

He set the glass down. He said, "A lady needs her servants."

Her eyes burned at him. Those incredible eyes. She said, "Don't give me fucking shit." She stubbed the cigar. She said, "Will you walk me? In the garden?"

He complied. His mind was curiously busy. He was remembering the small girl's tale. About the Dragonflies. He supposed he should report it. After all, things that lived in the air were the province of the Corps. But it had been reported often enough before. He frowned. He'd have to have a word with Raoul sometime.

She was clinging to his arm. She said, "You weren't there for a minute, were you? You were miles away."

He looked down. "Lady," he said. "Adjust your dress."

"I'm not a lady," she said. "The whole town knows what I am. You know."

"Lady," he said. "Adjust your dress."

She looked up at him wonderingly. She said, "You mean it, don't you?"

"Yes," he said. "I do."

She brushed at her cheek with a knuckle. "I'm a funny old soul," she said. "Things get to me sometimes. I'm sorry."

He set his lips. He'd expected the whoring; he hadn't expected this. He thought, *So it begins again.*

There were strange trees in the orchard. Medlars. He hadn't seen them since he was small. She snatched fruit from them. "You eat them when they're rotten," she said. "I like things when they're rotten. But some I prefer fresh."

There was a little summerhouse. She sat and stared at him. She pushed the dress down to her hips. Then to her thighs. She said, "It's adjusted now. Do you like it better?"

He didn't answer; and she took one of the medlars, squeezed. He watched the liquid trickle to her fur. She lay back. She said, "Do you like fruit juice?"

Velvet was picking pears. It being the season. She fell out of the tree. She used a very rude word, on the way down to earth. She sat up rubbing her behind. She'd turned her ankle as well. But the windows of the house stayed blind.

She got up, still swearing faintly. Grafted on to the wrong stock, those trees were. You'd need a Cody basket to get to the top. She wondered how the Gellerns coped. Maybe they didn't bother though. Like the cherries.

She walked round to the Kiteman's digs. Mistress Goldstar met her. "He ain't up," she said; but she'd already ducked under her arm. "Rand," she said, "it's me. Got a pressie for yer. . . ."

He was lying face-down in the bed. "Rand," she said, "it's me. Rand. . . ." She shook his shoulders, and he opened one eye blearily. "There's some money on the mantel,'' he said tiredly. ''For God's sake go away, Velvet. Come back later on. . . .''

She limped for the stairs. ''Cuntstruck,'' she said sagely. ''Bin goin' on fer weeks. Still, it was bound to 'appen. But then,'' she soliloquized, '' 'e wouldn't want me. Short legs,'' she whispered.

Mistress Goldstar caught her in the hall. '' 'Ow is 'e?'' she said. ''I gets worried about 'im. Goin' up the 'ill all the while. 'E ain't eatin' proper neither. . . .''

Velvet repeated her diagnosis, with some vigour. Mistress Goldstar picked up a broom. She fled, as fast as her injured ankle would allow. Later she put the truck away. She locked the little iron-barred door with pride. Master Billings had given her the lock. It was very fine, and made of brass. Nobody would get in there.

They walked in the garden again, the last fine day of the year. She'd put a leather collar on, and given him the lead. ''Snatch it if I misbehave,'' she said. ''I like being made to mind.''

He sat in the summerhouse with her. He said, ''What's the Master Kerosin like?''

She looked at him. ''He pays the bills,'' she said. ''It's what he's there for.''

''And doesn't he care?''

''Care about what?''

''Me,'' he said. ''And all the rest.''

''There aren't any rest,'' she said. ''I've rather gone for you.''

He smiled. He said, ''Can you hear the clock?''

''What clock?''

''The big one, in the house.''

''Of course not,'' she said. ''Not from here.''

''It's a machine,'' he said. ''It measures the seconds, and the minutes. Then the days, and years.''

She considered. She said, ''You think I'm a machine as well.''

''No,'' he said. ''I didn't say that.''

She brooded. ''I ought to throw you out of course,'' she said. ''I shan't. But you knew that anyway.''

He said, ''Perhaps.''

She got up, suddenly. She said, ''Let's go to bed.''

He glanced at the sky. He said, ''It's early yet.''

She said, "The earlier the better." Later she lay face-down, and talked to him. She said, "You're a strange man, Rand."

"How do you mean?"

"I don't know," she said. "Just strange."

He said, "Most people are strange."

She shook her head. He saw it in the half-light. It was still barely dark. She said, "Most people are very ordinary. The more you know them, the more ordinary they get." She pushed herself up on her elbows. "Don't fall in love with me," she said. "If you do, I shall destroy you."

"You're destroying yourself," he said. "You might take one or two with you."

"But you won't be among them?"

"No," he said. "I don't aim to be anyway."

She traced a little pattern on the pillow. She said, "You were badly hurt once, weren't you?"

He said, "Perhaps."

She traced the pattern again. She said, "Maybe she had her reasons. Most of us do."

He said, "I expect she had."

She half rolled over. "I ought to let you have me when I'm dry," she said. "You'd get more feeling from it."

"But you never are."

"That's your fault," she said. "You can't blame me for that."

He said, "I don't blame you for anything." He looked up at the sky. He said, "It's the most important thing."

"What is?"

"The thing between your legs."

"That's not very nice."

"Yes" he said. "It's proper, for a Lady."

"I'm not a Lady," she said. "I told you once before. Don't call me that."

"There are many sorts of Lady," he said. "You're the best."

She said, "An animal."

He nuzzled at her. "Yes," he said. "That's right."

Unexpectedly, she started to cry. He kissed her till the tears stopped. He said, "You're not being fair of course."

She rolled on to her back, lay looking up. She said, "What's fair?"

He said, "Very little."

She was quiet awhile. Finally she said, "I suppose it comes from the Kites."

"What comes from the Kites?"

"It changes your attitude," she said. "I could never really understand it."

"I don't fly the Kites."

"You fly them all the while," she said. "Every day the good Lord sends."

He considered. He said, "Do you have a family?"

She lay quite still. "What do you think?" she said.

"I don't know. That was why I asked."

"Three," she said finally. "Why do you think I'm slack?"

"Where are they?"

She said, "A long way from here." She brooded again. She said, "Even unto the seventh generation."

"What?"

She turned, impatiently. "We've married, in and out. To keep the money in the Clan. The stock weakens, eventually." She rubbed him. "I wouldn't want a great big thing like that," she said. "Flopping about between my legs. It would feel untidy."

He said, "You're just jealous."

She said, "A lot of us are. I've read about it." She dragged him on to her, dug her nails into his back. "Quick," she said. "I can't wait any longer. . . ." Later, when he pulled away, she gasped. He said, "I'm sorry. Did I hurt you?" and she laughed. She said, "You are a silly boy."

He went to G8. He'd heard some curious stories about the Station. He found it much the same as any other. Two hangars, with a standby; normal for the Salient. The Kites were streamed in good order, and the books were neat. He thought a lot about the Lady Kerosina. However they appeared, there was a human being underneath. Or was there? He remembered Janni, and instantly closed his mind. There was no Janni, he'd told himself that before.

He walked to the Perimeter. The Base Captain was with him. He stared at the Badlands. They were blueish even in daylight. He turned to him. He said, "Was there a Captain Manning here once?"

The other's face changed instantly. He said, "Are the books in order, Kiteservant?"

"Of course," he said. Later he said, "I'm sorry, sir."

The other shrugged. He said, "It doesn't matter. Get your rumours from somewhere else though. If you please."

They were walking back across the Base. Under the high strings of the Codys. He shivered. The winter winds were striking early. He said, "Are there any people still out there?"

"Out where?"

"Beyond the Frontier."

The other glanced at him. "There was one a year ago," he said. He held his hands a little apart. "It was about that long."

"What did it do?"

"Crawled under the wire," said the Kiteman.

"What did you do with it?"

"Nothing," said the other. "Stood and watched it die. Then we buried it." He pointed. He said, "It's just over there."

Rand shook his head. Somehow there seemed to be a relationship with Velvet and the Mistress Kerosina. But for the life of him he couldn't decide what it was.

He found out what an Easthold winter was like. It was grey, and howling. Waves smashed over the sea walls; a mile or more from land, the water boiled like yeast. The town closed in on itself, barricaded its windows and doors. He fixed the shutters for the Mistress Goldstar personally. She heaved a sigh of relief when he had finished. "My 'usband used ter do it," she said. "I can still manage; but I ain't so young ner more." She touched his arm. "You're good to me, sir," she said.

He was surprised. He said, "But anybody would have done that for you."

She shook her head. "No, sir," she said. "Not necessarily. . . ."

Kites were lost of course, and their Observers. Replacements were rushed from Middlemarch. Men, and *matériel*. Because Demons love the storms. The skies glowed, over Easthold and the Salient. Flier after Flier discharged his flares, into the wild night. He found the sight oddly moving. *"We're here,"* they seemed to be saying. *"We're ready, and we're waiting. . . ."* No Demons came.

The Master Kerosin returned to Fishgard. Which meant a month without his Lady's company. To his surprise, he found he missed her. He set himself to analyse the feeling. You could buy what she was offering, in any pub in town. Yet he felt no inclination. It was her, he decided finally. She herself. Something inside her, burning like silver fire. Something he had accessed. He shook his head. The trap was honeyed, obvious; yet also it was multilevelled.

She wrote a letter to him. *"It's boring without you,"* she said. *"I went for a walk yesterday. I kissed a sheep. It was only because he looked fed up as well. We were both soaking wet.*

"I asked the Master Kerosin to kiss my navel. He was quite disgusted. Yet you kiss me everywhere.

"I'd like you to fuck me again. I like to feel it squirt up in my tummy. Women aren't supposed to say things like that. I do though. Did she say them as well? The other one? I think I love you.

"Did I tell you my husband was bald? It's supposed to make men sexier. It doesn't seem to work with him though. But since he's given me three children I suppose he thinks he's done his duty. . . .

"You know the sort of things I really like. You're different though. I keep trying to tell you, but you never listen. I'll let you know when it's all right to come back. You probably won't want to though. I'm an old lady now; I've got a big fat bottom.

"Did I tell you Thoma plays the sitar? It's a great help to him, it stops him getting involved. He was playing it when my third was due: I was bleeding quite a lot, but he stayed upstairs. But after all he is an artist. He's very sensitive. . . ."

He put the letter down. He thought, *One day, I shall probably kill somebody. . . ."*

The Master Lorning's trade was definitely seasonal. From the solstice celebrations onwards, he progressively laid off his staff. They complained, with varying degrees of bitterness. But Velvet merely shrugged. "It always 'appens," she said. "Bound to, ennit? Stands ter reason. . . ."

There was a village a mile or two out on the Easthope road. She waited for the weather to set in hard and took the truck. There was a pond there where the ice got really thick. And

Kerosina had an ice house. There was a pond in Fishgard, but it was nowhere near as good. The ice from it was full of little worms; they woke up in the summer, started wriggling. All right for the Gellerns maybe; but not for the Ridge. Besides, she wouldn't cheat the Mistress. It wouldn't be fair; apart from that, she'd lose her best source of trade.

She heard the honking quite a long way back. She steered into the side of the road and scowled. Always somebody shoving people about. She turned, saw it was the Buckley. It pulled up beside her. The Kiteman slid the window back. He said, "Want a lift, young lady?"

"Can't," she said. "I got the truck."

He said, "And I've got an empty van." He got out, opened the back doors. It wasn't empty really. There was a stack of little Kitesails to one side; he was bringing them back to the Tower for mending. There was plenty of room for the truck though. He swung it on board. It didn't seem to cause him any effort. She realized he was much stronger than she'd thought. He lashed it into place. Kitemen were a bit like sailors; they knew all sorts of funny knots. He said, "Where are you taking it?"

Velvet said, "The Mistress Kerosina." She wished at once she hadn't told him. He didn't seem to mind though. He said, "Good. I can drop you then. I'm going past."

She glanced at him sidelong. "Better not," she said. " 'E ain't gone back yet." Her teeth started to chatter.

He looked across at her. He said, "Are you all right?"

She nodded. Rubbed her arms. "Funny, ennit," she said. "You gets in somewhere warmer, then you starts feelin' the cold."

He compressed his lips. "No shoes on," he said. "And that silly hat. . . ."

"It ain't a silly 'at," she said. "You bought it for me."

He shook his head. "Velvet," he said, "you're a summer creature."

She frowned. She wasn't sure she understood. "It ain't the summer," she said.

"No," he said. "It's not the summer." He changed gear for a bend. "I'll drop you at the end of the drive," he said. "Then I'll wait for you."

"Wait for me?" she said. "What for?"

"Shoes," he said succinctly. "And a hat."

"I can't wear shoes," she said. "They pinches."

He said, "Not if they fit your feet."

Fishgard showed ahead. She couldn't believe they were nearly back already. He coasted down a hill. Climbing the last slope to the Ridge, the van began to cough and splutter. She said, "What's the matter with it?"

"Getting old," he said. "Like me."

She glanced at him again. There always seemed to be things she wanted to say to him. But she could never really decide what they were. She didn't expect she'd know the words anyway. Words were difficult. Especially when you hadn't been to school. She expected he'd been to all sorts of schools. You had to, to know about the Kites. She said, "You wants ter buy Master Lornin's car."

He was surprised. He said, "The Falcon? He wouldn't part with that."

"Garn," she said. " 'E 'as to, every winter. Then 'e buys it back when 'e's got a bit o' trade. Be lorst without doin' that."

He looked thoughtful. "What does he ask for it?"

She told him. It sounded astronomical.

"And what does he expect to get?"

That seemed much more reasonable.

"I dunno," he said. "I should have to get somebody to look at it."

"It's all right," she said quickly. "They're a bit 'ard on bearin's. But 'e 'ad 'em done last year. Keep the oil well up, you shouldn't 'ave no bother. External pump," she explained.

He started to laugh. "Velvet," he said, "is there anything you don't know?"

She was surprised in turn. "I don't know 'ardly nothin'," she said. "That's the 'ole trouble."

They weren't shoes really. More sort of boots. Nearly like the Kitemen wore; and lined too, really thick. She hadn't seen a hat like that though. Furry, and with bits that even covered her ears. She walked round town in it, for the sheer pleasure of feeling warm.

Cook had given her a big box of goodies. Honey cakes, all sorts. She took some round to the Kiteman as a thank-you present. She thought he was looking moody; but he brightened when he saw her. She kissed him. She said, "Thanks ever so much." He held on to her. Anybody else and she'd have pushed away; but he was different somehow. She said, "I think I love you."

He smiled. He said, "I know I love you." She did stiffen fractionally at that; and he laughed outright. "Velvet, Velvet," he said. "There's many sorts of love."

She frowned. She didn't know really what he'd thought was funny. She hoped it wasn't her. She supposed it would be fair enough though. After all it wouldn't be the first time she'd been laughed at. "I ain't worth lovin'," she said bitterly. "I ain't no good. I'm a procure—procure—what you called me."

He held her by the shoulders. Looked down and shook his head.

He said, "You procure cherries too. They're always very good." He led her to the window. He said, "Have you seen the new Cody?"

She could just make it out against the dusk. The string of oval plaques below the last of the Lifters. They were twisting gently as it flew. "Yeah," she said. "Ain't seen one like that."

"No," he said. "Neither has anybody else." He opened a book. It was full of coloured symbols. He traced them with his finger. "V, E and L," he said. "V and E again; then a T. It's your string, Velvet; I had it streamed for you."

She knuckled her cheek. She said, "You goin' ter buy that car?"

He shook his head again. "He wouldn't sell to me. He doesn't like the Kites either. And I'm not all that fond of him."

"That's all right," she said. "I'll soften 'im up."

"Velvet," he said. "Velvet. . . ." It was too late though, she'd already dashed for the stairs. Letting herself out, she wiped her face again. She always hated crying in front of people. It made you look a baby.

The Master Lorning wasn't enthusiastic. Quite the reverse in fact. But she happened to know he was unusually strapped for cash. She hinted as much, delicately, but it brought no result. She considered, and leaned forward. She also knew the Mistress Lorning visited her sister this time of the year;

otherwise she wouldn't have dared walk into the "Dolphin" to start with. She murmured a certain suggestion; but he merely looked more irritable. "What's the good o' that?" he said. "I ain't got no PGs."

"I wadn't thinkin' o' the guests," she said. "It was fer you. An' it wouldn't cost."

She saw his eyes change. He said, "Could you fix it up?"

" 'Course," she said airily. "No problem." She only hoped she was right.

She headed up the hill, to the big school on the Ridge. She knew they were back, they'd come back the day before. On the way she glanced up at the Cody string. Too dark to see it properly; but she still felt a little rising of pride. Also the lump was back in her throat. She set her jaw and stumped on.

An orchestra was playing, in the big hall. She peered through a crack in the curtains. Winter and summer, the girls were always in white. She thought how smart they looked. She always fancied she'd have liked to go to a place like that. But you had to have rich folks. To start with of course you had to have folks. She listened to the music. She supposed it was very clever, but there never seemed much tune in it. She waited till they stopped, risked a sharp tap on the glass. The Mistress Hollan looked across at once. She'd been standing at the front, wagging a sort of stick.

She ducked out of sight. The other would know who it was. She waited. In time a side door opened, let out a yellow gleam of light. She hurried over. The Mistress Hollan was blonde, and tall; nearly as tall as Kerosina. Looked a bit like her too. She outlined her requirements, and the other considered. She said, "You'd better come in for a minute. I can't be long though, I'm taking Prep tonight." Velvet followed her down a corridor floored with shiny wooden tiles. It always smelled of lavender.

She laid out cash. A lot of cash. Even more than the hat and shoes. Though not so much, she supposed, as it would cost to fly a Cody. The Mistress considered, tapping her fingers. Finally she nodded. "All right," she said. "Let's make it next weekend."

She said, "Who else shall we use?" and the tall woman's eyes gleamed. "Who else?" she said. "Do you mean we need three?" She pulled her forward. She said, "We'll have to practice first though."

Velvet groaned, and shut her eyes. She nodded, set her teeth; and Miss Hollan lifted her skirt.

The deaf-mute ran his fingers along the car's block. He raised the throttle linkages, tested the vibration again. He concentrated, screwing his face up. He rocked the front wheels, crawled beneath the chassis. There were unidentifiable sounds from the direction of the steering assembly. He sat in, waved for the Kiteman to follow. He checked the movement of the gearstick, drove across the yard. He circled the town, drove as far as the Ridge. He frowned finally, pulled in. He opened the bonnet, made some small adjustment. *"Be—er,"* he said. *"Be—er. How Mu'?"* Rand knew a little of the hand talk. He gestured, and the other nodded. *"A—ri',"* he said. *"A—ri'."* He nodded again, vigorously.

He paid the Master Lorning cash, drove the sleek black motor away.

"Well," said Kerosina. "Gone up in the world, haven't we?" He turned his head. The Falcon was visible, through the tall windows of the bedroom. It gleamed. He'd worked solidly on it the last two days, cutting the layer of road film that had been allowed to collect. "Yes," he said, "I think so." He rolled over, lazily. He said, "I was surprised he sold it to me."

"You shouldn't have been," she said. "I know how it was arranged."

He said curiously, "What do you mean?" But she shook her head. She would say no more.

He fondled her, and kissed. "As a matter of fact I've fallen in love with her. She goes like a bird."

She shook her head, eyes closed. "No," she said. "It's just the ego thing. It's the long bonnet that does it. It reminds you of this." She squeezed him. He stiffened again instantly, and she began to pant. Later she sighed. "I'd love to go with you," she said. "Get in your big black car and drive and drive. And never stop."

Rand shook his head. He said, "I doubt it."

She sighed again, dreamily. "Can't you just imagine," she said. "If I was on my own. Say I was a Kitebase secretary, or that I worked at the school. And you'd just come to town."

He pushed himself up on his elbows. "Yes," he said, "I can. You'd be looking for someone like the Master Kerosin to marry, and someone like me to fill the time in with."

She opened her huge eyes. She said, "You can be so cruel."

"And you," he said, "can be so dishonest." He stared at the pillow. "I live in the real world, Mistress," he said. "Because I have to. Black's black, white's white; and red's red." He saw a tear form, trickle. He brushed it; but she pushed his hand away. She said, "You never loved me, did you? You never loved me at all."

He considered. He said, "That's a very difficult question."

"It isn't," she said. "It's a very easy one. Black's black, and white's white. So the answer's yes or no."

He smiled a little sadly. "Caught," he said. "I asked for that though, didn't I?" He lay down, attempted to pull her to him. She arched her back, pushing at his shoulders. "No," he said. "Don't do that. Don't do that Mistress, please." She relaxed.

He lay quiet. He was thinking about what she'd asked. And the impossibility of making a true answer. He was wondering why he'd gone to her in the first place. After all, her household was notorious; a byword, even in that town of rumours. Curiosity perhaps, curiosity that turned to lust? Or had it been simple desire for revenge, the need to take from someone else what had been taken from him? That was where the vivid boundaries ceased, the colours began to blur. You couldn't know someone as he had known her and remain disengaged. He knew the scar on her hand, where she'd cut it on glass as a child; he knew two toes of her left foot were crooked, because she'd been stepped on by a horse; he knew the foot hurt sometimes in the wet. He knew her back muscles knotted when she was fatigued, that her neck often gave her pain. He knew she sometimes voided blood. Between periods, and from the wrong outlet. He knew it frightened her. It frightened him as well. She'd ceased to be a puppet, become a human being; when she cried, her tears were as salt as his.

He put his mouth close to her ear. "Listen," he said. "I love you. I love each hair of your head; I love your breasts, I love your tummy, I love your fur. I love what's underneath it. I love your legs, I love your toes, I love your fingers. I love *you*. Is that white enough? Or black?"

She clung to him. "Don't go away," she said. "Stay, just for tonight. It will be all right."

He frowned. He said, "I don't know if I should."

"Please," she said. "Please, Rand."

"What's so special about tonight?"

She said, "I'm frightened."

He stroked her. He said, "What are you frightened of?"

"I don't know," she said. "I think I'm frightened of being afraid."

"It's all right," he said. "Hush there, hush. Shhh. . . ."

The Falcon waited, patient in the drive.

She was cool to him when he visited next. And again the time after. "The boys are coming home," she said. "It's going to get very difficult, Rand."

"No," he said gently. "It's going to get very easy." He took himself off to the G Bases. This was the dripping tap routine; he thought it had come about on cue. He didn't bother to return to Fishgard between calls; there was always somewhere or other he could stay.

The days lengthened. The spring came early and warm. Velvet called again and again at the house of Mistress Goldstar. But the Kiteman was never home. She realized she'd probably never see him again. But then, there was no reason why she should. " 'E's got what 'e wanted," she whispered. " 'E's got 'is car. . . ." She wept a small and private storm. When it was over she washed her face. She took her parasol, headed for the quay. She was summoned forth to the big house on the hill. Rik Dru went with her. When he came back he joined the Biguns' boat.

His duty tour ended, finally. The recall reached him at G12. A month's refresher course in Middlemarch, some leave, and then another posting. He made his formal farewells at the big Base, headed back. The Falcon, as ever, ran well. Soon she'd be on the smooth roads of the Middle Lands. The roads she'd been designed for.

He called at the house of Kerosina. After all they purchased air rights from the Church, it was on his official list of visits. He saw it was shuttered, empty. He met a disgruntled gardener. He said, "Where have they gone?"

The other shrugged. " 'Ow should I know?" he said. "Don't tell the likes o' me. New people comin' in next week. Least, I bin paid till then."

Rand got back in the car and drove away.

The fall of Velvet was brief and parabolic. She was stumping along the quay, parasol as ever at the ready, when her skirt was snagged. She spun round, alarmed. She'd forgotten she was passing the Biguns' headquarters. Rik Dru though had a longer memory; and he was experienced now. He twisted the boathook, and yanked. *"Eeee,"* said Velvet. *"Aaaiiieee. . . ."* There was a splash, and silence.

He packed his things at the digs, said goodbye to Mistress Goldstar. He left her a cash present, and the biggest bunch of flowers he could find. He called in at the Tower, but Raoul was away on leave. He drove down to the arch, and parked the Falcon. He ran up the steps, tapped the door. There was no answer.

He tapped again, waited a moment frowning. He tried the handle. The door was unlocked.

The curtains were drawn, across the single window. He had to wait a moment for his eyes to adjust to the gloom. Then he saw her. She was lying on the bed. A bowl of water was beside her; it was tinged with pink. So was the compress she'd laid across her forehead. He knelt, appalled. "Velvet," he said, "what is it? What's happened?"

She looked at him dully. "Gang-banged," she said faintly. "Thought they would one day. Allus somethin', ain't there?" She dabbled the cloth in the bowl, laid it back. "I don't know," she said vaguely. "I don't know at all. 'Ad a good trip?"

He was holding her, stroking her hair. Then before she realized he'd scooped the bedclothes round her, lifted her. She struggled feebly. "What you doin'?" she said. *"Rand,* what you doin'?"

She thought she'd never seen him look as angry. He said, "I'm leaving. And you're not stopping here."

"I can't," she wailed. "I got me livin' to earn. *Rand,* no. . . ." She jammed her feet violently against the door-frame. She said, "Me 'at. . . ."

"Oh, blow your hat," he said. "I'll buy you another." He

backed anyway, scooped it up somehow and plonked it on her head. He left the door swinging. Master Lorning could shut it at his leisure. He put her in the Falcon, tucked the blankets round. He started up; and she began to squall again. "The truck," she said. "The truck. . . ."

"You don't need the truck."

She said, "But all the money's in it. . . ."

He looked at her. Pulled up beside the arch. He took the key from round her neck, unlocked the little door. He hauled the handcart into the light, pulled up the false bottom. He stared at the inch-thick layer of notes. He said, "You crazy little creature. . . ." He grabbed them up in bundles, stuffed them into the Falcon's boot. He sat back in and wiped her face. He pushed her hair back and kissed her. He swung under the arch, headed up the High. She said feebly, "Where we goin', Rand?"

He glanced across at her, his lips still compressed. "You're a summer person," he said. "We're going to the summer.'

7 kitemariner

HE WALKED INTO town, in the early evening. The housebirds were squealing and trilling, swooping under the high eaves, making their last flights of the day. Nath glanced at them, vaguely. There were many types of housebird; he knew none of them. But then, there was no reason why he should. He was a mariner.

He looked up at the sky. Still clear, but with the faint greenish cast that always seemed to come at the end of summer. He saw clouds were massing, low in the west. A front was coming in; could be a blow by morning.

He headed down the steep, cobbled High Street. It was so steep the cottages and shops were set on little platforms, each stepped below the next. Six courses of bricks on the downhill side, zero at the other. In sight of the harbour, he paused. As ever, perspective made the sea appear to climb a reciprocal slope. He saw the occasional whitecap form, a long way out; precursors of the coming wind. Beyond, the first of the Inshore Units rode at their buoys; *Holdfast*, *Windwrack*, *The Lady Guardian*. He could recognize them by their silhouettes, even at this distance. They'd all be streaming of course; but the Codys weren't detectable in this light. Not even to his keen eyes. A pair of glasses would have brought them in clear enough; but he had brought none with him. He had no need of them.

He turned right, along the quay. *Kitestrength* was still at her moorings; but she wasn't due to slip till twenty-three hundred. He stared at the tall gantry on her bow. The Cadets would be aboard already, checking the Cody strings. The Pilots and the Lifters, the baskets and mancarriers. The priests of course wouldn't board till later; and by tradition the Fliers would come last of all. This time though she'd sail without her Second Engineer.

He saluted her vaguely, but there was no response. Old Toma would be on the bridge by now, probably enjoying the odd sip of the skipper's gin. Or fast asleep already. As a watchman, he was a joke; but he was coming up for retirement, and even the Vars could be generous on occasions. In any case there was little need for high security in the Southguard. Not as yet, anyway. There'd been rumours of unrest in other parts of the Realm; Militia called out in the Salient, and several times up north. There'd even been some nasty reports from Middlemarch. He shrugged. Things like that worried him sometimes; though he'd never essentially thought of himself as a thinking man. The Church held the Realm not by force, but fear. Fear of the grounding of the Codys, a sudden inrush of Demons. But the Codys had been grounded, time and again. And nothing had happened. So if that fear ceased. . . .

He twitched the jacket back round his shoulders. He'd been forced to wear it like that because of the sling. He hadn't really needed it, the evening was still warm; but he'd probably be glad of the dark blue reefer later on. He eased his wrist. His left hand was paining him, under the heavy dressing. But then, he only had himself to thank for that. He grimaced. About the stupidest accident he could think of; and him a Second.

Yesterday morning it had been. Preparing for his shift. He'd clamped the work to the drill bed, securely as he'd thought; checked his centring, brought the big handle down. Like a fool, he'd steadied the job; and the casting had lashed round, carried his hand between the bed and centrepost. He'd wrenched back somehow, stood and stared; then he'd called. "Denzi . . . Denzi. . . ."

The Apprentice had paled. "My God," he said, "What have you done?"

"Been a damned fool," Nath said between his teeth. "Will you get the Mate?" He gripped his wrist and stared; at the white bone showing, the squibbing blood. His third finger was shattered; he thought, "That's gone for certain."

The Mate was there in a flash. He always liked to be first on the scene if there was news. He said, "Don't worry, I'll sort you out." He came back grinning. "There you are," he said. "Drip into that." He slung a filthy bucket down, on the iron-ribbed deck.

Nath's sight had flickered fractionally; and to his surprise, sounds had become dim. When his vision returned they'd wrapped his hand in some sort of dressing. It looked like engineroom rags; but by then he'd lost interest. They put his jacket round his shoulders, took him ashore. He lay on a couch, somewhere in the Kiteport Tower, while a Medic attended to him. He clicked his tongue a bit. "I'll try and save the finger," he said. "But I can't guarantee a thing."

He turned his face away. He was feeling a little ashamed. There was a girl in the room; a nurse, in a long white gown. Only the richer Towers could afford them. "It'll be all right," he said. "Why don't you cut it off?" She approached, and wiped his forehead. "Don't worry, Mariner," she said. "You'll be fine."

He gritted his teeth again. He said, "Just get on with it." After which the clickings and the little scrapes were one. As were the twangs and stabs of pain. They could have been the effects of knives and scissors, could have been the antiseptic they used from time to time. "I don't think the guides are damaged," said the Medic. "We'll try it, Sister." He felt his finger being bound. Later they swathed his hand in a bulky, chalk-white dressing. They called a car for him, and took him home. For which he was privately grateful.

Kari was cold, when she opened the door to him. She said, "What is it this time?" Then she saw the sling, and shook her head. "Ah, the Kitetoll," she said. "Getting quite used to it, aren't we?"

"It wasn't the Kites," he said. "It was something I did myself. In the machine shop."

"What happened?"

"I hurt my finger," he said. "Nobody to blame but me."

She looked at him. She said, "You'd better come and sit down."

He swayed a little. "I think," he said, "I'd better go to bed."

A little wait. Then she said, "Do you need a hand?"

He shook his head. "No, thanks," he said. "I've still got one left."

She brought him a meal, later on. He was half-dozing. He managed part of it, to show willing. Then he slept, with relative soundness. Though when he woke at zero seven hundred his hand was throbbing like the Devil. His arm as well. He wondered if the wrench had been transmitted through the nerves.

He slept again. To his surprise, he was feeling better when he woke next time. He'd expected delayed shock.

The storm broke in the afternoon. As he'd known it would. She said, "How long must this go on?"

"How long must what go on?"

She didn't answer. Just set her lips, wielded a breadknife with unusual vigour. "Better be careful," he said. "You might cut yourself."

She threw the thing down, ran to him. "Nath," she said, "I can't stand it. Not any more."

"Stand what?"

"Not knowing," she said. "Not knowing what's out there." She swallowed. "When you go," she said, "I have to wait and wait. And wonder if you'll come back. . . ."

He said, "I always come back." He pushed her away, with his one good arm. "I'll be all right," he said.

She shook her head. "One day," she said. "One day, you'll go like all the rest. And where shall I be, then?"

"Kari," he said, "I hurt my hand, in harbour. It was a silly thing to do."

She looked up at him. The tearstained eyes, shoulder-length yellow hair. "You hurt your hand in harbour," she said. "The rest will happen later. . . ."

He took her chin. "Kari," he said, "do you remember? In the Northguard?"

She shook her head, confused.

"You married me for what I was," he said. "A Mariner." He pulled her to him. She was wearing bright blue trousers, like a fishergirl. They roused desire in him. The old desire.

He pushed his fingers underneath the waistband, reached to twitch at her belt. She wrenched back. "You'll have to choose," she said. "Between me and the sea."

"Kari," he said, "you are the sea. . . ."

"Not to you," she said. Later though she touched the dressing, gently. She said, "Can I look? I might be able to help. . . ."

"No," he said, "Best leave it alone for now. They knew what they were doing." He gripped her shoulder. "Kari," he said, "it's nothing."

"I'm nothing," she said, bitterly. "I can see that now."

He glanced up. He'd decided years ago the Southguard wasn't like the rest of the Realm. Not even the Middle Lands. There were the Yards of course farther along the quay, the Yards where they built the ocean-going ships; Kitevessels, the occasional small freighter. The other way, out of sight from here, were the pits and foundries. You could smell the stink from them way out at sea. But the westerlies carried the smoke away, so the villas on the ridge of hills weren't troubled. He stared at them; the roofs cluttering the treegrown slopes, as far as the eye could reach. Kites flew from almost every one; but that was understandable. For years now, money had been streaming steadily to the south. Why, he was not so sure. Except that the Middle Lands seemed less secure than they once might have been. He shook his head. He'd seen mobs shouting Middle Doctrine slogans. The last thing, surely, that mild Order would have desired. Or was it? He looked back to the harbour. The sea was calm tonight. But it still concealed a lethal fury.

He decided he was getting depressed. He glanced again at the endless plain of water. He was remembering a night with Kari, the first night ever. They'd sat and stared at the ocean; another ocean, stretching out for ever. "Look at it," she'd said. "What colour would you call it?"

"I don't know," he'd said. "It hasn't got a colour. There's not a word in the Realm, that would describe that."

He touched his wrist again. There was a word, of course. He'd realized, over the years. The sea was red.

They'd lit the lamps, along the front of the "Mermaid". Although it wasn't really dark as yet. He glanced at the pale, high frontage. Lights showed, in several of the rooms; and a sleek black car stood at the kerb. A Falcon. He walked to it. He'd fancied owning one himself, one time; but the chance had never come. They were getting scarcer now; this was well maintained though. He pushed open the big door of the pub, walked in.

The front bar was empty save for one other customer. He was tall and slim-faced; he sported a neatly-trimmed beard, a mass of curly black hair. He was leaning on the bar, studying a thick manual. It was bound in blue, heavy metal rings through the spine. He glanced up, nodded briefly. He said, "Evening, Mariner." He looked at the sling. He said, "Been in the wars?"

"You could say that," said Nath curtly. Ale was brought him; he swigged, set the cup down and wiped his lip.

The stranger looked up again. Then he closed the manual, set it aside. "Sorry," he said. "What happened?"

He shrugged. "A bloody silly cockup. Simple machining job. Nearly took a finger off. Don't know whether I have or not yet."

The bearded man sipped his ale. He said, "These things happen. That your line then?"

He nodded. He said, "Second Engineer. *Kitestrength*."

The other glanced at the windows. He said, "She's sailing tonight, isn't she?"

"Yes," he said. "Twenty-three hundred."

"Tough luck."

Nath stared at his beer. He was tempted to drain it and go. But somehow he wanted to talk. He said, "That your Falcon out the front?"

"Aye."

He considered. You needed a bit behind you to run a motor like that. He said, "What are you in then?"

The other smiled. He took a card from his pocket. He said, "Panvet-Hoyling. Chandlers extraordinary. Used to be Gib and Crossey."

He handed the card back. He said, "The one thing that gives me the shivers is the sight of a foul anchor."

The chandler grinned. "It's bread and butter to us," he said. "Anyway, we inherited it. Had to pay for it, thought we might as well keep it."

Nath knew the shop of course. Big handsome premises next to D7. The Kiteport Tower. Even had its own Cody mast; they streamed the foul anchor from that as well. It was a sort of permanent flying insult. Or a warning. He said, "I've never seen you in there."

The bearded man shook his head. "You probably saw my partner," he said. "I'm generally out the back. I fly a desk these days."

The Mariner glanced up quickly. He said, "Were you Kites?" That would explain a lot.

The tall man nodded. "On the civvy side," he said. "Came out about eighteen months ago."

"Why'd you jack it in?"

"It's a long story," said the other. He drank ale. "You get tired of counting spares for other people," he said. "Makes more sense to do it for yourself." He nodded. "Like another in there?"

The Mariner considered. Finally he said, "Don't mind if I do." He eased his position with a little frown.

"Look," said the Kiteman, "you want to have a seat? You don't look too happy where you are."

"Wouldn't say no," said the Mariner gruffly. He picked the ale up. He said, "Thanks a lot."

There was a corner table. He eased himself down, took his cap off and laid it on the side. He was a broad-shouldered young man with a shock of dark brown hair. He sported a full, luxuriant moustache. The other held his hand out. "Rand Panington, by the way," he said. "That first name's a bit of a mixture."

He said, "Nath Ostman." He looked thoughtful. He said, "I've heard of you."

The dark man shook his head. "No," he said. "You heard of the generation back. Where do you hail from yourself?"

"The Northguard, originally," said the Mariner. "Then all over. Just spent a season on the Easthold Station."

The other pursed his lips. He said, "That was my last posting. You know Josen? Commandant, Fishgard Tower?"

"God, yes," said the Mariner. "He was a drinking buddy. Helped make up for the rest. Bit of a dump, Fishgard."

The Kiteman nodded. He said, "In more ways than one."

"What do you chandler?"

"Anything that's called for," said Rand. "We do quite well out of the Kitebases actually. Easier to come to us than send all the way to Fronting." He patted the book. "Been trying to get to grips with that Seaking quad-expander. But I think I shall have to give it best. Leave it to the professionals."

Nath leaned back. His mood seemed suddenly to have improved. "A rich source of mechanical vitamin," he said. "Otherwise known as a plumber's paradise."

"You ever work on them?"

The Mariner nodded. "Aye," he said. "In the Northguard. They build 'em here; but then they're all exported. Which is the first sensible idea they have."

"You ever stream Dancing Bay?"

The other nodded. "Many a time. With a Seaking rig, that just plain isn't funny." He grinned. "Still, I was only a Third then. If we'd gone aground, it wouldn't have been my fault."

"That," said the Kiteman, "was no doubt a great comfort."

There was an irruption. Nath stared at the newcomer with faint disbelief. She was short; stocky, one might almost say. He put her age at somewhere in the early teens. She wore an elegant hat of black-glazed straw, its rim decorated with artificial flowers. It was attached at a rakish angle; he saw the head of a spectacular pin. Her hair was long and lustrous, hanging to her waist. Her dress reached to her ankles; from beneath peeped bare and somewhat grubby toes. "Thought I'd find you 'ere," she said. "I can't get in."

The Kiteman pointed. "Where," he said wrathfully, "are your shoes? How many times do I have to tell you?"

She leaned on her parasol composedly. "Can't wear 'em on the quay," she said. "They bin unloadin' fertilizer. It spoils 'em."

"What were you doing on the quay?"

"Just lookin'," she said in an injured tone. " 'Ain't no 'arm in that."

Rand sighed, and took a key from his pocket. "Go straight home," he said. "And don't stay up all hours. When I get back I shall expect you in bed, my girl."

"Ta," said the urchin. "See yer. G'night, sir," she added winsomely.

The Mariner watched her retreat. He said, "Does she belong to you?"

The other smiled. "In a manner of speaking," he said. "As a matter of fact, she's one of my partners."

"Your *what*?"

"Three of us put up equal shares," said the tall man. "So

she gets equal profits. Got quite a little nest-egg already." He smiled again. "She's got a strongbox up in her room," he said. "Spends half the night counting it. At least it's taught her to count beyond ten."

"But how the Hell could she put up money for a chandlery? How old is she?"

"She reckons she's fifteen now," said the Kiteman. "But I don't reckon she's anywhere near it. As for how she got it; well, that really is a complicated story. I don't know the half of it myself." He considered. "Fancy some grub?" he said. "The lobster's pretty good here. Guaranteed all caught by P and H pots."

The Mariner frowned. Kari would be looking at the clock already. Sighing, and setting her lip. He felt the first stirrings of anger. After all he hadn't asked to have his hand trapped in a machine. He'd still got the rough end of her tongue though.

"All right," he said. "So what the Hell. . . ."

Velvet let herself into the chandlery, went through to the back. She emerged from the yard gate a few minutes later, pushing a little handcart. You couldn't get as much in it as in her old truck, but it was rather fine. It had large spoked wheels, and paintings on the sides; anchors, with ropes twisted round them. She passed the first of the boatyards, turned up Groping Lane. The name was suggestive, but there didn't seem to be much of that sort of thing these days. She pushed the truck on to waste ground, hid it behind some bushes. There was another chandlers, run by a Master Fishley. The name suited him somehow. They had a delivery from Holand, always the same day of the week. It never arrived till late though. The driver had gate keys, but you couldn't lock the wicket from outside. She ducked through, made a quick inspection. She found a pile of new wooden blocks. Three-sheavers. The fishing boats used them, they were always good stock to carry. Farther on were some bottle screws. Small; but they'd stay a Kiteship's jigger. Or go for jury spares. You couldn't take too many though; Rand had more than once queried what seemed to be surplus stock. She shrugged. She couldn't sell them herself; after all she was in proper business now, they had to go through the books. She still didn't think he'd be happy though. He had funny ideas about that sort of thing.

On the way back she pushed the truck more brazenly. After all, that was what it was for. It had been made to carry things like rigging blocks. She dumped her finds into the storehouse bins and put the truck away. She got some milk and biscuits and went up to her room. She took her hat off, shook her hair out. She got to her knees, unlocked the strongbox. She got out the first wad of notes, began to count it contentedly.

The Mariner took to calling in at the Stores. At first he feared he might be in the way; but they didn't seem to mind. On the contrary, his knowledge came in very useful. Who for example knew that the valve gear on a Seaking quad was identical to that on a Dayle Marine unit? Or that both sets fitted some of the larger trawlers? The makers denied it strenuously; but they all came from Saltways in the Holand, and they only marketed one pattern. Spares were frequently hard to come by, even the boatyards sometimes sent round. Hardly a normal line in chandlery; but then, Kiteport was hardly a normal town. Rand commented on it one night, and the Mariner grinned. "You can say that again," he said. "But at least it's better than Fishgard. Those bloody dragons on the roofs gave me the creeps. I'd have taken a mallet to the lot."

Rand brooded. "Yes," he said. "It's a funny place all right." He glanced down. "How's the hand?"

The other frowned. "Coming on," he said. "At least it's out of that blasted sling. Don't think I shall ever bend the finger again. I suppose I'm lucky in a way though. At least I've still got it."

They were in the bar of the "Mermaid". Nath drained his beer, and ordered another round. He said, "Does your partner live in too?"

The Kiteman shook his head. "No," he said. "Just me and the brat. Cheers." He drank, and set the glass down. "I've got a lot to thank you for, Nath," he said. "You've brought us in a lot of trade. We'll be making you a partner next."

The other shrugged. "Glad to help," he said. "It gets me out of the house."

Rand didn't comment. The Mariner had hinted at tension before; but if he wanted to talk about it he would. In his own good time. He said, "You been at sea long?"

"All my life," said Nath. "Such as it is. All I ever wanted to do. Funny, I was born inland. My folk were farmers. Still are." He shook his head. "That's not really going to sea though," he said. "Streaming the Codys. That's coasting. Except you're not going anywhere. You can see Kiteport with a decent glass, even from the Outstations."

Rand smiled. He said, "I can imagine it could get tedious."

The engineer drummed his fingers on the bar. "That's the whole trouble," he said. "It isn't even that. All right if you get the Vars; but if you get the Ultras you've got problems."

He said, "Why's that?"

"They bring an armoury with them. You've never seen anything like it. I swear to God one day they'll ship a cannon."

"Why?"

Nath shrugged. "Who knows? In case of mutiny I expect."

He considered. No Middle Church in Kiteport of course; the wealthy didn't need them, and it didn't matter what the yards and foundries thought. But two churches still opposed each other. The Vars, and the Ultras. He hadn't had experience of the latter. He'd seen them strutting the quays though, guns strapped to their waists over their scarlet robes. He'd decided they were best steered clear of; he hadn't realized they ran the Kiteships too. He said, "They certainly don't look good news."

"No," said the Mariner darkly. "Best keep away from 'em. Keep your little girl away too." He lit a stubby pipe. "I used to do the Island run," he said. "That's a bit more like it."

Rand was intrigued. He'd heard about the Islands; as a trader he'd even handled some of their produce. Matting, some turned goods—they did a nice line in belay pins—coils of curious-looking rope. In the main the fishing fraternity distrusted it; but he knew from experiment it had enormous strength. He'd never seen a map of them though. Maps of the Southguard were rare enough, and wholly denied to commoners. The Corps had to have them of course, as the Mariners had to have their charts; but they were closely guarded, classified Top Secret. The reason the Church gave was that they would be of benefit to Demons; though he suspected there were other, darker motives. It wouldn't do to have the ordinary folk find out too much about the land they lived in; knowledge is dangerous, except of course in the proper hands. He said, "What are the Islands like?"

The other looked far-away. ''You wouldn't believe 'em,'' he said. ''You just wouldn't believe 'em. . . .'' He drank ale. ''The Warm Stream splits round Tremarest,'' he said. ''That's the biggest of the group. Gives 'em a lot of fog, some seasons of the year. The rest of the time. . . . There's plants you just don't see on the mainland. Big spiky things, they call 'em palms. You get some pretty funny animals too. Nothing very big though, and none of them dangerous.'' He considered. ''There's no industry,'' he said. ''Only the ropemaking, bits and pieces like that. And they don't bother with those unless they feel in the mood. Don't need to, they can live from the sea. The Warm Stream never varies; so the fish are safe.''

He said, ''Do they fly the Codys?''

Nath looked amused. ''What for?'' he said. ''They'd laugh at you.''

''You make it sound a bt like paradise.''

''It is,'' said the Mariner. ''Sometimes I think. . . .'' He drummed his fingers on the bar again. ''The people are brown,'' he said. ''Much browner than us. Should be, they spend all day in the sun. As for the women. . . .'' He drank more beer ''There's a mountain on Tremarest that spits out fire and smoke. It blows up sometimes. The rock runs down the sides. Like red-hot rivers.''

It sounded like a traveller's tale. Rand said, ''Come on,'' and the other looked at him. He said, ''I've seen it.''

Nath's eyes veiled themselves again. ''I'd like to have been an explorer,'' he said. ''It's the schoolboy in me. Just take a ship, and go. Follow the dolphins.''

''You mean they exist?''

''Of course they exist. Did you think they didn't?''

''You'll be telling me there's mermaids next.''

Nath Ostman looked at him, amused. He said, ''You should know. You've got a captive one at home.'' He looked thoughtful. ''I'd like to find out where the Dragonflies live,'' he said. ''That'd be worth doing.''

Rand looked up sharply. He said, ''Dragonflies?''

The other shrugged. ''Something else nobody believes in,'' he said. ''So we don't bother to talk.''

''Velvet told me she used to see them,'' he said slowly. ''I thought she was pulling my leg. Or making up fancy tales. She's very good at that.'' He drank ale. ''What are they like?'' he said.

"If she's seen them, you already know," said the Mariner. "Big. Long silver wings."

"Have you ever seen one close?"

The other shook his head. "They keep well clear of shipping. I still think they're watching us though."

"Have they ever done any harm?"

"No. They just watch."

"What are they?"

Nath shook his head. "I don't know," he said. "But I think . . . I think they're machines." He drained his beer. "There's another island to the south anyway. Beyond the Tremarest group. A day's sail at least. Big 'un too."

"How do you know?"

"Because we got blown off course once. That was in the old *Sea Trader*. I saw it in the distance."

"Did you make landfall?"

The Mariner grimaced. "Did we Hell", he said. "The skipper was a good Var. Put his helm up, went for Fishgard as if the Devil was behind him."

Rand finished his own beer. "Look," he said, "you want to step round for a bite to eat? There isn't much; but there is fresh crab. Velvet got it this morning. Said it was cheap as well. Which I wouldn't wonder at. *Very* cheap," he added.

"Fine," said the other. "Don't mind if I do." Two men brushed by them as they were walking out. He thought both gave them hardish looks. The Mariner quickened his pace. "Watch that pair," he said.

"Why so?"

"Ultras," said Nath. "They're not all in fancy dress."

There was a big sitting room over the shop. Its windows faced the sea. It was curiously furnished in parts; Velvet had started her driftwood collection again. She was sitting on the sideboard, barefooted as usual, drinking a glass of milk.

" 'Ello," she said.

"Fix yourself some wine," said Rand. "I'll see what I can rake up." He vanished into the kitchen.

"I'll do it," she said. She jumped down, padded across the room. "Somethin' I bin meanin' to ask," she said. "When you'd got a minute. . . ."

Nath all but dropped the glass. It had been a very basic question, about seamen on shore leave. He said, "How do you know about things like that?"

"Well," she said, "stands ter reason, don' it? An' it don't 'appen in Gropin' Lane, I checked."

"No," he said faintly. "It doesn't happen in Groping Lane."

Rand came back with a tray. Big dressed crabs, a pile of salad on the side. Fresh, crusty bread. Later they smoked a pipe in companionable silence. Finally Rand spoke. "I always say there's nothing to beat fresh crab," he said. "I wonder where they get all that flavour from."

"Dead sailors," said Velvet instantly. She looked guilty at once. "Sorry," she said.

The Mariner smiled. He said, "You're probably right." He tapped the pipe. "I'm not just paying back a compliment," he said. "I was going to ask the other day, and I forgot. How about coming up to our place for a meal? Kari's a damned good cook; and you could bring the littl'un."

Rand shook his head solemnly. "I couldn't do that," he said. "She wouldn't behave herself."

Velvet jumped up, instantly defensive. She clenched her fists. "I *would*," she said. "I *would. . . .*" She turned to the Mariner, appealingly. "I'd be as good as gold," she said.

The Kiteman laughed. "I'd love to," he said. "When?"

"Tomorrow," said the other. "Never spoil a good mind." He considered. "Tell you what," he said. "Why don't you stop the night? Save you the hassle of driving back. The Vars can get a bit stroppy after twenty-four."

"Right, you're on," said Rand. "Hear that, Velvet?" He snapped his fingers. He said, "Bath, young lady."

"Oh," she said airily, "there's plenty o' time fer that."

"No there isn't," he said. "I don't want any of your last minute jobs. I mean now."

Her composure sagged a little. "I was talkin' to the Mariner," she said.

"You can talk to him tomorrow," he said. "All evening, unless he gets fed up with you. Go on, scat."

She looked at his face, and decided he meant it. She stalked out with her nose in the air, slammed the bathroom door. He called after her. "There's some clean towels in the cupboard. Mistress Dolkin brought them in."

Her voice floated through the panels, plaintively. "Do I 'ave ter take my clothes off?"

He said, "It is customary when bathing." The Mariner chuckled.

Rand fetched more glasses of wine. "Thanks," said the other. "Can't be too long though. Got to soften Kari up for tomorrow. She's out at the moment; that's why I came round." He sipped. He said, "That's the oddest little girl I ever met."

"Who, Velvet?" said the Kiteman. "Yes, she has her moments."

Nath lit his pipe again. He said, "I can imagine that."

Rand looked at him, eyes narrowed. "What's she been saying?"

"Nothing," said the seaman. There was a silence, that lengthened. He shrugged. He said, "She was asking about the Gropings. Wouldn't have thought she'd have known about things like that."

"She knows," said Rand. He sighed. "I'm not exactly surprised."

The Mariner looked troubled. He said, "I probably shouldn't have mentioned it."

"It's all right," said the tall man. "I'm glad you did." He hesitated; then he began to talk. Nath heard him through. "I see," he said. "So you brought her back here. Did you adopt her formally?"

The Kiteman shook his head. "How could I?" he said. "She didn't belong to anybody, nobody wanted her. She was a piece of flotsam."

Nath looked thoughtful. "Still might have been best to check up," he said.

He was surprised at the change that came over the other's face. "Why?" Rand said. "She's an Innocent. They'd have sent her to Skyways."

Velvet was back. Wearing a large, ill-fitting bath robe. She eyed her protector balefully. "I'm goin' ter bed," she said. " 'Case I gets mucky again."

"Not with soaking wet hair," said Rand. "Come here, minx." He took the towel from her, rubbed vigorously. "All right," he said finally. "That'll do. Go on, I'll come and see you later." He slapped her bottom.

She stalked away. She paused by the Mariner. "Good-night, sir," she said. She kissed him.

Rand walked as far as the "Mermaid" when the other left, went in for a nightcap. He looked in on Velvet as promised.

The bedclothes were pulled to her chin, and her eyes tight closed. But he knew she wasn't asleep. He scotched on the bed. "Velvet," he said, "are you on the game again?"

She sat up, startled. "No," she said. "No, Rand. I promised. . . ."

"Then why are you asking funny questions?"

"What about?"

"The Gropings."

She pouted. " 'E tol' on me. The Mariner. I din' think 'e would."

"No," he said, "he didn't. It was someone else."

She traced a pattern on the blankets with her finger. "I just likes ter know," she said. "Force of 'abit. I ain't done nothin', honest. . . ." She hesitated. "I did nick them crabs," she said. "But they'd left 'em all just laid there, it were their fault reely." She looked up, hopefully. "Good though, wadn't they?" she said.

"Velvet," he said, "you're beyond redemption. One of these days I shall take a great big stick to you. Come on." He tucked the covers round her, kissed her forehead lightly. "Go to sleep," he said. "Or I shan't let you come tomorrow after all."

She lay awake for a while after he closed the door. He didn't trust her, that was what. She turned on her side, and snuffled a bit. She didn't like not being trusted. She rubbed her nose with the back of her hand. She'd show him one day. She'd run away to sea with that nice Mr. Ostman. She was sure he'd be kind to her. She felt better in the morning though.

He drove up in the Falcon. Climbed up the steep High Street, and turned left. Velvet was feeling very grand. She was wearing a new white dress with roses on it, and a little matching hat. Though they were ribbons really, rather than flowers. She sat up very straight, staring down her nose at everybody they passed. Finally she pointed. She said, "It's up there."

Rand glanced at her. He said, "How did you know?" and she shrugged. She said, "I gets about."

She was right of course; though he'd have found the place anyway, the Mariner had given him clear directions. He was surprised at the size of the house; an elegant, stone-fronted mansion, set in its own grounds and with Codys streamed from Towers at either end. He wouldn't have thought a Second could have run to that. Though Nath explained the paradox later on. "It belongs to the Master Helman," he said. "He's got property right through Southguard. Most of the Middle Lands too. He lets an awful lot to newly-weds." He grinned. "Very advantageous rates too."

Rand nodded. He said, "He must be quite a character."

"Yes," said the Mariner, "I suppose he is. Getting on a bit now though."

He handed Velvet from the car. She curtsied. He threatened her with a backhand. She grinned at him.

They had a ground floor flat. Rand pressed the bell. While he was waiting he looked out to sea. The panorama was spectacular. The whole of Kiteport spread out like a map, the quays and harbour, yards. Above it the Kites, flying like bright confetti; beyond, the great blue rising shield of water. Nath had told him from this height the nearest of the Islands was visible on a good day. Rand screwed his eyes up, but the horizon appeared unbroken. He'd probably meant with a glass.

Kari was much as he'd imagined; a slight, quiet girl, blue-eyed and with soft fair hair. She chattered readily enough, acting the hostess to perfection. She talked about her early life in the Salient, as the daughter of a moderately well-to-do farmer; her travels through the Realm, as secretary to this or that tycoon. She'd finished up in Middlemarch, where she'd finally met Nath. She'd journeyed to the Northguard with him for his first Kiteposting, spent two years in a cottage overlooking Dancing Bay. From her windows she could see the A-ships. She'd always known when it was him on duty, because he'd stream a special Cody for her. "It cost him a fortune," she said. "I kept telling him he was a fool; but he never listens to me." She turned to Velvet. "Where are you from, love?" she said.

"Oh, the Easthold," said Velvet in her poshest voice. "Fishgard, in fact." She toyed with her fork. "Not much of a place," she said. "Rather rough and ready down there I'm afraid. But I think I might be beginning to live it down." She shot a look at Rand. "You won't believe it," she said, "but in our house we didn't even have a bathroom." He addressed himself to his food, studiously. Reminded himself to clip her ear for her later.

It was all very pleasant and relaxed, and the meal was excellent. Yet underneath he sensed a certain tension. Mistress Ostman excused herself soon after dinner was over; to his surprise, Velvet went to bed soon after. She said she was feeling tired, and for once she looked it. Perhaps it was the strain of all that good behaviour. She stood on tiptoe to kiss him. He hugged her; and she whispered, "Sorry. . . ."

"That's all right," he said. "I'll beat you in the morning." He rubbed her bottom. He said, "Sleep well."

Nath crossed to a corner cupboard, came back carrying glasses and a bottle. He said, "Have a drop of the real stuff."

Rand eyed it. "If that's Kiteship liquor," he said, "no thanks. I've heard it's even worse than Salient sockrot." But the other merely grinned. He said, "Don't drink with your eyes."

He sipped. "My God," he said. "What's this?"

"Middle Lands," said Nath. "Even we get the odd perk. Dig in; I've got a few more bottles stashed away."

There was a long, glassed-in conservatory. They sat awhile and looked at the sea. Finally Nath shook his head. "It's the one thing I'm afraid of," he said. "Maybe that's why I keep going back. I sometimes think it's like having a tooth pulled out. It hurts to poke your tongue in the hole; but you keep on doing it."

Rand sipped. "Yes," he said. "My father told me once he felt that way about the Kites. We're a pretty cross-grained species, after all."

The Mariner nodded. "That's what's wrong with Kari of course," he said.

He waited.

The Mariner put his glass down. He sat forward, hands between his knees. He said, "I think we're going to split up. We can't go on like this."

Rand said quietly, "Is there nothing to be done?"

The other shrugged. "I don't know what. She wants me to come ashore. For good."

"But you don't want to."

For answer, Nath waved a hand to the horizon. He said, "Would you?"

"I'm not a Mariner."

"There's more to it than that of course," said Nath. "She wants to start a family. You know what women are like."

He wasn't sure he did.

The seaman leaned back. "It isn't that I don't love her," he said. "I feel the same about her as the day we met. But I just don't feel I'm ready." He smiled. He said, "I think I'd make a lousy father."

"I think you'd make a very good one."

The other glanced at him. He said, "You should know."

Rand said, "I'm not her father."

Nath reached to top his glass up. He said, "Well, if you're not I don't know who is." He replenished his own drink. He said, "She's a very lucky little girl. I hope she appreciates it. I've never seen a child surrounded by so much love."

He was vaguely startled. He'd never looked at it like that. He said, "It's strange. If you just think you've been hurt, you hate the world. If the knife's really gone in, you think more of people as a result." He took out his little tobacco pipe, struck a lucifer. He said, "I do what I can."

"You do a sight more than that," said the Mariner. "You wouldn't see a hair of her head harmed, would you? For all she deserves a tanning now and then."

Rand said slowly, "I wouldn't like to see any child harmed."

"I'm afraid you're going to," said the other. "Before too long as well. Did you hear about the riots in Middlemarch?"

"A bit."

"They tried to burn Godpath," said Nath. "Which wouldn't in itself have been a loss. The Vars are out in force, the Militia are armed from Fronting to the Northguard. I was talking to a guy the other day who'd just come down. He reckoned there's over two hundred dead to date." He shook his head. "They can't hold it much longer," he said. "Once it really starts, it'll spread like wildfire; everything will be up for grabs. The Realm will be a shambles; nobody will be safe." He slammed the glass down. "We were saved," he said. "Just us, out of all the world. What for? I sometimes wonder whether we were worth it."

Rand was silent. The fear had been in him of course a long time now; but he hadn't suspected the other of harbouring such notions. Somehow, hearing them from Nath's lips made them all the more chilling. He summoned a mental image of the Realm. The hills and valleys, towns; sour heaths of the

Easthold, rich fields of the Middle Lands. Over it all, the bright flags of the Codys. Proud, defiant, watchful. But what if all the time they'd been watching the skies for nothing? No Demons would plunge from the zenith; shouldn't they rather turn, and look into each others' eyes?

He pushed the thought away. He said, "Who are these Ultras, Nath? What sort of people are they?"

The other looked sardonic. He said, "I'd have thought you'd know more about that."

"I've heard of them," he said. "But you've had dealings with them."

The Mariner snorted. "You don't deal with them," he said. "Largely because they're mad."

Nath considered. "They're Vars I suppose, basically," he said. "But they've taken it to the limit. And the Vars are bad enough. You know what they say; a Church like nothing ever seen before. Which is why they're Variants of course. Though personally I doubt it. I don't think there's anything new."

He swilled the drink in his glass. "They've got some funny ideas," he said. "There's one rest day a week, you can't lift a finger. I've seen a man shot for landing a tub of fish. That was down in Stanway. They'd like to enforce it through the Realm, but they can't. They've only got a real grip in the Southguard." He glanced across. "Their big depot's near Stanway," he said. "Few miles along the coast. Hunter Trucks and Battle Waggons. Where they get the money from beats me. Extortion mainly, I expect. You mean you haven't had a call?"

Rand frowned. "We had a couple of odd characters in a few days after we took over. Wouldn't come out with what they wanted. I sent 'em packing."

"And you've had no trouble since?"

"No, not a thing."

"You're lucky," said the Mariner. "You supply the Kites though. They're Kiteworshippers to a man. But if they come back again, pay them." He heaved himself from the Holand fibre chair, walked into the lounge. He came back carrying a lamp. Under his arm was a big leather-bound book. Looked like a ship's log. He said, "You might be interested in this."

Rand turned the pages, carefully. He said, "I didn't realize you had to keep these."

"We don't," said Nath. "Skipper and First Mate only.

Except that our First Mate can't read. This is for private interest.''

He said, ''Good God. . . .'' Between the entries were sketches. Rough, but vigorous. The dolphins of legend, arcing through the waves; strange fish that almost seemed to have wings; great creatures blowing jets of water from their heads. He said, ''How big are these?''

''They vary,'' said the Mariner. ''Biggest I saw was twice the length of a Kiteship.''

He said, ''That's impossible.'' Nath shrugged. He said, ''I must have been drunk then.'' He pointed. ''There's some sightings of Dragonflies. Six days on the trot. They must have been busy that year.''

Rand studied the neatly-written entries. Bearings accompanied each, notes on weather conditions. He said, ''It always seems to be fine when they come. And always daylight.''

''Seems to be,'' said the Mariner. ''Couldn't really say though. If it was dark you wouldn't see 'em anyway.''

''But you never tried to draw one?''

The other shook his head. ''I can't,'' he said. ''I don't know what they look like, when it comes down to it. They're just a twinkle in the sky. Your little girl's seen one closer than me.''

Something swooshed out of the book. Rand retrieved it; and the other looked faintly rueful. ''Shouldn't really have seen that,'' he said. ''That's why I keep this thing locked up. Ought to get rid of it really; but I haven't got the heart.''

He stared at the photograph. The girl stood arms akimbo, legs braced apart. She wore a little kilt of patterned cloth. It scarcely covered her loins. The rest of her was bare. Her hair was long and dark; and there were flowers twined. He said, ''Who's this?''

The Mariner said, ''Addi.''

''Where's she from?''

''Tremarest. She's waiting for me.'' Nath jerked his head. ''I could go to her tomorrow. Leave all this. There's ways and means.''

''Why don't you?''

The other hesitated. He said, ''Because I don't duck out of my responsibilities.''

Rand sought his rest, finally. The room they'd given him was large, again with windows looking on the sea. Before them, on a tripod, stood a great brass telescope. He frowned. He'd heard the Ultras worshipped a female principle. Godmother, dream-woman, he'd never been too sure. He swung the great barrel, peered through the eyepiece. He shook his head. It must be the Midland hooch. He'd expected to see Addi of Tremarest; but the field was dark.

Velvet was excited, in the morning. She dashed through carrying what looked like a piece of shaped stone. "What's this?" she said. "It floats. . . ."

The Mariner smiled. "It's from the Islands," he said. "You can have it if you like, we've got plenty more. It keeps your skin smooth."

She stuffed it into her pocket instantly.

Rand took the Ostmans for a drive. Velvet for once was constrained to the back seat. He struck out west along the ridge, turned inland. He found a wooded village. There was a long, half-timbered pub. The food was excellent, the beer less so. Nath ambled to the bar to complain; but the landlord was unsympathetic. "What's wrong wi' that?" he asked, holding the cloudy glass to the light. " 'Saint's Bathwater,' we calls that."

The Mariner leaned on the counter. "Then," he said easily, "I suggest Her Holiness stops cutting her toenails in it. . . ."

The beer was changed.

They both seemed more cheerful, when he finally took his leave. Kari hugged Velvet, and gave her a little present. Yet another hat. She said to come again. Driving back through Kiteport, he wondered cautiously if he had at last done a little good.

The weather remained fine. It was only the shortening of the days that reminded him the season was drawing to a close. That, and the absence of the Housebirds. He wondered if they migrated to the Islands.

Velvet took to watching the ships. Very interesting things, ships. She'd never actually been on one, though she'd been born by the sea. Least, she thought she'd been born by the sea. She'd certainly lived there most of her life. She strolled the quays, parasol at the ready; but Kiteport wasn't like the Easthold, there was never a real need of it. She did have one nasty moment; but that was on Quay Four, the place she found the crabs. There were girls there, who worked the fishing boats; most of them younger than she was, she'd decided. One of them approached one day. "Fuck orf," she said forthrightly. "This is my bleedin' patch."

Velvet regarded her coldly. Her dress hardly came to her knees, and it was full of holes at that. "I am a businesswoman of this borough," she said. "If I chooses ter take the air, it ain't no concern o' your'n."

"Businesswoman," sneered the other. "I knows what you are. It's writ all over yer. . . ."

Velvet gripped the parasol. "You won't like what's goin' ter be writ orl over you," she said. She advanced. The other fled, precipitately; but there was a little knot of them farther along the quay, they were waving their arms and pointing. Velvet retreated. She'd found out long ago, discretion was invariably the better part.

She returned to her contemplation of the Kiteships. She knew all their names by now; *Holdfast* and *Windwrack, Spindrift, Guardian, The Lady.* Plus the others that had come round from the Northguard; *Demongroom* and *Demonbride.* They were sister ships, somebody had told her; though she wasn't too sure what that meant. All the people on board seemed to be men. They were the only two it was hard to tell apart. She couldn't read the lettering on their fronts, not as yet; it was annoying to have to ask. But she was beginning to recognize the shapes. As she knew the shapes of the ships.

Also of course there was *Kitestrength.* She was Velvet's favourite. She wasn't too sure why; except that Mariner Ostman had once sailed on her. Would do again very shortly, if what she'd heard was true. She watched her comings and going with particular interest. Her crew always debarked to a man, as soon as she docked. Left just one old watchman, and he was usually asleep. She observed them, counting carefully. It was useful being able to number. One day when she knew there was nobody aboard she tiptoed to the gangplank. She glanced quickly to left and right, and hurried up it. She jumped down with a scuff and thump, looked round her awed. At last she was standing on an actual, real ship.

She padded along the deck. Somehow *Kitestrength* seemed so much bigger than when she had been standing on the quay. She stared up at the great masts with their complication of rigging, the spars with their brown furled canvas. There was so much; she couldn't work out what half the things were supposed to do. By the mainmast though she stopped and peered. One of the steel shrouds had rusted, a yard up from the strainer. There were even some broken strands. The bottle-screw didn't look too good either. She prodded at it with her parasol. They ought to come and see Rand, and get that fixed. It was downright unsafe.

She half-pulled a belay pin from a rack, shoved it back. They sold things like that too; she was sure theirs would be better. There was good profit to be made here. She moved on. The deck was steel as well, with a sort of diamond pattern. It was so hot it was burning her feet. Crazy, for this time of the year.

The bows swept up, ended in bulwarks higher than her head. There was a massive winch, tall levers sticking up to one side. It was all gearwheels, their teeth covered with black grease. She thought it was the Kitewinch. It wasn't though, that was on top of the Tower. The Tower was braced to the deck by great tarred struts. She stared up at it. She didn't hate the Codys as much as she had. Not since a special String had been flown for her. They'd got this place in Southguard, afterwards; so she supposed sometimes they could do good as well.

Velvet edged round the winch. She thought how clever Mariner Ostman was, to understand things like that. She was sure she never could. She glanced back, over the high wheel-house. There was a dusty look to the sky. Yellowish, almost; and dark clouds massing, low down in the west. She'd seen skies like that often enough before. The weather would break soon; there was going to be a gale. It was lucky *Kitestrength* wouldn't be sailing yet; after all she'd only come in at thirteen hundred.

There was a little hatch thing. She tugged at it. It opened. Below was a steep wooden ladder. She peered; then she took a firmer grip of her parasol. She adjusted her hat, swung herself over the coaming. She descended, placing her feet carefully.

His duffel bag was packed and waiting. He dumped it in the hall, walked through to the kitchen. Kari was washing up at the deep old sink; clattering dishes, slamming them one by one into the draining rack. She didn't look round.

He waited a moment. He said, "Kari, I've got to go."

She didn't answer.

He walked forward. He gripped her shoulders, turned her. He said, *"I've got to go. . . ."*

She said, "Then go." She wouldn't look at him.

He took her chin, forced her head round and up. He said, "It's just one trip."

"I know," she said. "It's just this one. And then one more. And then another. . . ."

He felt a gust of anger. He pointed at the windows. He said, "The sea's been my life. And I'm giving it up. I'm giving it all up. For you. What more do you want? Tell me what else I could do. . . ."

"You could put your kit back in the wardrobe," she said. "Right this minute. It's just as easy as that."

He said, "It's not as easy as that. You know it's not."

She said, "It's easy enough for me."

He shook her. He said, "Everything's easy to you. When you want it to be."

She squalled at him. "Easy?" she said. "Easy? Running this place, and watching you go away, and wondering if you'll come back, and staying home in case you want a screw, and putting up with it if you don't. And washing your bloody shirts, and telling the neighbours no you're fine, and seeing bits of you cut off and wondering what'll be next. Yes, it's easy," she said. "It's easy, easy, easy. . . ."

He slapped her. He saw her hair fly out. It brought him up standing too. He'd never hit her before. He said, "Oh, Kari, Kari . . . What's gone wrong?"

She clung to him. He let her cry it out. Then he steered her, very gently, into the lounge. He sat her down, and took her hands. "Listen," he said. "I've been cleared for duty. And this is my last trip of the tour. After that, my contract's up. I can renew or not, exactly as I choose. But if I don't go, I'm Absent Without Leave. That means no pension, nothing. Everything I've done will be a waste. You know the Church, you know they don't give second chances. For God's sake, you were brought up a Var."

She didn't answer; and he shook her wrists. "We'll go to the Northguard," he said. "We'll go and see my folks. They'll find us something; or they'll know somebody who's selling. It won't be much at first; but it'll be a start. Afterwards . . . you can have your own family.'' He pushed her hair back. ''Kari,'' he said, ''have I ever let you down? Have I ever promised anything, and not kept my word?''

She looked up at him with reddened eyes. ''There's just one thing,' she said. ''You won't come back. Not this time.''

He brushed at her cheek. He said, ''Will you wait and see?'' He swallowed. He said, ''I need you to, Kari. Just this once. Otherwise, I can't go on.''

She hugged him. Then she pushed away. ''Come on,'' she said. ''You're going to be late.''

Walking down the High Street, he glowered at the sky. A storm was brewing; he'd known since zero eight hundred. Didn't even need to look up; he could smell it. Well, the sooner it came the better. Not even the Vars would order an offing then. If the voyage was aborted, he was through already. Nothing more to worry about.

He hefted the duffel. He thought about Addi, so many leagues away. Over the rim of the earth. What was she doing, now? Right this minute? What would have happened, if he'd gone with her? Would she have turned into a wife as well?

Kitestrength was in turmoil when he boarded. Cadets scurried about the deck, laying out cables and traces; others were atop the gantry in the bows. He saw a puff of vapour whirl above the winch. So they'd raised Kitesteam already.

He ran the First to earth in the wheelhouse. The Skipper was there, and the Mate. They were poring over a chart. The Chief Engineer gripped his hand. He said, ''Hello Nath, nice to see you back. How's the war wound?''

He said, ''Fine.'' He flexed the finger. Some mobility had in fact returned. He nodded at the foredeck. He said, ''What in Hell goes on?''

The other put his hands on his hips. He said, ''Judge for yourself.''

He stared. A group of scarlet-robed men had appeared on the Kiteplatform. He could see the guns they carried from here. He said, ''Oh, no. That was all we needed.''

The Chiefie nodded. ''Yes,'' he said. ''We drew a short course of Ultras.''

''When do we sail?''

The other looked grim. He said, ''Ten minutes ago. Better get below.''

The Skipper glanced at the sky. ''We can just about get on

to moorings before that lot hits us,'' he said. ''Given a bit of luck at least.'' He turned back to the Mate. ''Double hawsers, Mister,'' he said. ''We shall need 'em. . . .'' The other said, ''Aye aye. . . .'' He scurried off, bellowing orders.

Nath swung down the last of the ladders, to the gantry over the great gleaming engines. Like the deckplates, the walkway was floored with diamond-patterned steel. He glanced down. The oilers were at work already, each stripped to the waist, each with a greasy kerchief round his neck. They hurried from point to point with their red, long-spouted cans. He put his hands behind his back, checked the gauges quickly.

The Third was on duty; a slim, freckled youth. Came from the Easthold somewhere. He looked too young for the insignia on his jacket. But all Thirds were starting to look young these days. He said, ''We're not actually sailing?''

Nath said, ''Aye.'' He whistled the boiler room. He said, ''Give us more steam.''

The Chief Stoker was gruff. He said, ''You're getting it.''

''OK, Rall,'' he said. ''Thanks.''

''One day,'' said the Third, ''this bloody Land's going to blow up. I've got my little hit list. Starting with the bloody Ultras. . . .''

Nath rounded on him. ''Run this ship, Mister,'' he said. ''That's what you're here for.''

The wheelhouse speaking tube shrilled. He took the whistle from the mouthpiece. The Skipper said, ''What's our pressure?''

''Ten pounds under head, sir,'' he said. ''Building well. Five minutes at the outside.''

''Can't wait,'' said the other curtly. ''Quarter ahead.'' The telegraph clanged at once; Nath swung the big brass handle to acknowledge, turned the first of the great valves. The engines woke up; the silver cranks rose, slow at first, sank into their pits. He checked the gauges again, looked over his shoulder. He said, ''Quarter ahead. *Mark*. . . .'' The Third consulted his chronometer, made an entry in the engineroom log.

Velvet was appalled. She'd explored the first compartment, the vee-shaped space piled with big sausage-shapes of canvas. Spare sails, she presumed. A metal door opened on to a second, dimly lit by portholes to either side. There was a funny smell, like a garage. Steam pipes everywhere, shafts and wheels overhead. Flat leather belts led down to benches lined with machines. The drills she recognized; the others were strange to her. She shivered suddenly. She'd realized this was probably where the Mariner had hurt his hand.

She retreated. Better go back, before someone came and caught her. She gripped the ladder; and feet pounded overhead. She heard orders being called, then others.

Velvet clapped a hand to her mouth. This was what came of being nosey. Rand was always telling her, but she never listened. She wanted to go home now. Run to him and tell him what she'd done. He could spank her if he liked; he'd hold her then, and make a fuss of her. It was too late though, she was trapped.

She was seized by a wild hope. What was happening, what must be happening, was that they'd come aboard to make *Kitestrength* secure. They'd need to after all, with bad weather on the way. So she'd only have to wait a little while, then she could slip off. And never do a thing like this again.

There was a little alcove by the aft bulkhead. She huddled into it, gripped the parasol again. She looked up at the ports. It was getting dark already. She was sure even if someone did come down, they wouldn't see her.

She jumped. The deck beneath her was vibrating. There was a thumping noise too, deep and slow. It seemed to come from nowhere at the back. She stared round wildly. For a moment she didn't understand. Then realization flooded. The engines had started.

More feet scurried overhead; and there was an order. "*Let go forrard. . . .*" She heard it clearly, even in the little hold. They must be using one of those electric things to speak with. The engine beat increased; and the loudhailer sounded again. It said, "*Let go aft. . . .*"

She curled into a ball, started to whimper. She was going to sea then; into the storm.

The Chief relieved him, which was sinister in itself. In times of peril, the First Engineer took the gantry; and a Second doesn't fill a Running Log. Nath made his way forrard, to his cabin. On the way, he glanced through a port. The sea was grey as slate, whitecaps beginning to break; and rain was lashing down already. He put a waterproof on, climbed to the wheelhouse. They'd already lit the lamps; they were swaying to the motion of the boat. He glanced astern, through the big square windows. The land was all but lost; a darker shadow, fading as he watched.

The Skipper looked at him keenly. He'd understood of course the significance of the relief; but he made no comment. He said, "What's our offing, sir?"

The Master Heldon studied his wrist. "We've not done badly," he said. "Should be picking up our marks in forty minutes."

He glanced at the telegraph. Full speed ahead. Not that he'd needed the verification; the trembling of the hull told him the revolutions accurately enough. Nath almost smiled. On normal voyages, even of this short duration, they hoisted sail once clear of land; the wells round North Cape were drying one by one, fuel conservation was becoming a major factor. But this voyage wasn't normal. Even the Ultras, it seemed, had recognized that. At least the dispensation had saved him one unpleasant chore. The propeller was eight-bladed, ten feet or more across; raising it in its frame wasn't a job he relished, even on a calm, fine day. Lives had been lost at that, more than once; they probably would be again.

They contacted in less than forty minutes. *Spindrift*, the ship on Station, was firing rockets. He saw their answer arc into the gloom. The Skipper spun the helm. He'd pass her, turn against the tide, steam up to the buoys. A nasty operation; and with a crosswind too. Nath listened. He estimated half a gale already. He was glad, not for the first time, he wasn't Deck Crew.

One of the Ultras came in. He stood hands on hips and stared round. Nath left the wheelhouse, climbed carefully down the ladder. He couldn't stand their close proximity. Brave men's lives were being put at risk and for what? A whim, a fancy. There had to be a better way. He thought, not for the first time, "It isn't the Realm that's mad. It's them."

He took shelter in the lee of the bridge structure. *Spindrift* had slipped already; gratefully, he supposed. He knew he would be. A signal lamp winked from her stern. He translated the cyphers, automatically. "*You must be crazy. . . .*"

There was an Ultra on the Kiteplatform. He raised a weapon. Shots crackled across the sea. The light went out abruptly; the signaller had prudently dropped flat. *Spindrift* turned contemptuously, trailing a faint wake of foam. She headed for the land.

The buoys were ahead. Nath heard the telegraph ring for Quarter Speed, then Engines Stop. He watched with something like awe. Thug and bully Yarman might be; but he was a good First Mate. As Heldon was a first rate Skipper. *Kitestrength* sidled in, the platform rolling against the almost-dark sky. The buoys were picked up, somehow or another; deckhands scurried, dragging the second hawsers forward. Astern, they'd be doing the same; but their task would be easier. Steam jetted from the foredeck winch as the cables were drawn in. The motion of the Kiteship altered at once. The rolling ceased; in its place was a shorter, sharper bucking. She plunged and yanked, snubbing at the cables. He heard the faint tinkle of the wheelhouse telegraph. He knew what the message would be. Finished with engines . . . He glanced up uneasily at the topload of rigging, canvas. They should have handed topmasts and to'gallants, steamed under bare poles; but there hadn't been time.

A loudhailer crackled from the foredeck. He couldn't believe his ears. It said, "*Stream. . . .*"

Nobody but a madman or an Ultra would have thought of it. It was impossible of course; they'd even have grounded the Codys on the mainland. Nonetheless, they somehow managed to manhandle a Pilot on to the Tower. They coupled, paid out fifty yards; and the Kite collapsed with a crack. The cable snaked into the sea. They reeled it in; and the priest with the megaphone said, "*Stream. . . .*"

The second Pilot went the way of the first. A Cadet reeled to him, across the heaving deck. He said, "My Lord, we cannot do it. It is impossible. . . ."

They'd rigged arc lamps from the wheelhouse front. So every detail showed clear. The Ultra took the pistol from his belt, barrel-whipped the boy across the face. Then again. The other crawled away. The priest said, "*Stream. . . .*"

Nath retreated to the engineroom. He was feeling sick.

Velvet wasn't too good either. An extra buffet came; the ship rolled and corkscrewed, and she finally threw up. Messily too, she was off balance at the time. She brushed at her front, and whimpered. "Rand," she said. "Rand. . . ." She crawled back onto the canvas, lay staring into the dark. After a while she shut her eyes; but it didn't help, there were still little spots and flashes whirling about. She rolled on to her side.

She didn't seem to be frightened any more, she'd just stopped caring. That was natural though. When you felt as bad as this, you didn't have time for anything else. The spasm came again. And again afterwards. The third was worst of all. Oddly enough though, she felt better for it. She wiped her chin and spat. She fell asleep.

The wind continued to increase.

He stared at the gauges. Still full head. He said, "What about the Ultras?" and the Chief Engineer smiled grimly. "They won't go near the boiler room," he said. "A fire slice is about the only thing they respect." He glanced down at the slumbering machinery, shadowy in the swinging of the lamps. He said, "Your engines, Third." He jerked his head. He said, "Time for a refresher."

Nath followed, wondering. He'd never been in the Chief's cabin before. It was another of the unwritten rules. The other got a bottle and two glasses. The table was gimballed; the glasses still tended to slide about, one side of the fiddle to the other. He drank, and coughed. The Chiefie smiled. He said, "Keep going. It's better when the teeth are numbed."

He produced a box of the yellow, tobacco-filled tubes. Nath hesitated, and took one. Normally he didn't care for them; but tonight was different. In many respects. He lit up, and the Chief said, "How's that lassie of yours?"

Nath frowned. He said, "I don't know." He sipped again, cautiously. He said, "I'm going ashore after this trip. Did they tell you?"

The First looked at him. He said, "We'll all be going ashore. Unless we look lively." The wind roared; and he cocked his head. Tethered as she was, *Kitestrength* was helpless, exposed to the full fury of the sea. "God," he said. "Listen to that. . . ." Through the crashing of the waves came the first dim growl of thunder.

Nath took another drag of the cigarette. He saw his hand was vibrating. He made himself be calm. He said, "We're looking for a place up in the Northguard." He grimaced. He said, "Going back to the land."

The other glanced at him. He said, "If you're let to."

He nodded. "Yes, sir," he said. "I know what you mean." He set his lips. The folk of the Realm were like folk down the ages. Wanting no truck with Gods, and less with Demons.

Wanting to bake their bread, and till their fields, and raise their children in peace. He felt blind anger at the Ultras, at the Vars, at all who sought to impose their will on others. But maybe that anger was old as the hills as well. He said, "Is there going to be trouble? Do you reckon?"

"There's trouble already," said the Chief. "You know that as well as I do. If it spreads, we're all for the chop. I used to think it wouldn't come in my time. But now I'm not so sure." He drained the glass, poured himself another. He said. "How's your little Island girl then?"

Nath was startled by the intensity of the vision that came to him. She waved and postured, held her arms out. She dropped to her knees. He knew there were tears in her eyes. He said, "Chief. . . ."

The other waited.

He hesitated. Something he needed desperately to say. About Kari, and about Addi. But the words wouldn't form.

It seemed the First read his mind. He smiled again, briefly. He said, "I sometimes think a woman's like a ship. She takes your breath away to start with. The lines of her, the glitter. Then they send you manholing. You see the worst she has to offer. You find out then, what you really think of the sea."

He stared at his glass. He said, "Why did you ask me in?"

The wind howled again. The Chief glanced at the bulkhead. Measured the angle as the Kiteship rolled. He said, "It's never good to meet your Maker stone cold sober."

There was a bang. It echoed through the ship. *Kitestrength* surged sideways, sickeningly. A crashing and grinding began at once. It sounded from the starboard bow.

The other flung the glass away. "Bloody Hell," he said. "Come on, lad. . . ."

Before he reached the engineroom he'd realized what had happened. The port tackles had parted, she'd swung onto the other buoy. Only one hope. Release the starboard hawsers, winch astern. And hope the shortened moorings stood the strain. A few minutes of that pounding and she'd be holed.

The Chief glared at the gauges. "Get on deck," he said. "They'll need all the help they can get. I'll take over here. . . ."

Nath said, "Aye aye, sir." He ran for the ladder.

The rain struck his face like slingshots. And *Kitestrength* was bucking and plunging, more wildly than before. Lightning blazed; he saw spray break over the fo'castle, a silver shower higher than the gantry. He began to work his way forward, hand over hand.

He clung to the wheelhouse ladder, peered aft. Lamps were rigged there too. Some sort of confused fight had broken out. He saw running figures, saw an Ultra felled. He heard, dimly, the clatter of the stern winch.

He climbed. Level with the windows, he pressed back. The Skipper was there, and the Mate. Both were backed against the bulkhead, their hands held high. The Ultra had an automatic levelled; they were expostulating fiercely, though he couldn't hear the words.

Nath glimpsed the big chronometer above their heads, and realization dawned. It was twenty-four hundred. This was the Holy Day, on which no work might be done. To save a woman in labour, to save a drowning man; or to save a ship from wreck. He should have expected no more.

He edged back down. He saw the stern party had backed away from the winch. The action spoke louder than words. He saw a hawser part; the severed end lashed viciously across the deck. That was the finish then. The others wouldn't last more than minutes now.

What happened was unexpected. He could tell by the instant alteration in her motion that *Kitestrength* was no longer tethered. Yet he'd heard no more shackles give. He realized what had happened. The endless fretting had finally taken effect; the buoy itself was adrift. He saw men hurry to the winch. They'd pay out cable, stream the thing as a drogue. It might be their last chance.

He edged his way round the lee of the wheelhouse. The Ultras had formed a cordon, forward of the winch. He saw the guns. The arcs were still burning; but they were scarcely necessary. The lightning was continuous; it lit the sea almost as bright as day. A loudhailer brayed through the thunder. "*Will of the Lord,*" it said. "*Will of the Lord. . . .*"

He stared in disbelief. Passing to starboard was one of the Inner Markers. He wouldn't have believed their rate of drift. Even towing the buoy. But the tide was making, the gale itself had backed. It was blowing now almost straight onshore. He set his mouth. The Stanway wreckers would have good pickings, come the morning. They'd have no use for corpses though. They'd give them back to the sea.

He began to edge forward. Somebody must sacrifice themself, that was plain. If he could get near enough to their Bishop . . . He'd die of course; but it might distract the others. A few seconds was all it needed.

There was a cry. He stared again. Atop the launching platform capered a wild figure. A creature from hallucination surely, or a fevered dream. Its hair, which was long and dark, flew wildly in the wind. It was bare to the waist; the water gleamed on its breasts. It raised an arm; instantly a vivid streak of lightning seemed to grow from the sea. The thunder-clap was fearsome.

The apparition pointed, to the dark loom of the land. It crossed its arms above its head, a gesture of negation. It pointed at the ship, and the gesture came again. It struck a pose, one hip thrust out, waved an arm toward the open sea.

"The Spirit of the Storm," boomed the loudhailer. *"On your knees, Brethren. On your knees before the Mother. . . ."* The Ultras threw the guns down, cowered; and he wouldn't have believed the speed at which the deckhands moved. He saw a man's skull crushed; another writhed, a baling hook driven through his eye. Then mercifully the lights flicked off. The lightning blazed again; but the Kiteplatform was empty.

He swung back up to the wheelhouse. The Ultra lay groaning, blood plastering the side of his face. The Mate stood over him with a belay pin. The priest rolled over, tried to push himself to his knees. Yarman kicked him in the throat.

The Skipper was already blowing down the voicepipe. He said, "Emergency revolutions, Chief." A pause; and he shouted. "To Hell with your bloody valves. *Emergency revolutions. . . .*" A boiling began at once, under the Kiteship's stern. He grabbed a loudhailer. He said, *"Cut that bloody buoy loose. . . ."* He swung forward, slammed one of the windows wide. *"Emergency,"* he said. *"Jettison Tower. . . ."*

The charges had been well placed. Four thunderous reports; and the Tower sagged. It toppled, seemingly in slow motion. A mighty splash; and the Kiteship's bows rose high. Too high. The Skipper blew down the voicepipe again. He said, "Ballast forward tanks." He glanced over his shoulder. "Stay here, Second," he said. "You might still be needed. . . ."

For a long time, an eternity it seemed, it was touch and go. *Kitestrength* was throbbing from stem to stern, straining her every rivet; but she was already into the bight of Stanway

Bay, the tide sweeping her to leeward. The Skipper had the wheel hard over. "Come on, you bitch," he said. "Come on, you old sow. Come on . . ."

Slowly, agonizingly slowly at first, her head came round. The land, the dark loom of Mitre Head, was on her port quarter. Then it was abeam. She'd weathered the point. She wallowed in the cross sea; but the ballast tanks were filling, Nath felt a fresh stability. There was a sureness to her movement that hadn't been there before. She began to edge out from the land, to the safety of the open sea.

The Skipper heaved a long, slow sigh. He used the voicepipe again. "Thank you, Number One," he said. "Standard revolutions." He glanced down at the Ultra. He said, "My ship. My bloody ship. . . ." He looked up at the Mate. "Mister," he said, "she's still carrying too much deck cargo."

The Mate grinned, and nodded. He bundled the Ultra to the door, dropped him down the ladder. The body hit the plates with a sickening thud. He swung down, started lugging it to the side. Others followed suit. There was a plashing of priests.

The Master Heldon looked across to Nath. His face was still set grimly. "They all went over in the same big wave," he said. "One of the risks you take, going to sea." He rubbed his face. Suddenly he looked unutterably weary. "Thank you, Mr. Ostman," he said. "Will you relieve the Chief? Ask him if he'd have the goodness to step up here for a moment."

Nath said, "Aye aye, sir." He saluted, and headed for the ladder.

The storm had blown itself out as quickly as it had risen. The only sign of its passing was the long, smooth swell. *Kitestrength* edged up to the quay. Hawsers were thrown, and secured; the throbbing of the engines stilled at last.

The morning light lay grey across the town. Nath swung down the forward hatch, clicked on a big handlamp. The forepeak was empty. As were the workshops beyond. He edged into the Kitehold. "Velvet," he called. "Velvet. . . ."

There was a flicker of movement. She tried to duck under his arm; but it was too late, he already held her scruff. She wriggled ineffectually, subsided. He looked at her. Her face was still pale; her hair was draggled, and she smelled of sick.

"Well, Mistress," he said. "And what have you to say for yourself?"

"I couldn't 'elp it," she said. "I was only lookin'." She pouted. "My skirt's all wet," she said. "You feel. . . ."

He said, "You're lucky it's not a good deal wetter." He firmed his grip, began to march her toward the bow. He said, "How did you know what to do? Who taught you a trick like that?"

She shrugged, as well as she was able. "They were only Ultras," she said. "They're all a bit round the twist." She looked up at him. "Good act though, wadn't it?" she said. "I quite enjoyed meself."

"Yes," he said. "It looked as if you did." He climbed the ladder first, waited for her to emerge. He resumed his grip.

Rand was waiting on the quay. His face looked haggard. "My God," he said. "I guessed where she'd gone. If you knew what I've lived through. . . ."

"I'd have traded," said the Mariner dryly. He looked back at *Kitestrength.* Her soaring masts and yards. "She saved the ship," he said. "And herself, and me. I suppose that makes her a heroine. But it doesn't mean you can trust her."

"No," said the other. "I found that out already." He dropped his hand on Velvet's other shoulder; they frogmarched her solemnly away along the quay.

8 kitekillers

VELVET TOOK HER glasses off. They weren't her glasses actually; they weren't anybody's, she'd found them on a tip. They were very fine, with thin goldy-coloured frames. There was even a little chain, so she could hang them round her neck. She thought they made her look mature. There was only one problem; she couldn't see much through them. Everything looked all blurry.

They'd invested in one of these new fangled typewriters. It had seemed like just a toy at first; later though she'd realized how useful it could be. She twisted the big handle at the side, and the letter popped out of the top. She read it, carefully.

Dear Master Herringhold,
The bulbs what you ordered is ready.

She scowled. She'd known there was something wrong. She took another sheet of paper, retyped carefully.

Dear Master Herringhold,
The bulbs what you ordered are *ready.*

There, that was better. She signed it, *"PP Tremarest*

Holdings." She wasn't sure what the letters stood for; she sometimes suspected Rand didn't know either. But they were like the spectacles; they looked good. She addressed the envelope, stuck the flap with wax. She dobbed the big seal on to it, examined the results. That was the part of letter-writing she really liked best.

She put her hat on, headed through the shop. The air was full of cheeping; the little yellow birds they brought in from the Islands. Their cages lined the whole of one side wall. As she opened the door, a posh voice said, "Good afternoon."

She stopped. Then she scowled again. It was the big black bird they'd bought a few weeks back. That came from Tremarest as well. It was always catching her out. It seemed it could imitate anything; even the ringing of the door bell. She gripped her parasol. "Naff orf," she said.

The bird put its head on one side. It watched her stump off down the street. "Naff orf, Miss Velvet," it said.

She headed towards town centre. Not that Fronting had much of a centre really. Its name rather summed it up. One way, it fronted the Middle Lands; the other way it faced the Southguard. It belonged to neither. She'd been surprised when Rand had chosen it. Still, she'd been surprised at a lot of things. She'd been surprised when he'd given up the other shop. There'd been rows with Master Hoyland, certainly; they used to go at it hammer and tongs. Half the night, sometimes. It had still come as a shock though.

Very serious affair, it had been. There was even a solicitor, a Master Lanting. Tall and greyhaired, with a big shiny briefcase. She thought he'd given her some funny looks. She'd wriggled uncomfortably, wanting to get away; she'd never understood about things like this. It had been impossible though; there'd been papers to sign, all sorts of bits and pieces. She'd made her mark, frowning; a cross, like the Fishgard boatmen used to use. Later Rand had consulted her, very seriously, about what she wanted to do; but she'd merely shrugged. Her strongbox was nearly full; so it didn't matter. As long as she was with him.

The strongbox had been another slight cause of friction. Even with Rand. He kept his money in a bank; but she'd never fancied the idea. After all, if it wasn't there it wasn't really yours any more. You couldn't even count it. He'd asked her more than once, what would happen if the house burned down; but she merely shrugged. The bank might burn down as well. He'd said that didn't matter, it wouldn't make any difference; but she'd been unable to see that. The money would still go up in smoke.

The town was busy, for the time of the year. They held an Air Fair too; but that wasn't for weeks yet. She was beginning to see why Rand had wanted to come here. He'd been cleverer than she'd realized; with all the trouble in Middlemarch, and more starting in the Southguard, people had been moving out in a steady stream. There was a lot of money about. They hadn't had the shop long, but it had done really well.

She turned left, headed for the Var place. This posting of letters was a good idea. You paid so much a month, and they always seemed to arrive. They were faster than the carriers too; they had their own little vans, you often saw them about. They were painted maroon, same colour as the Launchers, with big insignia on the sides. She'd got to know their local man quite well.

She glanced up at the Codys flying from the Central Tower. She saw the wind had veered round to the south. Which meant good weather, for a day or two at least. Anyway that was what the Mariner always said. He reckoned on a good day you could smell the Island spice. Though she never had. She turned her nose up. He'd talked a lot about the Islands, particularly Tremarest; but she hadn't been fooled. He'd got a bit of spare down there; you couldn't tell her much about seamen.

She handed the letter in, saw it stamped and signed for. She signed her own name on the sheet. VELVET, in big square lettering. That last was an accomplishment of which she was very proud. Learning to read had been a chore at first; learning to write had been even harder. The most difficult thing, she thought, that she'd ever tried to do. Rand had tried to show her, times enough; eventually he'd hired a tutor, Mistress Harken. She'd disliked her cordially; she had a feeling the sentiment had been mutual. She'd persevered though; she didn't like to be beaten at things. She'd chewed her quill tip, made inkblots by the score; but this was the result. She twirled her parasol. She was a real businesswoman now; she could even write her name.

Velvet headed back toward the town square. She hadn't been sure she'd like the shop at first, and living away from the sea. After all the sound of it had been in her ears all her life. It was all right though; in fact it had grown on her. And anyway her seafaring days were over. One experience had been enough. Also, she wasn't totally cut off. They handled mostly Island produce; even the seed corn and potatoes came from Tremarest. Rand had some good contacts; the Mariner had introduced him to most of them. There were other things as well of course; exciting things sometimes, apart from the birds. Great shells, all spikes and blotches, strange-smelling fibre mats; more of the funny floating stone, bolts of cloth with beautiful hand-printed patterns. She'd considered having some of it made up into a dress; but she'd decided against it finally. The great swirling flowers, in pink and violet and blue; somehow it wasn't really her. She had found a hat though, with funny little cork things hung all round the brim. She couldn't work out what they were for. They annoyed her eventually, bobbling about: so she cut them off. The hat was very nice though; it was made of a sort of grass.

The cloth had sold particularly well. With the proceeds they'd even bought a little van. It went out on delivery several times a week. There was a handcart too of course; Velvet used it herself sometimes, for small drops. Rand had scolded her once or twice, asked why she thought they employed a lad; but she'd merely shrugged again. She liked to get out and about, see what was going on; and anyway she was used to trucks. One way and another, her life had seemed to revolve round them.

In sight of the square she hesitated. A Hunter Waggon was parked by the town hall; scarlet and high-sided, with guns at front and rear. She could see the barrels from where she stood. There'd been quite a few of them about recently; they rumbled through the town all hours of the day and night. They worried Rand a lot, though she couldn't for the life of her see why. After all, they weren't doing any harm. They sold corn and seed potatoes, vegetables in season, Island fruits. They were just shopkeepers, the Vars wouldn't be interested in them. She gave the thing a wide berth nonetheless.

There was a closed carriage, drawn by a pair of handsome greys. She eyed it vaguely. She hadn't seen that one before; must be somebody else new in town. She made to pass it, and the window was rapped. She turned, curiously. The rapping came again.

She walked back; and the door was opened. Velvet gulped. She said, " 'Ello, Mistress."

"My little helpmate," said the Lady Kerosina. "I didn't know you were here. Get in."

She hesitated; and the other gestured. She obeyed, unwillingly. "You livin' 'ere?" she said.

"We bought a little place a few weeks back," said Kerosina. "One needs the occasional breath of country air. I'll show it to you." She rapped the roof, sharply; before Velvet could protest, they were jangling on their way.

Kerosina sat back and crossed her legs. She said, "So what are you doing in Fronting?"

Velvet swallowed again. "We got a shop," she said. "Leastways it's Rand's really. I got a sort of interest." She gripped her parasol. "Corn chandlers," she said. "We sells a lot of other stuff as well though."

"Fascinating," said the Lady Kerosina. "Next time I run short of wheat, I'll come and see you."

The carriage turned right, and left. The horses increased their pace. Velvet clung to a little plaited strap. "I can't be long," she said. "Rand's expectin' me back. I only come out wi' the post."

"You won't be long," said Kerosina sharply. "It isn't very far. It's only on the edge of town. If you can call this place a town. But at least it's quiet." She eyed Velvet candidly. "You've grown," she said. "You're looking well. So Rand's still looking after you."

She nodded. She said, "Yes, Mistress. 'E's ever so kind." She looked down. "Bit like 'avin a Dad, I suppose," she said. "Well, sort of," she added.

The carriage turned again. She heard the crunch of gravel. The coachman reined; a brief wait, and the wheels clashed on to cobbles. Kerosina said, "We're here." She opened the door, climbed down. "Don't stable, Jehan," she said. "The carriage will be going back to town." The coachman said, "Aye, Mistress."

Velvet had followed. She stood and stared round. The house, as Kerosina had said, was not too large; but it was stone-fronted, with crenellations on the top and lines of big bay windows. A big Cody string flew from the eastern Tower. Velvet turned. Surrounding the entire place was a high stone wall, replete with more of the curious battlements. Men were patrolling it. They wore Kerosin livery, and each had a gun slung to his shoulder. It was more like a little fort than anything else.

The Lady Kerosina looked sardonic. "One must take precautions," she said. "Even here. We're living in quite interesting times." She opened a parasol. "Walk with me, Velvet," she said. "It's been so long since I saw you."

The grounds were really pretty; trees set all over, little twisty paths winding between. There were deep green pools, mossy headhigh cliffs; in one place she saw a little waterfall. There were tall bushes, some of them in bloom already; between them she saw Island flowers. "It's beautiful," she said. She caught her breath. She said, "What's that?"

They'd come upon the little house unexpectedly. It too was built of stone. There were tall crooked chimneys, windows with funny diamond-patterned panes; it even had its own Kitemast, from which streamed a tiny Cody.

"It used to be the Head Gardener's," said Kerosina. "But he moved out. Went with the other people." She took a key from her handbag. "It's empty at the moment," she said. She glanced sidelong. She said, "Waiting a tenant."

The door had a rounded top. Like the door Velvet remembered in the arch. She stopped just inside. There were deep windowsills; just right for her driftwood creatures. She could twine flowers round them; there were enough in the garden already, but there'd be a lot more come summer. She hurried round opening doors. There was a big cupboard that would serve well as a wardrobe, a tiny sleeping cubicle. It was lit by more of the diamond-shaped panes; outside, a creeper tapped the glass. There was even a bathroom, with its own loo. In Fishgard, she'd always had to use the common.

There was a big metal box on the wall. She said, "What's this, Mistress?" and Kerosina called back. "A geyser," she said. "It makes the water hot."

There was a brass wheel at the side. She turned it, and there was a *whoomph*. She jumped back, peered again curiously. Blue flames showed through a slot; and water had begun to pulse from a nozzle in the wall. She put her hand to it, snatched it away. It was almost scalding.

She turned the geyser off, went back. Kerosina sat on the settle, composedly. "Well, Velvet," she said, "it's yours for the asking. Your own little house. Even when I'm not here.

You knew that already though.'' She smiled. She said, ''What do you think?''

Velvet swallowed. ''I'm with Rand,'' she said. '' 'E needs me in the shop. 'E's bin ever so good to me,'' she said. '' 'E taught me ter read an' write.''

The Lady Kerosina sighed. ''This is such a tedious little town,'' she said. ''I'm bored with it already.'' She leaned forward, whispered; and Velvet's eyes grew round with shock. ''I *couldn't,*'' she said. ''I *couldn't.* I promised. . . .''

The other looked at her. ''But you promised me as well,'' she said. ''So you'll have to break your word to one of us.''

Velvet twined her fingers miserably. She wondered why life always had to be so complicated. It would go all right for a time; but something like this always happened. Kerosina had been good to her, she'd always been good to her; now she was offering her a real house, of her very own. But Rand had been good to her as well. She bit her lip. ''Look, Mistress,'' she said, ''I do know somebody. It'll only be the once though. Then you'll 'ave ter get someone else. . . .'' She twined her fingers again. ''I got the shop ter run,'' she said.

The Lady Kerosina smiled. ''There's nobody as good as you,'' she said. She sat back. ''Very well,'' she said. ''Just the once.''

Letting herself back into the shop, the bird spoke to her again. Velvet glowered at it. ''I tol' yer already,'' she said. ''Naff orf. . . .''

It cocked its head, and made a noise like a bicycle bell.

It wasn't just the once of course. It was again and again. But she'd realized that as well. Once Kerosina had you in her grip, you didn't get away as easily as that. Sometimes it was boy children, sometimes girls; usually they'd scuttle away in shame and terror, but sometimes they'd creep back of their own accord. Then Kerosina would lock her doors, and laugh. It made it even worse.

Velvet raised the matter with her, several times; eventually the other's eyes flashed. ''I think I need some flowers for the patio,'' she said. ''Perhaps tomorrow I'll call in on the Master Rand.''

She felt an instant surge of panic. "No, Mistress," she said. "No, please. . . ."

Kerosina stared at her. "Velvet," she said, "you're an ungrateful little beast. Haven't you been paid good money?"

They were sitting in the main hall of the house. She looked at the carpet, traced one of the flowers with her parasol. "I din' wan' it," she whispered.

"But you took it," said Her Ladyship. "You took it, Mistress." She sighed. "What does it matter?" she said. "What does any of it matter? We'll all be dead soon anyway. The wells are running dry; that will be the trigger."

Velvet pouted. She didn't want to know. About wells, and triggers, things she couldn't understand. She wanted to feed the yellow birds, and arrange her shells in the windows, and just be left alone.

The closed coach trotted, forward and back from town.

The Minutemen were out; even here, in Fronting. Little contingents of them paraded the streets, muskets on their shoulders. Some claimed allegiance to the Vars, some to the Middle Doctrine. There was uneasiness when they met; but so far there had been no outright clashes. There'd be mutual glowering, as often as not a hurled exchange of insults; but one troop or another would invariably cross the road, out of the enemy's way. The Ultras were another factor altogether. They were more sinister; because nobody, not even the Vars themselves, knew the full extent of their authority. Their influence had been growing, that much was certain; there were rumours they'd even infiltrated the Middle Lands themselves. Rand heard the stories often enough; the taverns of the town buzzed with talk. As the taverns of any town buzzed with talk. The words of the Mariner Ostman came back to him once more. *"We were saved. Just us, out of all the world. I sometimes wonder whether we were worth it. . . ."*

There were other whispers. At first Rand turned a deaf ear. But finally they became too persistent to be ignored. He began taking note of Velvet's absences from the shop. She always took the mail down to the post, she had done since they'd opened. She'd leave about seventeen hundred, be back before they closed. It was a couple of hours now though, sometimes three. Once she wasn't back till nearly twenty-two hundred. She said there'd been a queue.

He turned on her, finally. "Velvet," he said, "what's this I hear? About the Mistress Kerosina being in town?"

She wouldn't look at him. She stuck her lip out, stared down at the carpet.

"Velvet," he said, "what are you up to? Are you performing little services again?"

She pouted. She said indistinctly, "I promised."

"Yes," said Rand, "you promised." A wait. He said, "You're lying, child." He paused again. He said, "Look at me."

She wouldn't.

He shook his head. "All I tried to do," he said. "All the time I spent." He swallowed. "I'll tell you where I found you," he said. "In the gutter. You might not have realized it, but that was where you were. A thief, a procuress, a whoremonger, a liar. I made a home for you, I gave you a new start. The sort of chance you'd never had before. Not in your pathetic little life. For a time I thought it was working. I'd even begun to trust you. But you couldn't keep away, could you? You couldn't keep your fingers out of dirt."

He'd never actually seen her lose her temper. He saw it now. "What do you know?" she snarled. "What do you fuckin' know? You an' yer Kites, an' keepin' yer nose in the air, an' lecturin' me an' tellin me 'ow ter go on. You ain't ever lived, not really. You don't know what it's all about, you don't know nothin'." She jumped up, chest heaving. "I'll tell you what it's about," she yelled. "I'll tell you what it's all about. It's about gettin' little kids, an' floggin' their snatches, an' gettin' some more an' some more after that because the first lot's wore out already. It's about nickin' things, an' tellin' lies, an' makin' it 'ow you can. Because that's what people are about. . . ." She flung a vase across the room. It shattered. "I ain't never made myself out posh," she said. "Only what I am. I tried ter play it straight though. I ain't never nicked from you. Not one bleedin' penny. You wouldn't believe that though, would yer? 'Cos I come out the gutter. An' you don't believe nobody out the gutter." She pointed through the window. "Go up the church," she said. "Go an' light yer little lamps. Tell 'em yer 'oly. Make yer feel good, that will." She panted. "Made yer feel good what you done fer me, din' it?" she said. "Go to 'Eaven fer sure, you will. . . ."

If he hadn't seen her angry, she hadn't seen him. He was across the room in a flash. He slapped her, and again. She tried to bolt, but he took her by the scruff. He shook her, flung her down on the settle. "All right," he said. "If you want it you can have it. You've been asking for it long enough." He dragged at his belt. She writhed and yelled; later though she fell curiously quiet. He stood up finally. The rage was still burning. "Get to bed," he said. "In the morning you can get out. The Mistress will find you a room. Useful to have you handy." He blundered downstairs, slammed the outer door. He headed for the nearest boozer. His heels rang on the path; he heard the sound dimly, through the buzzing in his ears.

She didn't wait till morning. She began collecting her things at once. Clothes, the cashbox, a new pair of shoes. She filled the truck, hesitated. She dumped some of the little driftwood creatures on top. Just her favourites. She didn't see why she should leave them. After all they wouldn't answer back, or yell at her. She stumped off through the town. She wasn't crying; it was just that the tears would well and trickle. They dripped steadily from her chin. It wasn't the hiding. She'd had enough before, they never really hurt; the sting had gone off already. It was what he'd said. She'd had to go back and work for Kerosina, she'd been forced to; otherwise she'd have told on her, she didn't make threats like that lightly. He hadn't given her the chance to explain though, hadn't even asked. Just assumed the worst. She lifted her chin. If he didn't want her any more, she knew somebody who did. She'd get a house out of it as well. She'd be everything he'd called her; liar, procuress, thief. And never bother trying to be good again. There was more money in it anyway, than running a scruffy old shop.

At first light Rand walked down the Kiteport road. He found the handcart abandoned, by Kerosina's main gate. He pulled it from the ditch, stood looking at it. He stared up at the battlemented wall. Events had come full circle then, he'd known one day they must. "It was bound to happen," he said greyly. He trudged back into the town.

Summer was coming, but the days stayed overcast. He served in the shop, dealt with the occasional rep, worked on the accounts. After hours he loaded the van, went out on delivery. He saw no sign of Velvet. He was glad of that.

Now of course was the time for his Middler philosophy. Each act, dressing and shaving, eating, lying down, was an act performed; complete in itself, neither good nor bad. It led nowhere save to the next. The sum of awareness grew, the psyche altered; that in itself was of equal insignificance. It was useless though. The thought brought no comfort, didn't fill the nagging emptiness inside him.

Velvet's clothes, the ones she hadn't wanted, were still scattered about. She'd always been an untidy little wretch; it had been one of the maddening, endearing things about her. The woman who cleaned for him gathered them up. She turned to him finally, biting her lip. "Where is she, sir?" she said. "Where's your little girl?"

"She wasn't my little girl," he said. "She was never my little girl."

She looked helpless. "But what shall I do with these?"

The Middlers were always appealing for clothes for the paupers in their care. He supposed he ought to send them to the church. But he didn't have the heart. "I don't know," he said. "Do what you like."

The cleaning woman glanced at the bundle in her arms, and back to him. "I'll put 'em in the spare room," she said. She shook her head. She said, "She had such pretty things." He saw there were tears in her eyes. He wondered for a moment why.

It was true of course. She'd never been his, she'd been nothing to do with him. But nothing had ever been his. He'd loved his sister; and see what had happened there. He'd loved Janni, loved her with his heart and soul, loved her to distraction; and she'd been taken from him. Casually, by the crooking of a finger. He'd worked from month to month, from year to year; but for what? He'd ended as he'd begun, with nothing. The silence told him that, the silence of his rooms. The clock told him, with its ticking. He tried to remember happier times, set them against the gnawing loneliness; laughing with Janni, loving her, riding the horses. He failed again. Because those times had gone, ceased to exist. When the sun was shining, then it shone; when clouds eclipsed it, there was no sun.

He took to dropping into one or other of the local inns. Usually he'd make a night of it; though of course there always came a time when he had to leave. Let himself into the shop, and climb the stairs. So he started keeping a few bottles about the place. Wine and cider, even the Northland hooch. It did no long term good; but it dulled the pain a little. Like brandy on an aching tooth. He wondered what old Father Alkin would have thought. He'd probably have said it was a sensibe idea.

News came from the north. There'd been riots in Streanling and Barida; Var Militia had taken over the coastal wells, oil production was now controlled by the Church. Middlemarch itself was a town under siege. Roadblocks had been set up on all approaches; strangers had been fired on indiscriminately. Shooting had been heard inside the town as well and many fires were burning, seemingly out of control. All the factions were armed; Vars and Ultras, the Middlemen, the Corps, Militia of various persuasions. But which of them actually controlled the battered city was unknown. "It's the end of the world," said a grimfaced Kiteman, shaking his head. "It'll never be the same. Least, not in our lifetimes."

Rand walked away. A part of him understood. The strange G8 affair had shown the way; pointed out the lack of overall control, the true weakness of the central authority. Since then the Kiteworld had been simmering, waiting for just such an explosion. Sometimes though he felt isolated, remote. It was as if the events weren't really happening, didn't in fact concern him. But of course his world had ended already. Not once, but many times.

He took the Falcon down to the Master Hummin, filled her to the brim. He piled jerrycans into the boot, added a gallon of oil. As he left the forecourt a Var patrol swung in. By morning the garage was sealed, the line of handpumps guarded by armed militia.

He dreamed of the flying of a great Cody rig. Its wings dwarfed anything he'd seen; even the wire of the Trace seemed thicker than his wrist. Lifter after Lifter sailed up, to clang against its cone. The wire thrummed; finally the basket climbed away. He saw Velvet was aboard. Tiny, and pathetic. She called to him, her voice thin as a gull's. She held her arms out. He called back, spread his arms in return; but it was too late. The winch was clattering, she was being drawn away. Higher and higher, into the drifting clouds. He shouted, despairingly; and the winchman turned. He saw it was Rone Dalgeth. "I won again," he said. "I've taken her as well." He swung a lever; the pawl cleared from the ratchet. Rand grappled, despairingly; then he was awake, and sweating. He staggered to the loo. He saw there was no rest, by night or day; now, she had invaded his sleep.

He frowned. The clattering came again, and faded. He knew the sound; steel halftracks on cobbles. Hunter Waggons from the Vars or Ultras; a whole convoy of them. It was like an army, grinding through the town. He frowned again. There was a rattling; distant, but unmistakable. Someone was using automatic weapons. He clicked the light off, pulled the curtains back. He saw the glow of flames, reflecting from the clouds.

The war came to Fronting with shocking suddenness. Next night Rand woke abruptly, wondered what had disturbed him. He wasn't left long in doubt. The sound came again. Gunfire. This time it was close though; it sounded to be in the street. He rose, dressed hastily. He snatched a glance at the clock. Zero three hundred. He hurried downstairs, turning on lights as he went; but before he reached the shop there was a massive crash. It came again, accompanied by the tinkling of glass. He was being broken into. He snatched up a crowbar that lay on one of the storeroom crates. It was a useless gesture though. He ran forward, saw what he was facing and dropped it. He raised his hands, slowly.

The intruders fanned out, guns levelled. Six hardfaced young men, their hair tumbling to their shoulders. A silence; then Brad Hoyland walked forward. Rand moistened his lips. "Hello, Brad," he said. "Come for some seed corn then? I didn't know you'd gone back into farming."

The Ultra stared back. The pale hair, so pale as to be almost white; the sharp-boned face, equally colourless eyes. The face of a fanatic. He'd been like it at College; all he'd needed was a Cause. He said, "Where do you keep the Falcon?"

Rand gestured, briefly. He said, "Round the back."

"All right," said the other. "Open up. We're requisitioning."

He moved ahead of them, prodded in the back by one of the guns. He unlocked the garage doors, ran the car into the yard. He'd have put his foot down, taken his chance; but it was useless, the gates were locked and chained. He slowed, set the handbrake; and one of the Ultras jerked his head. "Right," he said, "out." He heard the click as the other cocked his gun.

Hoyland spoke quickly. "No," he said. "We can use a spare driver." He ran round, climbed in. He pressed a pistol to Rand's ribs. He said, "Do just what I say." Rand nodded. He realized the other had saved his life.

The gate was swiftly dealt with. A hammering from one of the automatics; and the gunman put his heel to the splintered wood. It swung back; he eased the Falcon through, into a scene from Hell. Fronting was in uproar. A building was on fire; it lit the street as bright as day. There were running figures; and the air was full of din. Shots, and screams. He saw a man felled with a pickaxe handle. The assailant turned aside, fled into an alley. Rand realized things like that would be happening right across the Realm; old scores being settled, casual murder committed.

There was a big, squaresided vehicle. Four of the Ultras piled into it; the others dived into the Falcon. The van accelerated, moving fast. He followed.

More bodies lay about, in the path and roadway. He swerved round the first, couldn't miss the second. The nearside wheels passed over it, with a sickening double thud. Hoyland bared his teeth. "That's it," he said. "You're getting the idea."

The looters were active already. A shop window had been smashed, they were scrambling in and out. A gunman in the lead truck opened up. One fell; the others dropped their booty and ran. Rand said, "What are you doing? What do you hope to gain?" and Hoyland said, "Shut up." The gun dug harder into his ribs.

The Middle Church was ablaze too; another big fire was burning behind the town hall. Hoyland said, "Turn left."

His throat dried. He'd realized where they were headed. "No," he whispered. "No, Brad, you can't. . . ." The Ultra laughed.

They pulled up short of the Kerosin Mansion, drew into the cover of some trees. The house was already under attack. Rand heard the clatter of automatic weapons, saw the answering flashes from the wall.

The van had pulled ahead. Two of the Ultras tumbled out, dragging what looked to be a heavy tube. They rammed the spiked tail into the ground, extended a pair of sturdy jointed legs. Hoyland prodded him with the gun. "Out, fast," he said. "Leave the keys. Put your hands on top of the car." He stepped back, barrelled Rand across the neck. He collapsed.

The first bomb was dropped into the mortar. A flash and roar. The missile fell short. The second though struck the big gates full on. Splinters flew, and one of the valves sagged inward. The gunner whooped, and elevated the barrel again. He began to bombard the grounds.

A man ran across, yelling. "You fucking moron," he said. "We're already in." He kicked the last bomb from the Ultra's hands. The other swore, rolled over sucking his fingers. Then he sat up. "Kill the Pigs," he said. He followed the rest, at the gallop. As he ran, he drew his pistol.

Rand hauled himself up slowly, leaned on the Falcon. One hand was to his head. He felt his neck, the warm stickiness there. He blinked giddily, stared round. At first things wouldn't focus; then awareness returned. He saw the shattered gates; beyond, the house was burning, shooting flames and sparks high into the sky. The flames caught the Cody rig, suddenly. Flashed from Lifter to Lifter. The String sagged, and began to fall.

The odd pistol shot still sounded; but in the main resistance seemed to have ceased. He staggered forward. One of the Ultras was curled under the gateway. The gun he had dropped lay an inch or two beyond his outstretched fingers. One of the new-style revolving arms as well. Rand checked it. One shot had been fired; the rest of the charges were intact.

He hurried through the grounds. There was a little house, set round with trees. He saw most of its side wall had gone.

He stepped through the opening. He had no torch; but the flamelight showed him as much as he needed to see. A body lay in the ruins. He recognized the dress. He'd bought it for her only a few weeks before. Other than that, identification was difficult. The corpse was headless.

Brad Hoyland was behind him. He licked his lips. He said, "This shouldn't have happened."

Rand straightened slowly, turned. "No," he said. "It shouldn't."

The other's eyes dilated. "Rand," he said. "Now wait a minute, Rand. We didn't want to hurt her. But people do get hurt. It isn't our fault. It's the Pigs. They started it."

He didn't answer, and the Ultra's face changed. "All right," he said. "So we got the bourgeois bitch. Might as well get her tart." He clawed at his waist, and Rand shot him through the heart.

They'd captured the Mistress Kerosina. They dragged her across the courtyard. One of the Ultras punched her in the face. She spat at him. They bound her to a kitchen chair, sat her where she could see her burning house. They ripped her blouse away, and the Ultra giggled. He laid her shoulder open with a knife. Blood streamed instantly down her arm, began to dribble from her elbow. She looked at it incuriously. He cut her again. "It's your tits next, Lady," he said. "Get ready. . . ."

There was a little pressure on his back. "Drop the knife," said Rand gently. "Step away. Slowly."

The Ultra did as he was told. Finally he halted. He said, "This far enough?"

"Yes," said the other. "I should think so." He pulled the trigger. The Ultra shrieked, and tried to writhe away. He didn't get very far. You don't though, not with a shattered spine.

The rest had stood transfixed. He turned on them, and they bolted. He hurried to the Mistress Kerosina. He slashed the ropes, tore the ruined blouse into strips. He bound her arm as tightly as he could, took his jacket off and put it round her shoulders. She clutched it across her chest. "I don't know why you bother," she said dully. "If you don't get me, the Vars will."

"I'm sorry," he said. "It's all I can do." She stared at him. Then she got up, walked off toward the flames. He ran back the way he had come.

A voice called, from the shadows by the gate. He hesitated; and she stepped forward. She said, "Hello, Rand." She swallowed. "I knew they were coming for you," she said. "So I came too."

He looked at her. Her hair was longer than he remembered it. She was wearing trews and a jerkin. A holster was strapped to her hip. So she was a gun girl too. "Well," he said, "it seems to be my night." He hit her. When she got up he knocked her down again. Janni crouched on hands and knees, hair hanging forward. He cocked the pistol.

Her voice was muffled. "Yes," she said, "you'd better use it. Do it quickly though." She shivered. "You won't believe me of course," she said. "But I didn't have any choice. I had to go to him."

He said, "You had every choice."

She shook her head. A drop of blood splashed on the cobbles. "No," she said. "We'd have gone to Skyways. Both of us. And not come out again. He promised me."

Rand set his mouth. "Nice try," he said. "You could always spin a good tale though. He wouldn't have dared. Too much would have come out at the hearing."

She shivered again. "What hearing?" she said bitterly. "He owned that place." She touched her mouth. "We were mad, doing what we were doing," she said. "It was obvious. It wouldn't have needed a hearing."

He nodded. He said, "I think I'm going to kill him."

"You can't," she said. "He's already dead."

"How do you know?"

She said, "Because I shot him myself. Then we let them out of Skyways."

He realized what he was holding. He flung it away, with loathing. He dropped to his knees, pressed with a kerchief and wiped. "Janni," he said. "Janni, oh my God. . . ."

She stiffened. But he'd already heard it too. The shrill, rising and falling wail; the siren of a Battle Waggon, coming fast.

She scrambled to her feet. "Quick," she said. "Quick, Rand. . . ." He ran with her, swung into the Falcon. He gunned the engine, moved off fast. Lights showed behind him, jizzing and bouncing. He hauled right, accelerated again. She said, "Where are you going?"

"Kiteport," he said. "I've got contacts there."

"It's useless," she said. "It's the same all over. Right through the Realm. . . ."

He swung the wheel. "I'm not staying in the Realm," he said. "I'm going to the Islands. Tremarest. There's bound to be a ship. . . ."

She shook her head. She said, "You won't make it, Rand."

Everywhere, the night sky had blossomed fire. The flames were shocking, poppy-red. He detoured again and again, avoiding burning villages. The Falcon jarred and shook, wheels bouncing over potholes. Finally he found a better road. It ran south and slightly west. He said, "This is for us." He gripped her arm. "We are going to make it, Jan," he said. "We've got to. . . ."

He stared. Ahead and to the right, a Cody string was rising. In place of the Observer's basket hung a great blazing symbol; the *ankh,* the looped cross of the Middle Doctrine. Beyond it was another and another. They stretched far into the west; the last bizarre signs of hope, in a crumbling world.

The night wore on. The road ahead became visible by degrees; grey cloud streaks grew overhead; between them was the lemon vividness of dawn.

She groaned. She said, "Oh, no. . . ." She pointed. Lumbering toward them, jolting on the rough, was an Ultra Battle Waggon. It was moving fast, heading at an angle to cut them off.

He said, "*Get down. . . .*" He shoved her; and she ducked beneath the dash. He stared at the thing. The gap was closing fast. He changed gear, pushed his foot to the boards. The Falcon responded. He slammed back into top, held her as she bucked and leaped. He beat the big machine by fifty yards. As he passed, its forward armament set up a hammering.

Rand swerved, desperately. And again. Something spanged from metal. The windscreen starred, disintegrated. There was a rush of fresh, cold air. He swerved again; and a bend took the Ultras from sight. The firing ceased abruptly. They were clear; nor did he think the Cruiser would trouble to follow. They'd seen the Falcon's speed.

Janni uncoiled, slowly. He said, "Are you all right?" and she nodded. She said, "Yes, fine." He gripped her hand. It was a miracle; the first of a very long night.

They rounded a further bend; and she pointed quietly. She said, "Look. The sea."

He glanced to the right. A pall of smoke was drifting from the west. His heart sank. That was Kiteport.

A mile on, the engine of the Falcon began to knock and miss. He coasted to a halt finally. The bonnet was instantly enveloped by a cloud of steam. He opened one of the long leaves and stared. The round that had passed between them had cracked the block.

Rand set his lips. He said, "Come on." He took her hand.

He only looked back once. The Falcon was finished; but she'd served her turn. There was no emotion, no sense of loss. Strange, when he'd once felt such a pride in her. She was nothing to him now; she was a piece of worn-out steel.

The land was deceptive in its vastness. They walked an hour, but the sea seemed to be no closer. The sun broke through, for the first time in days. Long searchlight-beams sparkled from the water. It seemed ironic.

The road dipped, climbed again. Tackling the slope, Janni stumbled. He looked at her. The blood on her face had dried to long brown stripes; her skin looked chalk-pale by contrast. He dabbled the kerchief in a little wayside pool, wiped her neck and chin. Later he washed her hands. She clung to him. After a while he said, "Come on. We can't stop now."

They were on the high downs. The wind seethed in the short, cropped grass. Ahead, seeming still distant, the land edge was sharp-cut against the blue. He said, "We're nearly there." He pressed on; finally she shook her head. "It's no good," she said. "I shall have to rest a minute."

He sat with her. Wished he had a cigarette. He said, "What happened to your folks?"

She looked at him expressionlessly. She said, "They're dead." Her eyes changed focus. "Rand," she said. "Rand. . . ."

He stared back the way they had come. He saw it too. The red speck of a Battle Waggon. He grabbed her wrist, started to run. At an angle away from the road. It was useless, naturally. They'd already been seen; the thing altered course at once to intercept.

She collapsed finally. He dropped to his knees and held her. She whispered, "I'm sorry."

Rand kissed her. "It's not your fault," he said. "At least I found you again. I'm sorry it didn't last longer."

The great scarlet truck moved alongside smoothly. A little wait, and the engine cut. Silence fell; he could hear now, beyond the high plain of grass, the wash and crash of the sea.

She groped for the holster at her hip. He caught her wrist. "No, Jan," he said, "it's useless. It only means you'd die that much quicker."

A port opened in the Cruiser's side. Steps were lowered; and a tall man moved down them carefully. He wore the full robes of a Kitemaster. He was very old, his face lined and gaunt; but his eyes were brilliant, and he held himself erect. Two aides followed. They were also clad in scarlet; but they carried no guns. Instead, one held a great Staff of Power; slung on the other's shoulder was the sending apparatus of a wireless telegraph.

The priest walked forward. He stood awhile looking down, it seemed compassionately. Finally he spoke. "Have no fear, my children," he said. "I am the Master Helman." He smiled. He said, "You gave us a long chase."

Rand blinked, and swallowed. "What's happening?" he said. "What do you want with us?"

The other shook his head. "What is happening," he said, "is that the Realm has become insane. But then, it always was a little mad. As to what I want with you. . . ." He turned, and gestured.

Rand knew his jaw had sagged. A figure had appeared, in the sideport of the big machine. It was short, and inclined to dumpiness; it clutched a parasol, and wore a straw hat at a fetching angle. It said, " 'Ello, Rand. . . ."

He left Janni. He ran forward. "Velvet," he said. "But . . . but. . . ."

She clung to him. There were tears on her face. "I wanted ter come back," she said. "I din' really want ter go. It was 'orrible. Bein' away from you. I daren't though. I din' think you'd want me."

"You little fool," he said. "You silly little fool. . . ." He shook his head. "But how," he said. "The summerhouse. . . ."

"Yeah," she said. "I know. Nasty, wadn' it? I seen it. . . ."

He was conscious of not making sense. "But who. . . ." he said. "It was your dress. . . ."

Velvet looked a bit guilty. "She liked ter do 'em up like that," she said. "Some o' the boys. Used ter turn 'er on." She swallowed. "I'd already scarpered," she said. "It was gettin' un'ealthy. Then the gentleman found me. . . ."

He looked at the Master. "But to do this," he said. "You're Vars. . . ."

Helman smiled again. It seemed though there was infinite sadness in his eyes. "The Vars, the Middlers," he said. "They're merely forms of speech. Folk see such things as the extremities of a ladder. But to me, philosophy is circular. Go far enough in either direction, and you meet your enemy." He nodded to his aide. He said, "Call them in." The other inclined his head. He unslung the wireless apparatus.

Rand turned. Another figure had appeared in the doorway. She was tall and slender, with a mane of bronze-coloured hair. Her grave, lovely face was that of a child; but somehow he knew she was older. She hesitated at sight of the group, half-turned to the priest. She gave a little mewing cry. Helman moved forward. "Her name is Tan," he said. "A *protégée* of mine for several years. She doesn't speak much; but she understands everything you say." He took her hand. The girl stepped down. She moved a little awkwardly. Rand saw one leg was a mass of white scar tissue. The Kitemaster said, "I want you to take her with you. A small boon."

Rand shook his head. He said, "Where to, Lord?"

The other said, "You'll see."

"Look," said Velvet, awed. "A Dragonfly. . . ."

Rand stared. It was moving in purposefully, over the sea. He saw the silver glitter of it. The long, slim wings. Tan pointed, gave the little mewing cry again. Velvet took her hand. She said, "She says it's pretty."

The creature held course towards them. He began to realize the sheer size of it. It swept overhead, with a whirr and clatter; and he all but cringed. Helman laid a hand on his arm. "Have no fear of it," he said. "It means you no ill."

Velvet said, "It's goin' ter *land*. . . ."

It had banked, and turned. It was so graceful. It dropped down, low and lower; then it was bumping across the clifftop grass. He saw that what he had taken for eyes were the windows of a driving compartment; he could see the faces behind them now. On the thing's nose was a great spinning blade. Up close, the wings still glittered. He saw beneath its body were delicate spoked wheels. It moved toward the group, swung half away and stopped. A hatch opened in its side. Two figures climbed down; a man, and a woman. Both were fair; both wore tight fitting one-piece suits, as silver as the machine. "They are from the World of Dragonflies," said the priest. "We've been in contact with them many years." He smiled once more. "You'll find it a very different place," he said. "You see they don't rob the earth, as we do. We began again, in the bad old way; and now we're paying for it.

They take the Lord's true bounty; even their machines fly by the power of the sun. It will be strange, at first; but you'll walk free there, and live without fear."

So there had been another people, all along. Rand said hesitantly, "Will there be . . . others? Others like us?"

Helman nodded. "We've been selecting carefully," he said. "For quite a long time now. Our world is dying; but many of its folk will be saved." He nodded briefly to the west. "A ship left yesterday," he said, "with some of your friends aboard. It was bound for Tremarest. It didn't sail under the Kites. They've served their purpose."

The strangers approached. The taller spoke. "I am Lanagro," he said. "This is Mada, my Lifepartner. Are these the folk you spoke of?" The Master said, "They are."

The woman made a little husky sound. She pointed. The stranger frowned. Then he hurried forward. He knelt at Tan's feet, looked into her face. He touched her ankle, placed his right hand gently on her knee. He moved the hand down, slowly; and she stared, amazed. Behind his fingers, the skin was no longer blemished.

One of the aides started back. He said huskily, "A miracle." But Lanagro smiled. "No," he said. "A skill we have acquired. We have many others."

Tan gave the little cry again. She pointed at the great machine. Velvet grinned. "She says, can we get in?"

The Master nodded. He said, "Take her, child." He turned to the sky people. "We send our best," he said. "We send Innocence, and Beauty. Cherish them." Tan moved away a pace; then she ran back, impulsively. She dropped to her knees. She said, *"Thank . . . you . . . Lord. . . ."* Helman touched her hair. He said, "Go with God. Quickly, the machine is waiting."

Rand said, "Come with us, Master." But the other shook his head. "No," he said. "My place is here. In any case, I'm old. My life has run its course."

He swallowed. He said, "Try to save her, sir."

"Save whom?"

Rand said, "The Mistress Kerosina. She didn't ask to be the way she is. She didn't ask to be born."

"I'll do what I can," said Helman. He touched his shoulder. He said, "Your feet are on the Way."

Janni unslung the holster, laid it on the grass. "Somehow," she said, "I don't think I'm going to need that any more." She took Rand's hand.

The priest stood back and watched. The whirring of the Dragonfly's engine increased. It began to move, slowly at first. Its tail lifted; and it rose, lightly as thistledown. It banked once, swooped low overhead. He saw them wave, raised his Staff in salute. Then it was fading, across the sea. The last Helman saw was the silver flash of its wings.

He turned, nodded sombrely to his aides. They climbed aboard; and the big machine started up, rumbled away from the coast. It turned toward the smoke palls, hanging sullen on the horizon.